The Love Life Of A Chameleon

Belinda Tobin

The Love Life of a Chameleon

Copyright © 2024 by Belinda Tobin

Published by Bel House Books

Paperback ISBN: 978-1-7637062-8-6

EBook ISBN: 978-1-7637062-9-3

For permissions or enquiries, please contact:

Bel House Books

Email: bhb@heart-led.pub

Website: www. heart-led.pub/bel-house-books

First Edition: October 2024

 A catalogue record for this book is available from the National Library of Australia

Other titles from Bel House Books:

I'm Sorry Juno

To The Heart of the Man

The Emptiness Algorithm

Crucifixus

I acknowledge the Yuggera and Ugarapul peoples as the Traditional Owners of the lands and waterways where this book was written. I honour the wisdom that lives within the cultures of our First Nations peoples and celebrate its continuity. I pay my deep respects to Elders past, present and future and send my greatest gratitude for all they do for the life of this land.

Always was, always will be.

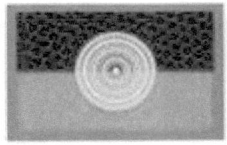 

For the psychiatrists, counsellors and nurses that helped me find my true colours.

Chapter 1

I have been abandoned by the person I adore. In my moment of despair, he just dropped me at the hospital. He watched as I went through the doors and left. He did not see me hooked up to machines and monitored for hours. He was not there to hold my hand and help me stay awake. He did not afford me the chance to apologise or tell him how much I loved him. And he was not there yesterday to see me transferred here to this hell.

What does that say about me? When a man who was once my rescuer now found me so disgusting that he decided to dump and run. How horrible must I be? When he left, there were no well wishes; he didn't even demand that I take care of myself.

He had rejected me at his home, and now he repeated this humiliation at the hospital. He had walked away that night when I said I wanted him. hopelessness guided me to take the pills. Parked outside his house, I could see the lights on and knew I would not have long. Only this would make him understand how much I needed him. He met me at the door, and I explained what I had done. He should have seen my desperation and decided he needed me, too, that he would save me again. But without speaking, he shoved me into his car and drove me to the ED. And then he walked away, offering no words in response to this ultimate plea.

I thought right then I had seen the full face of hopelessness. Now I understand it can get much heavier and far more horrific. It holds you down with hands of authority and turns your face to the wall. It makes you wait there for hours, with no will to wonder. Then, it lifts you and lines you up at the medication window for another dose of deadening. Then hopelessness drags you back and deposits you in the same spot for the next staring session, senseless and surrounded by only stale and stagnant air.

I knew I should feel something; sad or angry with all that had happened. I should be plotting my escape and mapping my next move. I should be working on a way to get Ben back or at least making a Plan B for a new man. I should be shaking off the sting and charting the course to regain control. I should be finding a way to punish the partners for declining my promotion; I should be seeking my revenge for them calling me "too soft".

But my mind was numb. Even if I wanted to, I could not make it work. The medicine had made it all grey and quiet, so I was at least peaceful but also purposeless. The only wish I could muster was that I had taken more pills and done the deed properly. Now, I also had this failure to contend with.

So, I spent my day staring at the wall, my back blocking out all the activity. It sheltered me from the screams, the stacking of trays and plates, the doctors' diatribes, the nurses' instructions, and my next-door neighbour's incessant shuffling.

I heard a nurse coming up behind me and waited for some kind of chastisement or commandment to commence. It was like being a child all over again. Instead of rebuke though, there were words of kindness.

"Hey, Nora. These might make you feel a bit more comfortable."

She placed a pair of socks between my eyes and the wall and waited until she knew I had seen them.

"Here, let me put them on for you."

There was no resistance on my part, but I also provided very little assistance. She pulled back the sheets and struggled to put the socks on sideways. But they were on, and then she tucked me back in and patted me on my arm.

"Sleep well, Nora. Goodnight."

The socks were soft but supportive. It was like my feet were being held with warm, gentle hands. I didn't know I was crying until the tears trickled down my nose. I thanked whatever god there was for those socks and reached down to touch their tenderness.

Then I thanked whatever god there was for my wall and fell asleep with my hand pressed against it.

I had hoped my second day would be just as simple, but duties were demanded. Trips were taken down to the doctor's room, where I had to replay the revolting events of the previous days. I sickened myself when I heard my story. What a pathetic creature I was. The nurse took me to the dining hall and instructed me to eat, but when she was called to other duties, I made my escape and went back to my wall. Later in the day I was escorted to the courtyard, comforted with the advice that it was much warmer outside. The sun seemed to sneer at me, so I absconded again to my safe space and snuggled under the blankets.

This dull, robotic drill happened again the next day, with one exception. A nurse found me after I fled the dining hall at lunch. She sat on the end of the bed and watched me watching the wall.

"Hey, Nora. I'm Maria. We really need you to eat something."

Silence shouted my intention to persist with self-harm.

"Nora, if you don't eat something soon, we will need to put you on a drip, and you will have to stay even longer."

This time, silence announced my apathy at the advertised course of action.

She left in a silence that suggested she shared my indifference. I congratulated my stubbornness for its success.

But Maria returned and wiggled behind me, distracting my wall-watching with a mug. The intrusion was unexpected and unsettling, scoring Maria a minor win. It was also impossible not to see the rosy, frothy liquid the mug contained and the straw that awaited my submission.

"It's a protein smoothie. They make them fresh here and I think they are fantastic. If you drink this, I will mark it as a meal and I can leave you alone. Otherwise, I am going to have to come back and keep annoying you."

I had to concede that Maria was clever. She knew of my aversion to attention and was willing to help me stay in my cocoon. I only needed to drink this thing, and then I could return to my stupor. For a moment, I considered casting the cup across the room, but not even my ire would allow me to be that impolite.

I sat up and took a sip. The chill was shocking, but I did not show my surprise. The sweetness was stirring, but I was sure I could soon suppress this stimulation. The thickness was tender on a dry throat, aggravated by air conditioning. But I would not allow myself to enjoy it. This was medicinal only, a means to an end, and that end was continued indolence. I finished as much as I thought I could get away with and then passed it back.

"Thanks, Nora."

She made a mark on my chart.

"Do you need anything else?"

I settled back in with the wall, the only one who truly understood, and my silence signalled that I was now sulking.

A few hours later, Maria was back beside me.

"Hey, Nora. I am about to clock off for the day, but I wanted to bring you some tea and cake before I left. Gosh, when was the last time you would have had tea or coffee? I thought you might be missing it. And you are in luck, the cake today is lemon. But please don't tell anyone I brought you some. It is usually first in, best dressed when there is lemon cake. But I wanted you to try some before it was all taken. If you like the smoothie, you will love the lemon cake!"

I so wanted to be rude, but Maria was right. I had forgotten about tea.

I sat up and made the mistake of making eye contact.

She engaged and sent a smile.

"I will see you tomorrow at lunch. Take care, Nora."

This was not the tea I knew and loved. This was a pathetic proxy. The mug was plastic and boring. There was no china or colours here. There was a tea bag string hanging out the side, which was, in my world, paramount to heresy. Two tiny white pods held the milk, and sachets supplied sugar.

Disgust was strong and delayed proceedings. It was a recollection that finally moved me forward. The only time I ever had tea in the afternoon was with mum.

At 3pm, on the dot, we would be seated on the front porch with a pot of tea, sometimes biscuits, sometimes cake, sip, chew and chat until the commuter train came. Services to the country had dwindled, so this only happened once daily and was a great source of delight. Mum's house was just a short distance from the station along the train line, so the speed was slow enough for us to see the people perched inside. As we watched through the windows, we would make up stories about who they were, where and why they were going. This was when I realised my mother had an imagination well beyond her small existence. I wondered how much of it was born from experience, but prying would have been improper.

She had bought the little house after dad died, serious about starting again with something that was just hers. She really did begin with a blank slate, selling or donating everything from the old house and decorating the new one with carefully chosen pieces from the op shop — except for the beds, which she brought new. Mum was a minimalist before it became fashionable, stating how much she enjoyed having space and not much to dust.

When I started university, I moved into a share house with some friends not far from the campus. But every Sunday, I would spend with mum. After I moved to the city, I came back when I could spare the time, but that was sparse and usually only meant Christmas. Until she got sick. Then, I would hike back every weekend. I started grieving when she could no longer sit outside for afternoon tea. That was the start of our separation.

The tea Maria brought was tepid, what my mother would have considered a sin. Although in a place like this it made sense. They wouldn't want to give someone the satisfaction of being able to scald themselves. It still had the familiar tannin taste, though, infused with relief that commenced well before the tea could hit my bloodstream. I was convinced the comfort would be transient, so I could spare a few more sips. The lemon cake didn't look as good as my mum's. It was obviously made in one industrial slab, each section identical and uninteresting. It came with a cardboard cutlery, and I could already feel the rough, repugnant touch on my tongue. To assuage guilt, I scraped off the icing. Then, I sectioned off a piece and picked it up with my fingers, preferring the taste of flesh over paper. Yes, there was a tartness that was noticeable but not noteworthy. And it was certainly sweeter than it should have been. For just one moment I wished that mum was here to critique this cake with me. But she wasn't and hadn't been for over a decade. I don't know why I kept hanging on to this nonsensical notion.

Maria had won another round. I had been tricked. I could not drink the tea without eating the cake, and once a piece of cake had been consumed, it was obligatory to have more tea. I was trapped in a complicity between these two commissaries. I would not congratulate her for her cunning though, simply wait for any pleasantness to pass and permit no more. That would be the last time I let her lure me out with sweet offerings.

The next morning, the rolling of trollies and clattering of trays could not rouse me. My back held firm. However, I could not stop the smells from seeping through. There was the fetid fragrance of bacon. Those poor pigs. And something similar to the scent of sausage. Eggs, yes, there were eggs in the air. And toast. The toast tempted me, thrusting forth an image of my mother, topping it with thick butter and marmalade. But hopelessness melted the mirage and covered me with contempt. I tried to convince it that I could just go and get a coffee, but it commanded conformance.

Only then did I notice the windowpanes beside my precious patch of wall. They started towards the middle of my bed and stretched across the room to the person opposite. They were made of thick tempered glass in a criss-cross pattern. The design distorted the view, and what would have probably been bright bushes on the other side were in here seen only as a blur. I sat down at the end of my bed and traced the lines. I thought about how much this pane looked like my life. There were many clear pathways in my past, but now, the future I had forged so carefully was foggy. I had been willing to be any line Ben wanted and even cross some, and I would have bent in any direction to make him happy. But he had chosen instead to abandon me. Now, I couldn't see anything clearly.

The doctor suggested that by now, my thinking should be somewhat clearer. He had reduced my medication and asked if I had noticed. I hadn't. He told me that I needed to attend the group sessions, that it was valuable to hear about other people's experiences, and that I would learn a lot. I did not respond. As far as I was concerned, I had learnt everything

THE LOVE LIFE OF A CHAMELEON

I needed to know. I was a complete failure and felt no need to share this fact with anyone or hear the variety of ways that other people had come to the same conclusion.

He told me his plans to transfer me to a private facility for at least the next two weeks. It would be more suitable than here for figuring out the next steps, where I could get more personal attention and make some plans. I thought I would feel delighted by the proposition of getting out of this place, but I had just gotten used to the rhythms and how to play the game, so I found the prospect of a move disturbing.

He then asked me a question that was the most unsettling yet.

"Is there anyone you would like to call?"

He may as well have just stabbed me through the heart; it would have hurt less. For he had just handed me the anguish of accountability. I was thrust into the real world, where I would have to let others know I was not well and admit my weakness.

"What day is it?"

"Tuesday."

"I would need to call my boss."

"What is their name?"

I noticed his prudent use of pronouns.

"David Ellison."

The doctor made a note on my chart.

"Anyone else?"

If he was writing a permission slip, I would make sure I was prepared.

"Yes, my partner."

"What is their name?"

"Ben, Ben Gray."

Another note was made.

I had never called Ben my partner before. But that is what I saw him as, and so that is what I said.

"I will get the nurse to give you your phone a bit later and you can make the calls. You can also let your boss know that you have a medical certificate to cover this week and the next two. That should give you a bit of time to breathe."

The doctor seemed very satisfied that he had given me a sense of space, but I thought him cruel for reminding me of my responsibilities.

"I will also need to pay my rent."

"Can you do that on your phone."

"Yes."

"OK. I will get the nurse to help you with that too."

There was no thank you on my departure. He only deserved my anger that day. I walked past the huddle of broken hearts, sharing their stories and averted my face so I could not see theirs. I passed the courtyard, the tables drenched in sun and the walls punctured with pink flowers.

"Piss off," I said with profuse passion.

Maria came again at lunchtime, interrupting my inertia with another smoothie. She stood there and watched me drink it, waiting to make a mark on the chart. With Maria, though, I did not feel like her prime concern was compliance. I could sense that she really did care. I felt a compression in my chest but held back the tears. Was this what the doctor was suggesting was a sense of clarity? It felt more like a callous confusion. I couldn't tell whether I wanted someone to hold me or hurt me, to tell me that everything was going to be OK or torment me with the truth. For a moment, I thought about what I might need to do to get my medication bumped up to what I had before. I was beginning to fear the feelings arising.

"The doctor said you can make some phone calls. I will go and get your phone and let's head into the interview room."

I met her there, mentally being dragged, kicking and screaming. I was imagining myself being restrained, and the phone held forcefully to my ear as I yelled, "Please, please, don't make me do this." My obligations had become a torture, and I was weak.

Turning on my phone, I felt my stomach churn. The smoothie was threatening to spew all over the table. With shaking hands, I scrolled through my unread messages. There were a few from my boss. The first told me that Ben had been in touch and told him I was ill. The second asked for an update when I could and if there was anything I needed. I was so relieved. I could now communicate by text and avoid answering any questions directly. I shot off a message stating that my doctor had advised I would be unavailable for the next three weeks, that I had a medical certificate to cover this period and that I would send it through when I could. One deed was done.

I then paid the rent and scanned the money in my savings account. This was where I was putting aside funds for a trip with Ben to Bhutan. It was to be a surprise for his birthday next year. He wanted to visit so badly, and I had built up almost enough to get there by business class. Maybe this could be the road to our reconciliation? There was no way he would be rude enough to reject such a righteous offering.

I felt addled as I trawled through the messages to see if one was from Ben. There was nothing past his advice that he was running a few minutes late for dinner. He had been held up with a client but shouldn't be far away. That was the night that my world had broken apart. There was no word from him since. But I had to let him know what was happening. Surely, he wanted to know. Surely, he cared. You can't just stop loving someone in an instant.

When I heard the ringtone, I was so nervous my legs started jiggling. It rang and rang, and rang, and rang. That's not right. Maybe he is on the toilet.

I rang again. It rang and rang and rang and then went dead. Ben had hung up at the other end.

He was there and listening.

"Let me just try once more."

I rang again. It rang once and then went dead again.

"Please, just one more."

"No. That's enough Nora."

Maria held me around the shoulders while I slumped on the table, sliding the phone from my hands. She lifted me gently, led me to the nurse's station, submitted my phone, organised my medication, and took me back to bed. I was blank, perhaps in shock, silent and stupid. But my wall was waiting.

A little later, she delivered tea and cake.

"It's carrot cake today, Nora. The cream cheese icing is wonderful. I'm sure you will love it."

I couldn't face any of them, not today.

Again, she came back.

"I bought you a colouring book. I nicked it from the art room for you. And some nice felt pens. The designs are gorgeous. It might help a bit, Nora, for you to do something."

I heard her pick up my tray of tea and cake and put down the book and box of pens.

I would pass on these, too. What was the point?

It was getting harder though to ignore the smells from the kitchen. The room was getting darker, and the shapes out the window turned to shadows, so I knew they would be serving dinner soon. My stomach was shouting for sustenance, but my body was on strike, shut down in sympathy for all the sadness and anger that was being imprisoned within. I simply told my stomach to "shut up" and tried to sleep.

Maria always seemed to know when I was at my weakest. I heard her move the colouring book and pens to my bedside drawers and place a tray on my table.

"Hey, Nora, come on. I am going to need you to eat. Please don't put at risk going to a nicer place. It's pumpkin soup, pretty good for a hospital. And I brought you some fresh bread and butter to go with it. I will come back later and check in with how you went."

Why? Why did they bother? And why did they keep bringing me things that only hurt me more? Mum's favourite soup was pumpkin. She would make it fresh, roasting the pumpkin first to bring out the sweetness. I liked mine with toast, but she always had fresh bread and lots of butter. So much so that after she had done a dip, a little ribbon of yellow oil would wander around the top of the soup until she scooped it up with her spoon. She would often slurp. Not because she was uncouth but because she knew it stirred me, following each repulsive sound with a side eye and a smirk. All I could do was tell her to "stop it", but through a smile. Her body gave in on her in the end, but her sense of humour never did.

She would be disgusted to see me here like this. I had failed her. I was not strong enough to stand on my own.

I heard her voice inside my head.

"Pull yourself together Nora. Please, do it for me."

I remembered laying with her, watching as she passed. She looked so peaceful, and her hand, as always, was so soft. I could feel that same hand now on mine, its placid pressure both pleading and providing permission.

I could ignore my hunger and punish myself—I was well-practised at that. But I was not willing to hurt my mother any more than she was right now. Even if I did not believe there was any hope for me, I would not hand her over this same heaviness. I would eat to please her.

The soup was just warm, and sour compared to my mother's. It was in a ghastly green plastic bowl, but at least this time, there was a metal spoon. I think I would have drunk it straight from the bowl if my only other choice was that cardboard rubbish. Maria had been kind enough not to give too much, so I easily finished it, using one piece of bread to scrape the sides. Butter was a step too far and a folly I could not forgive.

But the last piece of bread and the butter capsule kept staring at me, taunting me and testing my discipline. Desperate, I grabbed the book and pens beside my bed and flipped through the pages. They were all mandalas, filled with different shapes and designs, but all expanding black and white circles begging for colour.

One looked just like the print that Ben had on his wall. He also had a few textbooks about them in his bookshelf. He told me about a special ceremony he went to once where the monks built a big mandala on the floor using coloured sand. It took most of the day, and then, in the end, as the sun was setting, they blessed it and swept it all away. They bagged up the sand, and he brought some home and sprinkled it on his garden. What I had done the last few days was so similar. But the only souvenir I left with was shame. It would not allow itself to be dissipated. It just sat like a steadfast, solid stench. I wanted to scribble in every space with the ugliest brown I could find. But I sensed that this might hurt Maria, so I merely traced the lines with my finger, forcing myself to feel some kind of flow.

Maria came back and, after a "well done," made a mark on my chart. She told me that she would not be there the next day. She finally had a day off, and I was happy for her and comforted that she would have a day without me. Then she wrapped her arms around my shoulders.

"You're going to be OK, Nora. I know it might not feel like it right now, but you will be. And I know you might not believe in yourself right now, Nora. But I believe in you."

She kissed me on the head, picked up the tray and left.

The next day another nurse came and told me to go and get some breakfast. I found her tone to be that of a bully, so I decided to deny her the satisfaction of success. I walked down there but took a detour past the dining hall to the toilet. She was too busy to follow me, so I scored a point against the new player that day. I waited in the toilet for a while, then realised I was being a woos. I headed back past the dining hall but happened to spy the fruit platter against the far wall. It was the colours that caught my attention. The red watermelon triangles contrasted against the green oval grapes. The yellow pineapple chunks cut across the continuous orange circles cuddled beside them. The sweetness of the smoothies sprang to mind, and I shuffled forward, praying that I would pass by unnoticed. I piled a plate with a few pieces of everything, then hightailed it back to my bed. I decided if the new nurse was going to tell me that I had to eat in the dining hall with the others, I was going to tell her to bugger off.

Later that day, the doctor announced that I would be leaving the next morning. He had found me a spot in a private hospital with an outstanding reputation for helping people like me. What did he mean, people like me? I dared not ask. The patient transfer would take me over, and at this stage, I would be there for two weeks. This period was covered under the Mental Health Act and would be undertaken involuntarily. The doctors at the new place would decide what would happen to me afterwards.

"So, I am practically a prisoner?"

"You can choose to see it like that, Nora. You can believe that this is something bad being done to you. Or you can see it as a firm commitment on our part to care for you; as something being done for you."

Right then, the doctor sounded like a weird blend of Ben and my mother. Both expressed similar sentiments. My mother would bang on about the adage – cruel to be kind.

While I would whine about other's bad behaviour, she would always find a blessing in it, even if it was simply gaining greater intelligence. Ben would often repeat a statement he had heard on a podcast. A Buddhist Nun had said that boundaries are a kindness, and he tried to use this to convince me to start saying no more often. In this case, my boundaries were clearly being usurped, yet I was sure they would agree it was for the best.

The doctor wished me luck and walked me out. I felt like saying that I would be very concerned if he saw my mental health as a lottery. It almost came out, excited by the opportunity to have the final word and knock him down a peg or two. But I withheld this witticism, nevertheless, scoring it as a win for sarcasm.

On the way back to my room, I heard action in the kitchen. There were very few smells, which could only mean lunch. It was only ever a light offering of sandwiches and snacks. I snuck in again and grabbed some sandwiches in packets. I smuggled them under my sheets and returned for a cup of tea. I could have had coffee, but I did not want to be stimulated, only soothed.

Some of the sandwiches were egg, with the bread already made slightly soggy. They reminded me of the ones my father would make on our road trips, parcelled between ice bricks and frozen cordial. They always meant a picnic at a park, usually with a playground. They came with the knowledge that we would be seeing something new. I guessed egg sandwiches were fitting for today then, on the eve of moving on from what I had come to know. But I would not be wedged away from my wall that easily. I remained loyal, leaning against it as granted the wish of the wheels to be filled with colour. My choices were readily criticised by my conscious, but I was compelled to continue; to complete something before I left. To leave some kind of legacy.

When one was done, I found myself doodling on the page opposite. I drew the checkerboard I saw on the windows. My rows were not straight, and my columns were not symmetrical, but there was something satisfying about laying down lines. They provided a focus and a freedom. I wondered if they would miss this book if I took it with me and decided Maria had given it to me as a gift. I was content with this resolution and continued sketching until I smelt soup.

I could not sleep that night. It may have been the lack of sedatives. With the doctor's advice, I decided to try without a nighttime dose. Maybe it was the new girl in the bed beside me, incessantly snoring and farting, the communal curtain incapable of blocking the brutality bursting forth from her bum. It could have been the nurse's continuous chit-chat about the unseasonably hot weather and their latest hairstyles. As much as it was inane, part of me found it interesting. The nerves about my trip the next day to the new place could have also played a part in my insomnia. I hated change at the best of times. But my mind kept coming back to the book – the lines and the patterns, how they combined and evolved. They seemed so simple, but something about them I found impressive.

So, I lay there imagining lines and tracing them tenderly onto my wall.

Chapter 2

The next morning seemed to take forever to come. Finally, I heard the muted conversations of shift changeovers and the opening of the kitchen doors. I snuck out, made a tea and smuggled it back to my bed, behind the curtain, before anyone noticed. As the rest of the ward awoke, I watched the blurs out the window, drank my tea, and started on another colouring page. I felt anxious about what was to come that day. A departure and an arrival, and in between, a gathering of belongings. The structure of the day was simple, but each step felt so significant. I could not convince the nurses to allow me an additional medical solution to this stress. Choosing colours was a convenient distraction from my sense of dread and doodling a diversion from my discomfort.

The smells from the kitchen began to waft through the room, and I slipped in and scored a small bowl of porridge. It was stodgy and a sensible choice to sustain me through the next several hours. I was permitted to shower and provided with a towel. I had not washed in four days. I had not wanted to. And now, the nurse would summon me out after just a few short minutes. The shower room was sparse: a chair for my clothes, a fabric screen and a soap dispenser. There were no mirrors, and for that, I was thankful. I did not think I could cope with seeing myself at that moment – the monster that had messed everything up.

The water felt wonderful, and I switched it between warm and cold and back again to experience the change and to prepare for the shifts this day would bring. I had to dress in the clothes I came in. The last few days had been spent in a hospital gown and standard-issue undies. There was no one to deliver any alternatives. The feeling of denim on my skin came with a sense of normality, like finally, I was leaving and could simply return to my old life; my legs were ready for it. The t-shirt, though, was tainted with Ben's aftershave. Maybe it had seeped in when I snuggled close to him after dinner and started the seduction that ended with him storming out. Or perhaps it was transplanted there when he tied me down in his car with the seatbelt. The smell was a beautiful blend of sandalwood, spice and citrus. It was once so stimulating and satisfying, but now it was just so sad.

I returned to my bed, the aroma hanging onto me like a leech. There was a moment that I thought I would go into meltdown. I imagined ripping the shirt off and throwing it on the floor, shrieking like a banshee and jumping on it with everything I had. I could feel myself on the edge of an explosion, pulled back from the precipice by the stare of my socks. Their colour was ghastly, an orange that no one would ever choose to wear. Yet they were a gift, and this made them truly special. I plonked on the bed and packed the socks in the standard-issue hospital tote. They would come with me to the next place. I put on my shoes and went to the nurse's station to ask for some deodorant. I sprayed this thickly under my arms and all over the shirt, drowning out the demonic odour.

It was when I put on my cardigan that I felt the paper in my pocket. There it was, on the right side, a folded square. I thought it must be a receipt or scrap of a shopping list, but when I pulled it out to put in the bin, I saw my name. I knew it was from Ben. He always wrote the N with a flourish. He wasn't trying to be fancy; that was just his flow.

This could be it. This could be my redemption. He could be asking me to contact him again when my head is clear. He could be expressing his desire to be a couple. All I wanted could be written here; this note was maybe the genie that would grant my wishes. I closed the curtain around me and opened it carefully, to not let any hope escape.

It began.

"Dear Nora."

I breathed in those words. I heard him in my head, his low pitch creating a lull.

"Please do not try and contact me. If you call, I will not answer. If you write, I will throw the letter away without reading it.

I have taken your car back to your apartment and advised your work that you are not well. Now, the rest is up to you.

Use this time to find yourself, Nora. I know an incredible woman is within, but you keep running away from her. You trim and twist yourself to fit the shape other people want you to be. You are so good at this, so clever, so cunning, I almost let myself get sucked into the temptation of having you as a toy, a convenient creature for my own comfort. I am so sorry, because now I see all I was doing was enabling your continued escape.

Stop living through other people, Nora and start living for yourself. Stop letting others tell you how to shine and stand true to yourself. Stop conforming to what other people want and have the courage to claim your own sovereignty.

I know you say you love me. But you are incapable of truly loving anyone. Because you don't love yourself. I don't think you even know yourself.

I want love for you more than anything else in the world. But this is something you need to give yourself first."

I looked back at the words that were underlined.

<u>You are incapable of truly loving anyone.</u>

That stung. And it was completely false.

This whole letter was a load of absolute bullshit. Ben had the chance to give me love and he lost it. And enabling me? He made me sound like some kind of addict.

I walked out to the hallway and put the note in the big recycling bins outside, the ones with only a small slit for paper. I slid it inside, satisfied that I could not be lured back to it later. Not long after that, I left the building. But the letter was still lodged firmly in my mind.

The patient transport was excessive for a mobile adult. They could have just thrown me in an Uber, but perhaps they were worried I may abscond. There was no doubt that I had thought about it. The only problem was that they had my address and would know where to find me. If I thought I was embarrassed now, I could only imagine the shame of being escorted from your building and being loaded into a white truck. I would use the two weeks to find out what I needed to do and who I needed to be to get free.

So, I was strapped in the van, a solo passenger surrounded by a lot of space. It felt like a very unpleasant school excursion. Like not going to a modern art museum, but somewhere like the mint. Not to an innovative public park but to Parliament House. I stared out the window, confused about whether I should feel rebellious or resigned. Ben believed I did not really love him. I was stuck between finding a way to convince him that I did or leaving defeated. My last attempt at advertising my adoration landed me here. The next step may require a bit more thought. I parked this problem and focused instead on the places we were passing.

Slowly, the streets became more familiar, and I started to recognise the signs of my suburb. There was my local supermarket and bus station. A little way along was the café that grated decadent chocolate on top of the cappuccino. It would melt in your mouth as you took the first sip. Suddenly, I started craving coffee. But no detours were permitted. The van swung into a visitor's bay, and the driver came with me to see the building manager. I always left a key at the desk in case of emergency. I guessed mine were still in my car from the night I went to Ben to beg him to be with me. The building manager said a friendly hello, tried not to notice the driver, and passed me my unit keys and another envelope. He advised a man had dropped these off for me a few days ago. They were my car keys. No more notes.

Waiting for the lift to my unit, the last encounter with Ben replayed in my mind. I saw myself, just like Meredith Grey, clear, composed, and compelling, asking him to pick me, choose me, and love me. I could not for one minute consider that there was an alternative version where Ben was met with a bawling, babbling idiot shaking a box of pills in his face. I much preferred my rendition.

My apartment was exactly how I had left it, except for one small detail. The African violets on the kitchen bench were dry, droopy and dull. The once purple flowers had fallen off and made mulch in the potting mix. I had brought this plant to prove to everyone that I could keep something alive. That I was capable of care and sustaining a life. If all went well, I would progress to a pet. But looking at this pathetic pot, I am glad I had not raced into buying that rescue cat. Otherwise, I would be cleaning its decomposing carcass off the couch. In the entire scheme of this situation, the demise of a plant really was not that big of a deal. But walking past it on the way to my bedroom, it hit deep. This image sat in my mind as I grabbed a suitcase and filled it with comfy clothes. My makeup bag was already prepared. I had it eternally stocked in case of a sleepover or a sudden business trip. I crept into the bathroom and grabbed it quickly before I could be tempted to glance in the mirror. This action felt manic.

It was then that a thought flashed through my mind. I could start acting like a crazy woman, kick the driver out, and reclaim my space. This was my apartment, and no one could make me leave it again. However, the consequences of non-compliance were far more demeaning than obedience.

I pulled off my t-shirt, the one still with undertones of Ben and threw it in the wash basket. I would deal with that later. I dressed in a new clean shirt and grabbed a pillowcase off the pillow on my bed. There was something about the hospital-issue pillows that were so punishing. They seemed to ridicule your need for rest, dangle the offering then leave you in despair. The white flannelette was my favourite and still smelled of the lavender oil I would drop on it each night. If I had to sleep in a strange bed for two weeks, my head might as well be cradled by something comfortable. The whole packing process only took a few minutes. I met the driver back in the kitchen, and we made our way uneventfully over to the hospital. I did not see any of the scenery on the way. My mind was meditating on the plant, the lifelessness of the leaves and the fallen flowers, and what that said about me.

Again, at the admission desk, I considered simply walking away. I could quietly, peacefully just turn around and, without a word, wander out. Ben was right. I needed to stop doing what other people wanted, so this could be the place to start standing up for myself. But then he had also criticised me for continually running away from myself. I was so confused. Was staying here standing up for myself or was leaving how I would reclaim my sovereignty. Unfortunately, working through this conundrum delayed action. Before I could come to a conclusion, I was introduced to my nurse, Ranjani, and escorted to a separate room. Behind a closed door my vitals were checked, and my physical details recorded. I was given a breath test, blood pressure taken, and was measured and weighed. I glanced at my height. Good, I had not started shrinking yet. But I avoided my weight. There was no need to know that.

At home, I did not own any scales, a conscious choice after years of anorexia. At college it felt like the only things I could control were my grades and weight, so I set about overachieving at both. From both pursuits, I gained an incredible sense of achievement. However, while the former created great internal satisfaction, the latter was a persistent punishment. If I was not studying, I was weighing myself to check my progress, calculating calories, and making meal plans suitable for models. I could not stand to see a set of scales now, and just standing on them made me nauseous. As long as I did not see the result I could relax.

When I thought the worst was over, the nurse pulled out a Polaroid, stating they needed a photo for the medication chart. This felt like the greatest humiliation. I had always hated photos of myself, and now I would be captured, cloaked in four days of neglect and smothered in shame. I looked away as the film was waved and then was placed to wait on the desk. Within, though, arose a morbid curiosity. Just how low had I gone? Could this photo become a scapegoat to satisfy my need for self-hatred? Maybe I would look.

My attention was diverted by the call to confirm the details on my wristband and the process of its attachment. Then, the questions began. Ranjani flipped through pages, ticking and crossing boxes. She recorded my current mood and mental state, my desire for self-harm and special dietary requirements. I was assessed for a risk of falls and was asked to declare any injuries. I stated that I was no longer considering suicide. It felt like the right answer to give. Honestly, though, I was not so sure.

Ranjani showed me to my room, and she watched as I unpacked all my things onto the bed. She applied blue latex gloves and searched through the travel kit, taking the shaver and essential oil. I understood the first but thought the second confiscation was stupid. The smell of May Chang in a morning shower was like magic, but of course, this was not a place for the heavenly, merely for health. Honestly, how desperate would you need to be to attempt self-abuse with 10ml of essential oil? I knew the answer. I just didn't want to admit that I was well aware of how desperate one could become. She also picked up my phone and advised that its use was to be determined by the doctor. These things, she said, "can create such a distraction, and destroy what we are trying to achieve." She asked if I needed to check in with anyone and let them know the arrangements. But no one was waiting to know where I was.

Once the inspection was complete, the tour began. Packing away could be done at my leisure later. It was a short walk to the kitchen, well-lit with large windows and stocked with sandwiches and snacks. I saw the coffee machine and decided to return and recommence my relationship with caffeine. In the TV room sat a solitary figure, frowning at the events unfolding on the news. My god, the world could have erupted into war over the past few days, and I would not have known. I was too consumed by the conflict within.

There were more people in the room around the corner, seated in a circle, and all at various stages of animation. I could tell the leader in an instant. He was the only one really listening. The others were present but far from participating. As we stood outside, Ranjani showed me the timetable on the wall. The doctor would see me first thing in the morning and tell me which sessions I was to attend. It did not sound like he would be asking or advising.

The library was a lovely little space full of couches, cushions, and circular tables. A shelf spread across one wall, full of books, some looking brand new, others battered by many hands. There were windows here, too, all completely see-through and overlooking a strip of frangipani trees. I had decided at that moment that this would be my place and hoped desperately that the position near the window would not be popular.

Beside the library was a little art room, with tables formed into a rectangle and paintings and collages lining the walls. Basic supplies were available all the time, but anything sharp or toxic needed to be requested from the nurses and would be supervised. It was then that my heart sank. Even the means for creative expression could be corrupted and used to inflict cruelty. Was there nowhere I would be safe from my episodic impulse for self-destruction?

The site's set-up was simple and circular, so a few more minutes and we were back in my room, the paltry collection of possessions still piled on the bed. Ranjani alerted me again to the fact that the doctor would be here to see me first thing, and by that, she meant usually just after dawn. While so much of this place looked like a hotel, this alert reminded me that it was a hospital and that I had handed over many rights I once regarded as righteous. The right to privacy, to your possessions, and to choosing the time and nature for interactions. The Allied Health would also pop in later to meet me and walk me through the next few weeks. Dinner was at six, and my eating would be monitored. My gosh, these people were obsessed. I thought for a moment they were the ones in need of some therapy to alleviate their fanatical fixations on food.

Finally, I was left alone in the vast space that was my room. And finally, I had a chance to consider it fully. On one wall was a large print of sunrise over the ocean. It was a scene that would be so beautiful in person. Here, in two dimensions, on a hospital wall, it was just depressing. The bed was in the middle of the room, far away from any wall. It was isolated and alone, without any solid support on the side. Seeing it stranded like that made me feel sad. There would be nothing to snuggle against and touch while I fell asleep. Here, I would be adrift.

The bathroom was simple, shower, toilet, sink and mirror. Oh my god, a mirror. I had avoided looking at myself so far, but I would be teased by this one for two weeks. I may as well get it over and done with. I approached with caution; my concern justified. I looked like death warmed up. Which, if I were to be frank, was exactly what I was. My hair was frizzy, I had deep blue bags under my eyes, and even my skin looked sick after days without sunlight. I should not have looked. It only resulted in more loathing. I would now add another item to Ranjani's list of modern evils - the mirror. It was surely a means to madness. I was puzzled as to why they would take away a person's phone but still allow them to see their own reflection. Surely there was nothing anyone could say that was more critical than the words one uses towards themselves.

I left the bathroom feeling even more lethargic. I packed away my clothes, noticing the lack of hangers. I had nothing fancy anyway and doubted they would let you near an iron. I only hoped no one in here freaked out at folded clothes. Surely, there would be an OCD case that would be triggered by this. I wondered how they dealt with this dilemma. I put on my favourite pillowcase and special socks and instantly felt more secure. Both could do with a wash, but there was no way anyone was taking these away from me. I changed into track pants and put on a comfy jumper. Why was it that hospitals were always so cold?

I ducked out and had a speed date with the coffee machine, snagged a banana muffin, and snuck back before I had a chance to encounter any human. I stood at the window, ate and drank. The mocha was decent, and I decided to meet regularly with this piece of equipment. It was not delicious, but it did the job. While I let the caffeine work, I watched the people below from a bird's perspective. I wondered what our avian cousins would think of all our activity. How much of it was needed to survive, and how much was simply superfluous stress. The bird on the branches would doubtlessly think so much they saw below was silly. Being separated from it, in the stillness, the silence and the space of this room, created a confusing mix of sensations. At one moment, I was deep in dismay that I was being denied the busy life of details and decisions. The next, I was so grateful to be given the chance to get away from it. For a while, I felt like I was in a foreign land. And then, merely a few breaths later, I had arrived home.

Piling the pillows high, I parked on the bed and reacquainted myself with the mandalas. I had begun one before I left the other place, bridging the layers with shades of green and blue, brightened with some yellow bling. My contemplation of colours was broken by a calm but confident knock. A short, stocky woman bounced through the door, a beam on her face. She must have been about sixty, her hair stranded with silver, but she had an energy around her that belied her age.

"Hello, Nora. I am so pleased to meet you. I am Bev and I will be your counsellor for your time here."

She seemed far too happy for someone who worked in a mental hospital, making me wonder whether I should be hopeful or heedful. Bev asked to join me on the bed, sat down at the end, and admired the book.

"Oh, you like mandalas, and colouring. That is fantastic. I am an art therapist as well and we can do lots of cool stuff over the next few weeks. Sorry, let me start by explaining what you can expect while you are here."

Bev seemed too old to say 'cool', yet it was another sign that she was no simple stereotype.

With a lilt, she walked me through the process for each day. Meeting with the doctor, breakfast, meds, group sessions, lunch, meeting with her, homework, dinner and bed. And repeat. Everything on that list sounded tedious and terrible. I was sure if they left me alone for a few days, I would figure it all out. I was proficient at making plans and given space and time, I would work a way out of this. I just needed to figure out what this was.

Bev, though, began to poke. Her prod was so pleasant that I almost let my guard down. She asked me, gently and generously, what my goal was for being here. I wracked my brain for a decent answer, but it was still too tired to summon something that sounded satisfying. The truth would suffice as it did not unmask much. I advised Bev that I was unsure, as I was still trying to figure out why I was here in the first place. This answer appeased her, and she shifted forward on the bed, her face softening and showing sincere sympathy. This small offering of vulnerability was obviously of value to her. It also gave me great intelligence about how to wile my way through the next two weeks.

"Well, let's just start with where you are now. What brought you here, Nora?"

Oh my god, do I really have to replay this again? I had lost track of how many times I had retold the shameful story. I had no energy for embellishment, so I kept the portrayal plain.

"I had been seeing a man for about a year and a half. He dumped me, and I just snapped. I had a moment of stupidity and attempted suicide."

"I am so sorry, Nora." Gosh, this woman sounded like she really did care about someone she had just met. She was either a master of the mask or a natural mother. She did remind me a bit of mine—no pretence and effortlessly peaceful.

"It sounds like there must have been something brewing under the surface for such a long time though, Nora. Some problem that had been repressed but finally had enough and decided to roar. Do you have a sense yet of what had been going on for you up until then, something that you were constantly challenged by but hadn't resolved?"

My mind flashed back to Ben's note. He had accused me of being a shapeshifter and suggested that this was the cause of my stress. I remembered our conversation on the couch just a few months before we broke apart. We had camped with hot chocolate to watch a movie. The weather outside was miserable, grey, cold and raining hard. But huddling here in the gloom with Ben felt like heaven. As I was finding the film, he asked if he could share a worry with me. He was concerned with something he had observed over our time together. He leaned forward as he spoke softly and slowly. He felt I did not share enough emotion and was concerned that they would eat away at me. He also said it was hard to form a firm connection if he didn't know how I felt. He wanted to know all about me, even the bits I found uncomfortable. I spun him the tale of how, as a child, I had always been told to "settle down" and that emotions were an enemy. It was a part-truth and definitely plausible. Then, to placate even further, I admitted that I needed to unlearn so much and asked him to help me open up and be more honest. He hugged me and said he would be honoured. I could relax into his arms, for I had successfully avoided another attempt at accountability.

But here was Bev, pushing, just like Ben did. Why couldn't they leave me in peace to play this life my way? Again, I was swept into a foreign land full of fickle, filthy feelings. I much preferred my tidy town of thoughts. I could reside there, regulated and reliable. The alternative was far more erratic and unsettling.

"Nothing springs to mind at the moment. You are right, though. I have never really thought about it before. There must be something going on, and I would really appreciate your help to get to the bottom of it."

Bev's eyes brightened with the prospect of being of service. I filed that feedback away as well. I was starting to feel more in control.

It appeared that I would have a duo to deal with. Bev told me that she worked with the doctor to develop a treatment plan. She would be back tomorrow afternoon to discuss what they recommended. Until then, the library and art room were available, and "don't forget dinner."

Bev left with a wave, closing the door behind her. The snap of the latch let me breathe again and took me back to a place of belonging. The doctor was still an unknown authority, but I would deal with him the next day.

Chapter 3

The talk with Bev had brought back images of the pathetic plant in my kitchen. I seemed incapable of keeping anything good alive. I had killed the relationship with Ben, the first man in my life who truly seemed to care. He had saved me from Stephen and told me I deserved more. I hated him at first, although I didn't show it. We shared some mutual friends and had seen each other at several parties over the past few months. I never paid much attention to him; my time was dedicated to Stephen, supplying sustenance and support for his insecurities.

Yes, Stephen would get rough. Yes, Stephen would relish my humiliation. But Stephen also believed in me, that is, my ability to be a success. His means were not mainstream, but no one saw when he was warm, when he held me, made me tea in bed, stroked my hair gently and told me that I was his gift. No one heard him call me a good girl and that he was proud to call me his.

I was far beyond letting it hurt. I would let him think I was cowering to his power. He appeared satisfied with my performance. It seemed to please him. One night, though, as Stephen was in with his movie mates snorting coke, Ben came to the balcony and sat beside me.

We introduced ourselves, and I could sense something shift at the first shake of our hands. Curiosity led me to connect with his eyes, and they held an energy at once, embracing and enchanting. There were sensations that were unusual and unsettling. Pulling away at this point was proper, and I returned to staring out at the ocean.

He pointed to the bruises on my arm, barely showing under my shirt. He must have an incredible eye for detail, a sinister stalking streak, or both.

"Are they from Stephen?"

"That's none of your business."

"I will take that as a yes."

"Nora, I am sorry. I know I am butting in. But I have sat back and watched several times now. I can't continue to say nothing and condone his cruelty."

These words created a cramping in my chest.

"Seriously, Nora. You do not deserve the things he is doing to you. Goddamn it, Nora. I watched as he let a guy win you in a poker game and was almost sick as he followed you both into the room, taking off his belt. I have seen him pull out your breast in front of complete strangers, just to boast that yours were the most beautiful. I've seen the way he speaks to you when he is high, spitting in your face; how he pulls food and drink away from you so that you don't get fat. And now I see these bruises. Nora. It must stop."

"Ben, thank you for your concern. But it really is none of your business."

"Nora, that is where you are wrong. I am a witness to abuse, so are many more people here. Some are too scared to go against Stephen, but there are a few who I trust that said they would testify if you would like to report it."

Through the two years I had been with Stephen, I had experienced some pretty serious things. But nothing had shocked me as much as what Ben had just suggested.

These memories started a churning in my chest. I rifled rapidly through the coloured pens to find some peace, but even doodling could not distract me from the movie playing in my mind.

I was so torn. I knew what Ben was saying about the abuse was right. I did not believe him though when he said I did not deserve it. But here I was, stuck. Some people were ready to go against Stephen and support me to file a complaint. This would be disastrous, although not for the next girl. I had only seen him really angry once before. It was when I mentioned that one of the actors he represented was incredibly attractive. I had hoped he would take that as an invitation and that I might get a taste of such a treat. Instead, his fury was frightening.

"What do I have to do, Nora, to remind you that you are mine?"

He had slammed me up against the wall and pushed my face into the pure white paint. With one hand, he wrenched my arm up between my shoulder blades. With the other, he tore at my hair. Then, the biting began.

His hand moved from my hair to my mouth as I screamed, my pain muffled by his strong fingers pressing hard against my jaw.

I could feel the first drops of blood trickle down my shoulder and knew that I had lost.

"I will mark you, Nora, so you will never forget who you belong to."

He carried me into the bedroom, and for a moment, I thought he would get his rocks off, and all would be done. He ordered me to strip, so there was hope that all would be forgotten with a fuck. As I took off my shirt, I could feel the fabric being pulled out of the wound in my shoulder, and the pain was intense. I started to cry and plead, hoping that this would pander to his pathetic need for power. But he turned me around, pushed me onto the bed and tied me down with the shackles usually used for mutual pleasure and play. Now, this was war, this was wonton torture, and for the first time, I felt scared. He grabbed the gag and put it on tight. I could feel the straps digging into my skin.

I heard him undress in a rage; sounds that were not seductive but seething. He did not bother unbuttoning his shirt, simply ripped it off. His pants were thrown to the other side of the room. His socks used to begin the choking. He sat on my back, and I could feel his nakedness. As he crossed the ends of the socks and saw me struggle, I could feel his dick get harder. He got bored quickly and came to stand in front of me, showing me what I had done to him; his erection was my fault.

"Now, what can I do to you next? That scar on your shoulder is hardly enough."

He went and got his cigarettes, pulled over a chair, and sat, exposed, smirking at me while he began to smoke with one hand and wank with the other. The stench made me feel sick, and as I watched the ash fall over his thigh, I began to think about my escape.

He had decided his next move.

Stephen stood, a man determined and serious and started scratching up my legs. Not hard, but menacingly, teasing for what would come next. He stopped in the crevice between my arse and my thigh. Then he placed, ever so carefully, the burning cigarette onto my skin. What came from me was both a shout and a sob. I could not speak to ask him to stop; our simple safe word, which he often challenged but if I used consistently, usually consented to. It stung so badly.

"Now you won't forget, Nora. You are marked and you are mine."

He came to stand beside me again, blowing smoke in my face.

"Oh my god, this is gorgeous."

He reached for the oil, and I knew what would come next. He took me frantically, finally relieving himself over my arse and rubbing his cum into the burn, confirming his triumph. But he was not done. He went and got his stash of toys and kept driving me, inspecting the scene closely until he was hard again. The process repeated until he stopped for a rest.

Stephen left me there, with only fear for company.

I could tell he had gone and snorted more coke by the way he walked back in. I could hardly see through tear-filled eyes, but it was easy to spot. It was a sinister sway that promised suffering.

The next thing I felt was a sting on my shoulder. Stephen was using the crop on the cut.

"You are such a silly girl, Nora. Hopefully, this will teach you a lesson."

My squirming seemed to arouse him more, and he put down the crop and picked up the oil.

After the next round of penetration, he rubbed his cum into the bite on my shoulder. It was no balm but a brutal breaking open of what had already begun to heal. He lit up a cigarette and sat opposite.

"Oh Nora, I think you need just one more."

I tried to shake my head and shout no. I would have honestly begged if he had let me. But I was bound and my groans he only took as a goading.

The scratching began on the other leg, this time getting harder as it reached my crotch.

The cigarette was placed ever so gently. It started with a single but continued through searing until there was no more stinging. Only silence and my sobs.

He left again. I was alone with my self-flagellation, a fate far more ferocious than Stephen could create.

I heard the gate buzzer and thought, finally, there may be some reprieve. A guest may induce some guilt, and the torment may end. Minutes later, I heard the voices outside the door, drinks poured, and Stephen giving instructions; I knew he had one final point to make. The door opened, casting a bright light tunnel over the floor beside the bed. Stephen came and put on a blindfold.

"Now, Nora. You will have your last lesson. I choose Nora. You are mine. I own you. Every piece of you."

I thought about my mother at that moment and continued to cry. How I had let her down. This seemed to please the men greatly. I heard them chuckle and cast lots of turns. I could hear oiled hands already preparing their tools and some already starting to suck each other, groaning and growling like an animal about to attack. Stephen removed the ball gag and turned me over. It was when he replaced the gag with his cock that I drifted somewhere different. My body was being moved around, poked, pummelled and pissed on. But my mind was elsewhere. It was in the ocean, bouncing through the waves. Every sensation was from the pull and push of the waves and the scrape of the sand. All the voices were the people beside me, friends, having fun in the water. I don't know how long I spent at the beach that night. But I knew when it came to an end.

I was released and instructed to clean it up. He would return in the morning and expected the place to be spotless.

I did not ask where he was going. I did not care. Perhaps it was to another party, perhaps to a mistress. Regardless, I was left with his mess and mine. That night, I learnt many more lessons than the simple ones Stephen had spat in my face. Yes, the event was terrible, but it also gave me incredible intelligence and much greater leverage than I could have imagined.

I did wonder why I stayed with Stephen after this. Simply, I was outnumbered, for a large part of me sided with Stephen, happy to join him in the disparagement and to attest to the fact it was exactly what I deserved.

That was until Ben's intervention. Suddenly, people supported the small voice that whispered I deserved better. There was just no leaving Stephen, though; that was clear. So, I began to plot his departure. At the next party, when Stephen had gone off with the boys again, Ben came up to me, and I confirmed that, after some consideration, I knew he was right. But getting Stephen angry was risky, so I would do it my way.

THE LOVE LIFE OF A CHAMELEON

I had a plan and promised that it would work within six months.

"That's wonderful, Nora. But what can I do? How can I help?"

"Thanks, Ben. Honestly, you don't know how much I appreciate what you have done already. I've got this."

I looked into his eyes again, and my body felt like it was being invaded by butterflies.

"Well, I am here if you need anything."

He slipped me his card, Creative Director. Later in the bathroom, I added Ben's number to my contacts under Cardiologist because something weird happened in my heart when I talked to this man.

I learned that disgust and responsibility were weaknesses that ran deep for Stephen, so I set about needling at both. First, I stopped eating. My boobs began to sag, and my bones began to be displayed under my dress. Slowly, he stopped touching me and showing me off. Then I feigned a thrush infection, making sure he was watching as a smeared thick white cream around my crotch, apologising profusely for the smell. Unfortunately, this infection was persistent, so I was treating myself for months. With this, Stephen stopped sleeping with me and taking me to parties. And finally, when we were together in the same space, I started talking about children. I was not getting any younger and wanted to start a family with him. Now would be the perfect time, while I was in a good place in my career and while we were still young enough to really enjoy the energy of a child. Stephen stopped coming home, and it was not long before one day, he came back drunk from a party and demanded I move out. Deed done. Chalk another one up for Nora.

I had started preparing alternative accommodation at the beginning of this adventure and had secured a lease on a new apartment a few weeks earlier. I turned the lock on my new home, satisfied and steady. The next day I sent a text to Ben providing an update. We met for coffee two days later, and he helped me create a theme for my sanctuary. We had so much fun creating the vision for my space and watching it come to fruition. It was full of his great ideas and generous gifts.

But Ben never got to sleep in the bedroom or see the scars from Stephen's rage. We were never naked together. Despite my best attempts, my designation as a damsel in distress would never evolve into that of a lover. He was happy for me to play friend. But I was not. It was not a role I knew, and it was leading me to the point of panic. I tried taking on the role of his champion, but he did not appreciate having a cheerleader. He found it embarrassing and extraneous. Nor did he need a mother; he had no mess that he was willing to delegate. Neither did he want to be my father figure. He wanted me to stand on my own two feet. That Friday night, I had planned to push his buttons and him further into my life. I had cooked him dinner and would make my intentions clear. I would seduce him and secure him. I considered it inevitable. Ben, though, considered it impossible.

As he entered, he looked at the candles and creases began to form on his forehead. Darn it, I should not have gone out so hard.

"What's the occasion, Nora."

"Nothing, I just wanted to do a special dinner."

Ben didn't drink, so I could not even get him drunk. Instead, over dessert, I wiggled closer.

"Ben, there is something special I have to say."

"I know Nora, I could tell. But you don't have to sneak around it."

"Ben, I will just come out and say it." I leaned over and kissed him softly.

"I want to be with you."

He pulled away, making space between his chair and the table. I used the chance to place myself on his lap. My groin pressed against his, my breasts against his body and my hands around his neck. I kissed his cheek, his lips and his forehead.

"Nora, please get off."

The pain was greater than any burn could have been.

"This is not right, Nora. I love you; I love you dearly, but I can't be your lover."

"Why not? I don't understand! We get on so well."

My heart was breaking more than when I was a toy of torture.

"You are not ready, Nora. You still have so much to learn about yourself. You still have so much growing up to do."

My god, these were the same words my father's friend used when he was showing me how to make myself wet so that he could slip inside. But I was not a child and needed Ben to know that.

"That's not fair, Ben. Look at me. I have a great career, an apartment, I play my part in society and pay my bills."

"I know all that Nora. But what do you want?"

"I want you, Ben."

"You can't have me, Nora. I am not something to be conquered. I care for you Nora but can't be with you. You need to start caring for yourself. Do you even know who you are?"

"Of course, I do! I am your friend. I am the girl that has been waiting patiently for you to realise that we can be more. I am the girl that loves you, and the one who wants to be with you."

"And Nora, I am the boy who has been waiting patiently to find out who you truly are. You are wonderful to be around, so accommodating. But I don't know who you are."

With that, he stood up, and I slid off.

"I'm sorry, Nora. I think it best that we don't see each other anymore."

He headed for the door, and I did one thing I had never done before. I chased him. This honest, honourable man. I ran behind him, banging the door shut before he could open it too far.

"Please, Ben. Please. You are the only man that has ever truly cared for me. Please stay. I love you, Ben. I am sorry I crossed the line. Please forgive me. OK, you're right, let's just stay as friends."

"No-one is every going to truly care for you, Nora, until you start caring for yourself. Not about yourself, but for yourself. Until you find your passions you are just anybody's puppet. I thought after you got away from Stephen you would use the chance to become your own woman. But you are still stuck in people-pleasing. Nora, I have tried to ease you out of your shell, to provide somewhere safe. But I am not willing to invest any more effort in something you are not willing to do for yourself.

Goodbye, Nora."

As I saw him push past me and leave, my hospital door opened, and Ben was replaced with Ranjani.

"Hey, Nora. It's dinner time. Please go and get something to eat.

I reluctantly left my room and joined the line at the serving station, adamant not to make eye contact.

"Hello, you're new, aren't you?" said a short bald man, missing some teeth. "What's your name, love?"

Oh my god, I wish he would leave me alone.

"Nora."

"Sorry love. I am hard of hearing. What was it again?"

I felt like I shouted "Nora" the second time around. Great, now everyone here would know my name.

"Oh yes, Nora. I have a special meal ready here for you."

He bent down behind the counter, pulled out a plate covered in foil and placed it on a tray.

"Now, would you like some salad to go with that? We have a lovely Greek one today."

I could not imagine it would be better than the one I shared with Stephen on the islands, but I did not want to insult him.

"Sure."

"And dessert?"

"No thanks."

I had become so used to saying no to sweets with Stephen that the answer came out automatically. I was only allowed them if they were being sucked off him.

I knew I should have sat at the table and tried to be nice. But I just could not bear it. Instead, I smuggled the tray back into my room and closed the door. Ranjani followed shortly after with a curt knock.

"Nora, you are supposed to eat out in the dining room. But this is your first day, so I will let it slide."

There would be another nurse on in the morning, so I knew I could get away with at least one more meal in the sanctity of this room.

"I will make a note on your chart for the next nurse."

Bugger it. Ranjani was good. Seriously, why couldn't they just let me be alone?

"When you are done, come down to the nurses' station and get your meds."

"OK."

She left swiftly no doubt to hassle another poor soul.

I made it out and back from getting my meds without meeting anyone, brushed my teeth with relief, packed away my book and hopped into bed. It was so hard and small. I felt like a child all over again. I had no music to take my mind away. I just kept mulling over what being here meant and Ben's unbelievable declaration that he did not know who I was.

I must have been weary, for falling asleep did not take long. I was awoken a short time later by the sound of my door creaking open and a torch light touring the room. My first thought was that some crazed nut-job had escaped and was coming to kill me with cling wrap he had stolen from the kitchen. The light left, though, and the door snuck shut again. I remembered then Ranjani telling me they do checks several times a night. When she mentioned it, I thought it sounded like a massive intrusion. Now, after experiencing it, I had to admit it felt nice knowing someone was looking out for me.

The nightmares did not have the same compassion, determined to deliver dread. I had been free from them the past nights, perhaps because the medication had dulled my dreams. Now, the terror was back. I was huddled in the back of a huge cave, hiding from something or someone; I knew not what. I was ageing rapidly, more every minute. I was shrinking into the wicked witch from Snow White, but with no way to turn back.

My mother was there, in the shadows, taunting me and then walking away from me, out to the light and a lovely garden.

"You are dying a lonely old spinster, Nora. And it is all your fault. No-one will want you now."

These were the words she had said after I had brought my first boyfriend, Shane, home to meet her. When we were alone in the garden, she called him a loser and told me directly that I needed to find someone decent or that I would die a lonely spinster. She laughed when she said it, for it was so far away from the wonderful world she had built for herself. She knew it was not the only possible path. Mum did not take this stirring seriously. But I did.

Ben was there in the dream, too. He would run into the cave, cautiously poking me with a stick, unwilling to come close. He was treating me like some horrid creature, a leper, a freak, teasing me like a teenage boy would, with no remorse.

"You're a sad old spinster," he would laugh and prod some more. "No-one wants you, Nora."

When the dragon arrived, Ben disappeared. The dragon was black, seething, brutal, with eyes that would burn into my very soul. He would stick his head into the cave right up to my face. As it inspected me, I could smell its fetid breath and feel its heat blistering my skin. Once satisfied I was still suffering, it turned and blocked the entrance, trapping me in the dark. I was left to feel my bones begin to break under the weight of my own body, my bowels evacuating with no control, my skin starting to crack and bleed, and the ache of eternal loneliness. I could not die, only continue to deteriorate alone.

THE LOVE LIFE OF A CHAMELEON

Chapter 4

The sunrise was met with tired eyes and a mind reeling from the realism of the nightmare. My body was still echoing with the physical sensations of falling apart, and my insides churning from the visceral twisting of emotions. I would have loved to sleep some more but was bound by fear of returning to the cave and being unprepared to meet the doctor. Instead, I arose and dressed. I washed my face in the dark bathroom, so I did not need to see my reflection and snuck out for tea. Dangling the tea bags in the cardboard cup, I realised how much I missed my teapot. It was one of the only things I had kept from mum, and every morning I made tea in it, it reminded me of time with her. Having tea from that pot made me feel stronger like I was ready for whatever the day may bring. Today, though, the tea bags and throwaway cups were a testament to exactly where I was at.

I settled on my bed with the colouring book, turning to the last mandala and wondering what I would do next. For a few days, this book had taken the place of mum's teapot, and I was already feeling anxious about what would replace it when the last space had been shaded. This morning, instead of colouring, I was distracted by more doodling. Something was compelling me to try and capture the dragon, or at least its elements. While there was part of me that wanted to run from it and never look back, another part also existed. This part wanted to get to know and understand it - to find a way to be free from it. The evil in this beast was both excruciating and enchanting. A blank page became filled with sketches of scales, claws and eyes. I was satisfied with the shapes I had captured, and my success was shown by how scared I felt looking at them. I could not replicate its smell, but I did not need to; it still hung heavily around me. And while I was trying to avoid its acrid air, a thought struck me. Was this dragon there to prevent assistance or keep the world out so I could die in peace? Was its intent to imprison me, or was it protecting me?

My musing was interrupted by a sharp and serious knock. In walked a typical looking tired, slightly over-middle-aged man. He wore sensible slacks, a striped shirt, a shaven head, a tidy tie and gold-rim glasses. When I stood, I could look him in the eye. He placed a pile of files on the desk and shook my hand, introducing himself as Doctor Dempsey. He pulled at the chair beside the desk and signalled for me to join him. Bev had already shared the summary from yesterday, and he had a report from the previous place, so I did not need to repeat the events of the past week again. What a relief. Every retelling brought back such a sense of weariness like it was digging me into the same old hole. But he did ask if I knew why I was here. I wanted to say something smart-ass but could already tell that it would be ignored. I dutifully repeated what Bev had said about understanding the drivers that led me to the overdose. He nodded, acknowledging and accepting my answer, and in turn offered his purpose. He was there to help unravel the chaos that landed me here and to prepare a peaceful path forward. Between himself, Bev and everyone else here, they would help get me back on the road to wellness. He first needed to understand whether this was what I wanted.

I responded that I really didn't think I was ill. I just snapped. But it seemed Dr. Dempsey and Bev were on the same side, stating that this event was the sign of something much deeper. They were here to help me find the source of the stress and support me in dealing with it effectively, so I did not have to lash out like I had.

Over the next few days, Dr Dempsey and Bev would work to understand my early life and relationships. They were looking for patterns, events and responses that may have been helpful when I was younger but have now become maladaptive. What a strange word. OK, so maybe I was not mentally ill, just maladapted? I found this amusing but did not share my entertainment with the very dour Dr Dempsey. He seemed to appreciate a diligent student more than disruptive sarcasm, so I would oblige. However, I found the idea of patterns interesting. These are exactly what I had been working with since first opening the colouring book Maria gave me. Sequences of repeating shapes stacked in circles, each new mandala layer bringing forth a different design. Some would be slight evolutions of what had come before, others stark contrasts; both worlds sharing a solid black line.

I could see what they were trying to do. The mission then was to piece together the early layers that influenced the rest of the picture and paint the picture of Nora's psychology. For the next forty minutes, we went back and forth. He asked questions about my mother, father, home life, and early schooling. I provided succinct replies to his prompts, and he scribbled notes on his pad.

Were my parents still alive?

No. My father died when I was in high school, mum about a decade ago.

"What did they die from?"

"Dad died in a truck crash. Mum died of breast cancer."

What was my relationship like with my mum?

Really good. She was caring and supportive. No, no obvious signs of mental illness. I didn't say she would sob furiously when dad went away, but not because she missed him, out of sheer relief. She did not cry the day he died.

How did she make me feel?

Wow, OK. Interesting question. How did I feel around mum? I had never thought about it before.

Simply - loved, like no one else ever has. I was allowed to laugh and just have fun, although she also pushed me to focus on my schoolwork and make a better life than hers. She worked at a sandwich place during the day and sometimes as a cleaner at night to help pay the bills. She would bring home leftover slices for lunch box treats. My school friends were jealous of those, although not of much else.

The image of mum from my dream, frolicking through the garden, came to mind. That is exactly how she made me feel. Happy and hopeful. But she was gone.

What was my relationship like with my father?

This one created a twinge, and I tried to look away. It was then I realised there was a mirror hanging over the desk, and I was callously confronted with my own image. My reflection was watching me, making it much harder to lie or at least downplay the truth. What a horrible, underhanded thing to do. It was like the supermarkets that didn't trust you to scan all your items, so put a mirror in front of the screen. Seeing yourself would make you less likely to steal. Here, they suspected I may attempt to avoid handing over all the dreaded details at the bottom of my basket and paying the full price of honesty. It was a sad indictment of human nature and a truly sneaky act, although I also conceded that it was very clever.

I didn't really have a relationship with my father. I did not see him much. He was a truck driver and was pretty tired when he made it home. He was grumpy most of the time, so I tended to stay away from him.

"How did he make you feel?"

I was waiting for that question but could not have been prepared for the fear that began its deep drumming. Honestly, he made me feel scared. Every time I saw his truck outside the house would feel like throwing up. I knew it would come with a night of continuous criticism; over how I looked, my marks at school, the way I would smile, what I was wearing, why I didn't have a boyfriend, and how big my boobs were getting. He would follow me into my room; I was not allowed to close the door when he was home, waving his finger at me and finding new ways to humiliate me. There were days I was weak, when it all was too much, and I started to cry. I was told to toughen up, settle down and that I looked like a pathetic little girl.

Once, he had fallen down the steps at the pub and hurt his back. He couldn't drive and was stuck at home for over two months. That was easily the worst time of my life. It was horrendous, a living hell. I had not yet learnt how to deal with men, and certainly not my dad. I only made the mistake of putting my bloody pad in the bathroom bin once. I had wrapped it in toilet paper like mum had shown me, but this was not enough to placate my father's fury. I was dragged into the bathroom, my head pushed towards the open bin, told that this was disgusting, that I was disgusting, and to take my mess to the bin outside. I was worse than a dog leaving that filth in the house. The only respite mum and I would have from his vitriol was the grocery shopping trips. We took our time, sneaking some quiet space and sunshine in the park and sharing an ice cream before going to the supermarket.

Granted, he did try once to do something different. He saved up for a holiday by the beach, a little cottage a few blocks from the ocean. The drive there was promising; there seemed to be a pleasantness about him, an excitement about seeing something different. After about half an hour on the beach, though, he had enough. He hated the sand, so he went back to the cottage to hang out with his scotch instead. Mum and I stayed on, and that day created one of my most beautiful memories. Playing with her in the waves, watching her getting dumped but rising, laughing, letting herself float in the lulls and dive under the large ones. When we were worn out, we would lay on the sand and let the sun soak into our backs and our bellies breathe into the sand. In those moments, it felt like we were a bridge between heaven and earth, and I felt beautiful and like I belonged there.

I didn't want to leave, but the risk of him returning, tainting this space with his demands for dinner, and hauling us home was even more horrific. When we finally returned, he was still asleep, snoring on the sofa. When he awoke to the smell of sausages, he topped up his glass and started his rant about the sand. He treated it like an enemy. Over the next few days, we were seen as treasonous if we allowed any into the cottage and criminals if any sand succeeded in getting into the car.

What was my parent's relationship like?

I wasn't sure if you would call it one. I saw them cohabiting, but far from the couples I saw cuddling in the magazines mum would buy. They would sit together and watch TV when he was home. I would hear them talking about the weather, the house repairs, the bills, and his travel schedule. But every conversation would inevitably end in dad getting angry about something. The weather was always making his work difficult. The bills and house repairs always needed money we did not have, and he was just too tired to travel again, but he didn't have a choice. His frustration would be forced outwards; he would shove and hit, but never on the face. He would constantly put her down. Nothing she could do was ever good enough. Her cooking, clothes, and dresses were always too short, even though they were mid-calf. She never let him see her in pants. This was kept for his away days. She was never quick enough with the next beer, and the shots of scotch were never big enough. She copped the same as me but on a much grander scale; it was as if her bigger age meant she could accommodate more animosity. He would make her go to bed when she did, and I heard his demands and domination through the door. If he hurt her, she did not let me hear it.

The doctor asked me directly if he had abused me in any way. Was the belt abuse or discipline? Regardless, it was a feature of my early life, not so much when I was older. I remembered dad telling me every time that it was for my own good. A sudden shock sunk into my stomach and reddened my cheeks. I had never thought before how much Stephen was like my father. For a moment, I saw a flash of a creeping, thorny tendril traversing layers of my mandala, linking my life with a leafy malevolence.

He never touched me sexually if that was what he meant. Although when he was drunk, he did often make lewd comments to his friends, generally expressing pity for the poor man who had to take my virginity. It was embarrassing because there was one of his mates that I really liked. He was much younger than dad, maybe about ten years older than me. He was strong, tanned and stunning in his tight shorts and singlet tops. I kept sneaking looks at his arms and thighs; they were things of beauty, just like the statues of gods I had seen in the art books at school. He smoked like the heroes in the movies, and when he looked at me, I felt like I could melt. With mum at work, I was the one delivering snacks and drinks. In return, dad generously gave a range of demeaning comments, for which his friend would apologise later in the kitchen.

"Don't worry about them," he would say, "Any man would be lucky to have you, Nora."

He was the first to call me pretty, and I remembered the glow that erupted inside. Sometimes, he would rub my back reassuringly; other times, he would tuck my hair behind my ear and stroke it with his palm. Each time he caught me alone, he would compliment me, providing a counterforce to the contempt that I felt from my father. For him, I was smart, beautiful, my boobs were perfect, and he was sure the boys would be lining up for me. If dad had already fallen asleep when he was leaving, he would give me a kiss on the cheek as he said goodnight. This sensation seemed to seep into my very soul and stayed with me through all of the cleaning up and for the next several days. He was my first crush on a real person. In my room at night, I would imagine being romanced by Ronan Keating or George Michael. Still, this fantasy felt nothing like the ecstasy of being close to dad's friend. This man was the only reason I looked forward to my father coming home.

Was what happened with dad's friend abuse?

I know I was under the age of consent, but not by much, and I really liked him.

He had come around a few days after the funeral to check on me, which melted my heart. Mum was working more, so she was hardly ever home. His company was wonderful.

I did not know what to do when he started kissing me on the lips. I felt like a real loser; I hadn't had a chance to practice pashing. When his hands went to my boobs, I did hear some warning bells and did not know whether I actually wanted this. I just felt like I had no choice. He was so nice. I wanted him to like me, too, and I thought if I pushed him away, he would go away for good. I could not risk that. At that point in time, he was the best thing in my life, and I would not let it go. I had to grow up sometime, and it may as well be with him. In the beginning, when it was kissing and feeling through clothes, it was exciting. He became the centre of my nighttime fantasies, imagining him as my husband and wondering what our first night would be like together. The reality was far less romantic.

I felt so embarrassed when he asked me to lay naked with him. But he kept calling me beautiful and was gentle in taking my hand and helping me explore all of his parts. He smelt like old beer and cigarettes, but I didn't care. He showed me all the different sections of his penis, where it was sensitive, what made him feel good, and got me to practice until I got it right. He would take my hand and help me move it around my body, pinching, pushing and penetrating myself until I knew what it all felt like. He asked me if it felt good, and I said yes. That seemed like the right thing to say. I remembered the day he moved my fingers aside and slipped in his cock. It just seemed like the natural next step. It really hurt, though, but I hoped I hid the pain. I wanted him to feel good, and he seemed to really enjoy it. He told me he would pull out before he came and asked if I would swallow it? Of course, I would do anything to make him happy. I only hoped he did not notice how much I choked, was shocked by the taste and struggled to swallow the onslaught. After the final pulses, he assured me I had done great and was wonderful. He couldn't wait until I had got some more practice. Next time though, he would wear a condom so he could cum inside me.

Honestly, I felt so ashamed. It seemed so messy, not sexy, and my gags were just gross. But he was so generous and gentle, I would get better for him. No matter how incompetent I felt with dad's friend, I was superior to the girls at school, all silly and giddy in their chase of similar-aged boys. Most of them didn't even have muscles, let alone the maturity of dad's friend. Sure, I could not tell anyone about my older lover, but just knowing I had him was a great source of pride. I pitied the other girls who did not have the gift of a grown-up man. Because I did, he was all mine. I had a man, that is, until mum came home one day as he was driving away. I don't know if she was early or if we had spent too long making love, but either way, it did not matter. As he continued down the road, she pulled up at the door, looked at me, and knew immediately. I had never seen an expression so serious on her face. She jumped back in the car, careered down the road and didn't return until much later.

"He won't be coming around again, Nora."

I hated my mother that night. She had taken away something precious without even asking me what I wanted. I screamed at her that I loved him and slammed my bedroom door in her face, finalising any attempt for her to explain. In my room, I started plotting how to bypass her and find a way to hang out with him. I could go to his place instead, but I did not know where that was, and I was afraid she did. I prayed that he would fight for me, to come and talk with my mother and tell her how much he loved me. I made up movies in my mind about our reunion and my mother granting her support. I pined with each passing day, and when none of these events came to fruition, I was only left with the absence, an ache and the same old loneliness.

When I had settled into this sadness, mum dragged me to the doctor and explained to him that I needed to be on the pill. She said that my periods were very heavy, which they weren't, and that I was not yet sexually active, which I was. Mum lied to the doctor, but looking at him, I understood why.

He handed over the script in just a few minutes. Mum had not said anything to me until she watched me take the first one.

"I just want you to be safe, Nora. You have so much going for you. You don't want that spoilt with a child."

With these words, I wondered whether mum thought I had spoilt her life. Was I a disappointment, a distraction from her dreams? Or was it that she believed she had nothing else going for her and that motherhood was the mediocrity she deserved? But there was a more important consideration, and that was keeping me safe from another feared pregnancy, and this shared goal worked to cement our relationship back together.

"How was school? Did you enjoy it?"

It was OK—nothing special. Dad made me go to an all-girls school. He said it would teach me to be a woman and keep me away from the boys. We could hardly afford it, but he made mum work two jobs so that they could pay the fees. He would never let me forget it.

"What were your grades like?"

My grades were great. Learning was the only part of school I liked, and it seemed something I could do well. I won some academic awards and easily got the marks I needed for Uni.

"What about friends?"

I had a few, but not ones I wanted to share much with. I tended to move around a few different groups. I didn't mention the days I was teased by the boarders from rich farming families and the Country Road girls who got the best of everything. The sense of overwhelming loneliness from those days was back for a moment. It made me look again, briefly, into the mirror. I didn't feel like I really fitted in anywhere, but I told myself back then that I would one day.

"Were there any significant health issues throughout your childhood?"

"No."

I could not look at the mirror lest it compel me to disclose the time I thought I was pregnant. Dad's friend was always so careful with the condoms, but one day it broke. He brushed it off. "You'll be alright love." But when my period did not come on time, I began to pray. I apologised to God, admitting what I was doing was wrong. I asked for his forgiveness and that if he could make sure I was not pregnant, I would stop. I promised. I was never so happy before to see blood, and although it meant a few days of only hand and head jobs, it was the best feeling. I had spent the few days before racking my brain about how I could get an abortion. I even went to the library to research what I could take to cause a miscarriage. I remembered mum telling me once that she had one before me and had to take some medicine to get everything out. I parked that as an option, not knowing where I would get it. But I bled, felt blessed, and did not keep my promise.

The doctor called time on our talk, packed away his notepad and pulled out a timetable. Circling the boxes, he stated that I had to attend the two classes in the morning: gentle exercise and difficult emotions. After lunch, which I was to eat in the dining room (he did know), there were the healthy lifestyle and relaxation techniques classes. These were also mandatory unless I had a meeting with my counsellor. I was not yet allowed outside the building, but he would reassess over the next few days. A walk would do me good, but he needed to ensure I was in the right state of mind first. My counsellor would see me this afternoon, and then he would see me again tomorrow.

By the time he did his serious shuffle out the door, there was still another half hour until breakfast. This conversation had brought up a lot of stuff that I had forgotten, conveniently or purposefully, I could not tell. All of the bad feelings dad created were churning again. I began brooding over the lack of belonging, the loss of my first lover and how life could have been completely different. Scenes of life at school and my parent's fighting replayed as I stared out the window. See, this is why I did not look back. What is the use? It only brought up feelings you can't fix. It seemed so much more prudent just to keep pushing forward.

While disparaging the therapy, I learned much from this first session. The doctor's personality had been revealed. He was serious, sensible, disciplined, and detached — at least, that is how he wanted people to perceive him. His socks, though, told a different story. They were black but covered in colourful fruits that were wearing sunglasses. He had a quiet, quirky side, so my challenge had been set. Somehow, I needed to let him know that he was also being seen.

And he had not said anything about breakfast, so I smuggled that into my room with no shred of guilt. The cook was there again in the morning with a genuine smile and warm morning greeting. I reluctantly returned the gesture and got out of there quickly before he could start with any questions. The fruit was not quite ripe but had enough sweetness to be satisfying. The muesli pots were average but, topped with more Greek yoghurt, tasted much better.

Brushing my teeth in the dark bathroom, I wondered if I could use a headache as an excuse for missing the day's classes. Just then, though, I heard my mother's voice in my head. It was the same sentence she said, standing in the waves.

"Come on, Nora. Stop being such a scaredy cat. You're better than that. Just follow me."

I did that day. Diving under the waves when she did. Jumping over them when she did. Falling and floating when she did. What would she do now?

So, I went along and secured a mat right in the back row, against the wall. Finally, a sturdy sidekick. I begged for there not to be introductions, but I had to give my name, and being in the back, I had to go first. I said it quickly and looked down. I hated hearing my own name. Mum had made my name a dedication to her two favourite people, Nora Roberts, the author, and Nora Ephron, the filmmaker. Mum made me promise when she was sick that I would spend some time with their work. I saw how much joy it gave mum over the years to get the latest Nora Roberts book, so I agreed to give it a go. I could not admit to mum that I didn't make it past the second chapter. The characters just felt so superficial, so emotional, and so desperate. Instead, I told her I really enjoyed it and understood why she liked them so much. I hoped she believed me, but even if she doubted my honesty, she didn't let on. She looked delighted, and I was glad I could do that for her. In hindsight, I know I could have been honest. She would have asked more about my perspective, and then we would have had a healthy debate, likely ending in laughter. But it felt better to be on her side, to share this with her. The movies were better, only because we got to sit and watch them together. Some days, she was too weak to read, so we would snuggle up on the lounge and watch a whole range of romantic comedies. Thinking about it now, I had tried to make Ben my Harry, but he was no fictional character, and my amateur attempt at playing Sally had made a farce of this great film.

The stretching was great, and feeling the tension turned my mind to the present. I could push my body and sense the parts that were stiff. I could twist and know what was tight. Ben had introduced me to Yoga and it had become a dear friend. I had dabbled for much of my adult life, but Ben had challenged me to make it a discipline, one I had lost the past few days. As my body moved, I could feel my head begin to settle back into its proper place. Firmly seated on the ground, I reclaimed a sense of centre and calm. And as I cradled into child pose, my head tucked into my knees, I felt tears flow. For this felt like home. In my mind, I repeated the words the teacher had said earlier.

"Hello, Nora."

There was just enough time to go to the toilet and grab a green tea before the next class. After the exercise I felt pretty good, much lighter than when the doctor had left. Yet, I soon realised it was just a lull before another wild wave.

I didn't make it early enough to get the back seat in the class on difficult emotions. Wedged between two strangers made me very anxious. But I was next to a wall, so I wiggled the chair over and felt more comfortable. Bev was leading this session and the familiarity made me feel a little more relaxed. Then, she wrote up the emotion of the day. Shame. She wrote in big red letters on the board and began passing out a set of stapled papers. Shame, she announced, was the emotion that made us feel flawed, unworthy of anything good, like we were a lesser human being. It played an important role in keeping communities together but had a harmful shadow side. If we were shamed by the clan, we were outcasts, which meant certain death. We worked through the causes; childhood trauma, neglect, bullying, and excessive standards. And then we were tasked with ticking the boxes beside the consequences that seemed to play out in our lives. I could admit to people pleasing, but I didn't think I felt flawed, worthless, or empty; maybe a little lonely at times, but then it was my choice to withdraw. I didn't have any overt health problems, and I had never been diagnosed with depression or an addiction. I didn't see perfectionism as a problem; it was a source of pride. Why wouldn't anyone want to give their very best? Anything less was a waste. My self-esteem seemed to be just fine. I was a successful woman, so no problems there. Did I find it hard to trust others? Of course, but this was wise, not weak. And did I curb my voice in case I said the wrong thing? Of course, I did. That was just smart, not spineless. Look at what happened when I forgot this with Stephen and how badly it had gone with Ben.

There was not much on that list that resonated with me. But then we were all asked to think of a time when we had felt shame. What was the situation that caused it? How did we feel? What were the consequences – what did we do because of it? Had I felt it? Perhaps for a second with Stephen, but I snapped out of it before I would let him succeed with that. Maybe my father? Yes, he made me feel worthless, but this would have been well plastered over with the care I received from his friend. I dug into the past few days and realised there was shame around what I had done to Ben. While part of me wanted so desperately to get him back, there was a bigger part now wanting to run away, to hide, to never have to remember how my romantic attempts were rejected and the frustration on his face when he carried me out of the car. I would happily cast myself out of the tribe. Then something clicked. This same feeling of shame was what surrounded me in the cave. It was what I was left alone with in the dark when the dragon blocked the door. What did that make the dragon if it was intent on keeping me stuck there? These thoughts prompted the sketching of scales that thinned down into a single thread and tangled themselves across the page. Then, they stretched along the ground, growing into the shape of a tree. Some scales would broaden into bark, others lengthen into leaves.

It was then that I realised I was right. You can't fix feelings, but you could transform them. And yes, you do need to keep pushing forward, but with a clear purpose in mind. I found that a very interesting insight. I didn't know what to do with it, but I parked it on the page and packed up for the end of class.

Lunch consisted of salads, fried fish and chips, cake, and fruit. I decided to go against the doctor's orders and eat in my room. His reaction tomorrow would tell me more about what I was up against. I had finished when another nurse knocked on my door.

"Nora, you are meant to be eating in the dining room."

"Oh yes, sorry, I forgot. I will at dinner."

She scuttled off quickly; I wondered whether to write up my recalcitrance. I mean, really, what were they going to do? Take away some privileges? My peace was more important than their petty rules.

The healthy lifestyle class was positioned well to inflict maximum shame for poor lunch choices. The fish seemed like a great option at the time, but sitting through the evils of fried food would have made many feel bad about themselves. I scored a seat again at the back of the class and did my best to look like I was listening. I knew everything they were saying. From the beginning, Ben encouraged me to eat better and taught me many new recipes full of fresh veggies. I was a vegetarian long before meeting him, but he helped me become healthy. I really missed him. However, I now realised I would never return to him. Shame would keep me distant.

Bev found me filling my water bottle, and we settled back in my room for our afternoon chat. After the obligatory niceties, she asked me how I was finding the classes. I flicked through my notes, trying to find something informative to share. All I could come up with was that I found the shame one really interesting and had never thought about it before.

"It is so interesting isn't it! And I am so glad that you have started to think about it. Because shame will make you feel like you don't deserve love, health and happiness. And when we think we are not worthy of these things, then we do things that cause harm instead. We end up being with people, in places, and doing things that hurt us. It shows up in so many aspects of our life, and stunts our relationships and our personal growth."

So, with your permission, I would like to get a sense of where and how it has shown up for you. Doctor Dempsey gave me a rundown of your early years, and it sure sounds like your dad was a source of shame. "

"Yes, that's about right, Nothing I ever did was really good enough for him."

Even when he was away, the wounds his words caused were greater than mum could successfully smooth over.

"But you felt loved by your mum? Accepted for who you were?"

"Yes, she was great."

Having to speak of my mother in the past tense broke my heart, and I could feel the pressure in my chest, pushing up tears. But I held them back and shook off the sadness. I needed to play good student now.

"So, Nora. Is it fair to say that from a young age, you were taught by your father, maybe even terrorised with the notion that you were not good enough; that you were faulty and broken? Do you feel that it became your job to find a way to fix yourself?"

"Wow, Bev. You are good. I need to think about it a bit deeper, but on the surface, that sounds about right.

"So, tell me about your life at work."

"Well, I joined the consultancy after Uni and worked way up the ranks. I am aiming to make partner, hopefully in another two years. I tried this year but was passed over. "

"It sounds like a lot of pressure. What are the working conditions like?"

"Yes, it is, but we have to deliver for our clients. There are many days I work well over 10 hours, but I enjoy it. I can't remember the last time I took a holiday, but I don't really need one."

When I described the work environment, it sounded more like a sweatshop than a professional services firm. But everyone knew you had to put in the hard yards before you could go any higher. I remember a partner telling me, "If you can't stand the heat, get out of the kitchen."

"Oh, Nora. That sounds full on."

Bev saying "full on" sounded so out of place, but it was funny.

"Do you ever feel enough there?"

"No."

"So why do you stay?"

"It's what I know. It's what I am good at. It is secure. It pays well. I can see a pathway up. It is what I want to do."

"How about your finances, Nora. What are they like?"

"Really good. I have saved up a lot, especially after living with my last boyfriend. I can stand on my own two feet."

"Awesome, Nora. Congratulations."

Again, "awesome" was so out of place, but I was starting to get the sense that under her sensible haircut she was part hippie.

"Do you allow yourself treats with your savings; trips, or nice things?"

"No, they are not necessary. I don't need these things."

I did not tell her I would never spend money on myself if not required. Nice things were brought for me by my boyfriends, if they were so inclined. Having financial security was too important to throw away on trinkets. Although I did sometimes spend hours online shopping, putting thousands of dollars' worth of linen sheets and designer jewellery into my basket, before deleting them all and congratulating myself for my discipline.

"How about your social life? Do you have friends you see regularly?"

"No. I am too busy with work."

"And what about your love life? Do you have a boyfriend? Was he the one that brought you into the hospital?"

"No. He was just a friend."

"Have you ever had a boyfriend where you felt really free to be yourself?"

I had believed that this would be Ben, but now I was not so sure. He had accused me of not revealing myself to him. Had I? Or had I not tried hard enough?

"No, not really."

"Do you have a hobby? Any creative outlets?"

"No, there is no time. Work takes up most of my day and sometimes the weekends as well."

"That's a pity, Nora. I can see the designs in your book, and they are terrific. You seem to have a very natural artistic flair. Do you enjoy drawing?"

"Yes, I loved art at school, and would have loved to do more of it. But dad said it was just lazy, useless and there was no money in it. Mum would love what I did, but wanted me to have a better life than her. She said it was something I could enjoy in my spare time, when I was making good money and had some security."

"Now, what about spirituality, Nora. Do you practice any specific religion?"

"No. I prayed with mum to Mary when I was little and dad was away, and she still feels like an important figure to me. But when I went to a Catholic school, I realised how hypocritical everything was, and I could never live up to their expectations, so after I left I never touched it again."

Wow. I heard myself talk about expectations and saw Bev scribble in her book.

"That's really interesting, Nora. Right there it sounds like shame was huge for you at school. That's what it does, it holds us to account for standards. Some standards are really helpful and raise us up to be our best. Others are just stupid, and we end up having to hurt ourselves just to meet them. These kinds of standards, the unrealistic ones that cause shame, hold us down, or, even more sneakily, succeed at making us keep ourselves down, getting our own need for acceptance to do the dirty work."

Bev was excited about where this conversation was going and rustled around in her seat.

"This is excellent, Nora. Great work. I would like to set some homework if that's OK."

"Sure."

How could I refuse and extinguish this lady's enthusiasm? I did think about it for the moment, but she was one I needed to keep on side.

"Come with me."

Bev almost skipped to the art room, and I had to take many quick steps to keep up. She opened the immense cupboards, and what I saw made me smile. Shelves were stacked with canvases, paints, papers, journals, pencils, glue, coloured pens, fabrics, foils, buttons and art books.

"What size journal would you like?"

I chose A5; easy to fill up and carry around.

Bev then handed me a roll of fine-line markers. There were around thirty with multiple shades of every colour. I had not seen anything so impressive for a long time. Then came a pencil case full of basics—a little ruler and flick pencils because no sharpeners were allowed and only tiny erasers. She also popped in a gold and silver pen, the good ones that cost around ten dollars. What a treat!

When she was satisfied with my stash, we sat down, and she gave me my assignment.

"Until we meet tomorrow, I would like you to do two things. They will sound a bit weird, but bear with me."

I was getting used to her weirdness, so I was ready for whatever she might suggest.

"I want you to draw the shame you have experienced in your life. As you have seen it and felt it. Just go with whatever comes. This is not an assessment of any sort. It is a flow of expression. If you would prefer, just use words, or pictures, or both, whatever works for you. The aim is to show yourself what shame means to you."

"OK, that is interesting."

I learned that the word "interesting" was well received. It seemed to suggest some sense of introspection or insight.

"Now, here is the kicker. While I am giving you all of the colours, you are only allowed to use these ones."

She undid the roll of pens and pulled out five shades of red.

"Nora, Dr Dempsey and I very different. He is dubious about art therapy, but he has seen the help this can give. Art and colour are essential to who we are. They help us process, understand and pave a way forward. I have chosen red for a reason and will reveal that tomorrow. But I don't want to prompt anything. I want to see what comes out for you first."

She carefully placed the pens back in and bound up the roll.

"The second thing is, that before you go to bed, I want you to write down one thing you are grateful for about the day. Do you think you could do that?"

The last question sounded a little condescending, but I was willing to give Bev the benefit of the doubt. I said I could, no problem. Then she called me to stand back to view the full contents of the cupboard.

"Is there anything else you might need, Nora? Anything else calling you for this task?"

My eyes fell on the piles of coloured paper. They were so perfect and neat. Yes, I wanted to rip it to shreds. I was unsure whether it would form part of the artwork, but I knew I wanted to tear it apart. She handed me a few pieces of red paper and a glue stick. Then reached down and pulled out one of the art books.

"You might also find this interesting, for when you need to take a break."

It was a book on Frida Kahlo. I had heard of her briefly, but the book cover looked intriguing. I added it to my pile and followed Bev out. Before I returned to my room, she took me to the library and showed me a shelf that would also be worth exploring if I wanted to do something different. They were books all about self-compassion. It sounded a bit indulgent, so I initially dismissed it. Still, the beautiful seat by the window almost begged me to join it. I would think about it later. For now, I had a job to do.

We walked along the corridor while the relaxation class was finishing. Could missing that class be my grateful for the day? I suspect I would have made a fool of myself by falling asleep, so avoiding humiliation was certainly something to give thanks for. I made a mental note of this in case I could not find anything better. I said goodbye to Bev and returned to my room, sitting on my bed with all these wonderful tools to sketch some ideas about shame.

Chapter 5

Despite my excitement about embarking on this assignment, after sitting for half an hour with the five red pens, I had to admit I was stuck. I tried to think about how best to depict shame. I wanted to produce something smart and insightful to excite Bev and have her believe I was playing along. But there were no shapes, no words coming to mind. Ben used to say that I thought too much and felt too little. But now, I seemed incapable of either intellect or instinct. I picked up the Diary of Frida Kahlo to distract myself from this dilemma. Instead, I was hit with inspiration. A little girl stood at the entrance of a red building, seemingly being watched by an eye on the wall and trying to get inside. She had the same haircut I had as a child and a pair of brown boots, like the ones I wore in winter. Seeing this image of the little girl alone started an eruption, an enormous flow of feelings. I was sucked into that painting, with dad watching my every move, with him knowing how much I was scared and wanted to get in, but keeping me outside alone, just because he could.

I then knew what shape I needed to start with. I grabbed whatever red came first and sketched an eye on the page, with the pupil being a deeper shade, one more sinister and seething. Was this shame? The heat flowing into my cheeks told me it was. It was the same burning sensation I had in my face when dad would humiliate me in front of his friends. And it was the same blaze I felt with dad's friend when I choked and gagged giving him head.

From the eye came a chain of crimson. I could feel it pressing into my skin. It was cold, hard, and hurt whenever you moved, just like the one Stephen would use when he wanted to ensure my submission. I drew a rock at the end of the chain and put it under a maroon river. This was the sinking feeling I had when I thought I was pregnant. During that week, I lived in hell in my head. The ripples on the river formed into a womb lined with maroon. The blood flowed out back then, and now it began a bright red braid over the page. And the womb was left, laying empty. A triumph as a teenager. Now, though, I was at the old end of the breeding age range and not likely to ever be a mum. Yes, there was shame in that space.

The braids began to bend and became the outline of lips, a line of lips painted in different shades of red. These were the colours of lipstick I wore to work each night in the Cross and applied ardently in the apartment that doubled as the escort agency office. I came to the city with a curiosity and a romantic notion of what it must be like to make love for money, and like magic, I was given the opportunity to see if the romance was real. Colouring in these lips, I was struck by the irony – the night I was offered a job, I was wearing a long pink floral-print dress and a pink hand-knitted cardigan with pearl buttons. How quickly this persona was replaced once I stepped into the red light.

But the burn came back again when one night I bled with a customer. I was thrown out of his room, with him ranting at the security guard that I was disgusting. I was pushed into the "loser lounge" out the back with the others who could not work that night; one too drunk to stand, another shooting up in the corner, and another sniffling and sneezing snot over her dress. I was not allowed to leave until the club closed. That night, I learned that the bouncers were not only there to keep the girls safe; but to keep us in. When I replaced the club with an escort agency I felt much more in my place, but never at peace. I learnt that the thrill of being wanted, of being paid for, of being used for pleasure was in my own mind. It was not inherent in the profession.

The secret of being a sex worker seared scarlet every time I would go home and visit mum, but I kept it safe under my skin. I did think about telling her once. Part of me suspected she would be thrilled that I was exploring the world and its realities and being resourceful to get ahead. The other knew she would be saddened that I was letting men use me, and she would be so angry to find out I was not being safe.

The shape of lips then shifted into a string of S's. S for shame, for sex, for secret, for "settle down", and for Shane, the first guy that I settled down with. His guitar was red, and his energy on stage was searing. So was my face when mum called him a loser. Although it would have been a much deeper red, a burgundy; like the colour of the roses I placed on mum's casket as it was lowered into the ground, and the hue of the hate I felt at Shane for his absence.

There was one shade I had not used yet: an orange-red. How close this was to the city lights in Seattle that I passed on my way to a new apartment and a new life. Letters became light bulbs, blaring in orange-red across the page. I met Aaron in Seattle, and we began to map out our successful life together. He knew how much I loved these lights, so he brought me a pair of stilettos in the exact colour and, whenever he could find them, look-alike flowers. It was such a pity they had no fragrance. There was also the red sole of his mother's shoes, showing me her superiority and that luxury was her lifestyle, while for me, it was only a longing. There was another red I associated with Aaron, and that was the flush of his penis after a bout of frantic lovemaking. In many ways he reminded me of the guys at the Cross, desperate to prove himself, just not paying for it explicitly. This flush was also inside me, ingrained as a frustration, the burning begging for more attention and appreciation.

As the light bulbs transformed into flames, I remembered how they had been cared for by Daniel. His art was astounding, but his hands were awesome. He had seen my yearning, caressed it, expanded it and given me permission to explode. For he wanted emotion and exacting it from me was his excitement. After our passion, he would paint. I would watch him naked, mixing the existing to make new and aiming to get the post-sex shades of my vulva just right.

The flames also reminded me of Calli, her warm embrace, and her bright smile when she gave me the garnet ring. But then came lines; the ones I crossed when I returned it to her and walked away.

After the lines came red triangles. This was the red I knew with Rob and Tom, similar to the colour of the ties and cummerbunds they wore at their wedding. They adorned me with them afterwards, playing with me between their nuptial celebrations. Positioning me between them and calling me their treasured third point, the tip that made them strong like a triangle. But this triangle was not sturdy, smashed under the seduction from Stephen, with his orange-red glasses and goading as to whether I thought myself too much for just one guy. The orange-red flared on the end of his cigarette as he said I had obviously not had the challenge of him yet, and with that comment, I was captured. He was looking for a live-in lover, an independent woman but one who wanted to enjoy submission on the side. In return, he could introduce me to a world of success. I could shine in my career, and he would support me in whatever way possible. I could also mix with the rich and famous. What more could a girl want?

So, after the triangles came more lines, ones created and then crossed. These lines flowed back into burgundy blood like that crusted over the deep bite he gave me on my shoulder and that seeped from the cigarette burns on my legs when I sat down. I remembered touching these scars as I placed the lace red bodysuit on the bed. When I knew Ben was ready, I would seduce him, wearing it. That night, he would finally see the scars, and as he stroked them, we would be united. I would show him what he had saved me from, and he would become my superhero, shielding me from life with his scarlet cape.

The lines started to cut deeper into the page and turned into crosses. The only red seen that night had been from the lights beeping incessantly on the hospital machine. They kept flashing at me even when my eyes were closed. I started to feel so stupid, and in sympathy, the crosses converted into slashes. There were layers of loathing embedded into this memory and levels of revulsion that went so very deep. It needed more than just marks on paper. I went to the desk and grabbed a sheet of paper, ripping it into shreds and ready to stick it all over the red mess I had created. But my plans were paused when I glanced upwards and saw myself in the mirror. I watched, mesmerised by the mania that looked back. I really was a miserable wreck. Deep black bags begging for sleep and frizzy hair pleading for care. My lips sat in a sombre, straight line like they had forgotten how to smile. I did not recognise the eyes examining me, but they stayed still as the rest of my face began to shift and change.

Before me was the face of the child at the door; simple features, a short bob, and a smile. She seemed happy to see me and eager to know more. She quickly morphed into a teenager; hair and face lengthened, and the smile became more sedate. A string of plaits framed each side of her face, and I could not tell whether her portrait portrayed pride or pain. Soon, though, this confusion was replaced with the conviction of the uni student. The cheeks were broader now and brighter, and the eyes exuded excitement. The hair was wild again, but with a sense of freedom and focus, not from being forsaken. This student stayed for several minutes, saying nothing but everything. Too soon, it was tamed, the hair transformed into a tidy bob, the face coloured with muted clays. The features were covered with concentration and professionalism piled onto the sense of purpose.

Like a lightbulb flashing on and off, the face would switch suddenly, showing eyes encircled with charcoal, lips coloured crimson, and the mouth would morph into a sly smirk. This seductress gave way to the groupie, the hair held up by colourful clips and features framed with bold blues and sparkly purples. The shine slipped away to be replaced by shales and shades of seriousness. On the forehead were fine lines, deeper, darker ones under the eyes and a sense of seriousness. As time moved forward, the channels and imperfections were covered with a colour resembling, but not matching, the skin. The makeup became the face, flawless and firm. Slowly, fissures arose in the façade, and the canvas of my face began to crack. Deep etchings were embedded around my eyes, and my cheeks were covered in crevices. My mouth became surrounded by sickly seams, and my neck a column of corrugations. I was left staring at the spinster. And then it all faded away until all that remained was my true reflection, raw and ruined, and the rage arose.

The chair was a convenient weapon, and I wielded it like a woman possessed. It hit the mirror in the middle, making a sound more like metal than glass. There was no shatter, only a dense thud; there were no shards to satisfy my need for further harm. Now, even the mirror was mocking me. I struck it harder, this time supported by shrieks. The glass would not budge, and the chair bounced back, bringing no satisfaction, just sarcastic rebuke. I saw the nurse and security guard enter the room, and I screamed at them too. There were no further memories of the event, until I awoke in bed, a nurse seated beside me reading.

I rolled over before she could register I was conscious and clenched my eyes, trying to force a replay of the bits I had missed. I was not strapped to the bed, so it can't have been too bad. Yet, nothing came; there was a void. I prayed I did not hurt anyone. It was terrible to not remember but truly awful to contemplate the thought that I had harmed another person.

I had felt this uncertainty, this panic before. In Seattle, after another unsatisfying sex session with Aaron, my sympathy slipped away, and I was left with anger. I told him I was going to meet some girls from work at a club, but he didn't seem to care. My next memory was waking up in a seedy, smelly hotel room, naked from the waist down and with blood on the sheets. I scanned for another body, half expecting to see one dead on the floor. But there was no one. But maybe I attacked someone? Whose blood was this? The sting next to my navel as I moved reassured me it was mine. I don't know where I got the razor; maybe the same place as the half-drunk bottle of vodka. The fine lines told me this was not an attack from anyone else but my own meticulous madness. The relief was so immense that I thanked God that day. I went to the bathroom and purged myself of whatever pathetic things I had done, cum running down my leg as I leant over the bowl and thrust my fingers down my throat.

I tidied up well, though, and was feeling somewhat triumphant, then was hit with another wave of nausea when I saw my car. It was missing one mirror, a broken headlight, and a deep scrape of white paint down the passenger side. Had this happened while I was parked or from a post? Had I damaged someone else's car leaving the club? Or what if I had done something worse and hit a person or a pet? I drove back to the apartment, alert, waiting for the cop's siren and preparing to be taken into custody. I was already mentally prepared to deal with Aaron's embarrassment and the impact on my career. I began wondering whether I could afford a good lawyer.

But the ride home was smooth, and the sirens never came. By the time I returned to Aaron I just looked like I had a wild night out. If he wondered what I had done, he didn't let on. He was off the gym, giving me more time to get back to normal. I spent weeks after that waiting to be served with a warrant, thinking that every footstep past the front door was the police, ready to arrest me. But after a few months, and with the insurance covering the repairs to the car, this problem was packed up and shoved into storage, and I was left to live with the same old stress.

So, I was familiar with the fear that came after the fugue. It was here again with me now. A cyclone was going off in my head, and my body was hot and heavy. I was so confused. Was I a victim or an aggressor? My stomach cramped, my throat burned, and despite using all my strength to be silent, I could not stop the sobbing. The waves kept coming, but I could not go over or under; I just stood there and let them hit me. What the hell was wrong with me?

I did not know the nurse who came to sit beside me on the bed and who wrapped her arms around me. And for a moment, I wanted to yell at her too, to tell her to bugger off and leave me alone; to take her hands off me, and how dare she touch me? But no strength was left, and each stroke she made on my back felt like a blessing. Her waist was my wall and my hand on it creating a sense of hope. Each line she made deepened a lull, and it was not long before I was back to sleep.

I was sitting up with a cup of tea on my bed, staring out the window, well before the serious knock came. This doctor would not catch me off guard. The nurse was gone, and so was the chair, the doctor bringing his own from the corridor.

"Good morning, Nora. How are you feeling?"

"Fine."

"You had quite a wild afternoon."

"Yes, it appears so. Did I hurt anyone?"

"Your concern is admirable. And no, Nora, no-one was hurt. You were disarmed and sedated without any damage."

The relief washed over me and settled with the other weights in my chest, although the words "disarmed and sedated" sure stung, suggesting I was more of an inmate than an inpatient.

"Why is that important to you?"

"I just don't want other people to pay for me being an idiot."

"Do you think you were being an idiot, Nora."

"Of course. It is not the smartest thing to do to be screaming and slamming a chair into an unbreakable mirror, is it?"

"So, being smart is important to you?"

I could see what he was doing. I did have to commend this doctor; he was clever.

"Of course! Without it I would not have a career, be financially secure and be able to fend for myself."

"And yet, with it you are still here."

Silence. I could not think of anything to say.

"Do you know what brought on yesterday's event. What might have triggered it?"

"Maybe I just didn't want to eat in the dining room."

"Very funny, Nora."

His sarcastic tone told me he did not actually find my comment amusing.

"I can't help you unless you let me."

"Do you think I need help? Maybe I am just human?"

"You are human, Nora. One that is, from what I can gather so far, a sensitive one, living with an incredible amount of trauma. And the way you are dealing with it is destructive. So yes, I do think you need help."

I hung my head and rubbed my forehead. He was right, and I hated him for it. His calling me sensitive made me seethe. I had been denied the promotion at work because I was "too soft". Many adults and admirers had accused me of the same, taunting me to help me toughen up. I did not know how to care for it either, so had to build callouses over it to deflect their cruelty. Here, this doctor was not suggesting being sensitive was a shortfall. There was no damnation; simply a diagnosis.

"Do you remember what happened, Nora?"

"I remember hitting the mirror and the security guard entering. That's about it."

"Has this kind of thing happened before – you blanking out?"

"Yeh, there has been a few times."

I presented a synopsis of the previous, similar situations. There was the time I self-harmed at Uni. I was stressed out with final exams and lost a few hours. When I was working in the club and banished to the loser lounge, I couldn't remember if it was the drugs, but I had no idea how I got home or why the walls were covered with my blood. Then there was the incident in Seattle, but I was probably just drunk. I phrased the time with Stephen and his gang as politically correct as possible. It was an aggressive sexual situation. I spaced out then, too; I don't know for how long. After I split with Calli, I could not remember how I got home or why my clothes were wet on the floor. I think I blanked out for a while when Ben dropped me off at the hospital, but then it was probably just the pills.

"OK Nora, that is interesting."

Interesting? That word sounded great when I used it, but just sardonic when the doctor said it. Maybe this whole situation was actually fascinating from where he was sitting, but for me, it was just more evidence that I was capable of immense idiocy.

"What were you doing before this episode began."

An episode? He made my life sound like a sad soap opera. I guess it was not too dissimilar. It certainly was no fairy tale.

"I was working on the homework Bev gave me."

Why did I feel like I was ratting her out?

"And what was that?"

"Drawing how shame has turned up in my life."

"Can I see?"

I had not seen it since yesterday, too afraid to look. Opening the journal in front of him now I felt sick. It was a brutal, bloody mess.

"How did you feel when you were doing this, Nora?"

"I don't know."

"Interesting."

If he said interesting one more time, I swore I would poke him in the eye.

"I am starting to get an idea of what might be playing out for you, Nora. But before I make any conclusions, I would like to understand how your childhood experiences may be influencing you now; how the coping mechanisms you developed are hindering your health."

My health? Of course, I am in a hospital after all!

"Bev said you don't have many friends?"

"No, really just work acquaintances."

"And work takes up quite a bit of your life?"

"Yes, most of it. I am working towards partner."

This statement of fact set off a flurry of panic. Oh my god. I hope my colleagues didn't know I was in a mental institution. My chances would be sunk. They don't want a crazy as a partner. What have I done? Idiot! Idiot! Idiot!

I was left in silence for a few moments while he scribbled some notes. Or was it to allow me to sink into my stupidity?

"What about intimate relationships, Nora? How have they played out over your adult life. Have you had long-term, consistent partners, or spent time alone?"

"It's probably fair to say that since I started my consulting career, there's been a steady stream of relationships."

Were they relationships? Sure, we had something in common, but I was not convinced there was much of a connection.

"Around how long did each one last."

"I don't know exactly, maybe around one year, sometimes two."

"What is the longest you ever went without an intimate partner?"

"Maybe a few weeks."

I just knew he was going to say interesting!

"Interesting."

You absolute arsehole. I wanted to call him a cunt, but never could bring myself to use that word to describe anyone. Sure, I used it regularly to excite those who got off on obscene language. It seemed to work well to get them closer to climax. Still, I never used it outside the bedroom. The power this word held always surprised me, and I wondered why having one did not come with the same confidence. Before I could start weighing the pros and cons of poking him in the eye, we were interrupted, and the moment was lost. A nurse came in, excused herself, but explained the doctor was needed. I wondered whether there was another imbecile here making a dumb attempt at destroying the mirror.

"Sorry, Nora I have to go. But here's the plan. You are going to be under close supervision for at least today. Your door stays open. You will go to the classes and eat in the dining room, and keep doing the homework. Got it?"

"Yes."

"Bev is going to come and have a deeper debrief with you about what happened. And tomorrow I want to dig into your first few long-term relationships, so can you start thinking about those please?"

"Yes."

"Are you going to be OK with the mirror, or would you like us to mask it up?"

"I'll be OK."

"Good. Take care, Nora. I will see you tomorrow. "

The doctor left, dragging the chair behind him but not closing the door.

Oh god. I wish they would stop dragging up the past. Being reminded of my past failures was not fun. And then they were surprised when I got irritated? Why couldn't they just focus on the future? I wondered if the doctor got his rocks off hearing about other people's relationships. Perhaps he lived vicariously through the vices of others. They do say that people study what they lack for themselves. Maybe he wanted to learn about other people's minds because he was so monochromatic.

But then what does that say about me. I spent my days analysing other people's businesses and advising them on being more successful. Was this some vain attempt to make up for this missing reflective ability in my own life? Ludicrous. I buried that one in the pile of busted myths.

My belly started churning and calling for food. I had forgotten I had not eaten since yesterday's lunch and longed for something comforting. God dammit, I had to wait ages until breakfast. I decided to use the time to make notes for tomorrow, freeing up the rest of my day to get back to some mandalas. But how painful it was to dredge through my early relationships. They were just embarrassing. I had no choice but to play the game, so I put on my gloves and began to dig, promising myself I would stay at the periphery.

For there really was not that much to tell.

I would have loved to count dad's friend as a long-term relationship. It felt like years, but he was only with me for around three months before mum scared him off. We never went out anywhere together. So, was it really a relationship? I will never know if it had the chance to be more. There was nothing serious at Uni; lots of flings that didn't count for much.

I lived with mum, and she worked less, so there was little chance to host. Most guys were too busy getting on the beers with their buddies. I had a laugh with some, hung out a bit after class when I was not working and had sex with several in their darkened dorm rooms or seedy share houses, all extremely unsatisfying. Some of them suggested we should be a couple, but I was more concerned with my grades than getting trapped in that tedium.

When I moved to the city after graduation and landed a consultancy job, the freedom and sense of confidence were exhilarating. I considered a few guys at work as potential partners, but there was so much I wanted to explore first. I found a small place between the water and Kings Cross. It was a quick bus ride to work, so I could start early and stay late. And on the weekends, the street full of strip clubs and pubs was a constant source of curiosity. I was desperate to know what went on behind the darkened windows and bright lights. It took a few weeks for me to muster up the courage, but finally, one Saturday night, I meandered in. I sat a few rows back and watched the show – the strip, the snake and the sex with a dildo. When she squirted, the men cheered. I had never even known that was a thing. I thought she had urinated, but further investigation proved me wrong, and made me realise a new world was waiting.

As I went to get a drink, I scoped the scene and saw the row of women lined up near the stairs. Sometimes, a man would approach the bar and walk away with one. Upstairs, it seemed, was where the real fun happened. I was unsure why, but I wanted to be one of those girls. Back watching the show, I amused myself by drafting my application for the position of a prostitute. I wondered what my strengths would be. Would there be a practical test you would need to pass? Or perhaps you had to impress a panel? It was not so funny when I felt someone approach, and I looked up to find a burly guy in black looming over me.

"Get out. You need to leave."

I had no idea what I had done wrong, but I was not arguing with a guy who looked like he could snap me like a twig.

Just before the door, though, another guy barred my way.

"Wait. Do you want a job?"

Of course, I did. I was too stupid to ask what, but I was being handed an adventure and would not question it. And so, it began. I spent days in the consultancy and nights at the club. Most of the girls were great. They taught me what to do with the guys and a few tricks to keep for the special ones. One or two were just like the bullies at school, but I stayed away from them lest they beat me up. I had guys paying to be with me, and I felt powerful. But each night, a little fragment of the façade fell away, and I saw further behind the scenes. The power did not accumulate with age. Over time, the girls did not grow in happiness; they became haunted by human nature.

After my night in the loser lounge, I never went back. I moved over to the other side of the harbour and put my energies into excelling at work. I upgraded my briefcase and wardrobe and started planning overseas trips for advanced training. Still, there was something about making money from sex that was so enticing, so I decided to try something different. I signed up with an escort agency a few train stops away and added some expensive lingerie to my professional attire.

The trimmings of the apartment that acted as the escort office were stylish. A leather lounge suite, study desk, television and free drinks made the abode very comfortable, although the aim was always not to stay too long. There were drivers to take you to your client, ensure your safety, and collect the money afterwards. Yes, I did wonder what would happen if I met someone from work, but that was part of the excitement. This was where I first encountered the use of pain for pleasure. I was partnered with another girl and, on the drive, told what to expect. Her description of spanking, whipping, choking and slapping sounded horrible. I hardly expected to enjoy it as much as I did. Initially, each act was shocking and scary. But then the pain seemed to bring out a wildness, a wanting from deep within. Each stroke of sadism stirred me. From then on, I put my hands up for the pain jobs. I learnt so much more than the normal, needy lays.

There were six months of sleeplessness; career woman during the day, escort by night. About a month in, the gloss started to fade. I realised this was no better than the club; it just had better facilities. I still held the power over the clients, but it started to be less fun, leaving in the dark a crumpled mess. I was still beholden to the men waiting in the car and the women back at the apartment deciding who would get the next job. We were all disposable. It became clear that something had to give. I decided to concentrate again on my work. I had my fun. Now, it was time to get serious.

With my weekends free I found myself on Saturday nights down at the local pub, usually with some consulting comrades, otherwise alone, listening to the local bands. There was one that played regularly, and I had taken a shine to the guitarist. This was Shane and my first long-term boyfriend. Looking back, using the term serious in this description would be stupid. Shane exuded bad-boy energy. He had long hair and sultry eyes surrounded by black liner and wore mesh shirts so you could see his nipples and leather pants with a studded belt. His muscly arms and chunky rings looked like he could break a jaw if he took a swing, and when he held a pick in his teeth, I was definitely turned on. He was my challenge, and I casually started making eye contact, which he returned, then became consistent. He approached me at the bar on a break and brought me a drink.

"Would you like to enjoy that in the VIP room?"

That question held so much promise.

Bev disrupted my dot points and doodles. I felt bad seeing her. I felt that I had let her down somehow.

"Hi, Nora. I just wanted to come and see how you are going. How are you feeling?"

"I'm OK."

"I'm so sorry. I may have gone in too hard, too soon. Would it be OK to chat about it further this afternoon after class?"

"Sure."

"Again, I am really sorry that happened, Nora. Are you sure you are OK?"

"Yep."

"Alright, I will leave you in peace. But please grab me or a nurse if there is anything you need."

"OK."

"Promise?"

"Promise, thanks Bev."

Wow. She really was lovely. I was so tempted to let her take the blame for my outburst. But I knew it was all on me.

She bustled away, and I could smell the warm wafts of breakfast being served. But bloody hell, I had to eat in the dining room. With the door open, I would be caught for sure if I tried non-compliance, and I could not do any more drama. I grabbed my notebook and a pen and put my stuff in a spot in the back corner.

I was headed to grab some banana bread and yoghurt, none of which required interaction, but was interrupted.

"Hi, Nora. Nice to see you back. I didn't get to introduce myself yesterday, my name is Mark."

Mark was the man with the missing teeth, serving the meals.

"There is a beautiful fresh batch of hash browns if you would like one. And poached eggs today. You eat eggs, don't you, Nora?"

"Yes, sometimes."

"Awesome. Would you like me to dish you up some, there are herbed mushrooms too if you like."

As much as I wanted to tell this man to go away, his offer sounded delicious and much more filling than my first idea.

"That would be lovely, thank you."

I don't think I had ever seen a face light up as brightly as Mark's as he began serving my breakfast.

"Bon Appetit, Nora. And there are sauces on the side if you would like them."

"Thanks, Mark."

I sped back to my corner and, for a moment, was hypnotised by the steam coming from the food. It would float and flow, and I sketched some strands while waiting for it to cool. Cramped in this corner reminded me of my first visit to the VIP room, which was actually a small office out the back of the pub. I was parked on top of Shane's lap on an old kitchen chair and offered a vodka shot to supplement my shandy. While the other guys huddled together, Shane and I sat separately.

"So, you know my name. What's yours?"

"It's Nora."

"Hmmm, that's a bit old school, isn't it? We will have to think of something a bit cooler for a rocker's girlfriend. That is, if you would like to be one?"

"Well, let's see if you want me as one first."

With that, we kissed and sealed the deal.

"Whoa, Shane", said the lead singer. "OK, you win. To beat you I am going to have to find two to fuck."

We kissed and whispered in that corner, and when it was time for him to head back to the stage, he asked me to hang around. I did. I watched from the audience in awe of this man who had so much confidence and captured my imagination. As the music played, I tried to think of a better name than Nora, but nothing came. I parked this one to brainstorm in bed with Shane. That would be the perfect time and place. After the show, they had more shots, snorted some coke and packed up. Shane told me he wanted to spend the night with me but lived in a cramped share-house. So we went back to my unit, and until I moved away two years later, he hardly left.

It must have been the combination of nose candy and novelty that created such a cyclone of climaxes. The energy I saw on stage was brought to my body, and I was teased and taken in every room. The next day, I was excited for what was to come, a coupledom in which I could thrive. I spent the week working, but weekends were with him, cruising around on his motorbike, watching his gigs proudly, and feeling his warm, sweaty body after the shows. It seemed like the perfect blend of being apart and together. The nights he had practice, I would lie in bed patiently until I heard his bike roll down the driveway. With the shift of the lock, my heart lit, and as he came to nuzzle in behind me, naked, I knew what he needed, and I revelled in providing it.

This brilliance only lasted, at best, six sensational months. Then the band broke up, and Shane became housebound. From then on, the best word I could find to describe Shane was sedate. He became unsure about what to do next and unwilling to step out solo. Shane wrote fabulous songs, many of which I found scrunched in the bin. I tried all I could to buoy his confidence, but he buried himself in and had become my baby. He would not rise when I went to work and, on the weekends, only at lunchtime to ask what was for breakfast. He did not want to go out to watch other bands and do some networking; he just sat and watched TV. He rarely ever initiated sex, and when he did, it was only after sniffing amyl. I started to understand why. When I came back from work, I would find porn discs lying around the loungeroom and a whole load of washing waiting for me. It all smelt like cum. One day, desperately needing attention, I offered to watch the movies together. "Nah.", was all he said. I watched as his waistline expanded, his skin got dull, and his excitement to see me at the end of the day diminished.

I was so disappointed. I wanted the life of a rowdy, wild rocker; I wanted him to adore me like he did his guitar when he played it passionately, not now, not packed away and forgotten about. I wanted to see him break through this blockage and shine; I believed in his potential, I just had to help him find this faith for himself. I needed this to go somewhere. I needed him to be someone. I needed him to get out of this rut. There was one solution, and that was to take him home to meet mum. I knew she would see the same thing I did and have the wisdom to help me find a way to bring it to life.

Mum was excited to meet him and ensured his favourite food and drink were ready. She smothered him with kindness, and I waited for his shell to crack. He stayed silent most of the time, though, conversing in short sentences and seemingly ungrateful for mum's generosity.

By day three, she had written him off. While he sat inside watching sports, mum and I shared tea on the deck. I was terrified to ask but did anyway, hoping for a pleasant surprise.

"So, Mum, what do you think about Shane?"

"Oh Nora, I am not sure whether this is what you want to hear, but he's a loser."

"That's not fair, Mum. He has a lot going for him."

"That might be so, Nora. But he is not letting anyone see it. He is a loser because he is wasting his potential and is not doing anything to help himself. He is lazy, a user, and as much as you want it to be otherwise, he is actually not going anywhere.

She was right. The energy I wanted never eventuated.

When mum got sick, I went home to visit her almost every weekend, and, without fail, she asked how Shane was doing each time. My answer was the same.

"He's getting there."

I just wasn't sure where there was. Maybe there was a porn addiction, a life of purposelessness. I only knew that there was not out of my house.

During one of our last visits, she got really serious.

"Nora, I won't be around forever. You really need someone that will support you."

Then came the smirk.

"Otherwise, you will die a lonely old spinster, like me!" She laughed. I didn't.

I was overcome with fear. Just like the time she told me that lollies would rot my teeth. I never touched another one.

The wise thing would have been to back away from Shane, count my losses and kick him out. But I did not want to be the one to give up on him. He just needed a champion. Instead, I solidified my investment. I came home every Sunday and cleaned up his mess. I scoured opportunities for songwriters and sent them what I could patch together from his scraps. I sought courses where he could perfect his craft and compromised my savings to send him along. I did all I could to show him he was loved and that I believed in him. He started to make plans and promises. None were fulfilled. He was beyond pudgy now; he was fat, but sadder was that despite my support, he was still faithless.

After mum died, I was desperate to do something different. I had to get away. Running from the grief seemed all I could do. A training opportunity came up in Seattle, and I took it as a sign. On one of my last visits to mum, while she was still well enough to watch TV, we had a movie marathon made up of mum's favourite Nora Ephron films. Sleepless in Seattle was among them, and she had said she wished she could have gone there to live near the water and regular rain. This was my chance to honour her memory; the coincidence felt meaningful and magical. I begged Shane to come along. Seattle was alive with music; he could start fresh, writing songs and finding a new, creative crowd. But he was fine as he was; Shane did not need me to be his mother. He would go back to his share house and make something happen.

Interestingly, he didn't try and convince me to stay either, so I started to sense that despite my dedication to him, he saw me as disposable. In the end, we packed up and parted ways. I went to pursue my career and process my grief, him to go back to being purposeless. I was just glad that we had never got around to changing my name. I walked away as Nora, nothing else.

I brushed my teeth in the dark and went in early to secure the back corner for the morning exercise. With each breath in, I felt some space being created around this memory; with each breath out, Shane slipped further away, and I was left alone with the sound of air against my throat. My sense of failure and frustration was replaced with a focus on the tension in my thighs and finding the moment my muscles met their limits. For that brief time, I was no longer languishing in my head. I was grounded in my body. My only decision was whether to push past the friction or to balance myself at the boundary between where I was and where I could be.

By the next class, though, the barrage of thoughts was back. There was the delight and drive of the early days and the disappointment when he departed. Every moment played out like a montage in my mind and came out in the doodles on my page. There was the fresh flow of the breeze against my face on the back of his bike, the scintillating stream of notes that his guitar sang, and the pulse of my heart as I heard him come home. Then, there were so many low, straight lines. Every ray of light that would reach down to him was reflected, rejected.

Then the teacher listed on the board all the kinds of people we needed in our support network. As each on appeared I realised that I had played them all for Shane, hoping one would work to pull him out of his hole. I could see his greatness, but no matter who I was for him, he could not see that for himself. Was my support insufficient, or was he incapable of receiving it?

Then, the teacher mentioned the need to play these support roles for ourselves. That shut me up. I had never considered it before.

By lunch, I needed a distraction. I did not feel like doodling, not even to explore my dragon further. It was a demon that felt far too big for me at that moment. I picked up the book on Frida Kahlo. I had not known anything about this artist, but after I had melded with her child, I wanted to know more. The book was touted as an intimate self-portrait, yet there were so many faces. Perhaps she was using these sketches to practice for her next piece, or maybe they were parts of her she needed to express. Reading the introduction, I received my answer.

"I paint myself because I am alone. I am the subject I know best."

This made me take a deep breath. Ben had accused me of not knowing myself, and here was Frida, seeking to understand herself fully. Just like Seattle, this seemed like a crazy coincidence. I had just begun to read the essay on her work when Bev knocked and entered.

"Hi, Nora. Is now an OK time?"

"Sure, perfect."

I was thrilled. I would miss the next class and maybe wrangle out of the last one as well.

"Ah, I see you have started the book. What do you think?"

"It is interesting."

Yes, it sounded so much better when I said it.

"Bev, can I ask why you gave me this one?"

"Well, I wanted to show you how powerful doodles can be. Frida's sketches are not just stunning, they are saying something about her experience, what she believes, and what she was exploring. I thought they reminded me of your work. I wanted you to see that they don't have to go anywhere or become anything, because they are meaningful just as they are."

"OK, that makes sense. Thanks."

"So, how are you feeling after last night?"

"Still a bit frazzled."

"Yes, it would have been frightening. The doctor tells me that this kind of thing has happened before."

"Yep, unfortunately."

"Well, I am just glad you were here this time. I'm so sorry it happened, but at least it shows us where we need to help."

This lady was the epitome of optimism. I found it hard to know whether it was inspiring or just fucking frustrating.

"Would you like to show me where you got to with the homework; what triggered it all for you?"

I reluctantly went and got the journal, opening it up to the page in question, which was easy to find. It was overflowing with red, the paper pounded, and its place bookmarked by strips of torn red paper.

"Oh wow. Do you want to tell me about it?"

"Well, there is not that much to say. It started pretty straightforward. I had some shapes showing times in my life when I felt shame, and the colours really brought them back to me. I'm not sure where it turned nasty."

"I can see it, Nora. It seems like you started so organised and structured. I can see the shapes underneath. But you're right. Then it got really savage. Would it be fair to say that the shame you started with turned to anger."

"Yes, that sounds about right."

"It may sound right, Nora. But does it feel right?"

"What do you mean?"

"From what we know, you were never encouraged to deal with your emotions. It is no surprise then that they exploded like this. Emotions are like lava in a volcano. If you don't let them flow, they build up and then there is nothing else that can happen but that they come out in one big blow.

Do you remember seeing anything like this with your parents?"

I paused to process what she was saying and excavate for any examples.

"Actually yes. Sometimes when dad was home, he would go off his rocker for what seemed like no reason. We knew to stay well away from him then. He usually settled down after a day or two though. We never talked about it. Mum sometimes would spend hours sobbing, but then she would be fine too. Is that the kind of thing you are thinking?"

"Yes, Nora. Perfect. It just shows how you were taught to deal, or in this case, not deal with emotions. These were your role models, so it makes sense that you do the same thing. The good thing is you are aware of it, so now you can start choosing healthier responses.

How did it feel for you when you started getting angry?"

"Horrible. I tried to stop it, but it just took over."

"Why did you try and stop it?"

"Because I shouldn't get angry."

"Why not?"

"Because getting angry is bad. It means I have lost control."

"No, no, no, no, no, Nora. That is bullshit. Oh, excuse my language. Anger is awesome."

Bev was really excited now, and she started waving her hands like I had just won a grand prize. Her swearing was a surprise, but I was coming to realise she was full of them.

"Anger is actually great progress."

"What? How? I feel like I have failed!"

"Well, think about where you started, with shame. Shame sees you lying down and sneaking away. It is basically you surrendering to other people's standards. Shame is debilitating, but anger primes you for action. It is a step forward, because now you are not just going to stand there and take it. You are going to assert yourself. Do you see the difference?"

"Sort of."

"Anger tells us our boundaries have been crossed and it is time to renegotiate or reestablish them. Let's look at this."

Bev scoured through the picture to find the place where the pressure became profound.

"Here, what are these straight lines. They start to cut deeper."

"They represent time with my ex-boyfriend, Stephen."

"Did he cross your boundaries."

"Yes."

"How?"

"Sometimes he was abusive, violent."

"I'm so, so sorry."

Bev went over and put her hand on mine.

"This may be difficult, Nora. But did you let him get away with it? Did you let him keep crossing the boundaries."

"Yes."

I could feel my jaws clenching.

"Are you angry at him Nora for what he did?"

"Yes."

"More importantly, Nora, are you angry at yourself for letting him do it?"

I could not answer. All that came out was a moan, followed by a flood of tears. Bev came closer and cuddled me. Sitting with me in silence as I sobbed.

I knew deep down that being with Stephen was wrong. My own voice would mix with mum's and harangue me until it created headaches. Still, I prevailed, striving for success through him. I had seen how he looked at other women and men and was determined that I would not be disposable again. He could continue with his dalliances, but I needed him to need me. Yes, his treatment of me made me feel bad, but nothing as brutal as mum's begging for me to run away. That was another reason Ben was so special. He gave me permission to do what I had wanted to for so long but never thought I could.

"Oh Nora. I know this is so hard, but we are starting to unravel what is really important to you, not just to other people."

When that wave subsided, we worked through the other patterns in the picture, identifying how other people had trespassed in the past and how I had permitted it. I realised I was so angry at them for how they treated me. There was something more sinister, though, which was a seething rage at me for letting them. What kind of pathetic piece of shit did that make me? I never fought back. I never argued or asserted my rights. I simply shut up and slipped away. Except with Ben. Then I told him what I wanted but look how that worked out. He walked away. I was so confused. I was damned if I did stand up for myself and damned if I didn't. I was trying to figure out which one hurt less.

And then there was the anger at mum for dying. I was still furious at her for forsaking me. She was the only one who understood me and truly cared for me. Although Calli came close. Before now, I had not been aware of how much I hated myself for how I treated her and how much of this loathing was lingering. She was the only one that I had crossed the line with. I had always prided myself on being kind and caring for others. With Calli, though, I was cruel, and this was like a constant callous in my conscience. The only way I could get her to back off was by being a bitch. And I played this role to perfection. People do some pretty bad things when they are scared; she witnessed me at my worst.

There were more tears and minutes of silence while I struggled, spewing forth all the fury I had never felt. I was not the independent and strong woman I had told myself I was. I was merely navigating the boundaries of others. Bev sat beside me through it all, bringing me to a place of balance and sprinkling all my suffering with silver linings. Together, we rode the rollercoaster of recklessness and remorse, animus and acceptance, alighting after a long time at some kind of stable stopover.

"I'm sorry, Bev."

"What are you sorry for? This is exactly why I am here. I also want you to know that I am incredibly impressed."

Yep, this woman was insane.

"There are other people that would resist or reject the work you are doing know, and honestly, I thought to begin with that you might be one of them. But you are so courageous to work through it."

Right then, I saw my ruse had slipped. I was no longer playing the good student, so I could escape with permission. This place, yes, was a means, but to an end that I had not expected. The relief I felt after my rant told me I was on the right path and there were no other voices or vices here to contest it.

"Before we finish up, there was one other piece of homework. Was there anything you were grateful for yesterday?"

"Yes, that there was one day less I had to stay here."

I thought she would be insulted, but she seemed to completely comprehend my eagerness to exit.

"I get it, Nora. I really do. This is goddamn difficult stuff."

"We are not taught any of this, and it can really stuff us up. Try not to be hard on yourself. Just keep going. You are doing great. Just keep going.

Tonight, I suspect you might need some rest, but if you have any time, you could think about or list some red things that have brought you comfort or happiness in the past. We have given red a really bad rap with that exercise. But red is also the colour of reliability, power and courage. It would be great if you could balance it out and think about the red things that have provided positive memories and energy for you. Otherwise, you have more to learn about Frida and many blank pages in your book. But most importantly, try to get some sleep. This work is difficult enough, let alone when you put tiredness on the top."

She got up and gave me another hug.

"Please, if you need me, just get the nurses to call. They have my number, and I have told them you can call any time, day or night. Got it?"

"Yep, thanks Bev."

"It is my pleasure. Take care!"

Ranjani came a little later to get me for dinner.

"Hey, Nora. It is so nice to see you again. How are you?"

A shrug and a frown were all I could muster in response.

I was far too nauseous from the wild ride to consider eating. She asked me if I would like a pill to settle my stomach, which I declined, not wanting to have to digest anything more.

"Alright, but let me bring you something that might help."

She returned with a cup of ginger and lemon tea, a banana, and a packet of crackers.

I sipped on the tea as I turned the pages of Frida's drawings. What was it about ginger that seemed to provide strength? The smell was reassuring, and the taste told me everything would be OK. I could not face a banana, but the crackers were simple and salty, and the empty packet was shown to Ranjani when she came to check up on me later.

"That's great. Are you sure you wouldn't like some medication to help?"

"No thanks, Ranjani. I hope tomorrow I will be fine."

"What about to sleep?"

I hadn't thought that far ahead. She was right, though. I was still dealing with all of the drama; I did not want to have to deal with the dragon and a sleepless night as well.

"Actually, thanks, I think that would be a good idea."

We went to the nurse's station, where she recorded and passed over the pill. She then said goodnight and wished me a peaceful sleep.

Settling into bed, I scribbled out my gratitude for the day. There was one day less of living here. Two down, twelve to go. Now that I knew Bev was not insulted, I was free to tell it like I felt it.

While waiting for the medicine to work, I started thinking about red things that did not result in feelings of rage. Strawberries and tomatoes sprang to mind, the ones in mum's garden. We would sit on the ground together and care for them, picking the ripe ones and checking for pests. The fruit smelt so good, a very special blend of sunlight and sugar. Sometimes, I would find a lady beetle and beg mum to keep it as a pet. But she would remind me that all of God's creatures were born to be free, and besides, its mum would be so worried and miss it desperately, just like she would if someone came and took me away. From the moment I saw the king parrot, I was enchanted. It would come and sit on the bush, its red face and breast blaring. Mum told me it was always the blokes that had the bright colours to attract the girls. But I wanted to be that bold.

There were a few times at work when I felt things were slipping away, and I was about to give up. That is when I would go and buy myself a red shirt or a red suit. Wearing it, I felt like the king parrot and stepped proudly again into my place. Only it was not girls I was going after, but my goals. There was the red of the watermelon we had in summer. How it would crunch and make your mouth a sticky mess. Mum and I would eat it over the sink, slurping as we went and splashing each other with water afterwards when we cleaned up. We wore cherries as earrings, prancing around the kitchen to whatever song was on the radio. Then, we pipped them to make pies, our fingers covered and coloured by their crimson cuddles.

When I learnt to drive, I always loved the red stop signs. I had never thought about why before now, but maybe it was for the certainty they provided. I loved their clarity; there was no mistaking what they wanted you to do. And each stop meant a chance to take stock, to breathe at least once before beginning again. I remembered the redwood trees Aaron and I saw in Seattle Park; they were gorgeous giants, calling me to camp beside them for a while. But Aaron wanted to keep moving. There were times I had planned to go back to the park by myself and make the most of my time with these trees, but something always came up that seemed to be more important.

Red was also the colour of the lobster tail that told me I had stepped up in the world. It was a pity it had to die for me to deem myself some kind of success. But there it was, shiny, scarlet, seared, and served on a platter that provided far too much space for this single specimen.

When I returned to Australia, I was blessed with a trail of bowing noble bottle brushes, spikey, sassy grevillea and happy red hibiscus bushes between my unit and the office. When the need arose, I would take scissors with me and, on the way home, harvest a bunch of their beauty. My table would become a scene from a Margaret Olley still life, which gave me so much satisfaction. The hibiscus would fade after a few days, but the bottle brushes and grevillea would go on strong for almost a week before they started to decline. I admired them for their strength, their hardiness and how they would hang on to their colour despite being dragged out of their home.

With the onset of the drugs, sleep came, but so did the dragon, in snippets. The sedation may have made him seem less scary, but I was sure I saw him step aside from the cave entrance so slightly, just to let a little sunshine in. And did I detect specks of scarlet where the sun hit the scales? Still, there was the strong stench of my own shit.

THE LOVE LIFE OF A CHAMELEON

Chapter 6

I woke wearily, my head heavy from the sedation. For several minutes I stared at the wall and contemplated sleeping in. So what if the doctor saw me unkempt and unprepared? I was sure he had to wake other people up for their consultations, but I could not let him be the one in control. It was the same reason that I would rarely drink, not because of anyone else's expectations and not because I was better than the others and their excesses, but because I was afraid of forfeiting my power. I could work with weariness, not weakness. Moving slowly, I got up and made tea. Supported by its warmth and the knowledge that I would soon feel better, I began investigating the next entry on my list of intimate relationships.

When I first arrived in Seattle, there was so much exploring to do and a new me to be found. Just like the movie said, in Seattle I was going to grow a new heart. Unlike the movie, though, I was not mourning the loss of a wife but a mother, both my own and my failed attempt at being one for Shane. I worked hard during the days but made time to meet many American men. I went through a few fun weeks, figuring out how the dating scene worked and enjoying lots of meaningless sex. Each man had some noble characteristics, yet none challenged me or enticed me enough to follow up after the first few fucks. Until I met Aaron.

Aaron had the charisma of George Clooney and the same dark eyes bordered by brooding eyebrows. When he smiled, he even had the wonderful wrinkles that created whiskers around them. His suits were tailored, his pants tight enough to be tantalising, and his easy style a testament to inherited wealth. We met in a bar one Friday night, the atmosphere buzzing with the excitement of a long weekend ahead.

Our mutual friend introduced us and then left us alone, both of us suspecting a setup. Still, the banter flowed freely, and we even shared a laugh over the fact that he had a nice butt. Aaron could have slipped into an easy position at his father's finance firm but decided to make his own way, at least initially, as a stockbroker. He wanted to see how the world worked so that if he joined his dad later, he would have some real-life experience. He didn't want to feel that any position was just handed to him. He wanted to feel like he had earnt it. Aaron had the goal of making partner and I could see the passion in his eyes when he talked about his KPI and long-term plans. After trying to rouse Shane for so long, this was such a sweet song, and I got swept up in his story.

We clicked that night and exchanged numbers. By the next afternoon, we were having coffee and, the next night, dinner. Dinner was followed by dancing, and our first night folded in each other's arms. We celebrated the public holiday with coffee in bed, chatting between bouts of lovemaking. We started dating that weekend, and within six months, I had extended my stay, and we had moved in together.

Aaron's drive for progress was compelling. It burnt bright like the city lights sign I loved, and his mandate motivated me to be more. There was no doubt that I began this affair admiring him. After around a year, though, I began to see how much this passion masked a sense of powerlessness, and I began to pity him. Behind the fire was fear, and I got to see further behind this façade when we went to spend a weekend with his parents.

They did not have a house; they had an estate. They did not eat; they dined. And they did not care about how you felt; just what you did. For people well into their fifties, they were incredibly fashionable, his father parading around with pocket squares and his mother lauding around in Louboutin's. The whole time we were there, Aaron's parents did not once ask their son about how he was, but quizzed him constantly about his work. They did not inquire about his health or happiness, just his achievements and ambitions. They were best described as pleasant, not friendly, tepid, not tender. Their behaviour explained the increased agitation I saw on Aaron's face as we approached the gates. I had seen it pop up sporadically before, but over these two days, it was sustained and almost sickening.

There was one surprise, and that was Aaron's room, which was more like a gallery. It was full of paintings, some incomplete, and several sketches were stuck on the walls. What I saw was fantastic. There were abstract landscapes that made me long to be in them. There were portraits of people with fearsome features and others with love lighting up their eyes.

"Aaron, these are incredible. When did you do these?"

"When I was in school."

"So, you loved art in school too?"

"Absolutely!"

"Who are these people?" I asked, adamant to know more.

"Just people I saw on the streets when I was at school."

"So why don't you do any art now? You really have a great talent for it."

"Mum and dad would be furious if they thought I was frittering away time with something that would never make any serious money."

"But to make serious money, you have to be serious about it. And I think you really could be, if you wanted to."

Aaron just shrugged and started towards the door.

"Do you miss it? The process of making something, I mean."

"Sure, but I can't do everything. I can do this though."

He closed the door, took my hand and led me into his closet. His hands hurriedly hitched up my skirt and shoved down my undies.

"Aaron, your parents!"

"They are too far away to hear anything. Fuck them anyway. I want to fuck you and I will."

I could not deny that sexy smirk or the danger dancing in his eyes. The deed was done in a few minutes, and I left the room flushed and feeling like we had won one over on his parents. There was a sense of pride sitting at lunch, knowing I had their son's semen stains on my thighs and that I had defiled their decent home. The sense of victory, though, for Aaron lasted about as long as the sex itself. As soon as we exited the room, I could see the anxiety return, and it stayed with him all the way back to our apartment.

Most of the time, our sex was fast. Our diaries were full, but it was still done with feeling. When we returned from the estate it became flustered. I thought it weird when Aaron asked me to put on the special shoes and took me where I stood in the kitchen. I gave him the benefit of the doubt, considering he had begun to explore a new kink. But the novelty soon wore off, and I just found it sad. Flustered evolved into frantic, which evolved into fury. It was like I was playing the role of his mother and receiving the aggression he could not act out with her.

I had always admired Aaron's sense of adventure when it came to sex. There was no place sacred; we would do it in the change rooms in department stores, unisex toilets in offices, airline lounge showers, and shopping centre car parks. He would simply give me a longing look and a sexy smirk, and I knew the game was on. After a while, though, the game became less audacious and more obsessive. As the erratic increased, the enjoyment decreased, and as the pressure at Aaron's work became more pervasive, so did this pattern.

He began waking me at nighttime, nuzzling up behind me, fingering me until wet and whispering, "Nora, I need this. I need you, Nora."

After a frenzied few minutes, when he was finished, he would kiss me on the back, roll over and return to sleep. Sometimes, a strong spirit was sculled straight afterwards and he would come back to bed smelling of scotch. Other times, he would pace in front of the mirror for a few minutes before making it back to bed. Still, there was no longer any seduction, just release. In many ways, it reminded me of the guys at the Cross all over again.

I did all I could to help him relieve the pressure and make him feel more powerful. I would pander to his needs and praise him profusely. I attempted, unsuccessfully, to slow things down, to get back to the sensual, the erotic, the playful and the passionate partnership. But it seemed for him there was something more important.

Each of his achievements was applauded (literally) by his supporters at stylish dinners. However, after the party ended, he only seemed sadder, like he was one step closer to being stuck. He would put a show on to celebrate my successes, presenting generous bouquets of flowers and popping pricey champagne. But the night would always end with another sex scene in stilettos at the kitchen sink. It may have been meant as praise, but it always felt like punishment. I was confused about what role I should play – champion or scapegoat.

Was this success? I seemed to be ticking all of the boxes. I was living overseas and I had a smart, rich, handsome boyfriend who still wanted to have sex with me. I had lots of shiny new things and a clear career pathway. What more could I want? The reality was though, after almost two years, I was tired. Really tired. Truthfully, closer to the border of burnout, but I couldn't let anyone know. I sneakily suggested to Aaron that we take some time off on weekends to ensure we were refreshed to perform at our best. Perhaps we could take some art lessons together or tour around some regional galleries? He was too tired, and there was too much to do. Weekends were made for networking, getting ahead of the week, and not running away from it. He really wanted to win, and so I had to lean in further to this lifestyle, to truly commit, not come up with options for how to chicken out.

When I found out my project was winding up, and that my visa would not be extended, I feigned frustration, but in reality, was relieved. There was a valid reason for my departure so Aaron would not feel personally rejected. I was not surprised at the lack of emotion at my announcement or the lack of distress at my departure. My only worry was what would happen to him when there was no one to come home to. I was going home to the same city but to a new apartment and, after two years, probably to a new set of people. How I dealt with that was the only thing I could control.

The doctor wandered in, dragging his chair and placing himself near the bed. He then plonked the pile of files on the floor and picked out mine.

"How are you today, Nora? "

He didn't wait for me to answer before he asked the next question.

"Did you get some sleep?"

"Yes, thanks."

Perhaps my tiredness made me feel like throwing a tantrum, but I decided not to make it easy for him. I noticed his socks. He was obviously a football fan and a Saints supporter.

"I haven't had a chance to catch up on the footy though. How are the Saints doing?"

Dammit. I had made this one far too obvious, and he could see right through the ploy.

"Fine. You can find out in the newspapers in the library. Now, please focus, Nora. I have a busy morning, there is no time for niceties. "

"Wow, OK. I guess that is what Bev is for?"

He frowned a little, which I took as a tiny triumph.

"How is your mood today?"

"Hang on, let me ask it. Excuse me Mr Mood, how are you today? "

I nodded my head in response to the imaginary conversation.

"It says it's fine, thank you doctor".

"Very funny Nora. I wish that was the first time I have heard that one."

Prick. Now, he was even denying me that prize.

"Have you had thoughts of self-harm since I saw you last?"

"No."

I did want to say that I did – only when I saw him walk in, but from what I had already seen, this was unlikely to get me anywhere.

"I'd like to ask you about your friendships today. You have said that you don't really have any. Why do you think that is?"

I had to concede that he had won this round.

"I guess I have always just been too busy at work."

"Yesterday you worked through the positive traits of people you need in your support network. Who in your life provided some, or all of those?"

"That would probably be my mum."

"Anyone else."

"Some people have provided bits at certain times."

"Could you give me some examples?"

"Sure. "Then I had to stop. And think. There was nothing specific that sprung to mind immediately, so I improvised.

"In their own way each partner has pushed me to be my best, whether it was in my career, my creativity or just by taking care of me."

"Well, Nora. That sounds like a textbook answer. The only thing that impresses me though is honesty, and I suggest you start investigating how much you are being honest with yourself."

I came so close to expressing my belief that this man was an absolute arsehole, but before I could get the words out I was interrupted with yet another question.

"Is there anyone who plays a support role for you now?"

"Not at the moment."

"So, when you leave, who will be around to support you?"

"I'm not sure yet."

"Well, we will keep talking about this as you get closer to discharge."

I hated that word – discharge – it always made me think of an STD.

We spent the next while working through a group of the guys and gals I had dated, with the doctor asking me for one word to describe each. This was a truly difficult exercise, but even though I asked nicely, "pass" was not an option. So, there was "deflated" for Shane, "successful" for Aaron (said with sarcasm), "dramatic" for Daniel, "emotional" for Calli, I skipped Rob and Tom – this would be too difficult to explain, "sharp" for Stephen and "beautiful, yet brutal" for Ben. There could not just be one word for Ben – he meant too much for one mere term.

Listening to this list, I could feel the anger arise.

"I'm sorry, but please explain again why this is important."

"It helps identify patterns of behaviour that help me determine any diagnosis."

Identifying patterns? It felt more like imposing a punishment! What if I promised I would never attempt suicide again. Would they just let me go? Or was trawling through my failures, and facing this shit, the price I had to pay for my lapse of logic?

Thankfully, the topic was changed before I could voice my vitriol.

"Nora, why was it so important for you to make partner at work?"

"I have always believed that you should do your best. Besides, it was a great prize to make all the hard work along the way worth it. If you still had the stamina, you wouldn't bow out halfway in a marathon – I feel the same way about climbing the corporate ladder."

These words came out of my mouth, but I knew that my confidence in the corporate life was waning. I had seen what it had done to Aaron and Stephen and how I had been compromised. Still, it was all I knew, and this devil did offer some delights.

He wrapped up, informing me that the next day, he would likely be ready to discuss a diagnosis.

"Do I have to walk away with one? Is it mandatory to take one home with me?"

My mojo had returned.

"Of course not, but in your case, I think you may be leaving with a companion, maybe two."

Holy hell. Really? There goes making partner. They weren't going to hand out promotions to psychopaths. Although, from what I had seen, some of the partners sure acted as if they were deviants. Maybe they were just not formally diagnosed with a personality disorder, or perhaps they just chose not to share it with others.

"Well, doctor, I hope they can take care of themselves. I am a busy woman!"

"Let's discuss that tomorrow. Also, I will let the nurse know that you can have your phone for brief periods. Please see the nurse to arrange that. The door can now be closed again, although the same rules apply with the nurses able to check on you at any time. Oh, and I need to remind you to eat in the dining room. That is non-negotiable."

"Of course."

Could he detect my contempt?

"But can I ask why I have to eat in the dining room. I don't get it."

"Your ability to function in a social setting, and to interact with other people is an important part of our considerations. Isolation for anyone is dangerous, let alone if they have been suffering from a mental disorder. I need to see that you are able to cope in a community setting, otherwise I will not be letting you out into one."

"Hang on doctor, I am confused. On one hand I have Bev telling me that I need to care for my boundaries and not let other people tread all over them. I genuinely feel safer here by myself than I do out there with all the other mentals, but you are making me mingle with them. Aren't you then stepping over my boundaries? So why should I let you? Should I be applying the same skills Bev is teaching me and basically tell you to fuck off?"

"There is one difference in these scenarios, Nora, and that what I am doing is being done for you, not too you. I suggest you think about that while you have breakfast."

Bastard.

"Goodbye, Nora."

"Whatever."

For once small moment there was a sense of satisfaction with this response. Then came the immediate aftermath of remorse. Yes, I had been disrespectful to the doctor, but putting him in a mood would not help all the other poor souls he was to see that day. My mother would be disgusted. Just as the doctor placed the chair back beside my desk, I added an obtuse apology.

"Have a good day, doctor."

"You too. See you tomorrow."

Between his departure and breakfast in the dining room, I did some drawing — not of anything in particular. Coloured circles of excess, of everything, of bursting like bubbles into emptiness. Ticks showing that things had been tested and completed. Feathers, flying, freedom, forming into feet. Just two stepping forward.

I took these tangles into breakfast, claiming my usual window seat, my comfy corner chair. Mark made me the hot meal of the day, minus the bacon, but with some extra beans, and handed it over with a smile.

"I hope this helps you have a great day, Nora."

How could he be so happy?

"Thanks Mark, really appreciate it."

I said it, but I started to feel like I meant it. On the way back to my seat, I wondered how much this guy was getting paid. He seemed to do more good than the psychiatrist, but I bet he was only paid a pittance. I thought about sending a letter of praise to the director. Maybe it might get him a raise.

In front of me, a warm meal and well wishes. And yet, such a sense of annoyance. This is being done for me, not to me. It sounded like something Ben would say. I should be thankful that I was being held in a mental hospital, my phone taken away, made to each in front of strangers, checked on while I slept, and analysed for the sole purpose of identifying my abnormalities. These did not feel like acts of altruism. But then, what did I have to compare it to?

I started making a list of who else could provide care. Surely, there must be someone in my support network. There were some colleagues I could call on in a crisis, but no one constant. It confirmed what I always knew, that at the end of the day, I was the only person I could depend on. Yet here was the doctor suggesting that he was now part of my crew, a compassionate friend doing this for me. Well, I will show him that I don't need him. I will figure out how to do whatever he thought he was doing for me for myself. Now I only had to find a way to forge medical certificates.

All this thinking slipped away in the silence and stillness that started the gentle exercise class. In this space, I allowed myself to forget and focus on feeling my body. I brushed my hands along my legs, folded my feet together, caressed my toes and wrapped them in my warm breath. I bowed to this moment, free of memories, and melded my mind to the spectrum of sensations occurring with each stretch. Moving on from this class, I made a mental note to record this as my gratitude for the day. At least it would be something different from the countdown of the previous days.

I had expected little from the next class, an exploration of our values. It sounded like our religious education lessons in school, and I wondered if we would be starting the conversation with the Ten Commandments. Bev was leading the class, so I was willing to give it the benefit of the doubt. She described how our beliefs determine our behaviour, so getting clear about and connecting with what we truly believe about ourselves is important. We discussed the vexing issue of taking other people's values as your own and the conflict it can cause. Supposedly, acknowledging and acting on your authentic priorities would create a place of greater peace. I did not see any of this as a problem. I thought it was pretty apparent I was acting from my own agenda. I was an independent, resilient, professional woman, determined to achieve her goals.

When it came time to list our five values, I had them ready to go. Independence. Resilience. Professionalism. Success. Oh shit, that was only four. I scanned down the list of prompts on the page. Organised. Yes. That's my fifth, organised. That is who I am - independent, resilient, professional, successful, organised. That was easy. Now I could see why being in here was irking me so much. I held independence very dear, and this place was denying me that. I was still sure I would have sorted this all out if I had just been given the chance.

Bev had given us a few more minutes, though, so out of a mix of boredom and curiosity, I scanned further through the list.

Connection caused my stomach to crunch. This was the conflict Bev was talking about. I felt compelled to circle it, to add a number six to my stash. Isn't this what everyone says is the purpose of life, the core of being human? Isn't this what we supposedly all crave? But then, why wasn't it on my list? Was its absence a sign of me being faulty or fake? Connection. Connection. Connection. No matter how many times I looked at it, I could not get a strong sense of my feelings about it. In one second, it sounded like something I was longing for, and in the next, it was laughing in my face, exposing itself as a lie. My uncertainty unfolded as an underline, a reminder to consider this one again later.

With that placeholder, I was free to continue my exploration, and that is when I found creativity calling to me. I cannot explain why, but I had to circle it. But which one from my original list would I leave off? Which one would creativity replace? I realised then that it had been creativity that had been replaced. Somewhere in my time at school, creativity was cast off the list, and success was put in its place. No longer was it important to explore and express myself and make something unique to me. What was vital was remembering, reciting, being right and getting rewarded. Gosh, this is what happened to Aaron too. I could see then how much we were alike, Aaron and me. Only it led him to anger; it led me to adapt. Was creativity a core value? Could it be if it was crushed that easily? Maybe that makes it a hobby, not a value? I noted that question to ask Bev.

During morning tea, I flipped through Frida's diary, hoping to clarify what the value of creativity meant for her and how it was defined. Only when I was looking for the word in the index did I gain some insight into my idiocy. Here I was, hoping someone else could define my direction and provide a perfect answer. What a dumb ass. Anyway, it gave me a chuckle before heading into the class on grief. And I needed all the distractions I could get because I knew this one would get heavy.

And it did. We delved into talking about loved ones who had died and where we found ourselves within the five stages. My meltdown had shown me that I was still pretty solidly in anger. Still, the sense of hopelessness without having her in my life seemed to suggest I also straddled depression. It was interesting to peg my place in the grief process. Still, I could not quite see how this categorisation would help. I prided myself on holding back my tears but felt pleased that others could let them flow. Moving on, we discussed the grief that shows up when we lose someone or something in other ways. The examples came readily to me. Like losing Ben. Like losing my mind. Like losing my freedom. Like losing my chance at promotion. It was becoming apparent that there were many guises of grief goading this girl. OK, this may explain some of the rollercoaster ride of the past few months. Now, all I had to do was to work through it, and all will be well.

Except, wait, there was more. The teacher then taunted us with a more subtle form of grief; the loss of self-identity. She started banging on about butterflies and how to change, to transform into its full potential, it had to leave something behind. It had to leave the chrysalis to continue its journey. Supposedly, there are stories about ourselves that we had to let go of to become better versions of ourselves. Giving up these sides of ourselves can also cause the emotions of grief. All I could think of was growing up and how it meant leaving behind my immature, idealistic ideas. But apart from that, my page was blank.

Lunch came, and I cuddled in my corner, trying to conjure and answer for what creativity meant for me. Mark was missing, so it was a bit lonely. The fill-in serving lady was nice enough, but she obviously did not really care. I left early to spend the rest of the time in my room and was met by Bev coming the opposite way.

"Hey, Nora. Have you had some lunch?"

"Yep, just did."

"Wonderful. Is now an OK time to catch up?

"Yes, absolutely."

I said it sedately, but inside, I shouted, "Yay - now I miss the afternoon classes."

Bev pulled up a chair, and I went and sat on the bed. I had decided not to declare defeat and put a towel over the mirror, but I was also still feeling a little fragile, and it was best avoided for a bit longer.

"Did you just have the class on grief?"

"Sure did."

"How did it go?"

"Fine."

"Did anything come up about your mum?

"Nothing I was not probably already aware of."

"Yes, the anger came out really loud and clear, didn't it?"

Nothing else was needed but a nod.

"How are you feeling about getting angry now? Any better."

"Kind of. It is still really embarrassing."

"Ah yes, there is shame speaking again. Hi shame, come and take a seat."

She signalled to the air to approach and sit on her lap.

OK, it now appeared that Bev had lost it.

"I know you probably think I'm stupid, Nora."

Would I have said that? Never to her face, that is for sure.

"But sometimes it is so much easier just to call things out. You can name it, let it take its place, respect why it is there and care for its presence. It is a lot nicer process than trying to push it down or punch it in the face. We will get to that more when we get to self-compassion, maybe early next week. For now, though, when you hear yourself saying something like that, just try and name the unhelpful emotion that is speaking. Awareness is the first essential step.

Can you also see how you just piled embarrassment on top of anger? Anger serves a purpose; don't pile it under more layers. Burying it will only prevent it from passing on its message and melting away.

"Awesome. What about in the self-identity section. Did anything take you by surprise there?"

"Not really. I couldn't really think of any bits of myself I have had to sacrifice lately. All I came up with was a sense of sentimentality, like there was part of me that is missing being a child. You know when things were simple, and you didn't have to make so many decisions."

"Does being an adult make you sad?"

"No. I don't think so. Sometimes I just wish I could be a kid again and not have all of the worries."

"Understandable. But when you think about it, you could be grieving for the little girl that was left behind. I could also see how some of your relationships could be a form of bargaining behaviour."

"Really? How so?"

"Did you say that with one of you latest partners you played the role of a submissive?"

"Yes, that's right."

"Could it be that this took you back to that simple childhood state? You didn't have to make any decisions, just do what he said, similar to the role you played with your father?"

"Oh dear, are you thinking that Stephen was a substitute for my dad?"

"It could be seen that way, but only you would know whether that was the case. It certainly was a relationship where you played the role of a child, eager to please, and compliant in your punishment."

"So, being with Stephen was a way for me to bargain my way back to being a kid?"

"It could have been. You could have subconsciously been missing that little girl so much that you would even put yourself in harm's way to get a little bit of her back."

"Wow. You might be right. I had never thought about that before."

"And I could also be way off the mark. Maybe you are just a sucker for sadists. Or maybe it says more about your sense of self-worth? "

Another of Bev's surprises, but this one really stung.

"We will keep working that one through. For now, I am really curious about how you found the work on values."

"Yeh, good. I do have a question though."

"Wonderful. What is it?"

I came up with my five easily, but creativity still felt important, or at least early on, but not so now. If it drops off as a priority, does that mean it was really a value or just something you did at the time?"

"Creativity, cool! I can see that for you! Well first, of course well all have more than just five, and they do compete with each other sometimes, and we do have to choose at certain times. What does creativity actually mean for you though, Nora?"

"Good question, Bev. I don't know. I guess it is taking what you have and using it in new ways to make something unique."

"And this is what I see you doing so much with your drawings. Even if it might not feel like it, I suspect you also apply this value at work too, to come up with great strategies and solutions."

"Your right, I actually do. But I wasn't seeing this as being creative."

"I think creativity is a value that has never been lost for you, Nora. Sure, overshadowed by others at times, but if you are still hearing it now, I would suggest it is central to who you are. I actually think it is a really important way you process the world. The good thing is that you have the space to explore it further here.

Tell me, and this is going to be a strange question, but how much has sex played a role in your relationships?"

If anyone else had asked me this question, I would have found it stupid and told them to mind their own business. But with Bev, I could see her digging was done to lift me out of wherever I was rather than to push me further down.

"For most of them it has played a huge part."

"Ah. This is the interesting thing about sex. It can be used as a substitute for creativity. You know the desire you have to get intimate with someone; well, this does not always mean that you want to have sex. Sure, sometimes it does, but other times, it is an emotion calling you to be creative. When you think about it, sex is the ultimate creation tool, so your craving for it may just be your heart having the need to make something.

For so many reasons, you didn't think you could act on your artistic side, so it came out in sex because, in your mind, sex was more successful than, say, sketching. It gave you something that art or craft couldn't; it also gave you attention and, even for a short while, created a sense of attachment. Sex helped you fill multiple needs.

How does that sit with you?"

"I'm not sure, I would need to think about a bit more."

Behind this hesitation I was actually finding this stuff really interesting. She was right. I had never questioned the call for sex; I just acted on it. And I had the call constantly, so maybe this was creativity after all?

"Absolutely. No pressure. I am just putting some ideas out there for you to sort through. In reality, there are a lot of complex things going on for you.

Were there any other values that created questions for you?"

I paused, unsure whether I really wanted to broach my brokenness when it came to connections. Bev was always encouraging me to be honest so that she could help me. But this one just felt like I was admitting defeat and may be used to confirm some damning diagnosis.

"Nora, it looks like there is something really worrying you. Would you like to share it with me?"

Now, I had no choice. I really was conflicted, and this woman really did seem to care.

"It's just the value of connection. It seems like I should select it, that this is something we are all supposed to aspire to. But I just can't seem to connect with it. That's funny, I can't connect with connection."

Bev gave a little chuckle.

"Explain more as to why this worries you."

"I don't know. It just feels like if I don't care about connection, then I am just some cold-hearted bitch, some kind of psychopath."

"No, Nora, not at all. What you are is, to a great extent, a product of your childhood. It sounds like, apart from your mum, your early connections were full of conflict and fear. Why would you want to make connections if this is what they meant? Your reaction to the value of connection is not a sign of a psychopath. It is a sign of someone who has learnt that connections are not necessarily safe. Really connecting with someone takes vulnerability, too, to open up and let them in.

Given your experiences, I suspect this would not come naturally for you, so even if you wanted to, making connections could be difficult. Society, yes, tells us that they are important, but your experience tells you otherwise. It's no wonder you are confused. A couple of things here. First, we don't have to hold the values that society says we must. It is difficult to deviate but let me give you an example.

I always thought that I should have family on my list of values. I love my Mum, Dad and my siblings and will help them when needed. But this whole sense of forming a tight-knit community with them is just not important to me. They want to go on holidays together, have regular dinners, chat all the time on the phone, blah blah blah. But my work and time alone are more important than this continual interaction. I used to feel like a failure, too, so I understand how hard it can be when you don't subscribe to a value everyone else thinks is important.

It is hard, but you have to get real and honest. Ask yourself the hard questions – know yourself. Only then will you have the wisdom that can lead to true wellbeing. In my case, my family are negative, highly toxic people. Spending time with them would bring me down. My work brings me challenge and joy; time alone restores my energy and gives me time to know myself more. I choose these things over time with them. Yes, they think I am being selfish, and perhaps I am, but it is for a bigger purpose. Does that make sense?"

"I think so."

In reality, it was a resounding "Yes". These insights were incredible. Why didn't they teach this kind of thing at school? Although back then I probably wouldn't have listened anyway. Back then I figured I knew everything.

Your value of creativity opens up so many doors for you. I don't think you have to push connection. I think it will come as a natural consequence of exploring your creativity. That is why I would like to explore it further in your homework, if that is OK with you?"

"Sure."

Bev picked up the hesitation in my voice.

"Nora, I know you might be a bit worried after the last time, but this one is a lot more positive, and remember, you can stop anytime it gets too much."

Of course, I never would. It went against another core need, for completion. I knew what she meant, though, and thanked her for the reassurance.

"Coincidentally, the colour associated with creativity is orange. I love it when it works out this way!"

She pulled out three pens from the pack—a bright sunrise, orange ochre, and a shade like honey. While she said it was not technically orange, she also picked out the gold pen to add a bit more "pizzazz" if I needed it.

"Same concept, Nora. Express yourself. Show what creativity means to you. Is there anything else you might want from the art room?"

I thought for a while, and the small journal pages didn't feel sufficient for this assignment.

"Maybe a bigger piece of paper?"

"Come on then, Nora. Let's do it!"

We went and stood in front of the closed art cupboard.

"Nora, do you mind if we do a little exercise while we are here?"

"No, I don't mind."

"Fantastic. Could I just get you to stand in front of this cupboard. Close your eyes and take a few deep breaths. I just want you to try and get in touch with how you are feeling."

Bev stood beside me, and we took the breaths together.

"Perfect. Now, I am going to open the cupboard, and I want you to take a moment, look inside and tell me how you feel. 3-2-1."

The countdown made this feel very consequential.

As the cupboard was opened, I surveyed all the shelves. Slowly, I could sense some sparks of interest, inspiration, and intuition. I could feel some shackles of seriousness and stress slip away.

"So, Nora. What words would you use for how you are feeling right now? Just spit them out, don't think."

"OK. Free. Excited. Home – no that's silly, I mean..."

"Home is not silly at all, Nora. I completely understand and I think it is exactly what you meant. Now, I know you said you just wanted paper, but please, grab the first thing that is calling you. Don't think, Nora, just feel. Go with the flow."

"So just take what I want?"

"Absolutely. What is calling you, Nora?"

I reached down and grabbed a large canvas.

"Woohoo! That is so awesome. I can't wait to see what comes next. Scrap the pens, let's get you some paints."

Bev made a big pile of paints in the same shades as the pens, brushes, palettes, plastic cups, sheeting, and paper towels.

"Very clever, Nora. Now you can make your own shades as well. You are no longer stuck with the set colours."

I hadn't considered this before, but it opened many more doors.

Bev put everything in a box, and we returned to my room. The treasure box was placed on the bench beside the window.

"You are supposed to paint only in the art room, but just promise you won't make too much of a mess?"

"Sure."

"The paints are acrylic so you can wash them in the bathroom. You still also have a pencil for sketching and, remember, you don't have to use this. Just follow what you feel."

"Thanks Bev, this is great."

"Good girl!"

If anyone else would have said that I would have crapped on them for being condescending. But when Bev said it, it actually made me feel good. She wandered out, saying she looked forward to seeing me the next day, reminding me to do my gratitude practice and call anytime. The door closed, and I stared at the big blank canvas. Sneakily, I thought I could submit my homework just as it was. It, all by itself, seemed to sum up how I felt. Camping in front of the canvas, simply considering it, I could feel the pull of it, the pleasure of simply delighting in it, and the push, the passion to produce something. These dual forces played freely until I got frustrated and turned to Frida.

I searched for instances of orange. How had Frida used this colour? Then, halfway through the book, I came across an orange circle inscribed with the word Tao. I knew this word from my time with Ben when we toured Buddhist art exhibitions. I remembered it being something about the natural order of things. The Tao was about being alive and wise. And here it was in an orange circle, waiting for me to respond. I thought both Ben and Bev would find this hilarious. In a way, I actually felt a bit haunted.

The orange in the books was beautiful, so I began blending colours to see if I could get close to it. I was not going to confine it to a circle, though. I was going to cover the canvas with it. No particular reason. Just because I could. The mixing process was mesmerising and felt more like a meditation, more a treat than a task. I touched the paint, rubbing it in my fingers. I rubbed it on my arm and saw it soak into my skin. This was special. I took a short break for dinner and, while eating, doodled a few designs to put over the top of the orange base.

I stepped back into my room and looked at the expanse of the orange canvas, streaked with some variegations where I had not mixed the paints in properly. There were raised lines and some small clumps. It was far from flat and far from perfect. And yet, it seemed enough. Looking at the ideas to add, each of them was deemed superfluous. This simple, singular frame held all I wanted to say about creativity. Right now, it felt like finding the colour that was true to you, not trying to dazzle people with delicate designs. Thank you, Bev. Message received. Although I decided to also show the pallet as part of the piece, making it a mixed media submission. All of the blobs on the board, their simple separateness, and their intimate mingling also felt meaningful.

Ranjani came in when I was just washing the brushes.

"Hey, Nora. Nice colour! Bev mentioned you might be doing some painting tonight. It is really great to see you engaging with the process. Between you and me, Bev is a bit of genius. She has this way to see right through you and know what you need. She has helped me so much; I am so glad you are getting some guidance from her too. Hey, am just finishing up the evening meds round. Would you like anything to help you sleep?"

"Thanks, Ranjani. I think I'm OK."

"Sure?"

"Yes, I am feeling OK tonight."

"OK, Nora, well just come and get me if you change your mind. Goodnight. Oh, and for goodness' sake, don't leave a drop of that stuff on the bench. The cleaning ladies will kill me!" She left with a little cackle.

In the shower, I washed the orange paint off my arm, and enjoyed watching the watery hue circle down the hole. Slipping into bed felt awesome, like I had accomplished something, scored some goal, or done something good.

However, in my dream I was no saint. I was still a shrivelling old spinster with shedding skin. Only now, I was wrapped in an ochre blanket, and the dragon lit a small fire to keep my mangled body warm. I am sure I spied some golden flecks in his eyes, replacing the black of before, and the sunlight at the side seemed to grow and move towards me, or was this just the torchlight from the nurse's checkup? Instead of pure panic, there was a sense of sadness. I did not want to surrender to this suffering anymore, but I could not see a way to get strong or sneak past the dragon to escape. It was not loneliness or death that danced around me that night, but the acrobatics of anger and acceptance.

THE LOVE LIFE OF A CHAMELEON

Chapter 7

I was not sure what was worse, feeling groggy from the meds or being naturally tired from my nightly torment. Ben used to be my source of wisdom regarding dreams, telling me that everyone in it represented a part of yourself. I could see how the spinster was, that one was obvious. Even Ben was clear; he was myself, mocking me for my stupidity. Mum, though, I was not sure about. Was this part of me desperate to be like she was, so happy alone in her home, with her books, movies, and garden? That would make sense. I often envied how simply she lived and how content she was to die alone.

The dragon also had me beat. I still could not put a finger on why it was there. But there were more important things than to dwell on this; I had to get ready to deal with Dr Dempsey. Especially today when I may be presented with what he believed was wrong with me. It was hard not to spend some time staring at the painting. There were flecks of orange so similar to those I had seen in the sunrise and so many other subtle shades that I had not before noticed. I leaned closer to look at where two colours had tenderly touched, creating a tiny combination, one completely unique and very understated.

Pulling myself away from inspecting the intricacies of the painting, I made a quick trip to the kitchen and made tea.

Returning to the room, I was hit with the smell of paint, which took me right back to Daniel's studio. Standing at this door was just like being at the threshold with Daniel, and the same excitement arose within me. It was the thrill that came from seeing his art and being close to him.

I had just returned from Seattle with new things to add to my resume. There was a period of adjustment before I could fully get back into the swing of things, and I had no social circle to spend the weekend with. I decided that if I could not do art with Aaron, I would do it alone. I enrolled in an exclusive art class with an award-winning master. I started the classes intent on creating something for myself. I ended them being consumed by Daniel.

Sitting amongst the other students, I felt completely out of my depth. Not with the work; I could follow instructions, and my piece seemed to flow, but with my desire for the teacher. This man was not my usual type. He was old, almost double my age, and had grey hair and a beard, making him appear distinguished. His bravado at the beginning belied an immense insecurity, exposed through the wringing of the hands and the bowing of the eyes. That display of fragility just made me want him more.

I spent the classes doing what he said but also watching how he moved, how he held his brushes, and how his face lit up when someone gave him a compliment or congratulations. His wedding ring was simple, solid silver, and sang to me like a siren. How stimulating was the notion of subverting the social moral code. At a break we sat together discussing ideas for how my piece may progress. I looked into his grey eyes, and the deal was done. The only thing left was the logistics.

When Daniel announced the details of his upcoming exhibition, I knew I had found my way in. My dress screamed seduction but in a very simple and stylish way. Something about the ankle straps on the stilettos made it clear I had an agenda. As he passed me champagne, he said I had a real talent. The blush behind the makeup was real. Daniel suggested it would be good for me to visit his studio to get a feel for the creative process. The invitation was obviously for intimacy, not artistic inspiration, with the former being exactly what I wanted.

The next afternoon, we met for coffee close to the studio. We chatted about his latest projects and how I was finding the classes. He walked behind me as we climbed the stairs, the suspense already building. His hand went around my waist as we entered, and he would touch my arm every now and again as he showed me around. The conversation was calm and confident, and I could not help but be overwhelmed by his talent. He seemed thrilled when I told him so.

Once the circle had been completed, he asked if there were any questions. There was only one I wanted to ask.

"Can I kiss you?"

He did not use words to answer. Just grabbed my waist and pulled me in. The beauty was barely disrupted by the bristles from his beard. I had never kissed a guy with a beard before. A few clients had one when I was in the Cross, but I never bothered doing anything other than fondling their faces.

Ben said that guys with beards were hiding something. If this was a façade to something deeper, then I found that fascinating, not fearsome. There was no hesitation on his part, no mention of his wife or concern about the consequences, so I took it that this was condoned.

"You are a beautiful woman, Nora."

He unbuttoned my blouse and tenderly touched my breast through the bra.

Slowly, we undressed each other, appreciating every part that was revealed, the act a work of art in itself. Standing naked in front of him, I felt so awkward, so vulnerable, but I was encouraged by his comfort and sense of confidence.

He stood back and admired me, and I became his object of adoration.

"Magnificent."

My eyes looked downwards, daring to believe what he had said.

He took my hand and lay me down on the single bed he used for sleep in between sessions. Sitting beside me, he traced my body.

"I want to touch every piece of you."

He treated my body like a treasure, stroking and kissing. His cock was already hard, and I held it with my hand, but he would not be distracted from his exploration. This was unusual. This was truly special.

He kissed all of my crevices; my neck, my elbows, the bit of my hand between my fingers and thumb, behind my knees and then when I was getting weary with the process, he bit my breast, not hard, just enough to make me squirm, and smile. He would not go harder, though; he was there to please, not to hurt. I had not known attention like this, and when he went downwards, I experienced a new level of pleasure. I could feel myself getting very wet and very warm, and I was waiting for him to take me. But he kept going, gently, generously. I had no choice but to give in. That was the first time I had ever orgasmed from oral. Daniel, it seemed, was a master at many things, including both art and the female form.

As I recovered from the fireworks show that I had surrendered to, he stared lovingly between my legs.

"Beautiful."

He licked the liquid from around and inside and came up to face me.

"Taste yourself Nora. This is what art tastes like."

I did not like the taste of myself very much, but taking it from his tongue made it magical. The least I could do was to repay the favour, and I was desperate to feel him inside. I twisted until I was on top, then just as he had done, gently took all of him in my mouth. I knew men liked it deep, the back of the throat feeling like a thrill. I gave Daniel this depth, matched with slowness and interspersed with tickles from my tongue. It did not take long to achieve success. I felt his throbbing, testifying to his impending climax. I swallowed his cum, calmly and confidently and kept him safe in my mouth until it was all over. Then I cleaned him up carefully and, just as he had done for me, shared his taste with him, too.

We lay silently for a few minutes, enjoying the sensation of our skin touching and the openness the expansiveness that comes after orgasm.

"Can I paint you? Please, Nora?"

I was so scared of seeing myself through his eyes, but this was necessary to cement our connection.

"Of course. It would be my honour."

He arose, his penis still seeping, leaving a sticky smudge on his thigh.

"Just stay, exactly how you are. You are beautiful."

I hoped that the more I heard this, the more I would believe it, but it had yet to work with the other guys. Yet this felt different. There I was, hoping to snatch him, but instead, he was the one who seduced me.

For over a year, our spare time was shared between Daniel's studio and my apartment. It was a relationship but also a respite. Daniel offered me a different perspective, a pleasure outside the pressure of work. However, we would never wake up together. There was no sleeping over at his studio, that was just not practical. And when he came to my apartment he would sleep for a while but then always leave in the early hours. It worked well, given my work commitments, but I always wondered whether he was going back to his wife with the scent of our sex on his skin. Or perhaps he would head back to the studio to process our passion through his paints. Whatever he did, we never talked about it. It was so much easier to avoid the anomalies in our relationship. There was so much of me that felt the talking here was senseless. Why drag up the dirt if it was only going to cause distress?

Speaking of distress, Dr. Dempsey knocked and marched on in, pulling up a chair near the mirror. I moved one over near my bed, making seeing myself in the mirror almost impossible.

"Any particular reason why you have moved today, Nora?"

"I just find the mirror distracting. Honestly, it is a horrible place to have one."

I tried to deflect my decision with small talk, but he was determined to bring the conversation back to the purpose of the consultation, which was obviously not comradeship. He did not indicate he noticed the painting. Perhaps he did, but he didn't say anything. It was bloody difficult to miss. Dickhead. Was he prodding me on purpose, hoping for an outburst of pride to make his files more "interesting."

Again, we went through the rigmarole of checking in on my mood, appetite and sleep. I said I was not sleeping well and was told it could be because of the meds. The doctor didn't ask about any nightmares, so I didn't tell. He merely offered some more pills to assist. Here it was, the escalation of intervention being evidenced in my own room. I thought these people were here to help remove the layers of shit in my life. But it seemed they were just piling more on top, although I am sure they would insist that their prescriptions were there for therapeutic purposes.

He asked how the depression medication was working for me and whether I was having any problems with it. I mentioned about the nausea, and he told me to see the nurse to get something to help.

"Surprise! More meds"

"Nora, there is no need to be sarcastic."

The doctor was right. There was no need to be sarcastic, but it did make me feel better that he knew of my dissatisfaction. I had once heard someone say that sarcasm is the lowest form of wit. It may well be, but in my books, it was also the funniest. Well, at least I found it amusing.

"So, Nora, I have been working through all that you have told me, and what I have witnessed over the past days and I today I want to talk through what I see happening for you. It is clear to me that you are experiencing a moderate level of depression. But I believe there is something deeper that has affected a lot in your life. I believe you are also dealing with Borderline Personality Disorder."

A smile spread across my face. It sounded amusing, but the smile was also a shield against the anxiety.

"Well, that sounds.... interesting." I highlighted the point by putting my finger on my chin and frowning.

"More sarcasm, Nora. This is actually serious."

"Sorry doctor. It's just that.... a personality disorder? I don't think so. I think it sounds ludicrous. A bit of depression, well, I think I would agree there. I reckon 99 percent of the population is joining me in that diagnosis. But Borderline Personality Disorder? I think that is a bit much."

"Do you know what it is, Nora?"

"OK, no, but..."

"So let me go through my reasoning first. There are nine criteria for BPD, and I can see that you display at least seven of them. You have made extreme attempts to prevent what you saw as abandonment. Apart from your persona at work it also seems like you have a very unstable sense of self-image. I see that you have impulsive tendencies, specifically related to sex and with drugs and alcohol. You have difficulty with intense anger, and we have had an example here of how it can take control. Your string of relationships has been what I would classify as unstable, and you seem readily able to split yourself away from them. You have shown suicidal behaviours as well as self-harm. I think some of the desires for self-harm you may have also delegated to others, especially in one of your latest relationships where the abuse may have played this role. You have also given several examples of dissociation, some of which have led to very dangerous situations. "

Silence. Struggle. There was so much evidence, it was difficult to comprehend.

"Sorry doctor. That is a lot. Can you repeat your list again please."

I grabbed my notebook and pen and wrote down the keywords for each of the seven criteria I had apparently succeeded in achieving.

"Is there anything there that you disagree with?"

"I, um, I think I am going to need some time to work through this. It is a bit unfair just to throw this on me and be able to defend myself straight away."

"First, I absolutely agree. This is just the first of many conversations, and I want you to do a lot more research and question, challenge anything. This is not the conclusion, but the start of some constructive conversations. Second, do you think you need to defend yourself?"

"Absolutely. You are sitting there delivering a diagnosis that could put my whole career in jeopardy. Even murderers get the opportunity to prove themselves innocent, and I think I should have the chance to do the same. This diagnosis sounds pretty damning, and I should have a chance to defend myself against it. Because I don't think it is true."

"I understand, Nora. However, I think it's important to acknowledge that by not dealing with some of these things your career is already in jeopardy. You are very good at compartmentalisation, but it may not be long before some of the behaviours listed start impinging on your professional life, if they haven't already."

They had. I knew they had. I was lucky that he had not called witnesses from my work.

"Here's what I would like to do. Because I know this can all be really daunting, and this is a serious condition, although you already know that, it is what landed you here. "

"No, that was just me being stupid."

"Not when you look at it in the context of everything else. It tells a pretty clear story. This condition would have started showing up in your teenage years and made you feel pretty different, like you didn't belong. I see it as a key cause of your social isolation and unsettled relationships. I can see how it has also led you to focus really hard on those areas where you can maintain some sense of control, in your case, your work. Although I think your fear of abandonment is showing up here too, you don't want to get left behind by your boss, so you are breaking your back to prove yourself."

Silence. Struggle. I have to show this guy he is talking shit.

"I would like you to take some time today reading through this brochure, and going with Bev to get a book on BPD from the library. I want you to read through and understand this condition a bit better. Then I want you to come up with questions, concerns and challenges tomorrow. Does that sound OK?"

"Sure."

Here was my chance to prove this guy wrong, and I was going to take it and do it well.

Still scanning the brochure, I went back to the list of symptoms.

"Hmm, so which ones have I missed? Perhaps I should be aiming for a perfect score."

"Nora, I know this is difficult, and you will need time to process it. Bev has a lot of great knowledge about BPD too, so you will work this through with her as well later today.

Any other questions for now?"

"So, are you telling me I am crazy?"

"No, and please don't use that word. BPD is a condition, caused by you adapting to circumstances the best way you knew how at the time. It's just that these adaptations become problems in themselves. BPD can be treated and there are a number of really effective techniques."

Oh my god. Now I needed treatment as well? It sounded like I had bloody cancer.

"OK, say if this is true, what would I need to do, and for how long."

"The condition itself has been formed over many years, so the treatment has a lot to unwind. So, it a long-term process. There is a method called Dialectical Behavioural Therapy, DBT, that is shown to be really effective, and I will give you a list of people that you can contact to get into their programs."

"What do you mean by long-term? A couple of months."

"No, Nora. This will take years, maybe around five to help you manage the symptoms really well. Although the treatment wouldn't be full time, just a few hours each week, but would need to be regular."

No way. Now I was getting worried. I slumped down in my chair, for a moment succumbing to the doctor's damning sentence.

"I know how important work is for you, so over the next few days we will figure out the best thing to do there."

With these words, I sat back up straight. This guy was not going to mess with my work.

"What do you mean? I am here for two weeks, then I can go back, right?"

"I think it may be risky to jump back into the pressure you were dealing with previously. With what you have just been through and what we are seeing in terms of patterns, it may be better to take some time to process everything and get you to a more stable place.

"Or work could be a really helpful distraction."

"You don't need a distraction, Nora. You need to deal with this. In fact, I would say that distracting yourself from these destructive behaviours has been your modus operandi for decades, and has just caused you more problems."

I could hear myself repeating "modus operandi" in my mind, in the mocking voice of a child. I would have loved to stick my tongue out at him right now and needle him with a "neh neh neh neh neh", but it would not benefit my case.

"Do you have any sick leave."

"Sure. Stacks. At least a few weeks, but I can't be away for long."

"OK. What about income protection?"

"Yes, it is part of my super. But I am not sick. What are you getting at?"

"I would like you to think about taking some more time off. I am happy to support an application for income protection where you could get a few months to start working through the treatment and get a process in place for support."

"What? A few months? I could get away with it if was cancer or something. But not for anything bloody mental!"

I was already imagining the conversations around the conference table about me and my "mental condition." They would crucify me for sure. How could they let anyone who was unstable deal with clients directly?

"Nora, you don't need to make any decisions now. Let's talk this through further next few days. The only thing you need to concentrate on right now is your research. I know you would be a whiz at that, so come tomorrow to challenge me with some constructive questions."

I agreed, but through suppression of red-hot rage. This man was trying to meddle with my hard-earned position. I would beat him, but I had to be smart about it. In here I had to play by his rules. When I was back out, I could play by mine again.

"Oh, and now you will have access to your phone for one hour before dinner each day. I know you may need to deal with some things, pay bills or provide people with an update. But try and keep it simple, don't get caught up in any drama."

"I don't do drama, doctor."

As soon as I said it, I realised how wrong I was. So many episodes of my life would be suitable for a soap opera. I had said it seriously but hoped the doctor would take it as another attempt at sarcasm, not self-delusion.

"Is there anything else for now, Nora?"

"No."

"OK, so normal routine. Phone before dinner. Work with Bev. And I will see you tomorrow."

As he got up to leave, I could see yellow lions on his red socks. Yes, you are providing a formidable opponent, doctor, but this is not over yet.

Sitting on the bed, the door closed, alone, I was confused by what I felt. I should be relieved to have an answer, so why do I feel so angry? It was something that was known and could be fixed, so why did I feel so faulty? I have a disorder. A diagnosis. A mental condition. Did this make me more human or less? All I knew was that it made me less hungry. I could smell the hot breakfast, but it turned my stomach. I knew that it made me feel less friendly. I did not want to face Mark and his stupid smile. Besides, shouldn't people be afraid of me now? Maybe I should make a sign and put it around my neck to alert people and make sure they stayed away from my insanity lest it lure them in and leave them injured.

Bugger it. If I was a psycho, then I had an excuse not to follow the rules. I went to the kitchen, grabbed a coffee, and returned to my room. I kept my head down, avoiding contact and turning my back towards Mark. Did I feel bad for it? Honestly, yes, but it was for the best.

No one came to get cranky at me for not having breakfast. Maybe they knew too and didn't want to come near. While I drank my coffee laced with a good dose of wrath, I looked at the painting again. Right then, I wanted to tear it all up. Why was I bothering with this? What will this one piece of pathetic art do? I have been just told it would take years to rectify this condition. It seemed like the orange canvas was sneering at me, ridiculing me, relentless in its derision. Standing there, scoping out weapons with which I could destroy it, I suddenly knew how Daniel had felt.

The first time I saw him unleash anger, I was afraid. His hands would cramp into claws, the veins on his neck would pop out, and his head would shake. He would scream and slash at the canvas with his palette knife. It was not good enough. It would never win the prize. When the work was torn, he would toss it at me. He would shout at me, blaming me for not sitting right to get the shadows he needed or not having the right shape to make the statement he wanted. He would pace, prod, pout, punch the bed, and then come to sit, stating how sorry he was and starting to sob. He would chug down some antacids, tell me his stomach hurt so bad, and then curl up in my arms. I would stroke his hair. Tell him how much I admired him, how much more talented he was than all the other try-hards and that I believed in him. He never used the word, but in many ways, I was his muse.

Where was mine now? Who was coming to rub my forehead and tell me to forget about that demonic doctor? No-one. Fucking no-one. Who was there to stand from the sidelines, chant my name and cheer me on? Fucking no one, that's who. Then a knock.

"Hey, Nora. The doctor just told me he spoke to you about the diagnosis. How are you?"

A shrug was all that would come out.

Bev came over and put her arms around my shoulders.

"OMG Nora. Your painting. You go girl! I can't wait to talk to you more about it. I know it might not feel like it right now, Nora. But things are going to be OK. We are here for you. Just keep going."

Oh my god. Was this woman listening to my mind?

"I will catch you later, but please, if need anything, call."

"Thanks, Bev."

She parted with a cuddle.

The next morning, the gentle exercise felt more like an excruciating goading. There was no peace, only Madonna pounding the same lines over and over again in my head: "Borderline, feels like I'm going to lose my mind." Accompanying the words were ceaseless images of her prancing around in baggy jeans, chewing gum. If I wasn't crazy before, then I certainly would be soon. I had never been glad to leave that class, but the break was a great relief.

Despite caffeinating again, I could not concentrate in the next session on sleep hygiene. I wondered if I would have Madonna singing me to sleep that night as well. I doodled, but all I could get out was the dragon's eye. Was the dragon the part of me that knew who I really was, and is that why he shut me up? He may have felt sorry for me and let some sunshine in, but that didn't change the need for me to be separated from the rest of society. Maybe the doctor was right; maybe I should stay away from people. Maybe this was the message coming from this recurring dream.

A class on courage and confidence came next. I chuckled to myself. I was neither. Just crazy. If anyone could hear my head right now, they would concur. The teacher talked about each one and what held us back from being our best. Deficiencies in skills and experience can prevent us from moving forward with what is important, but these are overcome with action and practice. The more pervasive ones are fear and excessive self-judgement, and that is what we would focus on for the session.

We were told that to face our fears, we first have to be aware of them, so we were asked to take some time to list the things we were afraid of — well, the ones we knew of. It was suggested that there would be several sneaky subconscious ones, but we could only work with what we knew. I honestly did not think I was afraid of anything. The doctor had suggested my identity was unstable, but I figured fearlessness was a foundation. Then I began to think.

This morning showed me that I was actually afraid of losing my job. My dream was a clear display that I was petrified of becoming a spinster. I was concerned that people would think I was crazy, but what was worse was that if I thought that too.

We were counselled, or was it consoled, with the fact that these fears in themselves are not a problem. It is our relationship with them that led to destructive actions. Instead of working with the fears as they arose, we would panic, and it was this panic that caused problems. When had I ever panicked and did something I later regretted? Well, that was obvious, I was afraid of losing Ben, so I took the pills. But what did I really want? What was my goal? Well, I wanted Ben to see me as more than a friend, for him to become my partner. But what ended up happening? I embarrassed myself and put him in a really difficult situation. And the ultimate result? He ran away.

What? Oh my god!

"Can you see what happens when you let fear take the reins of your decision making? So often, what happens is the exact opposite of what you had hoped for."

The teacher then rattled off her own example, something about her teenage daughter and drugs, but I was still reeling from the revelation to engage with her experience.

"What is important is that we care for our fears, not fight against them. When we have a positive relationship with them, we can take helpful action to build courage and confidence."

Working through my list, I watched it all play out. If I let fear take hold and panicked about losing my job, I would go back as soon as I left here and show them that I was OK – there was nothing to see here! Just like the films of the gymnastic girls falling off the balance beam but recovering with hands in the air, a smile and a mental "ta-da". I would paint over the problem with professionalism.

The cons of this approach? What if the doctor was right, and the pressure did make me fall apart again? What if keeping up the façade was too much, and I would freak out again. Could it create the same problems that I was trying to avoid? Could trying so hard to restore their faith in me cause me to unravel? Would it result in more drama and destruction of my future with the firm? Shit. The doctor was right. I was so afraid of losing face that I might just do the thing that caused me to corrupt it completely.

Then, the teacher asked us to stop and think about what was really important. What was it exactly I was trying to achieve? I wanted to maintain my role and reputation and stay on the pathway to partnership. Would reacting out of fear give me this? Or could it end in disaster? What would be a more proactive approach, with less likelihood of disaster? I got it then. Taking some time and ensuring I returned strong seemed like a smarter approach. Congratulations, doctor, I will chalk this one up for you.

Next, my fear of being a spinster. Oh dear. Oh wow. Yes, I have let it lead me into so many useless relationships, using the term very loosely, of course. Fear had forced me to grab onto any guy (or girl) so that I would not be alone, and just hope like hell it would work. Sure, there were pros to this plan. There was always the probability that my promiscuity would put me in the right place, at the right time, for a perfect partner. The cons? I knew these well. I was constantly compromising. I lost myself. Even when I was with someone, I still felt alone. Suddenly, there was a surge; a wave of emotion washed over me, bringing me down hard and washing me clean. Was this what the revelations Ben talked about felt like? Was this what he meant when he said I did not know myself? What have I done!

My hands came to my mouth; I could not tell whether out of surprise or to suppress a scream. I looked up at the teacher and was met with an understanding smile. She used the chance to make an important announcement.

"Please, take your time with this one. And realise that there may be a lot of emotions that can get brought up once you start understanding how fear has driven your past. Please. Please. Please. Don't use this exercise to get down on yourself for what you have done. Let's use this awareness this time for learning. Let's use anything uncomfortable to strengthen your commitment to move forward with love, not fear.

It is so important to focus on the goal. Think about what you are trying to achieve."

What did I want? What was my endgame? I wanted to be strong and confident within myself. I wanted to be this way whether I was with someone or not. I did not want to have to depend on someone else for my happiness. I wanted to be like mum.

"Excuse me, I have to use the bathroom."

"Of course."

I raced back to my room, banging the door behind me and lunged into the bathroom. I had to brace myself on the toilet to get some stability through the sobbing. I think the only times I had ever wailed before was when dad whipped my bum with his belt, and when Stephen had burnt my skin. Today, though, the pain came from within. And it was so much worse. I saw it all so clearly, how giving into being scared had created so many scars. I was not a strong, independent woman. I was a terrified little child covered with a mask of maturity. More moans. More tears. Ranjani was beside me, rubbing my back and holding me against her hips. She took me to lie down and sat beside me, just allowing me to be, bearing witness to this breakdown.

By lunchtime, nothing was left, no water to waste on tears, no sustenance to support further sadness. I sat up.

"Thanks Ranjani. Really. I'm sorry."

"Do not be sorry, Nora. It is my honour to help you through this. It looked like a process you really needed."

She was right. I had just never known it until now.

"Lunch is on, and could I suggest you use the chance to get some strength back? This is not easy stuff, and you need all the energy you can get."

"Thanks, I will."

Ranjani left, and I went and washed my face. I was not going to look in the mirror, but curiosity challenged me, and I contemplated the red, raw face in front of me. Was this the face of my future? I was used to layers of crimson around my lips, but today, I had splotches of scarlet around my eyes. Reality was so much messier than the roles I played.

If Mark was miffed about me ignoring him at breakfast, he didn't show it.

"Nice to see you, Nora. We have a really nice Greek salad today. I make sure they don't skimp on the olives and fetta. Would you like it with some falafels and hummus?"

"That sounds really nice. Thanks, Mark."

"My pleasure!"

Mark served lunch with a smile, and for a moment, his kindness seemed like the most special sustenance.

The forms flowed freely, coming onto the page as I chewed. Some teardrops turned into dew drops on leaves that became bubbles floating in the air, shifting into the sun and the moon. Wow, did someone give me a hippie pill this morning, or was this the result of healing hormones. Who could tell, but it felt satisfying, and with the circles, I felt complete. I realised I had not done a mandala in days and decided I would do some more colouring back in my room to help me calm down.

Bev got to me before I could begin. I had just pulled out the book and pens when she came in.

"Hey Nora, how are you? Ranjani tells me you have had a big morning."

I thought more tears would come, but I was still dry.

"Yep, it seems like there is a bit going on."

"There sure is. It has been a huge few days here, and a wild time before that. It is going to take some time to understand how it all fits together. What you are doing is really tough, so you need to take care of yourself."

Take care. Those were the words that I would have loved to hear from Ben before he walked away.

"Because believe it or not, I think you will be working through a lot of grief, and not just finally processing the death of your mum."

"What do you mean?"

"Nora, I can see that you define yourself as a strong, independent woman, tough, solid, successful. The diagnosis strips away some of the black and white view of who you are. You are also starting to see how much fear has played a role in your life so far. It is bringing into question things that you thought you knew about yourself. I don't think it would be any surprise to see things like anger, denial, bargaining and depression coming out, as you try and adjust to this new awareness. You need to care for these things, Nora, to use them to grow, not push the away and pretend they don't exist."

What was going on for me, though, didn't feel like grief; it felt like giving up. But then, maybe this was the acceptance they spoke of? Did acceptance feel like exhaustion?

"Let's start with the diagnosis from the doctor. The BPD. What are you feeling about this."

"Honestly Bev, it feels like something I have to fight. I want to do my research and prove Dr Dempsey wrong."

"Good on you, Nora. Use the skills you have to learn more, to gain knowledge about this condition. Knowledge is power. There is just one proviso with this approach though."

"What is that."

"Well, you have to be honest with yourself. You can read the books that will outline all of the objective criteria. But you have to be really truthful about your own behaviour. Us humans are masters of self-deception, but lying to yourself, or ignoring certain issues is not going to yield the outcome you want."

"I see. So, my self-deception could be diagnosed as delusion, damning me even further?"

"Oh, you are funny, Nora, and very smart. I just mean that you have a chance here to come clean, to start with a blank canvas, if you will. You would not want to taint that with mistruths. Even if you find it hard to admit things to others, please do it for yourself. At the end of your analysis, if you can, hand on heart, say these things are not me, then that is meaningful. If you are continuing to lie to yourself, then you have lost a very valuable chance at moving one step further to the person you truly want to be.

Speaking of which. Did you find the courage class helpful?"

"Well until I cracked up. You guys are really clever, putting this class in when I was coming to terms with being crazy."

"I will take that as a compliment, not the cracking up bit, but being clever. We have done this a few times before, and know how scary it is for you to work through this process. So many people that come in here think they have their shit together. They are striving, tick all the boxes of modern success, family, cars, careers, holidays, but then they end up in a downward spiral. Remember the first day I said that there had to be something behind the event with Ben?"

"Yep."

It felt like a few years ago, not just a few days.

"Well now we are getting closer to really understanding the cause. When we do that, then we have a chance to care for it, to address it, so that you can live really well, Nora, but not just live, thrive."

Thrive. What a funny word. It was the same name as the fertiliser mum put on her garden. I laughed at myself, thinking they should make medicine out of it. They would make a lot of money in this place.

"What fears came up, actually specifically, what was the one you were working on that caused all the emotion to erupt?"

"It was being alone."

"Tell me more."

"Well, I realised how much I had lost myself, starting and sticking in relationships that were pretty meaningless, just to make sure I was not alone."

"I get it, Nora, and excuse the pun, but you are not alone in this one. When we were tribal creatures being ostracised meant death, so it is hardwired into our brains to fear being an outcast. So many people run to others out of fear. Did you get to work through what happened when you did this?"

"Yes, I just created more of the same problem. I ended up feeling alone with the added drama of dealing with someone else as well."

"Good on you, Nora. That is a huge revelation. No wonder you needed a release after that. Did you make it to the part where you thought about building skills then?"

"No."

"Well, that is next. Instead of fighting the fear of being alone, panicking and causing more problems, what skills do you need to deal well with being alone? How can you be more confident and capable in being by yourself?"

"I'm not sure."

"I heard a great saying once. It said if you are feeling lonely, then you have not yet spent enough time alone."

"I don't get it."

"The skill of being confident alone is a practice. You get better at it the more you do. And I have a theory why. Because it makes you find all the fantastic parts of yourself that are hidden when you are too busy dealing with other people. Nora, I can see so many awesome things about you. The purpose of alone practice is to come to see them for yourself. When you can be excellent company to yourself, when you can love yourself for all you are, then you can love someone else. I am sorry, but I believe that until you can love yourself, any relationship is at best mutual admiration."

"That's what Ben said."

"He was very wise. And I know you might hate him, but his care for you has brought you here."

"I don't hate him. I just miss him. He felt like my first true friend."

"Well Nora, how about you becoming your next one? Do you think it sounds like a plan?"

"I don't think I make a very good friend."

"Ah, well that is because you haven't had enough practice yet."

"So where do I start?"

"Great question. Well, if you had a friend that was just given a diagnosis of BPD and was struggling with it, what would you suggest?"

"Oh, you are good, Bev."

"Thankyou! So..."

"I would tell her to understand what it meant and come up with some questions or concerns. "

"Nora, you underestimate your friendship ability. Great advice.

If it helps, you can also think about it like your work. You would never propose a strategy or solution that was not evidence-based. Use your great skills to work this one through, too."

"Thanks Bev."

"No, don't thank me, it was your friend that came up with the idea."

We both smiled. How wonderful it would be to have Bev as an older sister. I could see what she was saying about getting better at being alone. But gosh, it would be wonderful to have someone to lean on.

"Nora, remember we are going to help you set up a lovely support network, so you won't be the only friend you ever have."

I swear Bev was a mind reader, or maybe like she said, she had done it before. I kind of found it sad that so many other people were also on this path.

"So, let's do it."

Bev stood and signalled for us to leave the room. We walked to the library. She pulled a book off the shelf and handed it to me.

"Oh, there is only one left. Someone must have the other one. Honestly, this is not my favourite."

The title leapt out at me like a madwoman's long, scrawny fingers- I hate you, don't leave me.

"What the hell?"

I couldn't tell if my shock towards the title was because it sounded like a crazy person or whether it sounded just like me.

"Yes, this one is pretty harsh, and in places damning of people with BPD. There is some really relevant stuff in here, but it also creates so much negative stigma as well. There is a lot I disagree with, like that people with BPD have no empathy, and are purposefully manipulative. In places it makes them out to be bad people, but that is not the case at all, and I need you to know that. I would be worried about you taking this information the wrong way. Yet a lot of people find it helpful. What do you think. Would you like to read this one, or just stick to the brochure?"

"Thanks, Bev. I think if I am going to get well-informed about this, then I need to know what's in it."

"OK. Perfect. Just do me a favour with this one. Remember that it is written by a doctor looking from the outside in. Take notes of what seems to fit and what doesn't.

Contest what he says with your own experience. Come to the meeting with the doctor tomorrow prepared with any questions.

We headed back to my room, book in hand.

"Now, were there any other fears that you worked through?"

"Yes, losing my job."

"Ah, yes, that would be a biggy for you. Did you find some way forward?

"I am thinking about what the doctor suggested, about taking some more time off."

"That sounds like a wonderful idea. Perhaps you could think of it this way. You have an incredibly important job right now, and that is working on getting well. When you nail that, everything else will take care of itself. Does that make sense?"

I nodded reluctantly.

"Awesome, although don't take my word for it. You may want to talk it over with Nora later."

I liked this playful side of Bev. I spent so much time in the professional world I had forgotten how pleasing it was.

"Is there anything else worrying you?"

"Oh, sometimes I get so frustrated that we have to dig all this up, my past I mean."

"I get it, Nora. Have you ever had a garden?"

"At mum's, yes."

"Then you know that digging is dirty work, but it is necessary for two reasons. You have to pull out the weeds, those things that don't serve the health of the garden, and can actually harm the plants you need. Then of course, you have to dig to make holes for the new, purposeful plants, those that will bear fruit, flowers, bring you food and joy. Digging is not nice, but it is necessary."

"Thanks Bev, I see."

"You sound sad."

"Just so tired."

"I understand. This is exhausting work. I hope you can get out soon and get some fresh air. It is so helpful to walk these things through. But for now, let's do some cool stuff. Tell me about the painting. What did you enjoy about the process?"

"I really loved mixing colours."

"I can see from the palette. Awesome. Is that what creativity feels like for you."

"I hadn't really thought about it. But yes, kind of. It is like taking ideas, shapes, colours and mixing them to make something new. I really like doing that."

Bev's eyes lit up, and she practically leapt at me. Who was the crazy one?

"Beautiful, Nora. That is exactly the process you are in now. You are the master with all manner of mediums at your fingertips. You have a vast range of skills, your experiences, your goals, your resourcefulness, your resilience and your creativity all waiting to be used; it is up to you to pull them together in a way that is meaningful for you.

In reality, you have been doing this all your life. Now that you are becoming more aware of the patterns and how they play out, the trick is how to make this creation process purposeful. You can choose what you want to work towards, and could I suggest it is something far more important than making partner at work or securing a partner at home?

Now, I know you have a lot to do to research the diagnosis. If you have some spare time or need a break, the next colour on our list is yellow. And you will not be surprised to learn that it is the colour of courage."

"Hang on, I thought yellow meant cowardice?"

"It is interesting, isn't it? In the western world it is a symbol of cowardice. But in more ancient traditions, it represents our personal power, confidence, sense of self, our purpose. Hang on, maybe that is why people associate it with cowardice, because they need more yellow in their life? Huh! I just thought of that."

"I get that. It makes sense to me."

"Great! Gosh we make a good team, the two Nora's and me."

Both of us gave a chuckle and she came again and gave me a cuddle. She pulled a single yellow pen from the packet and placed it beside my journal.

"With everything else going on, we are going to keep this really simple. Your task, if you have time, is to answer the question – Who am I? Is that OK?"

I gave a nod, already starting to think through what my answer would be.

"Oh, and I almost forgot about the grateful exercise. Did you find something yesterday to be grateful for?"

"Yes, I really appreciate the exercise class. I was a bit messed up in it today after seeing the doctor, but I do like having the space to stretch."

"That is fantastic. Just remember you have that space here too. Space is not just a place but a state of mind.

Nora, congratulations. You are doing wonderful work. I know it may not feel like it, but you are doing great. Thank you so much for working with me on this. I will see you tomorrow to set you up for the weekend. Until then, though, please call any time, OK?"

"OK, thanks Bev."

"See ya Nora, Goodbye to you too, Nora's BFF Nora."

Bev walked out, leaving me with a much lighter heart and a smile.

Were there people like this in the real world? If so, I don't think I have ever encountered them.

It was raining heavily, the day outside dull and depressing. I would have loved to sleep until dinner, but there was something more important. Just like my work, Bev said. At work, I would push through the tiredness to deliver a deadline, and today would be no different. I went and made a hot chocolate then started in on the book. Several times, I could not believe what I was reading. It was like this guy was describing my daily life; he even saw me pushing away those I was most desperate to connect to and observing my angry outbursts. The behaviours he described were damning and portrayed a person with BPD as pure evil, scheming, manipulative, lying, not caring about anyone else, and the epitome of promiscuity. Was that who I was? I didn't think so; I really didn't, or was I just in denial?

Then came the ultimate exposure. I was outted as a chameleon, taking on whatever character I needed to survive the situation. It seems I was so good at camouflage that I had even hidden this ability from myself. And then there was a knock at the door I had to answer.

A nurse came in, one I had not met before. Ranjani must have gone home for the day. That was a pity; I really wanted to thank her again for the time she spent with me. Anyway, the nurse told me I could have my phone for an hour. My disappointment surprised me. A few days ago, I could not live one moment without it, my eyes seeing more of its screen than the sky. Now, it felt like a distraction from finding out who I truly was. And yet, there were domestics to do. I sat in the interview room and paid some bills, checked my balances, and tried to avoid checking my messages as long as possible. I could not miss one name on the list, though, and that was Calli. Her message said the boss told her I would be away for a while, and she wanted to know if I was at home or needed anything? She would be around my place on the weekend, and did I need her to check on my unit?

Perhaps it was the lesson on courage, or maybe it was Bev's beautiful aura still hanging around, but I did respond. In the past, I would have ghosted her and maybe, just maybe, felt guilty about it, but I would have done it anyway. Not today. The new Nora was not going to run away. And there were probably a few things in my fridge or cupboard that were feral by now. Could I ask her to do that? Actually, no, I couldn't. Not after all I had put her through. But it would be great just for someone to check in on the unit and confirm my car is still there.

"Calli, thanks so much. Yes, I am away at least for another week. It would be wonderful if you could check on my apartment and make sure my car is still in the garage. I am probably being a bit paranoid, but I would really appreciate it.

I will let the building manager know you will be passing through and that it is fine for him to give you a key.

I'm sorry if I can't respond to you quickly. I am only allowed my phone for an hour at about 5 p.m. I will get back to you then. Otherwise, if there is an emergency, you can call me here.

Then I had to pause.

Should I tell Calli where there was? Should I give her the number to a mental hospital? No, that's too much. I scrapped the last line and referred her to the building manager in case of emergency. Then, I sent a message to the building manager.

My work emails were banked up, well over one hundred already. Part of me wanted to dive in, to respond to a few so they wouldn't forget me. But the other Nora said no. For the moment, this was OK to run away from. I returned the phone quickly before the first Nora found a way to evade the second Nora's edict.

Dinner was dahl, already served on a tray, with chutney, raita and a note that said: "Nora - Enjoy!" And I did. I always found dahl so satisfying, especially when it was thick. The spicy smells, the creamy texture, the warmth of it going down my throat. It made me think that I must have been an Indian in a past life. Sometimes, I would smell incense, and it would make me feel like I was home. The only person I ever told was Ben, who seemed to understand. However, then we joked that if my past lives were solely based on the food I liked, then I had also once been Greek, Japanese, Turkish, Italian, Thai and French.

I smiled again when I saw the dahl tonight was yellow. This place held far too many coincidences. It was starting to feel less like a hospital and more like the Twilight Zone. Bev was right, it was interesting that one colour could have opposite meanings. Coward was a word I had used to describe Daniel. Actually, I remember shouting it through his studio door one night. We were going along really well, enjoying our clandestine rendezvous. I was fine not mentioning the existence of his wife for a while, maybe around eight months, but inevitably it came up. I told Daniel, casually and calmly, that I wanted the chance to be more than just his inside friend. I would love to be seen out in public, to play a more prominent role in his life. Of course, he was married, and it was not possible in a traditional sense, but I thought we could work something out to allow me to be alongside him. I wanted to mingle more in the art scene, go to his shows, stand beside him, and be seen. I told Daniel I wanted to be more than just an invisible inspiration.

Daniel told me he understood and that I was right. I was to leave it with him. He would work something out. He had been thinking about telling his wife about me for a while now, and this was the prompt he needed. He slipped away in the early hours of the morning, leaving me hopeful.

Then he never called again.

When I called him, he just hung up.

At first, I was really worried. I thought something had happened to him, so I called his agent. I was advised in very formal tones that he was just fine; it was just that he didn't want to see me again. That was the conversation that preceded me standing on his studio door, banging, shouting out the word "coward" until I was asked to leave by security.

Stalking seemed like a feasible plan, so I snuck into some exhibitions, hoping to see him. I did at one, on the arm of his new muse, a young male. I considered causing a scene, but I was satisfied seeing Daniel shrink when he spied me and goading the new guy with "good luck" as I passed by. I knew Daniel was steeped in insecurities and this intimate interruption was all that was needed to make my point. Then, I resigned myself to the fact that I was replaceable and that I would simply need to replace him. Although I also allowed myself some private rage for this new lover getting the publicity I never did. I knew Daniel was a coward for being unable to dump me in person, but I also knew he was gentle and, in many ways, so good to me.

I knew a lot about Daniel. But who was I? What word, what shape, what yellow thing was me?

As silly as it was, I picked up the book about Frida, seeking inspiration. The whole idea was to show who I was, not copy from someone else. I did amuse myself with my own stupidity. This artwork was meant to be authentic. Still, I needed some ideas for how to interpret my "I".

Frida used quite a bit of yellow, but one page grabbed my attention. A pile of random shapes was washed with yellow. The plate's explanation stated that Frida associated the colour yellow — known as Amarillo — with madness and mystery. Now, this was magnificent.

Who was I? I was told this morning that I was mad. And I was angry about it, so the definition of madness fitted perfectly.

I wrote "Who am I" at the top of the page in yellow.

I thought about the words I would use to describe myself. Independent, professional, intelligent. But who am I?

Frida was right. I was also a mystery.

I went to bed with a blank page. Something might come after sleep. And there was still gratitude to do. Now that I had done the exercise one, I had to think harder. What the hell was I grateful for about that day? My mind skipped back to the tally. Another day down, eleven to go. But then the nurse popped in to see if I would like anything before bed. Did I need something to help me sleep? While I declined the offer, I accepted the reminder of what I was grateful for. Care - the care I received from Ranjani, the other nurses, Bev, and Calli. I was truly grateful for these people.

The nightmare was there again, and yet each time felt as scary as the first. It was not like the horror movies that had you desensitised more after each viewing. Each time I lay in the cave, it felt like I was really crumpling into a corpse. The dragon was shaded in yellow tonight, like Frida's drawing, and the same watercolour wash was over me, hanging like a cloud, holding me down. It was like he had breathed his flame into steam to surround me, to keep me scared and shackled. Or was the colour we now shared telling me that, in a way, we were similar? I could not comprehend what this dragon represented; was it an enemy, or was it me? Or were these the same thing?

Chapter 8

I watched the dawn through the window, tea in hand and with tired eyes. The drink roused my body, and the sunrise stimulated my mind. I saw the colours start strongly, with distinct warm hues, strengthening and blending, and then bowing to the blue. This process was perfect and determined to capture it, I started sketching with the coloured pens. Lines of red and orange became yellow lace, floating and folding into a broad expanse of azure and evolving into the circle of a sun.

Still, I could not come up with an answer to this most fundamental question—who am I? Staring at the blank page, I started to rattle off the list of what I am—a professional woman, an orphan, a person with a mental condition, apparently. Still, nothing came forward to tell me who I was. I would just have to tell Bev this one was too hard. For further inspiration, I wrote, "I am Nora."

Still nothing.

Maybe that is what I was. Nothing.

So often, I felt that way, like a shell or some kind of tin man. Oh gosh. I had skipped over the criteria the doctor didn't mention. But there it was, motioning wildly towards me.

The shape came easily then. Underneath my name I drew a yellow circle.

It was just like the emptiness I felt and was exactly like the diagnosis described. Now, I had escalated to eight out of nine matches against the criteria. The book described the consequences of this emptiness perfectly. When I was with someone, I had a heart, I had a sense of purpose. I was their partner, their champion, their mother, their muse, their child, their slave, whatever they wanted. Giving them what they wanted gave me what I needed, a sense of identity, a colour to cling to, portray and perfect. But when this would wane, or when I was alone, I had to do something to feel, to prove that I did exist. This was when I would break out, do something stupid and harm myself. All of this was self-medication for the nothingness that was Nora.

The day before, when I sat down with the book on BPD, I was arming myself for combat. By the time the doctor walked in, I was waving the white flag. I could pick apart the details of the painting that was my diagnosis. Still, the whole picture was sound and a very realistic representation of my life.

Dr Dempsey walked in to find me slumped in the chair, holding half a mug of tepid tea. I was swinging between the joys of revelation and the frightening prospect that I had just been found out. When I had walked in these doors, I believed I was fine. Now, I believed I was "afflicted."

For the first time, I did not care about the doctor's socks. I was not sure what I really cared about.

"Good morning, Nora. How are you?"

"Honestly, I don't know."

"Why, what's going on? Is it something about the diagnosis we discussed yesterday?"

"Yeh, I guess so. I have been reading the book and brochure."

"And...?"

"Oh god. So much of it sounds like me."

"I see."

"Do you? Do you really? Do you know what this means? I have read what people think about borderlines, and I may as well just put myself in solitary confinement right now. No one will want to be around me, and if work finds out, well, they will get rid of me for sure.

I thought I was doing OK, apart from the stupid thing with Ben, but now I find out I am actually pretty sick.

It is fine for you to sit there and hand out a diagnosis, but you have no idea, none at all, about the consequences for me."

"That's unfair, Nora. I do, and that is why we need to get you some more support. Because if you keep going on without paying this the proper respect, you could make things even worse for yourself. This is a really bitter pill to swallow, I know. But now you can do something about it, rather than just get swept along with it and cause more destruction."

"I don't want to have to do this. I really don't."

"I do understand. This challenges so much about who you are, and what you had planned. But it also gives you so much more knowledge to take better care of yourself and your future."

"My future as a fucking chameleon."

"It doesn't have to be that way, Nora. Did you read the bits about treatment and how successful they are? You can strip away the harmful parts and live a really great life."

"As a fucking chameleon you mean."

"Nora, please stop. I know you are angry. It is OK."

My anger turned to sarcasm in a swift second.

"Oh, and there is something you missed."

"What is that?"

"I also fit the criteria of emptiness. You may want to make a note of that. I am now on a score of eight out of nine. I am improving."

It felt so good to finally have switched roles, to have the doctor on the other end of judgement and have to justify himself for a change.

The doctor did make a scribble but then looked me in the eye.

"That's huge, Nora. Thank you. I am sure that would be an excruciating experience. How does that play out for you? How does it make you feel?"

My anger was deflected and diluted with the demand for more information.

There was one big breath, attempting to expel the malice and inhale a more helpful intention.

"Honestly, scared. So many times, I wonder if I do really exist. Sometimes I feel like an alien."

"How has this affected you?"

"I can see how it made me do things to get a reaction and some feeling. Playing a role for people helped ease it for a while, but it still came back. Work helped fill the void too, and I was hoping making partner would fill in the final piece of the puzzle.

"Nora, this is really good work. You should be really proud of yourself for getting to this level of self-awareness."

Silence was the only reaction I could muster, my mind swinging between a sense of achievement and anguish at what the awareness had revealed.

"This will take some time to process, and to work through what to do next. I would like you to take the weekend to think about the way forward and then on Monday we can talk about the plan for how best to navigate treatment and your work. Would that be OK?"

There was only enough energy left for a nod.

"I think it will help for you to get out for a while too – take a walk, grab a good coffee. You will have two hours leave on Saturday and Sunday to get some fresh air and see something different. Bev will have some ideas about how you could use the time, so please talk this through with her. You will need your phone, and I have advised the nurses to make sure it is charged for you, but you might want to remind them tonight.

Does this sound OK?"

"Uh-huh. A walk would be nice."

"Absolutely. Enjoy it. Now, anything else?"

"Actually yes. Can I have my oil back? It is aromatherapy stuff I use in the shower. The nurses took it when I came in."

"The doctor flicked through my file."

"Yes, I see it listed here. May Chang. I don't know that one. It seems fine. Sure. I will make a note and you can grab it later."

"Thanks."

"My pleasure Nora. Now, you take care. Have a good weekend, and I will see you Monday."

"Ok. You too."

He gave a small smile as he left the room, closing the door gently behind him.

Everyone kept telling me this would take time, but it felt like something I didn't have. Yes, I was stuck here, but the world was going on without me, and the longer I stayed away from work, the weaker my position became. I would take this weekend and use it to make a plan. There would be a way to fit it all in. There was the force again, to prove myself, to play the role of superwoman. But looking around me, here in the hospital, there was another role I was already in: patient. How the hell was I going to reconcile these competing roles? Which one would I choose?

Mark met me in the dining room, acting as if I had crossed the finish line at a marathon.

"Hey, Nora. You made it to Friday. Congratulations! I have made a celebratory breakfast. How about pancakes?"

Pancakes sounded great, but I didn't think I could deal with the guilt of a sugary breakfast. Yet here was Mark, so excited about the prospect that I could not refuse.

"Thanks, yes. Wonderful."

"Strawberries?"

"Definitely!"

"Deal."

I watched as he piled two pancakes onto the plate and positioned the strawberries, pointy ends up, into the shape of a face: two eyes, one nose, and a five-strawberry smile.

"There are sauces and cream at the end."

"Thanks, Mark."

"Have a great Friday, Nora."

I could resist the call of the chocolate hazelnut spread and cream, which would be far too indulgent, and instead soaked the smile in syrup. There were no nuts, which must be an allergy risk, so I had to skip the protein component, noting this deficiency in the morning's diet to be addressed at lunch.

The pancakes sat in front of me in perfect circles. Sure, they were not yellow, but with the syrup on them, they were close enough. Was it another coincidence that beside my breakfast was my own drawing of a yellow circle? The only differences were that the one on my plate was decorated with a smile and had layers, while the one on paper stood empty and was a simple, single dimension. The idea of layers prompted me to put aside time on the weekend to do a mandala. I would have so much time and needed to keep myself busy.

As I brushed my teeth in the dark, I wondered whether I would ever do it with the light on again. Of course, I would, but it didn't mean I had to look. When I returned to work, makeup would be a different challenge, but I didn't wear much, and I was sure I could just focus on the features rather than the whole face.

The gentle exercise class gave me a chance to breathe after the morning's battle. Was this why they did this first each day? To calm our minds after the confrontation with our doctors and the confusion about our futures? Again, very clever. BPD sat beside me but, for a moment, bent with me, like the bow before a wrestling match, a moment of dual respect before the contestants for the championship tried to destroy each other.

It was convenient that the class on self-compassion came next before Nora and her neurosis could beat each other up too badly in the break.

Suffering. Supposedly, we were all suffering. We didn't think we were, but whether we called it fear, frustration or stress or self-sabotage – it was all suffering. It was what the teacher said, but working through how each of these states made us feel, I could see that it was true. Compassion was what we did to help ease the suffering of others. Self-compassion, then, is the same thing, just directed at ourselves. We were asked to consider why it was that we could help other people so easily, and yet found it so hard to be kind to ourselves. Why could we take care of other people but only judge ourselves for not being strong enough? That was a great question.

Sketching out the word suffering in my journal, I began to see where my lack of self-compassion had sprung from, at least initially. Dad didn't make me think I deserved anything. Maybe then, I had been making the choices all along that were acting on this belief. When you didn't think you deserved care, you wouldn't give this to yourself. But now we were told it was the time to change this and become our compassionate friend.

So much of what the teacher said was the same as the push Bev was giving me to be my own BFF. Is this why I didn't have any friends – because I had not yet learnt how to be one to myself?

After all the theory on self-compassion, I seriously needed a coffee. I couldn't wait to get out on the weekend and get a real one.

Supposedly, it was common for people to find it difficult to be their own compassionate friends, so there was a first step — creating a proxy until we could provide this for ourselves. Who could I trust that I could conjure in my mind when I was finding it hard to care for myself and needed advice? I went through the prompts they provided — it would be someone wise, caring, courageous, and who we know always had our best interests at heart.

The word heart made my mind spring to Calli. The garnet ring she gave was in the shape of a heart, and she was definitely all of these things. I remembered when I had met her for the first time. I had been back from Seattle for over a year and was posted to a new client. A few projects were working out of the shared space, so we kept bumping into each other.

Calli had seen some sketches Daniel had done for me on my desk and knew that I was dating an artist. We would chat whenever we crossed paths. She was just so easy to talk to, always asking questions but never prying, so joyful, never judgemental. Calli was also so caring, so it was perfect she was in change management. And she was courageous. I had seen how she advocated for the needs of the client's staff, and I really admired her for that. She was wise, knowing that the project would fail without the people's support, and she worked hard to make it happen. Sometimes, we would go for drinks after work on a Friday. She had a great sense of humour, always telling jokes and had such a lovely laugh. Her gorgeous green eyes would hold my attention, and I could not or did not want to look away.

When I broke up with Daniel and we went for celebration (or were they consolation) drinks, the mutual attraction was acknowledged. We both had imbibed far too much champagne, but it only helped with the flow of what we both felt. Intimate interactions with other women were not new to me. I had played around with some in the Cross and as an escort to arouse the guys. They would get off on us kissing and fondling each other, but I had never developed feelings for one before, and I had never ever spent the night cuddled in their arms.

Calli was like a big warm coat on a winter's day. She was passion personified – arousing slowly, seductively, and then expertly answering the call she had encouraged. Calli loved receiving as well, expressing her ecstasy without fear and making me feel like I had given her something truly special. With Calli, it felt like a partnership of pleasure, not a performance.

The next morning, she made me tea, and we sat in bed, me stroking her gorgeous golden hair and both of us smiling, unable to believe what had just happened. Then she looked serious.

"How are you feeling?" I knew she was enquiring about more than my physical form; that she understood this was a first for me.

"Calli, I am good. Really good."

"No regrets?"

"None whatsoever."

The kisses that followed came naturally – they always did in our little cocoon. And it was in this little cocoon that I began to seriously contemplate Calli's dream of having a child.

I could even see it when I closed my eyes; I was snuggled into Calli's back, and the baby was lying in her arms. There was such beauty in this and such hope. In this little world we shared, things were simple.

After a long, frustrating day at work, Calli was always there to listen. When I doubted myself, she was always there to counter my self-criticism. She was all that a compassionate friend could be. But she was more. She was the most luxurious lover and a place of safety amongst so many storms. Calli was my sanctuary.

Until we stepped outside.

Then, she was simply a problem.

I could not see how I could make it work. Being a lesbian was just not the done thing. There was still so much stigma about it, and it would be seen as a stain on my reputation. So would having a lover in the same firm. Calli said it wouldn't be a problem. We worked in different areas, but if the need arose, we could declare a conflict of interest. Still, I could see how there would always be the potential for questions and suggestions that my credibility had been compromised. I knew how these people thought – I was one of them, and there was just too much space for gossip and sneaky doubt. Calli thought the partners would understand. I was far too uncomfortable about coming out. I was not brave enough to blaze a trail for others, but Calli was, and Calli did. I so admired her ability to be authentic. Even when I started pulling away, she was so kind; her love was so captivating I could not break free. She even forgave me when I did the Judas thing and denied our relationship three times.

"Are you and Calli together?" asked a colleague.

"No, not at all! What makes you think that?"

"Oh, just the way you look at each other."

Then, another when we were chattering about our dream dates.

"I think you and Calli would make a great couple, if you were that way inclined."

"Oh, you are hilarious. No thanks, I am more of a Colin Firth kind of girl."

The third betrayal came in the same month. I was packing up after a presentation when a partner declared he had heard a rumour; that I was with Calli. My response?

"Yes, I have heard it too. And I would like to shut it down now, once and for all. It is incorrect and downright insulting. So, if you please hear it, could you tell whoever is spreading it that it is not true."

At that moment, I had drawn the line in the sand that would split the ground between Calli and me. This was no longer paranoia about being found out. It was the raw reality of being with her.

I went home that night and did what needed to be done.

"Calli. I am sorry. But this is not going to work."

"You mean you are not going to let it. Oh Nora, how many times do I have to tell you that I love you. Come on honey. Let's keep going. Things have been wonderful. Don't we deserve to give it a really good chance. Otherwise, we will never know what could have been."

She was so optimistic. The only way to counter it was with cruelty.

"Calli, you sound like a goddam movie. Stop being so idealistic and naïve and step into the real world."

"Yes Nora, I am idealistic. And I take that as a compliment. But I am not naïve. I know how hard it is to be in love with another woman in this world. It might sound like a movie, but you want to live in one, Nora. You want the type of love, where it is all straightforward and easy, and the couple can live happily ever after. The real world is not that simple, especially not for us. You have to fight for it, Nora. You have to fight for the people you love."

Calli was not going to let me get away with running away. It was better that I ripped the band aid off before she could get into my head or heart any further. I had to shout it to make her hear.

"That's what I am saying Calli, I don't love you Calli."

"Don't, or won't, Nora?"

"I don't love you Calli. Full stop."

I twisted off the garnet heart ring. This was the little secret we shared in the outside world. It had sustained me through so much. Now, I threw it towards her face.

"It's finished."

I walked out and never went back.

When she called, I didn't answer.

When she sent a text requesting to talk, I simply kept responding with, "No, it's over." Then, after several times, I stopped replying at all.

What was over, though? Was it the relationship with Calli or the illusion that I had integrity?

Because I was doing to her exactly the same thing Daniel had to me. I had demanded that she split herself in half; make her integral nature invisible outside of our cocoon. I was expecting her to play two contrasting roles: my inside intimate lover and my outside cool colleague. Then, when she wanted more, I had cast her away.

I would not have blamed her if she had come banging on my door and yelled, "Coward." She would be right. She could have also yelled, "Shame," and she would have also been correct — I was ashamed of my shallowness.

She never did, though. Calli would never be callous and certainly would never seek retribution for my decision. Calli was the personification of a compassionate friend, but I could not hear her voice in my head right now. It would be counterproductive.

Ben also met all the criteria. I could still see him in my dream, though, poking fun at me being a spinster, using his voice with such venom. I could not have him as my compassionate friend either. There was too much pain, too much embarrassment. He was intertwined with my trauma, so he could not help me out of it.

I was left with mum. Yes, mum would be my compassionate friend. She was so much of one when she was alive, and this exercise suggested she could still be. That gave me a great sense of comfort.

The next part unravelled this, though, and I was left feeling exposed all over again. We were asked to think of something we were finding difficult to deal with. After just reliving the drama with Calli, my example came readily. Even though it had been almost five years since we broke up, I still felt so bad. We weren't in the office much together, but she would still offer me a smile whenever we passed in the corridor. I was sucked into her green eyes again. Forcing myself to look at the floor was my only chance of staying clear. Calli never stopped being kind.

It was my behaviour that I still found unbearable. So, I sat with the suffering I had caused her, how I had screamed at her, shunned her and belittled the love she had for me.

"This is a moment of suffering."

I repeated the words but felt like, "This fucking hurts" was a more honest depiction of this distress.

"I am not alone."

And I wasn't. I suspect that underneath all that compassion, Calli was also bruised. We were asked to think broader about our common humanity, and I considered all those people who felt they couldn't be themselves and were waking up today burdened by someone else's expectations. I suspected this would describe everyone sitting here for a start.

Hand on heart.

I couldn't believe I had never done this before.

Deep breaths.

I was sinking into my own support.

"May I be kind to myself."

I needed to add, "May I forgive myself". I said it, but it didn't seem fair. In fact, it felt indulgent, like I was condoning my own cruelty. But I was willing to try the process—make amends with me first, and the rest will follow.

I didn't think I could forgive myself, not yet, but the intent was there, and for the moment, that would have to be enough. Mum came to sit beside me, my guide for where to go next. What was the kindest thing I could do for myself right now?

Why was this question so difficult? Perhaps, as the teacher said, I had so much practice at responding with self-criticism and choosing my punishments that I had even forgotten there was an alternative. Before mum and I could come to an answer, we moved on. And I was moved to tears. In this, I really was not alone. As each of us crafted and then shared our self-compassion letter, there were long silences and sometimes sobs. My words felt more like torture than therapy.

Dear Nora,

I can see you are being so hard on yourself for what you have done in the past and for ending up here. You are beating yourself up about not being strong enough but also not soft enough. You are so worried about being seen as sick and stupid and never making it to success. I can see you covered in scars from self-criticism and still slashing away.

Nora, remember you are not alone in these feelings. Look around you; there are so many other people who are also struggling, who feel like they have failed, and who wonder if they will ever get their act together. We all let fear take over at times and do things we regret. There are so many others who have lost themselves and long for love yet don't believe they really deserve it.

Darling girl, let's step back and look at where you are. You were made to believe that you were not worthy of happiness, so understandably, you have done things that have caused you and others pain. Your father forced you as a child to believe that your needs do not matter. But you are grown now, honey, and are on an exciting adventure shaping a life you can be proud of – your life – not a life lived by the expectations of others. You are in control now, and you have the power to shape the life that you want. You are in the right place, with the right people to help you start on a new path.

Besides, I have already seen you score some great successes, so just keep going. This letter is a wonderful start! And just like this letter, I know you will find a way to channel and transform this negative and wasteful energy into something beautiful.

I believe in you, darling.

Perhaps it is time to start believing in yourself.

Your Compassionate Friend

And just like torture, there was an immense relief when the reading was done. In part because other people hearing about my problems was truly horrendous. But also because it felt like a burden had been removed. With this letter I had dropped the mask I had made for myself. The letter in itself held so much power, but the process created so much potential. Could this become the way I would be – from wicked to warm?

I greatly appreciated taking the three big deep breaths we were instructed to before we departed. There was a lot to let go of. The movement out of this session was slow, a shuffling born from the heaviness of our shared experience. But as disturbing as it was, as I exited the room, it also felt like I was walking through a brand new door.

At lunch, Mark was making jokes with another patient, one I had seen so pained through the letter exercise. I wondered whether his heartiness was based on something more than just a sense of humour, whether self-compassion allowed him to share so much of himself so honestly.

Over another great salad, this time with fish to make up for the protein missed at breakfast, I started building layers on my yellow circle. Then a light came on. That letter meant so much. Maybe I should send one to Calli to ask for her forgiveness.

With some help from mum, I started writing something simple. I finished it in my room, sad, my face streaked with tears, but satisfied that it said all I wanted and what I needed her to know. I would post it on my walk tomorrow and then wait.

Now I could see how the mandala worked, how it rippled outwards, but how the influence of the outside world also filtered in. Creating a mandala was not only about choosing what would go in the middle but also what you would surround yourself with. Ah hah! That is who I was – a system. Nah, I would not present that conclusion to Bev. It was far too wanky and far too scientific.

And just like that, she appeared.

"Hey, Nora. Well done. Friday! How are you?"

"Alright thanks."

"You look a little washed out. Everything OK?"

"I am still not sleeping so well, and the last sessions were pretty intense."

"Yes, self-compassion. It sounds so easy, but it can be so sad when you realise how little you have for yourself.

Speaking of yourself. How did you go with the homework? Who are you, Nora?"

"Bev, that is a very good question."

I showed her the simple diagram, the layers of yellow circles.

"Honestly, I could not answer that question. I actually don't know. I am not even sure why I drew the circles. I guess because part of it shows the emptiness I feel. Then the other layers show who I am as a cause and effect relationship. I am probably not explaining it very well because I don't understand it for myself.

It was a shame that sat with me as I showed Bev the diagram. How can someone not know who they are? There was nothing meaty, nothing complicated, or clever. If I handed this over to one of my bosses, I would be fired on the spot, but at least here, I had more freedom to fail.

"That is perfect, Nora."

Bev looked genuinely excited. She was like some goddam eternal optimist. There were times when this made her seem like such a peaceful pundit. But then there were those times she was more like a prancing Pollyanna, and this annoyed me. This moment was like the latter. How could anyone be impressed with something so vague, so incomplete?

"What? Why? How can this be a good thing?"

"Well, if you presented me with a full picture of who you were, I would have considered you delusional. You are here Nora because you lost yourself somewhere along the way, and this shows it so succinctly. The whole point of this exercise was to show where you are at, right now. This is a perfect picture of it, and of the adventure ahead of you."

Bev sat on the bed, holding the yellow circles before her, contemplating them and smiling at me.

"You have captured it, Nora. Here you are right now, a product of your past, of your own and other's actions. But the circles are like blank slates. You have a chance to fill them up with what is meaningful to you.

Think of it like a vase. The value is not just in the structure but in the space. It can't do its job unless there is emptiness. The problem your picture makes clear is that the circles are going to stay empty because they are closed in. If you need to put in an opening, could I suggest one of self-compassion? This could help you shed a light to see the contents more clearly."

"Oh Bev. Are you sure you were not a Buddha in your past life?"

"You are so sweet. But no, I don't think so. I can tell you though what I was a decade ago. I was an addict, desperate, disgusting and dangerous."

"I can't believe that."

"It's true. After my second child and a few medical issues I became addicted to pain killers. It was a really horrible time. I spent many years in places like this and there were many court appearances where I had to plead for my children not to be taken away. I was a mess, and caused so much harm, especially to my kids. There were so many therapies I had to work through, but the only thing that really made a difference was practicing self-compassion. If there is only one thing that you take out of here Nora, let it be the practice of self-compassion."

I could not imagine this woman being addicted, admitted, and struggling for years. An image passed through my mind of celebrity mug shots, but it was not a rockstar. Instead, it was Bev holding her prisoner number and turning to the side to have her picture taken. I really could not envision Bev crying for any other reason but out of sheer joy or empathy. Yet she, too, had walked through the path of self-hate and now stood before me, an inspiration, and I told her so.

"Thank you, Nora. That means so much. But can I tell you something, seriously, so are you."

Now, she was just being nice, I knew it.

"I know you are probably thinking that I am just being polite..."

Bloody hell. No, not polite, a psychic.

"But you have been through so much. Yet here you are, putting in the work when this is not easy, not at all.

You have now become aware that you are what you choose to let into your circles. Your life is not a closed system. It is influenced and impacted by everything in your environment, so choosing where your centre sits is incredibly important.

Opening up, though, to let the light into your circle is tough, especially for someone who has been taught, as you have, that vulnerability is a weakness. Letting down the layers of protection will take practice and needs to be done with the right people. The first right person is yourself. Being honest with where you are and what you need will open up a whole new world for you. Living through your values will create this light."

"There is so much to this, Bev. It is a bit overwhelming.

"Yes there is, and yes it can be. But you have time, Nora, and it is a lifelong journey. Some may suggest it can take many lifetimes for us to come to know who we are, and then many more for us to come to appreciate and love ourselves. There are no deadlines on this. It is too important to put a timeline on. The only success is progress."

Bev could tell that I was becoming a bit bewildered. In fact, I thought Bev could see into my very soul.

"Sorry Nora, too much talk. Come with me."

We went back to the library, and she grabbed a book on self-compassion.

"Self-compassion is really an essential skill for anyone, so we stock up on these. It could be a bit lonely in here for you on the weekend, so if you get sick of your room, come and camp here. The morning light is really lovely. Although you have some time out don't you! That's fantastic. You could always take it and read it under a tree in the park."

How nice it would be to park my back against a tree trunk. The thought got me excited, but there was more to come. We returned to the art room, where she stood in front of the cupboard with a wide smile.

"Ready?"

I nodded, but she didn't need any encouragement.

She flung open the doors like she was a clerk at the after-Christmas sales, moving back to let the mania begin.

"So, your task for the weekend. This time, the only restriction is the colour. I am not going to give you any prompts, with the exception that whatever you do has to all be in green. All good?"

"I guess so."

"That's my girl."

"Green. Wow. I guess I should have seen that coming. Looks like I am going to spend the weekend with grass and granny smith apples in my head. Oh, but then there was also broccoli, and basil, and beans..."

"And spinach, and tree snakes," said Bev, bouncing around more ideas.

"And asparagus..."

"And avocado, and grapes, and capsicum, and chameleons..."

"And..."

"What, Nora?"

"Nothing. I forgot."

There was that word again: chameleon. I did not know what was worse, having that one inserted into the list of ideas or the fact that the next one I was going to say was Calli's eyes.

"Well, we should stop talking about food. It is starting to make my belly rumble. Let's think creation. What would you like, Nora, paints, pastels or pens? Canvas or paper? What is calling to you?"

Nothing sprang to mind, and I just stood there surveying the shelves. So, Bev delegated the decision-making to herself.

"I have an idea. Let's give you everything. Let's not box it in at the beginning. Let's grab a box instead!"

She went to the corner and grabbed an old paper box, filling it with canvasses, green paper, some large A3 sheets, a box of pastels, green paints, another plastic cup, a few more brushes and some plastic sheeting.

"You are good to go!"

"Excited?"

"Kind of."

"That's good enough for me."

We walked all of the supplies back to my room.

"Well, have a wonderful weekend, Nora. I hope you have a great time out and about. Again, as always, call if you need me."

Bev reached down for her bag and bounced up.

"Oh, I almost forgot. Silly me."

She pulled out a little box and placed it on the desk.

"Happy birthday for tomorrow, Nora," she said, giving me a big hug.

I had no idea what was in the box, but her thoughtfulness brought me to tears. I should have waited until tomorrow, but just couldn't.

"Do you mind if I open it now?"

"Please do!"

I undid the ribbon, which was shiny silver, and opened the royal blue box. Inside sat a tiny crystal fairy. She was kneeling, her wings shimmering, smiling upwards towards me and holding a little green heart.

"I couldn't believe I found this, Nora. It just sprang out at me. I wasn't even looking, but it was like it was looking for me."

So, my theory was confirmed. Strange things happened around this woman. In the olden days, she may have been burnt as a witch. I was judging her as simply wonderful.

"It's so beautiful, Bev. Thank you."

I gave Bev another hug and then put the fairy on the windowsill to let the light dance through her wings. If I could choose who I had in my environment, then I wanted it filled up with Bev's. How I wished that could be an option.

"Gosh, I almost forgot again. What about your grateful?"

"It is you, Bev. I am grateful for you."

"Aww...you are so sweet."

Another hug, and she reminded me that gratitude was my homework for the weekend, too. Then she waved goodbye as she walked out the door.

When Bev left, so did some of the bliss. Yes, tomorrow was my 37th birthday, and I was far from my preferred party location. But it could be worse. Like when I turned twenty-six. Mum had died the day before, and I spent my birthday that year at the funeral director. Today was the 11th anniversary of her death. This is why I never wanted to celebrate birthdays. It always seemed like so much more of a sad time. Now, without Bev here, I felt the pain. Mum could be the voice inside my head, telling me to stay true to my values, but mum was not here to visit, hear me out, hold me, and take me home.

If there was a time I needed some of the self-compassion skill, it was right now. I sobbed the words, "This is so shitty." Then thought about all the other people who had lost their mothers, who would miss the chance to see their own children cuddled into them, and who had felt love leave them the day their mother died. I could not explain why I started twirling. I was trying to think of the kindest thing I could do for myself through this misery, but instead just started moving. The rhythm of the rotation seemed to settle my distress, and the movement made me feel a sense of strength. I would walk tomorrow. Until then, there was something to look forward to.

There was also my oil. I had forgotten about that, and it was almost five o'clock. I went to the nurses, got my oil and phone, and proceeded to the interview room. I sniffed the May Chang and felt my whole body melt and my mind become brighter. Was it possible for an aromatherapy oil to also be a compassionate friend? Well, I was going to say yes, and May Chang was mine.

It was with a sense of hope then that I checked my messages. There was a thumbs up from Calli and an assurance that she would follow up if there were any problems. I also sent an update to my boss, letting him know we should have a way forward by mid-next week. I checked my sick leave balances; I had well over a month. And then my savings to make sure they had not been hacked. Seeing how much money I had in the bank added to my cheer. There was enough in there to tie me over for a good few months, so I did not need to panic in case I was pushed out.

The only surprise was a message from the real estate agent who managed mum's house rentals. The current tenants had a posting overseas, and they must move quickly. They were trying to find someone to take over it but with no luck yet in securing another lease. The house would be free in about three weeks, and he needed to know if I wanted to list it now or wait to see if they could find a replacement. It all felt a bit too hard at the moment. My mind was hazy, and this problem sounded a bit too complex. What would be the kindest thing I could do for myself right now? Yes, this self-compassion thing was helpful. I needed to give myself some time to work through it. I wrote back and told the agent to hold off doing anything until mid-next week. I would advise them then of the course of action to take. Then I took one big breath, gave the phone to the nurses, asked them to charge it, and went for dinner.

Of course, pumpkin soup would be offered as the entrée that night! That was the kind of thing that happened in the

Twilight Zone! I ate in honour of mum, contemplating whether this meal really was a coincidence or a message to work through the grief lesson again.

Back in my room I showered with the oil flowing into the steam, making it fragrant. I had missed this so much. Then, I was ready to start designing my ideas for the green assignment. Pushing away the image of Calli's eyes and drowning out the call of the chameleon was difficult. Still, I landed on the concept of leaves. What do leaves do? They take in the elements and convert them into energy. They were such clever creations and so critical, yet so easily taken for granted. Leaves were also so easily injured and made ready sustenance for predators. But leaves were also where the light gets in. Maybe I just need more leaves in my life, literally and metaphorically. Although the last time I attempted taking care of plants I failed miserably. I was unsure where this one was going, and it was becoming more of an intellectual than artistic exercise, so I let it rest for a while.

I settled into bed and started into the self-compassion book. I immediately knew I wanted this author in my support network. She was just so authentic, and seemed to understand so well the struggles I was having with the thought of being kind to myself. She put forward so much clear evidence about its effects and gave me a new resolve to investigate it further. Could it be, as Bev suggested, that this might be a magic pill? For the moment, though, my eyes were closing, so this medicine would have to take second place to sleep. Although that was an act of kindness in itself, wasn't it? Or was it? If you knew, like me, that it would probably end up with you shrinking into your own shit, then one could consider it more like masochism. The truth is I did not have any choice but to step into this suffering.

The nightmare began no differently. There were no dramatic colours, just the humiliation of the mocking, the dread of having my body decompose and the emptiness inside and out. But while I was succumbing, two people snuck through the crack, the same one I could see the sun through. It was mum and Calli. They came and sat beside me, putting their hands on me, holding me together.

"We will take care of you.", they said as they tried to stop my skin from slipping and my joints from falling apart.

The dragon awoke and saw them. I was so scared when he started shifting, fearing that they would be burnt alive. I was waiting for it, ready to hear their screams, resigned to the fact that they would have been massacred because of me. The dragon turned some more, putting its head into the cave entrance. Just as I thought the flames would come, his head flopped onto the floor, and he stayed there, simply watching, then smiling, and sleeping. This should make me happy, but I was overcome with anguish.

I was so angry that I did not have any strength to stand because right now would be a great time to sneak out. I could escape. But then my body became something completely different. Instead of a sagging spinster lying in the arms of these ladies, they were touching a chameleon. I had a green, leathery, bumpy body with legs that looked like they didn't fit. My mouth was flat, ferocious in its display of displeasure, and my chunky claws could only clumsily clasp my carer's hands. My tail was twirled and lay heavily across mum's lap. I could see her wriggling to try and hold the weight. My domed eyes darted around the cave, scanning for danger, a damning display of my insecurity. Mum's and Calli's hands moved around to my chest, caressing it with their caring hands. Until they realised, it had been cut open. They looked at each other and nodded their agreement to enter. Each pulled apart a side to reveal a hollow cavity, a blood-lined barrenness. There was no heart.

Chapter 9

I didn't think my dreams could get much worse, but seeing myself as a heartless chameleon, while sounding comedic, was actually quite dramatic and disturbing. Calli's scream at seeing my gaping chest woke me, and there was not much sleep again until the sun came up. Being Saturday there would be no Doctor Dempsey or no Bev, so the day already sounded very boring. It was hours until breakfast, so I made tea, did some reading and ended up dozing off for a second round. I was woken with a shock when the nurse knocked on my door and swiftly swung it open announcing breakfast. It took a while to get my bearings again, hazy from a mixed-up sleep cycle. It was like I was lying in a hotel on a holiday. Well, apart from the fact that there was no bath, I was only allowed out for a few hours, room service was banned, and there were certainly no "do not disturb" signs available for the door handles. Although maybe they thought we were already disturbed, so we did not have to abide by the common rules of decency. Still, I could get out and feel like a real person again today. I decided to do it after lunch to prevent an afternoon that dragged on.

Mark was not in the kitchen today, so it felt strange and far less friendly. What was more frustrating was that a young girl had taken my seat. I thought I saw her getting admitted yesterday afternoon when I went to get my oils. Obviously, she didn't know the rules; the unspoken ones I had imposed included my claim over the most distant left-hand seat in any location. This ordinance covered the territories of the dining room and all classrooms. Non-compliance would not be tolerated.

So, I stood there for a moment like a stunned mullet. What to do now? The poor girl, though, looked so very fragile, close to fearful. I could not possibly follow through with my fanaticism. I did consider leaving her a note in the dead of night. I had an immediate image of me sneaking through the corridors Spiderman style, slipping the instructions stealthily under her pillow before returning to my room, crawling along the ceiling and bundling into bed just before the nightly torch intrusion. There were some times when my brain amused me, so I could not be all bad!

No, today breakfast would be had in my room. It was the weekend, so I assumed the regular routine was relaxed. I was sure the nurses would tell me otherwise if I had assumed wrongly. The food didn't taste quite as good this morning, either. It looked a bit dull, not exuding Mark's energy, and it was not served with the sauce of his smile. I picked at it for a while and put it aside, avowing to make up for it with a treat on my walk later. I would only get out much later, not for another five hours. There was only one thing to fill the time, and that was to catch up with Frida.

Green was not a colour that Frida used a lot in her diary entries, and I was surprised at that. And yet, the bits I found were some of the most profound prompts. There were a few pages where she had written solely in green ink and, when translated, stated her wish to do whatever she liked behind the curtain of madness. Was Frida also crazy? Had she been diagnosed with a mental health condition? I hadn't read anything so far, but from all of the surgeries she had to endure, I am sure she would have been at least a little depressed.

Well, if Frida could use a diagnosis as an excuse to do exactly what she wanted, then maybe I could, too?

What would I wish to do behind the curtain of madness? I did not have to think long, the ideas inundated my imagination. I would call Shane and sound like a sadistic personal trainer, telling him he was a sloth and a shame to mankind. I would call Aaron and preach to him that he was a pansy and needed to stand up to his parents, that he really needed therapy for a severe case of Oedipus complex, and to improve his pathetic sex skills. I would call Daniel's wife and rat him out about having lovers, although she probably already knew. Instead, I would stalk his studio and give him a severe case of anxiety. He was already a nervous wreck with a stomach full of ulcers, so it would not take much effort to excel at this and make his life excruciating.

I would call Calli and tell her I had changed my mind, that my decision was clouded by my condition; that I was clear now and did want a child with her and to hell with anyone else. Then, if I ever had to backtrack, I could again blame it on the BPD. I would tell my gay guys, Rob and Tom, to man up and stop using middlemen (or women) to pass on their messages. And Stephen, yes, Stephen, I would press charges and scream at him in the courtroom. It's OK, they would say, she is crazy. The best part would be they would think Stephen caused it. But what to do with Ben? Well, I could bang on his door until he heard my apology. In fact, I could do it this afternoon. It would push my time allocation, but it could be done if I got the right transport connections. There was so much I could do, that I wanted to do, and every action could be condoned by my condition. I could make this work for me. Besides, why should all these people get off scot-free when I had to carry around this curse? I considered myself a generous person, so why not share the craziness and get what I wanted?

This plan sounded fantastic, so much drama! But what did Frida choose? Reading on, Frida said she would use her madness to get away with spending her days arranging flowers, painting pain, love and tenderness, and laughing. Frida would sacrifice sanity to make things, to create, not to crush and destroy. She would channel her condition into creation and offered a great sense of compassion.

Now I felt really bad. Frida's approach was so altruistic and committed to her art, while mine was simply selfish. Yet I could not see how my form of madness could make anything good.

Then it struck me. Was this what the doctor and Bev were suggesting? To use the curtain of my madness to do something different? Could I use what I have learnt to get out of my chaos and start again? Was it possible to take time to arrange flowers, paint and laugh? It seemed indulgent but also incredibly idealistic.

These ideas floated around for a while but got lost in the lethargy that came with a lack of structure. I was so used to a regime that without a routine, I was feeling really anxious. I could start on my assignment, but I had lost the flow of thought. Or was it because I was trying to avoid thinking more about Calli's eyes?

Bev had said the morning light in the library was good, so that sounded like a great place to go. Thank goodness there was no one else in here. I was not in the mood for banter. Bev was right, the rays of the sun split as they came through the window, creating streams of various shades of gold. It made it feel like an ancient university. Each golden strand carried a family of dust downwards like the sun was giving them a lift to the library floor. I could imagine the little particles jumping off like an escalator at the end, with the parents pulling the children off so they did not trip. They were all here to witness this marvel of human wisdom.

I left the tiny visitors to their own devices and found another book on self-compassion. Flicking through, the concepts were pretty much the same, but there were some new and really relevant case studies. The other book on BPD was back, too. I almost put it down after the first few chapters. It painted a terrible picture of promiscuity and self-harm. The similarities were almost too painful. This author, though, found solace in spirituality, especially mindfulness, meditation, and no surprises here, self-compassion. But there was something else that stood out; the role of curiosity. I had never stopped to pay attention to what was going on for me at all. I just acted, whether it was appropriate or not. Sure, sometimes I could suppress what I wanted to do, but others, it just burst forth. This author suggested an alternative and productive pathway - being aware of what I wanted to do and attending to it with wonder. I wondered myself whether Bev had read this book, and wrote some notes to discuss with her the following week.

I had soaked up quite a bit of time in the library but now felt recharged and eager to get cracking on my homework. I passed the young girl in the corridor. It looked like she had been crying. Our eyes met for a moment, and we shared a smile. Instinctively, I wanted to ask if she was OK, but I shut that down quickly. I had my own madness to deal with, so I kept moving.

Back in my room, I started to conjure something clever, but all I could come up with was leaves. Frida had some in her diary, all slightly different shapes. That's right, they are all individuals. I made a mental note to take a pencil and get some inspiration on my walk — to examine how much the leaves varied even on the same tree.

Amor.

This was the word sitting above the leaves. This word translated into love. Love and leaves. That would make a great name for a painting, but I was unsure if I even knew what love meant. Green was also the colour of the wings Frida drew on herself. In one dramatic self-portrait, they were broken, but the text underneath declared that she was not leaving. Then, in the last painting she ever did, these wings were carrying her poor, broken, bloodied body up into the sky. The wings had healed and were now doing their duty of taking her beyond the chaos below.

Leaves, love and wings. There was something in this, but it took a while to come out of its shell and strike its sad blow.

"Love lifts us up where we belong."

This was the song that played as mum's coffin was carried out of the Church. She used to sing it all the time and asked that this be her final farewell. She had demanded that there not be much else. Mum had asked for no photos, no displays or drama. Not even a eulogy. She said everyone there would know her, so they didn't need to be told who she was. Just a few prayers and songs were the extent of the ceremony. A few cuddles after the cremation and some visitors over the next week, and then it was all wound up. I returned to work, and to Shane, the house was inhabited by tenants.

I often wondered whether the death of her hero, Nora Ephron, caused her heart to break or whether it was a source of strength. My namesake had died in June, and mum passed three months later. I have never been able to watch a romcom since. I tried once with Calli, but the whole way through, I kept thinking if mum would like this one. It hurt too much. And it hurt too much now. A fiery battle was going on in my heart, enflaming my arms and preparing me for attack. I wanted to hurt something, or me, so badly to banish the heat and the hate. I had the chair in my hands before I realised I had another choice.

Holding the chair in the air, I saw myself in the unbreakable mirror. This path was useless. Looking into my own eyes, I saw the thirst for destruction, and right then, I decided I didn't like it. I didn't like this person staring back at me, primed to punish anyone and anything around her the pain. I put down the chair, collapsed on the floor, and cried out for my compassionate friend.

"Mum, please, help me. I don't know what to do."

My eyes were dry, and my body was heavy with despair.

"Draw it honey. Capture your reality, and then show it some compassion."

The last time I tried the drawing route, I had to be disarmed. But mum suggested an alternate ending: I had another skill to apply, one more constructive than anger.

This is what Frida did, too, in all of its messy detail. She captured her reality, and here I was, learning through her. So perhaps drawing was also my pathway to power.

I felt sick as I began and even sicker when I had finished. Before me lay a sketch, all done in scarlet. This colour had called to me, and I did not have the energy to resist or return to the pile of pens and negotiate the use of one more neutral. There was the heart, the one ripped from the Chameleon's chest. It was still beating, but only faintly. The heart was held by a claw, the talons full of viciousness and vitriol. The owner of this claw knew its power and used it to squeeze this heart so hard that it cracked, causing a gaping crevice. Not satisfied with this single act of destruction, a talon ran along the inside of this rent, scraping more flesh from the tender meat inside. It was excruciating to see and even worse to feel.

When it was done, the tears came, one dropping into the rift, dampening the page and the colour, diluting the ink. I could not help but think there was a message in this. Ben always used to quote Rumi and told me once that wounds are where the light gets in. He also used this as support for his argument that I should open up more and that I should share so that he could help. Was Ben the light I didn't let in?

Light. Light. It was coming into this heart through the hurt. Light: it was what the leaves used to create life.

Light. Leaves. Love. Wings.

How did all of these things hang together?

I picked up the green pen and sketched a few more shapes, but I could not find a way to string them together. I tried morphing them into each other, like some kind of transformation process, but it felt too forced. It didn't feel right. The leaves were so earth, and the wings so heavenly. I was finding it hard to find their middle ground; the structure they shared. Then it struck me - they could exist as layers. Yes, they could come in circles. Circles always felt right. Although I really should be doing something different, but then, like mum always used to say, "If it ain't broke, don't fix it."

Maybe circles were just my thing.

With the green pen, I started a mock-up of the canvas. There would be two concentric circles taking up the whole page. I did not have the brainpower to figure out what to do with any space left outside. The inner circle would be leaves in all different shades of green. I would collect some shape and shade ideas later in the park. The centre was the environment, the place that lets in the light and creates energy. The energy would exude to the outer layer, flowing forth to wings, to flying. The two sections were like the separate earthly and heavenly realms. One was rooted in the dirt, the other in the sky. One was the mundane, where men walked; the other was the magical, the realm of angels.

Wow, I was really happy with the concept, but I was worried someone had slipped hippie juice into my tea. I was not sounding like my corporate consultant self. If I had explained this to my colleagues, they would have thought I had lost it.

I got in early for lunch, making sure I got my seat back and not daring to look around lest eye contact exact a challenge. Eating was not a priority, though. I was too busy dealing with the excitement of getting out for a walk. The latter was not helped by the formalities involved in signing out, including a lecture about returning on time. Otherwise, the police would be called, and this privilege would be revoked. Was this how they treated all the patients, or was this a special condescension they saved for the borderlines? Why did they have to spoil this freedom with fear?

However, a few minutes later, I was instilling fear myself. I thought about the disastrous situation of running into someone I knew. I was not beyond lying, but it would still be awkward. The exit was swift, and I made it to the post office without incident. Calli's letter was sent, and now, being surrounded by shops, I could relax as I could come up with a more realistic excuse. The safest place was the park, so I grabbed a coffee and found a quiet space under a shady tree. Gosh it was good to breathe the fresh air, and I sat for ages just looking out at the scenery.

There was so much I had taken for granted before now. While I never made it out on the hikes, I always knew they were a possibility. Locked up in the hospital, without the option, I was beginning to understand just how precious freedom was. Closing my eyes, I could hear so many sounds, things I could not hear behind tempered glass. In the hospital, there were corridor conversations, banging doors, and stacking of plates. Here, there were birds, cicadas, children playing, and the subtle whisper of the wind in the trees. When I opened my eyes, the world seemed brighter, and I was overcome by how much green lay under, beside and above me.

My butt was getting numb, so it was time for a walk. I went to the bubbler and rinsed my coffee cup, then wandered around collecting leaves of different shapes and shades. I also found a few feathers, none green, plenty black and white, but still perfect to get the detail right for my outer layer. This took me back to the high school art projects I loved so much. They never felt like work. I did miss them when it came time to concentrate on the academics.

Why hadn't I done any art since then? I was an adult now and was in charge of my own time. Although there were many days I felt owned by the firm. On the weekends, there were always client deadlines, travel to attend a Monday meeting in another city, or pressure to improve my billable hours. All of that was so thrilling in the beginning. Now, it felt more like a burden. This, though, was wonderful; the investigation and assembling of ideas, the seeking and receiving of inspiration. It just felt so right. It made me feel so free. Still, it would not pay the bills. It did make me contemplate the possibility of a better balance.

I was surprised when the phone rang, almost panicking that I had lost track of time. It was Calli, and seeing her name made my heart sink. I really didn't want to have to talk to her. Why didn't she just text? Again, a panic thinking that she may have read the letter. Don't be stupid Nora, you have just sent it! Maybe there is a problem with my apartment. With that thought, I pressed the green button and answered her call.

"Hey, Calli."

"Hi Nora, how are you?"

"I'm OK thanks." I tried to sound noncommittal, given that I was already technically committed.

"How are you?"

"Good. Really good. It is great to talk again."

"Thanks, yes. It has been too long."

I suspected this would be the extent of our conversation, facts and pleasantries, so I started to relax.

"Well, I checked your unit and car, and everything was fine. I hope you don't mind. I also did a fridge clean-out. It was starting to get a bit stinky."

"Oh Calli, thank you. You didn't have to do that. You are really kind."

I had never said that to her before, even if I had thought it a thousand times.

"It is my pleasure. But more importantly. Happy birthday, Nora!"

"Thanks, Calli, really..."

Her sweetness made me smile until I heard a child singing it in the background.

"Who's that, Calli?"

"Come here, Grace. Let's sing happy birthday."

The song made me cry, not just because it was so thoughtful, but because I realised then that she had moved on, that there was now a child in her life, and that she had done it without me. I couldn't blame her. It had been five years.

"Nora, this is my foster daughter, Grace. Grace, say hi to Nora."

Grace said hello in a precious, innocent, little girl voice.

"Hi Grace. That is a beautiful name. Thank you so much for singing happy birthday to me."

Then Grace went shy and silent.

"Calli, it is wonderful that you have a child in your life. I am so happy for you."

I don't think I had ever said that to anyone before. And I meant it, for a while at least, until another green-eyed creature appeared. This one was a monster that made me mad in many ways. How could Calli do this without me? She said she wanted to have children with me. Was she lying? But I had left her. I pictured her laying with another woman, snuggled together and with both of their hands holding Grace. This was my dream, and I had let it slip away for stupid, superficial reasons.

I thought about leaping into what I had written in the letter, but Grace started saying something to her mum.

"I'm sorry Nora, I have to go. Grace needs to go to the bathroom. Let's chat again soon. Until then, please take care and let me know if you need anything at all."

"OK, Calli, I will, thanks."

I hung up, knowing that I would never speak to Calli again. I only hoped I had masked any malice that was creeping up inside. It was like an acid, burning a hole in my stomach and making the coffee churn. All I could do was lay down on the grass and breathe. The burning took a long time to subside, but finally, there was space to consider self-compassion. Yes, this was shitty. Seriously shitty. More than that, this fucking sucked. Yes, I was so happy for Calli in one way, but why did her happiness have to hurt me so much? Common humanity? Fuck humanity!

OK, alright, you're right, mum, so many other people have hearts breaking right now. I get it, I am not alone. Was this how Calli felt when I left her and when I moved on with Rob and Tom? Payback is a bitch, isn't it, Nora? Kindness? Do I deserve any, really? OK, mum, seriously! What is the kindest thing I can do for myself right now? The tears flowed as I realised what the answer was. I needed to face reality. I had screwed things up. And I was going to keep screwing things up until I did just what Calli said I had to do – take care of myself.

As the tears cleared, the blades of grass beside me took shape and seemed to breathe with me. I watched the ants on their adventures and admired their tenacity. But I didn't want any marching down my shirt, so I sat up and watched the light dance through the trees and lean into the leaves. For a moment, I imagined the life the leaves were creating, flowing through the branches, down into the trunk, and transferring into my hand. Far too much hippie juice for Nora today!

The alarm went off on my phone, and it was time to return. The closer I got, the more scared I became of being found out. I slunk back in successfully without being seen by anyone I knew and signed back in. Laying out my leaf specimens made my room look like a science lab, which gave me great satisfaction. It was much more interesting than my usual pile of papers and laptop. I felt refreshed after being in the park like I had a different perspective and more physical energy. Starting to sketch out the painting, I could see how it would all come together. Leaves and wings, surrounded by love. However, what form the latter would take was still a mystery.

I had no time for dinner; I was too transfixed in the details of my layers and getting the light and shades just right.

Only when interruption came, in the form of Ranjani doing the final night rounds, did I realise how heavy and tired I was. I would have a lot to do the following day to finish it by the deadline of Monday, but this goal made me feel good, and what I had achieved already felt awesome.

"Nora, I was looking for you. I have something for you."

She walked over to where I was working and put down a little cupcake with a candle.

"I'm sorry. I wanted to get it to you earlier, but this evening has been far too busy. I hope you have had a lovely day, Nora. Happy birthday."

"Oh Ranjani, thank you."

There was no specific reason why the tears came then. Was it from fatigue? Or the fact I did not feel deserving of such kindness.

Ranjani gave me a hug and wiped away the tears.

"You are doing fantastic, Nora. Now, do you need some medicine for tonight?"

"No thanks, Ranjani. It has been a big day. I am just going to have my birthday cake, shower and go to bed."

She gave me a pat on the back as she said "Perfect. Goodnight, Nora."

The cake was so lovely, chocolate mud, my favourite. I would never have usually eaten something sweet straight before bed. Still, I knew this celebration would not corrupt my sleep. I was far too weary.

After a shower to wash off all the paint, I could only think about my one grateful with my eyes closed. I was grateful for green, even the manic monster kind. All of it helped me understand what was truly important.

If I dreamt of the dragon that night, I did not remember it. I was far too exhausted and far too excited for what the next day would bring.

Chapter 10

Another quiet morning, and this place was definitely feeling more retreat than treatment. I was up early and got stuck into my painting, only stopping to grab some breakfast which I ate between applying more strokes. I could not spare the time for a sit-down meal if this painting was to be done by the next day. As I hunched, squinted, and steadied my hand, I congratulated myself on the detail I had chosen to include. This would certainly keep me busy. Every leaf was a little different, every wing done in its own unique way. Yet they seemed to be coming together, despite their separate circles, to give the feeling of flow.

Hours later, I had to take a break to give my back a rest. I would have to advise Bev that some easels may be beneficial to save WH&S claims for back injury. I am sure she would agree. Coffee was calling, and as it cooled, I contemplated how I would spend this Sunday afternoon. It looked like a stunning spring day and would be beautiful in the park. But there was something about talking with Calli yesterday that created a conclusion. Yes, I was so angry and sad afterwards, but facing reality was like ripping a band aid off. Now, I felt more settled about the whole situation. It kind of felt like a 12-step process of making amends. I remembered when I got a random phone call from a guy I had only seen for a few weeks. We parted quite dramatically, but months later, he rang to say he was sorry for how he had treated me. He was now in AA, and I was on the list of people he had harmed. He asked for my forgiveness, and I gave it willingly. It was clear to me that the guy was troubled, and it was great that he was getting help.

I had not spoken the word sorry to Calli, but it was in the letter, and now I understood what a relief it was to voice your remorse and to ask for pardon. I had joked the other day about using my diagnosis as an excuse to go banging on Ben's door. But now it was becoming clear that it was a credible act, just without the banging bit. Amends were to be made with this man, and while I could spill it all out in a letter, it seemed like taking the easy way out. I chickened out with Calli, but I needed to build my courage and confidence, and talking with Ben was how I would do it. Besides, he needed to see that I was well. I didn't need him carrying around any guilt or anxiety about how I was going. There was my mission. To reassure Ben, and to seek forgiveness for my deplorable deed.

I painted again with renewed vigour; I had a vision and would make it happen on the canvas and in my life. After only a short break for lunch, I signed out and then snuck to the bus station, keeping out of sight as much as possible near the hospital. I laughed at the contrast between my cowardice around this place versus the bravery I was determined to show to Ben. There was no being on a borderline here; it felt far more like leaping between two extreme boundaries.

I jumped on the first bus heading towards the interchange, looking out the window at all the life around the city. There was movement and energy around the shops, the art galleries, and the water. It really was a wonderful city.

As I got off the first bus at the interchange, I saw my second connecting service was already slipping away. Bugger. Now, I would have to wait another 15 minutes. It would cramp my time with Ben, but I had no choice. I sat and watched the buses go past, all advertising some new fashion item, some new flavour, another exciting exhibition or event. There really was a world out there that I was not aware of. I had been so single-minded, set on success, pushing myself to make partner, I stopped seeing anything I decided was a distraction. Oh my gosh. I had done what my father had done to me. I had become my own prison guard.

On the second bus, I began to get nervous, playing out all the possible scenarios in my head. He could slam the door. I decided then I would not bang on it. I would respect his wishes and walk away. This would show him I was well. I preferred the second scenario, though, the one where he would be so glad to see me, hug me, hold me, and tell me he was so happy that I was there. He would say he was sorry for leaving me. I would sob and say I was sorry for doing that to him. Then, over tea, we would talk about all the work I was doing on myself. Then he would offer to drive me back, giving me a big kiss on the cheek as I got out of his car and maybe even ask to see me again the next weekend. Yes, this was the scenario I wanted and the one I was preparing for on the walk to Ben's house.

His car was not in the resident's car park. I looked and looked and looked again. I turned and checked up and down the street. There was no sight of it. The slump I felt was both physical and mental. But then, his car could be in for a service, so I buzzed. No answer. I buzzed again. No answer. I had no idea what I should do. All of my certainty collapsed into confusion. I had come all this way and would wait as long as possible. There was nowhere to sit apart from in the gutter of the guest car park. When a car pulled into it, I had to move. The woman looked at me like I was a weirdo.

"Can I help you?"

"Thanks, no. I am just waiting for a friend. They are running a bit late."

"Oh, OK. Have a good day."

"You too."

I thought about calling Ben, but I knew he would not answer. I found another gutter and continued imagining Ben's car coming up the street. But none were his, and the bus back would be here soon. I had to go.

Goddamit. Now I was furious.

I wanted to stay longer; I was not afraid of the police so much, but of losing the privilege. I could not stand being locked up for longer without the chance to sit outside, lie on the ground and be surrounded by green. I marched back to the bus stop, feeling seriously mad. As I saw the bus approaching in the distance, I also saw Ben drive past. I waved like a wild woman, not helping my cause much, yet it was an honest display of excitement. I could run back now and catch him. But it would mean waiting longer for another bus and being late back to the hospital. The decision was doing my head in. Then something snapped, and I did the only thing I could. I ran. I ran to Ben. I made it back to his unit a few minutes later, out of breath but ecstatic to have the chance to apologise in person.

But his car was not there.

Where was he? Had he driven past on his way to somewhere else?

Or had he seen me?

I scanned the street again, but there was no sign of his car.

Had he seen me?

I screamed out the word "bastard" and frantically buzzed his unit. No answer. So, I just kept buzzing. Someone was going to pay for this.

The next thing I knew, Ranjani was calling me for dinner. I was smothered in paint and had almost completed one layer of the painting.

"Hey Nora, dinner time. Did you have a nice time out today?"

I put down my brush and backed away.

"Nora, what is it? You look terrified."

I found myself whispering like I was in the middle of a horror movie and the killer was close, but I had to call for help.

"Ranjani. I don't remember coming back. Oh my god, I don't remember this afternoon. Ranjani, please help. I think I am going crazy."

Ranjani quizzed me on what had happened. I told her I remembered buzzing at the door but then nothing more. She held my shaking hands.

"Come on. Let's go and figure this out."

She led me to find the nurse who signed me in. The nurse relayed the details. A taxi driver had brought me up ten minutes after the cut-off time. He had seen the hospital bracelet and wanted to make sure I made it back OK. Yes, I looked a bit wiped out, but nothing too weird, so she signed me back in, and I just went to my room.

A taxi. I got back by taxi. Did I call it? Or did someone put me in one?

Ranjani sat me in the examination chair and knelt in front of me.

"Nora, I can see that you are really scared. Has this kind of thing happened before?"

"Yes."

"Have you talked to the doctor about it?"

"Yes."

"Well, all you need to know is that you are safe now. I am just going to do a quick check over and make sure you are OK. Then I will make a note for the doctor so you can talk about it with him tomorrow. He might order some tests, even an MRI just to check for anything like epilepsy that might have not been picked up before. It's alright Nora. We've got you."

I sat sobbing while Ranjani scanned my skin for any wounds, my eyes for reactions, and my heart and blood pressure for signs of acute stress. Nothing was significant. As she took the cuff off my arm, the young girl who stole my spot came to get her nighttime meds. Someone else had seen me in this sorry state, which sealed my fate – I was now sinking into shame.

So, I did not eat dinner. Ranjani understood I was nauseous. Still, despite her very polite proposal, I refused the pills. What was the use, really? I deserved to feel bad. I was a lost cause, and it was just better that no one bothered with me.

I spent the next hour sitting on my bed, depressed, staring out at the dark night. I could not even look at the painting. What a farce. I didn't fix anything. Bev would have to accept it as unfinished. Anyway, fuck her and these bloody assignments. They were futile. And fuck being grateful.

I gave in, went and got sedatives and went to sleep.

The nightmare was there again, but tonight, it was almost all dark. Mum and Calli were not there. I was alone, and with the lack of movement, I figured I was dead. And I was glad about that. The dragon just turned its back to me and walked away, opening the cave to the dark night and the wolves.

Chapter 11

I had only just made tea, and parked again on my bed to stare out the window when Dr Dempsey arrived. He pulled up a chair beside me, clicking his pen and opening my file.

"Hi Nora. It sounds like you had a bit of a scary time yesterday."

"Yes, you could say that."

"I see that you went to see Ben, and then you lost time between buzzing on his door and being back here."

"Yep."

This was starting to feel like an interrogation. Could it be that I had done something else? Something they had only just found out about, and something that was missing from my memory?

"I am going to get you to do a few blood tests, and I will organise an MRI. I was going to do it this week anyway as a precaution. We just need to check there is nothing else going on in your brain that we need to know about."

"Ok."

"Did you sleep OK last night?"

I wished he would shut up about sleeping. It was really starting to piss me off. I wondered what he would say if I told him the truth; that I wanted to go to sleep and never wake up.

"Yep. I took sedatives."

"And I can see that your mood is a bit flat. Is that a fair description of how you are feeling?"

"Yep."

"So, what's going on for you today, Nora. What are you thinking after yesterday?"

"That this is just useless. None of this is working. I am obviously unwell, and instead of getting fixed I am here painting bloody wings."

"Nora, like I said, the treatment for BPD takes time and patience. You have not even really begun it formally yet, so there are years ahead of you."

"Then just put me on the list for the loony bin, because I am not sure I could be bothered."

"Don't you want to get better?"

"I just don't see the point. My work is going to find out some time, and there goes any chance of making partner. I will keep having these episodes and put myself and others at risk. And honestly doctor, I am exhausted. Yesterday I saw how much I go back and forward between extremes. It is like I am spending my days being bashed around like a tennis ball and it is just so tiring. With work I can concentrate, but with everything else I feel like I am screwed. I just think it would be easier if I was sedated and shoved away in a cave somewhere to die alone."

Did I just sentence myself to my own nightmare?

"I know you might feel like this now, Nora. Yesterday would have come as a shock. How did you deal with this situation when they happened previously?"

"Well, it was much easier. I didn't have anyone to report to. I just picked up and kept moving."

"I see."

I didn't.

He gave a great big sigh and crossed his legs, revealing his socks. They did not match. Did I just catch the doctor on a bad day?

"What's going on with your socks?"

There was a bit of me that felt bad about bringing it up, but at least it would deflect the attention from me for a while.

"Oh yes," he said with a smile. These are crazy doc socks. They sell them to raise money for mental health charities.

"I see."

I didn't mean to repeat his own words so sarcastically, but I couldn't stop myself.

"Do they make crazy patient socks too, or is that not politically correct?"

He chuckled. He actually chuckled.

"You know, Nora, you are an incredibly intelligent, disciplined, funny and, I can see, creative woman. You don't have to let this define you."

"But it has created me."

"Only up until now. Now you have choices."

"I really just don't think I can do this." I started crying and he reached over to the desk and placed the tissues beside me.

"Well, I'm sorry, but permanent sedation is not an option. Realistically, what other choice do you have?"

"I could run away."

I started to think about mum's house. It would be free soon. I could run away there.

"I think you have actually been doing this most of your life, and how has that been working for you so far?"

He let that thought sink in. I wanted to argue with him, to not let him win, but deep down I knew he was right.

"You have another option, Nora, to take control of this, and not let it control you. You can take the reins. Do the treatment and dedicate yourself to building a really great life."

It was as if he was suggesting that I had not had such a great life to date. Again, if I was being completely honest with myself, I would have declared his observation was accurate.

"Today you will have a few interruptions with the blood tests and MRI, but I want you to continue, Nora. Go to the classes, work with Bev. I know you might not feel like it, but it is important. Do I have your word?"

What? He was making me promise. Were we back in primary school?

I agreed, but only to get him off my back. I would play it out when the time came.

"And then tomorrow, we will talk about next steps and make plans to get you out of here. OK?"

I nodded but wondered why I felt so sad. Suddenly I did not want to leave. What once was stifling now seemed safe.

I stared out the window until breakfast, seeing the world outside in a very different way. I had once looked upon it as a challenge, something to be conquered, to be tamed and twisted to my will. Now it appeared that instead of a captain, I was more like the cyclone that was causing the chaos. I was the storm that made sailors get sick over the side. The captain's job was to merely clean up the mess afterwards.

My own stomach was still squeamish, so breakfast didn't sound like such a great idea. When I smelt the toast though, it went from nauseated to needy. As much as I had thought about it, starving was also not an option, well at least not here.

Mark had made poached eggs and declared directly in a cheerful voice that it was an excellent way to start the day. I thought for a moment that starting today dead may have been better, but he did not need to hear that. He served me up a plate, putting a smile on the eggs with BBQ sauce.

"It looks like you could use this today, Nora."

Now he was just going to make me cry. I said a quick thanks and sprinted to my seat before anyone could see I was shaking.

I sat in my seat and sketched, not any particular project, just so people would leave me alone. Back in my room the unfinished painting was annoying me. It was teasing me with the thought that I couldn't complete it. I could have simply turned it around, or torn it up, but neither of these options would satisfy the need for this thing just to be done. So, I invested in each vein, and gave life to each leaf.

Moving around the canvas felt like a kind of rescue, and I began to embellish the simple steps. My arms followed their own tune; forward and focused on the canvas, and free, full and flowing as they floated away. This movement seemed to mediate the melancholy, although it also came with an air of embarrassment when the pathology nurse walked in to see me prancing around. She was right, she should have knocked. At least I was not naked, although that would be normal for a nutter. I noted this option down for further contemplation.

As I watched the vial fill up with my blood, I wished that they could simply just pull the BPD out as well. I would go through the trauma of a full transfusion if this would work. Surely there has to be a quicker way than years of psychotherapy. I made another note to ask the doctor about electric shock therapy.

When it came time for the gentle exercise class I stayed in my room. I knew it would make me feel good, so why was I resisting it? Of course, I knew why. Why would someone poke themselves in the eye on purpose? They simply wanted to hurt themselves. And why did they want to hurt themselves? Because they didn't believe they were worthy of anything good. This morning, I did not believe I was worthy of even gentle exercise. But the doctor was prepared for my recalcitrance. He must have told the nurse that I needed a minder today, and she came to tell me to go. I did so under protest though, and took the teacher up on the option of spending the lesson in child pose. I thought it would be a reasonable act of rebellion, but in fact it was more rewarding than I could have imagined.

There was something about feeling the breath expand in my back that was so reassuring. Cuddled up to my knees felt like being home, and my head on the ground made me think, even just for a little while, that something or someone had got me. Here I was in a sanctuary within a safe place. It was also true to its word; restorative. I rose feeling somewhat renewed, and little more alert.

I missed the next class, being taken downstairs for an MRI. I was hoping the procedure would take a long time, but damn their efficiency! I made it back just before the next class and one that was to be extremely confronting. The teacher outlined a whole range of different diagnosis and went through the behaviours, causes and treatments. The aim was to reduce the misconceptions around each one, and help us become better informed about our own, and others unique form of insanity. Well, she didn't say it like that, but that was how I interpreted it. There was no electric shock on the list for BPD, but I decided I would ask anyway. Although a home-made version was always possible.

Then all my nightmares came at once. We were divided into small groups to go through the challenges and insights we had gained around our own mental conditions. Before I could fake a gastro attack, I was put together with the same young girl I had seen several times now, and another guy, who also seemed grouchy about the task we had been given. I was the oldest in the gang, and so I felt it fell on me to go first. As I introduced myself, I could feel the cringe, and was still considering faking a vomit. Yes, it would be embarrassing, but not as much as being exposed to these people.

Then came Jess. She seemed so nervous. I completely understood. It is hard enough to deal with yourself, let alone share your weaknesses with others. Tom rounded out the group, although he sat back, keeping his distance and looking mentally detached. I gave him credit for doing what I couldn't. These two were both so young and in their own ways so fragile.

The first question to be addressed was what we were struggling with. There was no explicit instruction to reveal our diagnosis, but it was impossible not to. How quickly I reverted to my consultant's tone, telling them factually and formally that I had been diagnosed with BPD. I saw Jess sit up straighter. Then came the more difficult bit. What was I struggling with? Acknowledging that I was having a difficult time just felt like torture. I had spent so much of my life proving to everyone that I was purposeful, professional, capable and adaptable, and now I was being forced to admit that, here and now, I was floundering. Maybe being vague would be a good strategy. Then I would not have to reveal too much.

"What am I struggling with? Gosh, where do I start. There is a lot to deal with. I didn't think anything was really wrong. But since being here I realised there is.

In terms of specific things, these would be the blackouts. Sometimes I lose a bit of time. I also find it a bit hard to manage my anger. Oh, and yesterday I just realised how much I spend my days flip-flopping between two sides of a coin, and that is making me feel really crazy. That's about it for me."

Should I have used the word crazy? These two didn't seem to care.

Jess seemed eager to go next. Her hands moved from under her thighs and clasped together upon them.

"I have BPD too and I really get where you are coming from. I don't get blackouts, but I freak out. Sometimes I see familiar things like it is the first time I have seen them, like my parents, or my pets. It's like I have just landed in there for the first time. It makes me feel so strange and scared. I am also struggling with self-harm. It's how I ended up in here."

How horrendous was it that I started looking for her scars, although I knew that they would be well-hidden. They were there because of torment, not for attention.

Tom stayed stuck in his seat through all of this and did not shift when it came his turn to speak. When he did, it was really slow and unsure. He told his tale, one of depression where most days he could not get out of bed. He had lost his job, and his girlfriend and now was back living with his parents.

"I was sent here from the psych ward after trying to top myself."

"Oh Tom, me too."

I didn't want that to be spoken, still it slipped out.

"Really?"

I was able to maintain silence then, pressing my lips together and sharing only a nod.

The teacher interrupted just at the right moment, when otherwise we would have sat in silence feeling stupid.

"I hope that this short chat has helped you know that you are not alone. I know you don't like being social, but at the other end of the spectrum, isolation is not healthy. There are other people that are going through the same things, and sharing your experiences can help you and them. I would really encourage you to take some time to talk further, maybe you could sit together at lunch. Because before you leave you will spend some time with your counsellors preparing the way forward to build a support network. This is your chance to start – to practice.

We ask though, that you don't share any private details. I know you are all wonderful people, but there have been cases in the past that during an episode someone was put at harm. So please, no private details.

Any questions?"

Wow, we were being treated like potential stalkers. It was like they had read my file, or my mind.

Jess spoke up.

"But why can't we share details. We might form really good friendships here."

"I do understand. The reality is that you are all struggling with something, and so we need to be really careful about where you find your support. Sometimes what you see as helpful can end up being more harmful, it can result in misinformation, bad advice and even more dependencies. Sharing with people who have similar problems is so essential, but it needs to be done in a safe environment. We will help you put a plan in place where you can do this. Does that make sense?"

It sure made sense to me. It was becoming apparent that this was a fitting explanation of my romantic life to date.

As we headed to lunch, Jess said she would love to talk more, if that was OK with me. Honestly, I would have rather stabbed myself in the foot, but I would get the niceties over and done with. I braced myself for the banal, however, Jess was actually lovely. She did most of the talking which was fine by me. There was a lot she needed to get off her chest and was so excited to have someone else that understood. In some ways she reminded me of a younger version of myself. It made me wonder; Where could I be now if I had this information when I was her age? I would have finished my treatment, been pronounced a normal woman, probably made partner and living with my husband and children behind a white picket fence.

Instead, here I was, headed to forty and only beginning to understand the damage done, and the drama that lay ahead. I remember the doctor looking a little deflated when he gave the diagnosis, mentioning that he wished this had been picked up earlier. But of course, that would have required me to seek out help. He didn't say it, but I knew he was inferring that this late disruptive diagnosis was my fault. I hated it when he would use facts against me.

"Nora, I saw you the other day in the nurses station. Are you OK now?"

"Yeh, thanks. I just went through another blackout, and it was a bit scary."

"I'm so sorry."

Her empathy was real.

"I just want to be normal; you know. I have always wanted to work with kids, but I don't know now whether I am going to be able to."

"Jess, you would be great at it. I am sure if you just keep going you will get there. I have been told it takes a while. But I am sure you could do it. Kids could use someone as caring as you in their life. I know it."

"Thanks, Nora. What do you do for a job?"

"I'm a business consultant, and I was planning to just go back. But now I am not so sure. It is all a bit messed up. The doctor thinks it would be good to take a bit of time out."

She thought that sounded like a great idea, and so I was encouraged to run another idea by her.

"My mum's place in the country will be coming free soon, so I am actually thinking of moving back there for a while. I want to get away from it all and work on myself, maybe do some art and figure this stuff out."

"Nora, that sounds awesome. What about the isolation though? The teacher said that can be dangerous. What would you do for a support network?"

"Good point, Jess. Thanks! I haven't thought that one through yet."

I didn't want to tell her that the whole idea was to be alone, for right now it was the second-safest place I could be. And when they kicked me out of here in a few days, alone was my only option.

Bev came and tapped me on the shoulder, apologising for the interruption, and asking if it was OK to catch up. I was pleased to have an escape from Jess. She was a breath of fresh air, but there was only so much exposure I could take in one day and only so much empathy I could muster.

Back in the room Bev was beaming.

"It is so great to see you socialising a bit, Nora. I know you hate it, but it shows a huge step forward."

"Thanks, she is a lovely girl. It is just so sad."

"In which way?"

"Well, that someone so caring, so beautiful thinks the only way she can cope with things is by hurting herself. How messed up is that? She really doesn't deserve this. I only hope she gets all the help she needs so she can be happy."

"Did you just hear yourself?"

Bev gave me the look – the one that suggested I had said something meaningful and should be taking my own advice. It was so funny how one of her expressions could sum up an entire speech.

I had heard myself and knew from halfway through that this was not just about Jess. It was also a self-directed sermon.

"It sounds like you had a really rough afternoon yesterday. How are you feeling?"

"Still really worn out to be honest, and worried."

"Do you want to tell me what happened?"

"I just went to Ben's to say sorry. He wasn't there, but I thought he saw me when he drove by. I guess I just lost it. Then I didn't remember getting back here."

"I understand, Nora. And your intention was very noble. I have a question for you that you might want to think about for a while. Have you forgiven yourself yet?"

"I am not sure I can."

"Then don't go asking anyone to do something you are not willing to do for yourself first. Otherwise, it is a bit hypocritical, isn't it?"

Bev could have left out the "bit" bit. It was without a doubt massively hypocritical and all I could do was hang my head.

"I'm just going to let that one sit with you a while, and I would like to work through it a bit later in the week. Now though, I want to see your awesome painting."

Bev opened her arms wide like she was about to cuddle the thing. She asked me to tell her about it and I explained the inspiration of the leaves and wings from Frida.

"That is fantastic! Tell me though, does this painting feel true to you?"

"It did, Bev. When I started it Saturday it really did. Now I am not so sure. It seems like this is just a world I wish for. All I can think about is that it is not real, and will never be."

"It can be, Nora. I have every confidence in that. It is going to take effort though."

"At this stage I am really not sure I have the energy."

Bev came and wrapped her arm around my shoulders.

"This painting is telling me that you do. You might not right now – you have been knocked for six. But if you are kind to yourself, and do the right things, then it will come again. I heard a saying once that the thing you want to do the least is what you need the most. I think as much as you don't want to go there, painting may be exactly the thing that pulls you through and gets your energy back."

I did hear what Bev was saying. I just wasn't buying it. Painting felt more of a burden then a blessing.

"What are your dreams telling you?"

"That I am dead in a dark cave, abandoned to be eaten by wolves."

"Wow. That sounds scary. But it is also so insightful."

"Sorry? How so?"

"We are taught to fear death, especially in our dreams, like it foretells disaster. It is the same with tarot cards. People freak out when they get the death card. They take it literally. Think about it though; death, decimation, decay, it is all needed if something new is to begin. Something has to die; something has to be let go of to make space for the new.

The alchemists always knew this. They spent months allowing their mixtures to rot because this stripped away what they didn't need. When the decomposing was finished, they were left with the essence.

That's why I think this dream is fantastic. I think it shows that you are in the process of letting go of the old you; and all of the expectations that were keeping you stuck in self-destructive patterns. Let it go, Nora and grow something new.

Your dreams are telling you it is time to let the old stuff die. And your painting is telling you what your new will look like – it is light, life and love. That is what you have the chance to create now. It is so hard to let go, but you have to let it die to achieve this new dream."

I know Bev was being brutally serious. Still, I could not help picturing her as the little mayor of Thneed Ville, dancing around singing "let it die." I had watched the Lorax with Calli on rainy Sunday afternoon, and had "let it grow" going around in my head for months afterwards. I let the little voice of death win with Calli though. Maybe Bev was right, maybe it was time to plant some different seeds.

"Think of all those preconceived notions, the beliefs and identities that do not serve you as clouds. They will cover your sun and cause your suffering. You need to let them float away to let the light on your leaves and shiny wings. Does that make sense?"

"I think so."

"Sorry, Nora. I am rabbiting on, and you are tired. I think the message today is to just keep working on your painting. It is terrific. Just wondering though, how do you feel when you are doing it?"

"Sometimes there is such a flow, it feels so natural, like something I should be doing. Other times it is battle. Like this morning. My brain was telling me that this is stupid, that it is not going to make any difference."

"And all of that is completely normal. Do me a favour though Nora. Next time the latter one comes up, tell it to shut up. It is wrong, and science proves it. Art therapy does take time, but is proven to be incredibly effective at helping people deal with their thoughts and feelings, and find new ways to move forward. When he or she starts at you again, battle back with evidence and tell them to bugger off. I would not be here, Nora, if I did not know that this would work for you. I would not waste my time, and I would certainly not waste yours. OK?"

"Yep, thanks."

"I was wondering – do you want to take your paintings home? If not, I would love to put them up in the corridors here. They are such an inspiration, and so well executed. You don't need to let me know now, just have a think about it. All I would need is a little artist statement. But let's chat about that more over the next few days. We still have this week.

So, I will let you go and get some rest. In summary, just keep going. You have got this. It may not feel like it from where you are standing, but from my perspective you are making incredible progress.

If you do have time, and want to do something a bit different, grab a black pen and start making a list of all the things you think you might need to let go of to move forward. These could be beliefs, thoughts, behaviours, ideas or identities. Anything you think is standing in the way of this painting becoming a reality. Is that OK?"

I wasn't sure, but agreed. I would not argue with one so wise.

"Oh, and finally. What about your grateful for yesterday? Did you have one?"

I nodded.

"And..."

"Excuse my language here Bev, but fucking nothing."

We both laughed; her a lot, me a little.

"Fair call, Nora. It was a huge day. Could I suggest one though? You should really be grateful for your sense of humour. Hang onto it. Don't you dare let it be something that dies. It will hold you in really good stead. Let's see if you can come up with your own grateful tonight though. OK?"

"Sure." We were still both smiling when she left the room. After she was gone, I just might have sensed a little bit of magic she left behind.

Jess joined me again at dinner. As much as I wanted to draw or start on my list of things that had to die, she looked a bit desperate for company. We didn't say much though, between eating and both being pretty tired it was a quiet time. But not awkward, more reassuring than disturbing. It felt natural to give her a hug as we left the dining room and wished each other good night. The words meant something, even if we both knew that saying them would not be enough to make it happen.

After dinner and soaking in a hot shower with my friend May Chang I dedicated some time to think about the things I needed to leave behind. Was the dragon one of them? I still had no idea what it represented so I couldn't say for sure. With this exercise I really struggled. I did not want to write down anything. I wanted to live in the delusion that everything was just as it should be. Besides, I had fought so hard to get where I was in life, why should I let anything go?

The only inspiration I found was in thinking about those things I had left behind to come here, those that had disappeared and in doing so had helped me feel like this was a safe place. Firstly, I had forgone independence. Here I had to drop the idea that I could do it all myself, and admit that I needed help. That one was really hard. It was such a source of pride for me, especially showing mum that I was making it on my own.

The past week I had also seen that I was much more than just a capable professional. I could also be a painter if I really wanted to be. I was also a patient, someone paying others for their advice. The singular, focused image I had of myself would also need to shift if I was going to move towards this more expansive future.

Here, I had also become had a student, forced to give up the thought that I already knew everything and offered a new way of seeing. There is so much more I needed to learn.

Then there was this hope I had for a fairy-tale relationship. These don't happen in reality, let alone for someone who's emotions were erratic and constantly living in fear. I could not see how I could form any positive relationship with the way I was. And with this went my hope for kids and such other symbols of success.

When I was done there were, five black words on the page. Independence. Singular identity. Arrogance. Fantasy.

I was having a really hard time understanding how Bev thought that this would be a helpful exercise. Thinking that I had to let go of these things really hurt. Not as much as mum's death still did, but pretty darn close.

After this, coming up with something I was grateful for seemed one step too far. Still, I trawled through the day to find the highlights. As much as I hated to admit it, talking to Jess was good. I felt like somehow I had a chance to help. That was it, that was what I was grateful for today; the chance to help someone else.

I didn't realise how tired I was until my head met the pillow. I seemed to plunge into sleep like it was an oasis after days in the desert. My dream too, was refreshingly different. I was sitting beside the dragon this time, on a cliff, overlooking the sunset. The ocean played beneath us, an endless dance of ups and downs. As the sun slipped slowly, it cast colour onto the waves and created rainbows in the spray. The dragon had huge sparkly wings. Mine were much smaller, but just as shiny. On the other side of me sat a knife. There was only one thought then, that the dragon must die. Without hesitation I picked up the knife and stabbed and stabbed and stabbed and stabbed. The knife cut the dragon deep, but with every withdrawal the wound would instantly heal. This did not stop me though. I kept stabbing, angrily, savagely, crazily, until it was clear my actions had crossed the line from courage to stupidity.

The dragon looked at me and I dropped the knife. I was certain that it would now crush me or cast me off the cliff. Instead, it laughed. The dragon let out the biggest belly laugh I had ever heard. It was a roar, but also a rejoicing. I started laughing too. What seemed so serious was now deemed simply silly. And despite my every attempt to kill it, the dragon reached out calmly and cuddled me into its smooth warm body. Despite trying to assassinate it, and put it through a painful death, this dragon did not see me as a bad person, and was so willing to forgive my hostility. It was concerned for my care, not my condemnation.

As the day became dark, we both lay down and the dragon tucked me under its arm. I could not sleep though, for fear that the dragon may still change its mind and crush me. While I was gently rocked by the inhales and exhales of my guardian, and listened to its giant purrs, I waited for its hold to loosen and my chance to make a getaway.

Chapter 12

After this dream I lay awake, disturbed at the intensity of anger with which I had attacked the dragon. I could still hear the furious shrieks that came with each stab and feel the veracity with which I wanted this thing dead. Even my arms ached from the effort, and when I rose, it felt like I had waged this war in reality. It took two cups of tea before I could think, and for things to become clear. I began to understand what I needed to let go of and those things I had to hang on to. They were still hazy concepts though, not clear enough to capture in pen on a page. Instead, I decided to put the finishing touches on my painting and was almost done when the doctor came. I was frustrated by the interruption, which faded from his first statement.

"Bev said your work was fantastic, and I can see why. That is wonderful, Nora."

He had never noticed my art before, and this made his compliment even more meaningful. I felt sorry for how mean I had been to him and how much I had mistrusted his motives.

We worked through the usual questions, and yes, everything was the same. Then I noticed the doctor's socks, and I could not concede this chance to return his prior recognition.

"Hey, cool socks. Is that a real dog?"

"Yes. That is Dido. She died last year, so this is my little tribute to her."

I wanted to rib this man for naming his dog after a singer, but I thought such a comment would be cruel.

"You're probably wondering about the name. Well, that was my wife's choice, but it did suit her."

I was so glad that the doctor explained and erased any opportunity for me to reconsider the ribbing, which would have been done for no other reason but to push him down and exert some of my own power. There was another thing to let go of, and I made a mental note to record this revelation later.

"She really was a lovely dog, sometimes the only thing in the house happy to see me."

He gave a little chuckle, but I could tell this was no joke.

"So, these socks remind me of her good qualities and, in a way, help me be a better person."

"Wow, all of that in a pair of socks. I should get myself a pair with..."

Then I realised what I was about to say. With mum on them. And my heart sank. How superficial did that sound? But how deep did it hurt? I realised then that I did not have any photos of mum on display. Not in my wallet, in my apartment and definitely not on my socks. Socks. Like the ones that Maria had given me, that I still treasured. Perhaps I was still in denial that mum had died. Seeing her picture would make it real, and I was not ready to face the fact that I could not go home to her.

"Sorry, Nora?"

"Oh, nothing."

"Ok. So good news. There are no significant brain or blood issues. Your thyroid levels are a bit low, so you should check that up with your GP next week. There are also similar markers in the brain seen in many other BPD patients. Nothing serious though, just some small decreases in grey matter in certain areas."

"What? Has the BPD made me dumber."

"No, not at all. It is uncertain still which way the cause-and-effect relationship works when it comes to brain and behaviours. But yes, your brain works differently. Some of the emotional processing centres are stunted, and this makes sense if you have not had a chance to use them. Our brains have an incredible way of compensating though, and I suspect your intellectual capacities have become even stronger in response."

"How did this happen. I don't understand."

"It is always a mix of nature and nurture. It is likely that you were born with brain far more sensitive to the world than others. That in itself is a gift. But put it in a context that doesn't appreciate it, that tries to crush it, and the person is forced into internal conflict. In your case you were invalidated in so many ways and for one who is sensitive this creates great trauma. If you don't get support to process and help regulate your emotions then they become an enemy, and stop being used. Like the saying goes, if you don't use it, you lose it, and so the brain capacity in these areas decreases."

"But mum was there for me."

"Yes, she was a blessing. But as a sensitive child, you would have needed more support than just one person could give. When we lived in tribes you would have had a whole community around to care for you. But these days we are so isolated, and so the sensitive ones can get lost.

Sometimes, there is a genetic element, so maybe one of your parents struggled with this. They might have been born with heightened sensitivities, but they were made to feel like it was a fault. The way they learned to cope may have been passed onto you."

I thought about mum and dad. Both were tormented in their own way. However, looking back, it was so hard to tell what was brought on by everyday life battles and which from more sinister mental problems.

"Nora, it is really great you want to understand this more. Knowledge is power. That is why moving on with treatment is so important. Did I talk to you about Dialectical Behavioural Therapy, DBT? I think I did. Anyway, it has been shown to be really effective. It was developed by a doctor who battled with BPD herself. Here is a list of all the DBT practitioners in the area. My assistant checked yesterday, and they all have spaces in their programs at the moment, although some are getting close to full. When you have your phone later today, I need you to book into one that suits."

I scanned through the short list, already picking the names that sounded good.

"Whoa. $600 for a few weeks of group sessions?"

"Yes, I told you it would not be cheap."

"Why? I hope you get a gold pen with that. What do the people do that can't afford this?"

"There are some public clinics but certainly not enough. Most people don't even get to understand they have a problem in the first place, or only do, like you, when you come to a crisis point. For some though, the crisis makes them a criminal and they end up in jail."

I thought about how close I may have come to this myself in Seattle, when I stalked Daniel, or even just a few days ago when I had gone to Ben's.

"It is so sad. It's like they get smashed around by the world and then just told to suck it up."

"You're absolutely right. It's not surprising then, that without support many simply self-destruct."

The doctor said "simply" like self-destruction was a single act. I knew, however, how lengthy and complex this endeavour actually was.

"I guess this is your way of reminding me that I am one of the lucky ones."

"You are, Nora. Hopefully you can see now that being here, and the treatment yet to come, is not something nasty being done to you."

"I think I am starting to understand that."

"Now, your work. What should we do here? As your doctor I am suggesting that you take six months on income protection to work through the treatment and get back to a solid place. This would be for a start, and of course we would need to assess as we go along. I am happy to fill out the forms for income protection, and from my experience with this, it should not be a problem. Your work will need to sign off, but I think the insurance people organise that."

"So, work will know what's wrong with me."

"Yes of course. It is important as well for when you return, in case we need to put some supports in place to help you stay well in the workplace."

"Oh no. That's not going to happen. They will think I am impaired. That's horrible."

I shuddered at the thought of my colleagues tiptoeing around me like I was a loony.

"I am really not sure I should do this. Couldn't I just take the sick leave I have. That would be enough, surely? I can still do the treatment and work."

"I know you can, but I don't think it is enough. I really think you need time to process all of this and put some positive supports in place. How about you think about it overnight and we will make a decision tomorrow."

"I just don't want them finding out."

"I understand, Nora. Here's the thing though. If you don't deal with this positively, they will anyway, and it may not be pretty."

I hated this man for making so much sense.

"So, let me know tomorrow, which DBT you are in and what your decision is regarding work. In the meantime, today, stick to the same routine. I know there are things you are going to need to organise, so your phone time has been extended. You can pick it up straight after classes, and now you don't need supervision to use it. But please Nora, use it wisely."

Yes, that last comment was condescending. Still, I knew exactly what he meant.

When he left, I was left alone with an even greater weariness – my worry about work. The only thing I could do was distract myself and hope that all would come clear as the day went on. I put onto the painting what I declared were the last green strokes. Superb. Then I saw the bits that needed fixing up. I finished those. Then I realised the shading on some of the leaves was not complete. When that was done, my eyes were drawn to the circle boundary. It needed to be bolder. The wings, the wings too needed to look wispier. I could hear the voice in my head, my compassionate friend, saying firmly, "Walk away, Nora. It is done." The kind voice though was drowned out by the demand for this painting to be perfect. The two sides were having a mighty battle, neither willing to concede. Was this suffering? It sure felt like it, even if it was all inside of me. What was the kindest thing I could do right now? It would be taking a break, breathing, and getting breakfast.

I turned the painting around. Went and washed my brushes and walked out to go and see what Mark might have for me.

Arriving late meant my seat had been taken. Luckily, it was Jess who was in it. Mark was not around, so I made some porridge and sat down. We were both tired, so the conversation comprised of stunted small talk, but it was still satisfying.

"Is this your last week, Nora?"

"Yes, thank goodness. And you?"

"No, they are making me stay one more."

I realised then how people's questions, while looking completely innocent can be driven by an issue that irks them.

"Oh, I am so sorry."

"It's OK. I agree. I will miss you being here though."

"Thanks Jess. Yes, I will miss you too."

I often said things like that purely to be polite. This time, I meant it. She had such a great smile and was so encouraging. Part of me wished I could swap details and play the role of big sister, but the compassionate friend was very clear — I was not the big sister she needed right now.

We both searched for Tom, but he was nowhere to be seen. Sharing our hopes we would see him in class, we cleared our plates and went back to our rooms to get prepared.

During the gentle exercise, I made a decision. I was unsure how, but I would keep this practice a part of my day when I got out. Sure, I doubted I would have the discipline, but it sounded like a solid idea at this stage. Then, all thoughts slipped away, and I rode the gentle waves of my breath. What word would I use to describe this? Beautiful.

In the first class, we went through information on medication and the effects of drugs, including caffeine and alcohol. It was so interesting - all the array of chemicals that had been developed to alter how we really felt. It made me think that my adaptations were really no different. I had self-medicated myself to cope, and now I needed someone else's chemicals to clean up the mess and get me back to something deemed more normal. I wondered whether I would ever be normal or whether this would always be Nora.

Communication was the topic of the second class. I did it daily for a living, so I expected it to be quite dry. I pulled out my doodles, ready to be distracted from the humdrum. That was until we were all asked to identify our default communication type. There was a list to choose from. Assertive, yes, definitely assertive. Then, I read the description of this style and the explanation of the others. OK, coming clean, I had to admit I was a passive communicator. Yes, I readily submitted to others. This was clear right throughout my childhood. I never argued, never pushed for anything. I asked, then shut up and submitted to whatever answer I was granted. It seemed that for me this had never gone out of style.

Although, hang on, if I was being really honest, I would have to say passive-aggressive. Oh gosh, I really was. I put on the face of obedience, but underneath the mask were expressions of contempt. If I could not get my way or be in control, I would make them work to try and understand what I wanted. It was a game I played perfectly. Reflecting on my relationships and career, I gained plenty of practice. It showed up in the snide comments or subversive actions I took against my lovers when I was too chicken shit to tell it like it really was. And it came out in the covert chats and emails that politely brought my boss's attention to some anomalies or risks I had noticed in the work of those I did not like. I was not an assertive communicator. I was a coward. Yet no one else had ever suggested that I seek out alternative skills. Here, I was finally being challenged with a different style of communication – real assertiveness, not my deceptive version.

The teacher told us how communication is the tool we use to get our needs met. What I found really interesting is that she saw the passive forms of communication as self-punishment, a way to sabotage yourself from achieving what you really wanted. Some may call it martyrdom; she called it malignant – a disease that destroys relationships. I could see how this may be the case, and I was saddened by how much of my life had been spent being spiteful when I really thought I was being strong. I noted the following words down to add to my blacklist later – self-deceit.

The skill we were asked to practice was a sentence with three steps: "When you...", "I feel..." and "I would like..."

Jess and I worked through some provided examples, enjoying a joke along the way and putting on voices to cover our own embarrassment. I played the boss talking over the staff member, and Jess played the lowly labourer. Then she acted out the rude retailer, and I was the shocked shopper. I hated teamwork—I always have. I would rather figure things out on my own. Yep, there was another idea to be logged in black later.

Returning to our seats I wished Rob and Tom were here. This is exactly what they needed. They were such lovely guys. I was on the rebound from Calli when I met them, and in a way were my crude attempt to show her that I needed much more than she could give. They were on my dependable dating site, hugging each other, smiling, and seeking a unicorn. I had never been with two guys before, so this would be a new adventure, and I was hoping, one that would extricate myself further from Calli. I never expected to get so embedded.

Our first meeting was at their place. Rob was a great cook and served up the most gorgeous gourmet meal. It all seemed so comfortable and so expected that during the desert, the touching began. Both would brush past me, squeezing my shoulders or stroking my hand. And then it was no surprise that during the clean-up, there were caresses. Rob and Tom would kiss each other and ask me how it made me feel to see them express their love. I had to be honest and told them it made me feel honoured, happy, and horny. Rob came up to me and kissed me so gently. Tom followed; his kisses a bit more forceful. The hugs that came next were so lovely like I was surrounded by two solid supporters.

As I watched them have sex that first night, I was intrigued. I had been trying to imagine how sex with two men could compare with the natural fit between man and woman. These guys made it look effortless and did it with so much love. This was not the porn playhouse I had ploughed through to prepare myself for this moment. It was a passionate play, set on a stage of tenderness and deep respect.

I was proud that they wanted me to join their partnership. I felt like a wife with two husbands; truly wanted. I surprised myself with how much attention I had to give them and how much stamina I had to satisfy them. It was inevitable then, we became a threesome, and I began to spend a few nights a week over at their place. They never came over to mine, but that was not a problem. Their place was a palace compared to my cramped unit, and any attempt I made at entertaining would, knowing Rob's ability, be embarrassing. So, their place was where the threesome was based.

We used to play this game called entrée. While Rob was cooking, he would say what he would love to see, and Tom and I would do it for him. Between the chopping, stirring and turning, he would watch, and we would enjoy him doing so, sometimes asking for further instructions to keep him involved. Then would come the game of dessert. Tom would get to dictate the next deed. He would decide whether he would like me to be their voyeur, a vixen – taking both, or whether he would simply watch a duet and then play jealous lover seeking his vengeance with fake violence.

More often than not, they would get me to video them so that they could watch it again when I was gone. On the rare times I stayed, I would fall asleep between them to the sound of their sex being replayed in the background. The next morning, Rob made a magnificent breakfast, and Tom loaded me with leftovers. They said their job was to ensure I had enough love and food to keep me fit and healthy. It felt like heaven, or even better, home.

It was so ironic then that these guys were so skilled at saying what they wanted when it came to sex and yet could not interact on other menial matters without an interpreter.

"Nora, could you tell Rob we have had fish far too often lately."

"Nora, I need your help. Could you tell Tom that he should not go to the shops in holy shirts."

"Nora, I know you get it. Please explain to Rob about the importance of being with family at Christmas time."

"Nora, back me up on this one. Could you please tell Tom to be more spontaneous."

"Nora, I need you to convince Rob that moving to the country would be wonderful."

"Nora, Tom seems to think that having a cat in an apartment is a good idea. Could you please talk some sense into him."

For the first month or so, it was fun, and I was helping them navigate the nuances of their relationship. A few more months on, though, they needed me.

More months passed, and I spent my days trying to manage their misunderstandings. I began to feel meddlesome; like I was a convenient messenger for things they were not man enough to tell each other. I decided then that I no longer wanted to be needed. I stayed longer than I should have because talk began about me being a surrogate for their child. It sounded like such a perfect arrangement. I would get the chance to experience having a child without any attachment, responsibilities or career-crunching routines. But it became evident that even the promise of being a surrogate could not save my sanity.

Each day, my enjoyment of playing all the various parts dwindled, and I got embroiled in more debates. I could not raise my concerns; what would they say when I was not there? I could become an outcast. I knew I had to do something, though. I was no longer feeling loved, merely exploited. Rob and Tom were using me to patch up their problems, and I no longer wanted to be a part of it. Playing mediator and martyr for these guys was fun for a while, but the teacher was right. It became malignant and destroyed our relationship. What was worse was the realisation that came during the class - that I had not offered any alternative role model. I condoned and even encouraged the delegation of their discussions. Yes, they had used me, but I had let them.

Speaking of being used, wasn't it the same at work? There were so many long hours and hard slogs to meet the deadlines, and they paid me a pittance compared to the profit they made. In a way, these partners were using me too, and when I became one, I would be no better than a pimp. I would love to try this communication technique on the partners, to tell them how I felt. Although I knew what the response would be. I would be accused of being aggressive, promptly asked to pack my things, and suspended on the spot. I had seen it done before and knew just how brutal they could be.

This was no longer just about a job. It was about my health. Now, I needed time and had to assert myself to take it. Otherwise, I would have learned nothing.

At lunch, there was still no sign of Mark, and Jess had been called out by her counsellor before the end of class. Tom was there alone, and although he was not inviting me to join him, I thought it a strange coincidence that right now, I would be met with this name and the opportunity to use my words wisely. I asked if I could sit with him, and we started some very awkward and non-controversial chit-chat. The weather looked great outside. He was here for another week, too. Yes, the classes were boring, but I was learning a few things. The food was better than I expected. I had the chance to slip in a few words of support before things started feeling too strained, and then we parted ways. That was heavy. Was that what the doctor felt like talking to me? No wonder he didn't stay long.

Back in my room, I waited for Bev, scratching out a to-do list for when I got my phone and updating my blacklist with the insights from the previous classes.

"Hey Nora. How are you? And why is your painting turned around?"

"Hey Bev. I'm OK. I just didn't want to look at it anymore."

"Ah, are you a bit of a perfectionist? I am not surprised. It makes sense and is probably a great source of stress for you.

When you leave, do you want to take it home with you? If not, I would love to keep it here and put it up on the wall."

"Oh Bev, I think it better that I don't take it home. Otherwise, I would be tempted to spend the rest of my life tinkering with it. I would love for you to have it."

Bev was beaming and came to wrap her arm around my shoulders.

"Thank you. Thank you. Thank you. Yay!"

She was such a funny woman, going from counsellor to child in less than three seconds.

"Right, now we need to get serious. We need to work out the plan forward. What do you think about taking six months off?"

"It really worries me, Bev."

"Why?"

"I just worry that they will think that I am disposable."

"You are."

"What? Oh Bev, that's harsh!"

"Harsh but true, Nora. We all are. You would have to be pretty arrogant if you think that you can't be replaced by something or someone. They will always find a way to go on without you. They will probably recruit some green bean who is eager to please and won't ask questions and burn them to the bone just like they were doing with you. Then, when they have had enough, they will end up here too, wondering what just happened. Life will go on for them, Nora. The most important thing you need to consider is the life you want to live.

"What is the other Nora, or your compassionate friend saying?"

"Ok, Bev. Point taken. You win this one. I am going to progress with the income protection process this afternoon."

"Great! But it is not about me winning, Nora. It is about what you have to lose. You have spent your life trying so many different ways to succeed. You have continually pushed yourself past what is healthy for anybody, let alone one who has to really care about their mental health. And look at where it has landed you. I am just saying that it might be a smart idea to try something different."

Oh, she was good. She had me there. She knew I prided myself on being smart, and now she had used it against me. Sneaky, Bev. Very sneaky, indeed. But I knew that her cunning was based on care.

"How did the classes go today?"

"Good. It was a rude awakening, though. I could see how my lack of assertive communication has put me in some bad situations.

"Hurrah. I love a rude awakening!" She gave me a wink, which made me laugh. Bev had shifted from surprise to shock.

"Sorry, I jest. I think you may have a larger concern though."

"Really?"

"It is one thing to tell people what you want. It is another to know what you want in the first place."

"Sorry, Bev. I don't understand."

"Well, think about it. You have shifted and changed your identity continuously to satisfy others. You have stripped them off and on so many times it is very possible that you have lost sight of what the Nora underneath really needs. It may take some time to find again what is true for you. There are things you need and want that may come easily, that sit on the surface and can be seen by everyone. There are others though that have been buried and may take more work to bring to out into the open."

Does that make sense? Please tell me if you disagree." There was another wink. Was she goading me to argue with her?

"Oh Bev, you are hilarious. And yes, it does. I kind of felt that way on the weekend; a bit lost. There was no-one to take care of, no deadlines to deliver, apart from your homework. I ended up just doing what you suggested, at least the first day. We all know how my choice of activity worked out the next day though."

"Don't be too hard on yourself, Nora. You went there with good intentions, no-one got hurt and you have learned lots from the experience. Yes?"

"Yes."

"Now, how did you go with the list of things to let go."

I showed her the ten black words on my page. Independence. Singular identity. Arrogance. Fantasy. Self-deceit. I know everything.

"You are brilliant. Now, keep this list. You have a whole adventure ahead of you, and I suspect many more things will need to die in due time.

Nora, these are some things that you need to move away from. But let's shift your thinking towards what you want to move towards.

Your next task, if you choose to accept it, may really challenge you. The colour, probably no surprise here, will be blue. The title of the work will be "What I Want." How does that sound?"

"Yeh, fine, I think."

I knew Bev's assignments sounded easy but were usually a little pretty doorway to the complex and profound.

"Could I be so bold to suggest a different medium this time?"

"Yes please. Maybe pastels?"

"Perfect. Now, would you like a canvas?"

"No. Just paper for this one I think."

"Awesome, so you have everything you need?"

"Yep. Apart from the answer."

"Oh, ha-ha. Seriously though. This is not a test, Nora. This is your life. You won't find any of this in a textbook. It comes from a lot of trial and error. You have lived long enough to have tried many different things, so this exercise might be about stripping away first those things you now know you don't want. And remember, you have your list of values as well. These might be a good guide.

This will become more important as you move out of here and start making choices again about what you do and how you use the precious gift of time. It is about finding those things that make you feel good and create energy rather than destroying it and yourself.

Tomorrow, we will start discharge planning, so what you come up with here will be a really important input into building the networks and routines that will help you live your best life.

Sorry, I have been blabbering on."

"Not at all, Bev. I really appreciate what you are saying. And I get it. I really do."

"That is fantastic. But before I go, what about grateful. Did you come up with anything last night?"

"Yes. Only three more sleeps before I get out of here. No, only joking. Or am I? Actually, I was grateful for sharing some time with Jess yesterday. She is so lovely. The poor thing though. I felt good giving her some support."

"You are wonderful, Nora. And I am sure she really appreciated it. There is an important takeaway for you in this, too. It does us the world of good to help others. What we give out, we get back. It is a real win-win. Maybe this might be something to consider for your next six months.

But for now, I better let you get to making some phone calls. Have a great night, Nora."

Was it procrastination or my love of planning that saw me sit down when Bev left and start scratching out ideas. I was doubtful of her assumption that this task may be difficult. Writing the title on the page was quick and painless. What do I want?

But then the stabbing in my stomach began, and the scarlet of shame began burning my cheeks. This was exactly what Ben asked me before he walked out the door. I gave him an answer then. I wanted him. But now, this answer was off the table. I was so stupid. How could I not see that he was trying to help me find myself? I was too focused on trying to fall into him. I was such a goddam fool. I was not a powerful, independent woman. I was a puppet, or even worse, a parasite, using other people's lives to save me from having to build my own. Oh god, I was pathetic.

Ben also asked me who I was; even now, I was still unsure. All I could come up with was two pitiful yellow pancakes. This did not bode well for me in identifying what I wanted. Bev suggested I refer to my values, so I pulled these out. Independent, resilient, professional, successful, organised. What a load of shit. Seriously. I had really bought into them the other day. Now, I could see straight through them. There was connection, underlined, and the cramps in my stomach intensified. And there was creativity again seeking my attention. I thought about Frida and what she wanted, and it came to me.

Space. I wanted space; to understand what I really needed, to understand myself. I wanted space to find the environments that would bring me energy and help me come into my own power. I wanted to be a chameleon that chose the context to suit her colours, not one forced to fluctuate for other people's fancies.

I would not forget this word, but wrote it down anyway. Space. It sat there staring at me, and I smiled back, then I went to get my phone.

I called my superannuation fund and chatted about the income protection process. The lovely lady sent me through the forms, and Ranjani helped me get them printed. Then I sent a message to my boss, advising that I would apply for income protection, which would see me out for around six months. I hoped to have the forms to him early next week, but for now will apply to take my full sick leave balance. I sat there for several minutes, contemplating whether I should say more. I could offer up some information to secure a sense of trust and maintain our relationship. Who was I kidding? Trust had been blown the first time I saw him bully a graduate to tears. Mum's voice came clear into my head.

"This is not about them, Nora. This is about you. Only give them what they need and move on."

I hit send without adding another sentence.

After the sick leave ran out, I would have to go without pay for two weeks. It would sting and require me to withdraw some gems from my treasure chest. But I was lucky. How did other people do this that did not have reserves? I noted that one down as my grateful, and I truly was.

I did not have to get back to the real estate agent about mum's place until the next day, but I just had to do it now. The message instructed him not to take on another tenant, that I would be coming back, and that I needed to know what date it would be vacant.

Next, I found a DBT provider that offered virtual services and booked myself in. Done.

Finally, I called my landlord to confirm the notice period. 21 days. Perfect. It was meant to be.

I went to dinner with my brain buzzing and a sense of hope I had not felt for a long time, probably since I stepped foot in Seattle. It seemed my value of organisation was still working and actually being of value, not just a word I used to make myself feel good.

My excitement made it hard to concentrate on the conversation with Jess. She was feeling really down and looked like every cell of hers was depressed. She said the only reason she came to dinner was to see me. They had changed her meds, and it was really messing her around. She asked how I was, but I chose not to share my news and declare I was feeling neutral. This decision was made not out of cruelty to me but out of compassion for her. We did not stay long; it was obvious she needed to sleep. So, I gave her a hug and told her I was there to help if she needed me. Jess managed a small smile. I wish I knew then that it would be the last time I saw her.

Back in my room I started picking out blue shades for my depiction of the space that I was seeking. I thought about putting in specific shapes, but like creativity, this was a concept that felt amorphous. The sky. The sky was the space I needed. I didn't want the space of a big office or a luxury apartment. I needed the space of the sky. Somewhere for the leaves to grow towards and somewhere for the wings to fly. Before I could counter this idea with criticism, I scribbled on several blue gradients. It was so satisfying to blend them in with my fingers and watch the scratches become smooth. I wondered if it would ever be possible to plane over the problems I had caused. I thought about breaking Bev's rules and introducing some white clouds. I really wanted to use them to represent those things that did not serve me, like the white version of my blacklist. But I was too tired to make a decision, so I let that one sit to be dealt with tomorrow.

It took ages in the shower and much scrubbing to get the pastel stain off my fingers. And yet, I did not find it painful; it was definitely pleasing to be covered in a new pigment. In bed, I reminded myself of what I had to be grateful for. I was so thankful for the time, money, and space to help me figure this out. I knew so many others didn't. This thought developed into a depression as I drifted off to meet my dragon again.

While the night nestled against my window, I sat beside the dragon, watching the sky. We did nothing. Said nothing, just watched the clouds roll by. Suddenly, the dragon jumped up and flew off into the distance until all I could see was a tiny speck. Then, it sprinted back again, revealing its speed and strength. It landed beside me and picked me up, getting ready to propel me off the cliff. Every single part of me froze, including my wings. I knew I could not fly. This was not training; it was to be an execution. Did it simply want to show off before it slayed me; to mock me with something I would never be? The dragon's eyes pierced into mine, and as they widened and the pupils expanded, I could sense its excitement.

"No."

I only had to scream it once.

The dragon put me down, hugged me and then held my hand. I removed it, fearing it could still hurl me into the air and accomplish the assassination.

The dragon's eyes became sad, and it sat down. I thought about sprinting away. Instead, I slumped beside it.

"I just want to watch you for a while. That's what I want."

And we both cried.

THE LOVE LIFE OF A CHAMELEON

Chapter 13

I was actually still crying when I woke up, unsure whether it was relief from escaping my murder (at least for the moment), from using my voice, or from being heard. It was probably also exasperation at my inability to be satisfied. There I was, in a cave, left to die, and I was depressed. Now, I was out in the world, given the chance to fly, and all I could feel was anxiety. I should be running free in my dreams, either away from the dragon or soaring across the sky. Instead, I was still bound by fears. Continually afraid - that seemed like a perfect summary of my life.

Well, not anymore. I took this conclusion as a challenge and decided to put clouds in my sky. Yes, I wanted space, but I also wanted to see what was in the way and then, over time, watch them as they floated away. I didn't want to pretend that my sky was perfect. Self-deceit was another thing I had to give up, so I can't continue to deny that there are, and will always be, clouds. All I want, though, is to not let them consume me and leave me in the dark. I want to see them, respect them, and learn to fly with them.

So, I pulled out the white pastel and added the clouds, shifting across the sides of my sky. I smiled, wondering what Bev would say, and was still smiling at the thought of my rebellion when the doctor came in.

"You seem like you are in a good mood, Nora. Are you excited that you are down to the last few days."

"You bet."

He started through the regular list of queries, but I beat him to it.

"Mood, fine. Appetite, fine. Sleep, same. Meds, fine. Attend all classes, check. Eat in the dining room, consider it done. Phone privileges, understood and appreciated."

"Well, Nora, thank you for saving me all that talking."

"My pleasure. I was wondering though if I could record you asking all these questions tomorrow. The mornings just won't be the same without them, and it may assist in my transition back to the real world."

He didn't have to say anything. His look of condescension said it all.

"So, let's get down to business then. How did you go finding someone to start DBT with?"

"Good. It's all sorted. I found one that does virtual sessions which is great. And I am booked in for a meet and greet with the psych next Wednesday."

"Well done. Although, and sorry if I had not mentioned this before, but in-person is certainly preferred. Why did you look for virtual services?"

Now, there was disdain in his words as well.

"Because I am going away for a while."

"Please explain."

"Mum's house is going to be free in a few weeks. I have decided I want space and to get out of the city. When the income protection gets approved, I am going to head there for six months."

"Nora, that is a bit impulsive."

"Well from what I am led to believe about BPD you should probably not be surprised."

"I just wish you would have talked to me about it before doing anything. We need to do regular check-ins, and setting up a support network is important, probably more important than space at the moment."

"Well, we will just work out a way to make both happen. We can meet by video, phone, or I can come back for a day or two. No biggie."

"I really don't think it is a good idea. Do you know anyone out there?"

"No."

"Then you will be isolated. And that can be dangerous. It can create stress that could impede your progress."

"Doctor, I take your point. But the reality is I don't know anyone here either. I can't socialise with colleagues, and the only people to help are you guys. This is a great opportunity for me to do something different and I am going to take it."

"Against my advice?"

"Yes."

I had a smile back on my face. I was so glad assertive communication had been part of this course of treatment. The doctor thought otherwise.

"You did assertive communication class yesterday, didn't you?"

"Yep."

"Makes sense. This always happens. I will have to get them to rethink that one.

Right, well, let's just focus on the next few days. I would like to see you next week and will get my admin to set up a time. Please confirm it with her when you can access your phone this afternoon."

"I will do. Oh, and I got the insurance forms through and printed."

"Well, Nora. You are really owning this, aren't you?"

"It is about time I did."

"I congratulate you for your commitment. I will have these back to you tomorrow. Until then, you know what to do. The classes today and tomorrow will be important to help you map out what life is going to look like for the next few months, so please give them your full attention."

"Yes, Sir."

"That's unnecessary."

"And yet apt."

This time, the doctor shot me a smile as he walked away. Bugger. I was so preoccupied with showing off my planning prowess that I did not even get to look at his socks.

Mark wasn't at breakfast again, and the hot options looked sad and slimy without him. Jess wasn't there either; the poor thing was probably still sleeping. I heard that medication changes can be brutal. Tom wasn't there either, although I was not surprised. I suspected he was like me and took every opportunity to eat alone.

I grabbed some porridge and my seat and resigned myself to a very quick and quiet breakfast. This was funny. I had decided that I wanted space and was taking action to be in a place where I could be alone. And yet here I was, feeling lonely when a few acquaintances were not around. Was I sure that space was the right thing for me? The doctor did not seem to think so, and sitting here, I also began to doubt it.

To distract myself from the doubts, I started doodling. In my decisive state, I had also put a mandala on my to-do list and wanted to test out some shapes for the layers. With each stroke, my certainty came back, and when I returned to my room, the sky I had drawn secured the deal. I loved the blues and how they had blended. I wanted more of this in my life, and I was not going to get it in my apartment or in an office.

Standing back from it, though, something appeared missing from the picture. It needed some grounding, some context, some frame, and a floor. It was bright, blue, and beautiful but a bit boring.

"Well, Nora," I thought. "This is the space you are seeking. You can't have everything. You can't have the expanse of the sky and the excitement of the street all at once. You need to choose."

Feeling my body flow in the exercise class, my choice was confirmed. I wished I could record this class, too, and take it home with me. The teacher was one step ahead of me. At the end of the class, she handed out a list of websites that offer similar sessions, all free and that can be done anywhere and anytime.

The next class built on the first, working through the mind-body connection. We were told that a healthy body means a healthy mind and were pressed to identify all the things we would do back in our daily lives for both. To stay well, there was much to consider – diet, exercise, sleeping, medication, social interaction, posture, breathing, purposeful work. It was this latter one that got me stumped. Social interaction was easy. I would not have any, which is how I wanted it. But purposeful work? For six months, I would not be employed; I would not be a professional. What would I do?

I would take Frida's advice. I would arrange flowers, paint and laugh. Yes, I would do some courses on flower arranging. I knew there would be a craft shop somewhere near mum's and at least one florist, so I would definitely do this. I could even grow flowers of my own. I would have time to care for them. Yes, I would paint and draw. I also always wanted to learn pottery, and make mosaics. As I listed these ideas, the space started to shrink into something far less scary. Then, there was Bev's idea about finding a way to help someone else. I could volunteer somewhere. That would be great, too.

I had no doubt I would fill up my time at mum's. For the next few weeks, I would be super busy getting ready for the move. There were things to pack and store, and some that held too many memories and needed to be sold.

Lunch again was another short, solo snack. It made me think just how much impact one person can have after such a short time. Even if I had known Mark for only about a week, he made the start of my days truly wonderful. And Jess, while not a friend, was someone I was fond of. On the other hand, Tom was just a source of worry, but even this made my day feel more worthwhile.

Back in my room I started the paperwork for the insurance. It was all pretty straightforward until I got to the part asking for the name and cause of my illness. I was stuck. What was my illness? Should I write BPD? Then, if so, what was the cause? An atypical brain and childhood trauma? Or was the illness depression and the cause of excessive life stressors? Should I mention suicidal tendencies? I may have owned this claim process, but I was confused about my condition. Bev saved me from having to dwell on this any further; it would be one to ask the doctor tomorrow.

"Hey, Nora. How are you going? Are you excited to be leaving? Only two more sleeps!"

"Yes, there is."

My monotone response seemed to surprise her.

"Not excited?"

"Yes, I am, well kind of."

"We will dig into that further in a minute. But first, I can't wait to see your pastel creation. What do you want, Nora? Show me!"

I held up my space, my sky, now concerned about Bev's reaction.

"Nora, the clouds are not blue."

"I know. But I wanted to put them in."

"Why?"

I explained the concept of the clouds being those things I found troubling and that as much as I wanted a perfect sky, it was impossible. I wanted to see them and watch them flow away, rather than, through ignorance, letting them impede my judgement."

I was confident in my explanation. Still, Bev frowned, and I awaited castigation.

Her frown flew away, replaced by a resplendent smile.

"Congratulations to you, Nora! I was wondering when you were going to break the rules and follow your heart. I was hoping there would be one day when you decided to listen to your own inner voice. The picture makes perfect sense. Amazing work, really, incredible, Nora."

"Thanks, Bev."

I didn't feel like my creation was anything special, but Bev made it sound like a long-lost Leonardo da Vinci.

"Speaking of using your voice, oh that's funny, the doctor tells me that you have made a decision about taking time off."

"Yes, and I am going to move back to mum's old place for six months as well."

"That sounds wonderful. How are you feeling about it all?"

"Well, some moments I feel great, really looking forward to the change. Then a bit later I want to change my mind and just stay in the city. I go from wanting space, and then not, from being so confident then feeling so shit scared. I can't seem to keep up with how I am feeling."

"Ah, welcome to the wonderful world of human contradiction. I need you to know that this is not just you. We are all complex creatures, and, if we were to be honest, flip and flop around all the time. Now, you will tend to be a bit more black and white than other people, so this is something you are going to have to be aware of, and maybe manage more consciously. But remember that singular identity you were saying you wanted to let go of? Well, this is a part of it. It is about accepting your dualities and seeing yourself as a whole person. Let me show you what I mean."

Bev grabbed a large piece of paper and a purple pastel, drawing a circle that took up most of the page.

"Now, stay with me on this one. This circle, this whole simple circle is actually an interplay of opposites. Take a look. There is North and South, East and West. And to have the full circle you need all of the directions. You may live in the East, and that is all you can see, but that does not mean the West doesn't exist. Does that make sense?"

"Sort of."

"Our bodies may be a better analogy. Our brains have two sides, and so does our heart, both of which have different functions. Our environment, too, is full of opposites. We also have contrasting seasons, hot to cold, wet to dry, and night and day. These opposites exist in the whole, and we can't live without both.

What is fascinating, though, is how these contrasts play out within us. Think about your relationships for a moment."

"Oh god, do I have to?" The pretend, painful look on my face made her laugh, but she continued anyway, determined to make her point.

"Do you like excitement in your relationships, Nora; the thrill of the chase? What about the bliss of the first few days of being in love?"

I was unsure whether I had ever been in love, but I knew what she was getting at. It was the butterflies that started in your stomach when you thought about kissing someone. The cramp that came under your belly button when you imagined getting really close. It was the playfulness that came from pushing each other's buttons before it became annoying. It was seeing their sheets for the first time and smelling their cologne. It was the exploding pleasure when you saw their name on your phone and the passion with which you first explored each other.

"Sure."

"But is having a sense of security, stability, safety also important to you?"

"Of course. Oh, I think I am getting it."

"Good. Let's try another one. Think about your work."

Another pained face, yet she proceeded.

"Do you want recognition and reward? Is that important to you?"

"Absolutely!"

"But are there also times you want to be left alone, to be ignored, and to just hide away?"

"Yes. I see."

"Perfect. One more. Is there a part of you that is looking forward to getting out of here?"

"Yes."

"But is there also some of you that wants to stay?"

I could not help but look solemn. For Bev was right. These people, yes even the doctor in his own way, were precious.

"How do you know?"

"Remember, Nora. I have been where you are now."

It took me a moment to remember about her stays in rehab. That is right, she too has had this experience and had endured these extreme feelings.

"So, for today's exercise, we are going to get the full picture of you. We are going to acknowledge, accept and appreciate all the bits that are Nora."

Bev drew a line down the middle of the circle.

"On one side I want you to list all of your good qualities. If you don't like the word, if it is a bit too primary school for you, then make these your positive or helpful characteristics. And then, on the other side, these will be your bad, or alternatively negative or unhelpful qualities. Got it?"

"Yep."

"Now, don't get freaked out. Just let them flow. There are likely to be lots, and knowing you, Nora, you will come up with a lot more bad than good. We all have so many negative qualities, because simply, we are human. Most of them don't impede us at all. There may be one or two that we need to work on, that might be sinking our boat, but mostly, they just exist as one extreme of our quirky wholes."

"Yes, I see."

"OK then you wonderful woman, I will leave you to it. I am sure you have a lot to organise for your move."

"Yes, I do."

"Gee, I almost forgot again. Grateful?"

"Yes. For space and support to help me through this."

"That's beautiful, Nora. And I get the sense that these are becoming less about satisfying me and more about seeing the wonderful things that you already have. Same again tonight, OK?"

"Indeed."

"You go girl!"

Bev left, waving her hand in the air and with a skip. She left me not only with homework but on a high. What would I do without her? I wondered if she would let me record one of our sessions. Just to be able to hear her voice would be so comforting. And there it was, the space feeling scary again.

There were jobs to be done, though, so I got my phone and began. There was a request for an appointment next week with Dr Dempsey. Done. There was the confirmation of my introduction to DBT next week as well. Done. The real estate agent said how wonderful it would be to have me in the house, although I sensed it was sent through gritted teeth as it meant losing a commission. Done. I searched for a message from Calli. She should have got the letter by now, but nothing. However, there was a message from my boss. Reading the title felt like my heart was being squeezed again, and a claw of sharp talons ripped it to shreds.

"Regarding your absence."

The blood pouring from my heart ran to my stomach and made me feel sick. How could three words wreak so much havoc? I knew why. It was not because they were careless. It was because they were so carefully chosen. Absence, while technically correct, was also so accusatory. This man was a master of giving facts a nuance of negativity. I had experienced it in person many times. While I was relaying evidence, he would spin it and suggest that it was relying on emotion. What I saw as success, he only ever saw as me being second-best. He had also copied HR into the email, which I knew would be protocol, but still felt like he was making a point about my incompetence.

The message started by acknowledging my intention to take leave. Standard spiel. He advised HR would be in contact to confirm the request and process the paperwork. I held little hope that this would be all they would be doing. He stated that my health was important and that he wished me well.

Nice. I knew he didn't really mean it, but it was helpful to have it in writing anyway.

If he had left the message there, everything would have been OK. But he went on. Surely, I realised I had left them in a very difficult position. They had a full project load, and I had not provided any notice. This showed a considerable lack of concern for our clients and also my colleagues. He had advised all of the partners of my absence so that they may begin the process of reworking their forward plans. However, if there was any way I could continue to work, it would be recognised and appreciated. They were willing to make any adjustments necessary to accommodate my needs as long as they were not too disruptive, placed undue pressure on or impacted other people's productivity.

What the hell. Wasn't I only one person? He made it sound like the success of the entire firm was floundering because of my selfish actions. What happened to Bev's belief that I was disposable? When I started reading my messages, I felt hopeful and happy to be on the path of self-care. Now, I felt harassed, horrified and hopeless. Why did he have to make it so hard? And why did they have to give me an option, an out. They were offering me the chance to come back. I could forget all about this, concede defeat and just return. The doctor advised me not to go away anyway so I could pull back and use this to get some breathing space. Who was I kidding? That would never happen. I knew I would be sucked in again, but this time made to feel even more faulty.

A few minutes ago, I had been so confident in what I wanted. Now, I felt like a complete coward. I could not win, and I was not sure I even wanted to try.

Looking up into the mirror, I met the face of an idiot.

"Nora, did you really think this was all going to be OK? There is no blue sky in reality, you stupid bitch."

Ripping the pastel record of what I wanted was cathartic. Yelling out "No" was what I really needed. I needed a place of safety from this storm, and it was down low, on the ground, the only stable base I could find. I hunched over my knees, hoping the chaos above would not find me down here. But it came searching, and the suspense had me scratching at my legs; the scarlet strips were already becoming bloody.

Ranjani came running in.

"Nora, what's going on?"

"Get out. Just get out. Leave me alone."

"You know I can't."

She came and sat down beside me, cuddling in close. I wanted to kick at her, to push her away, but I could not hurt her. I would need to hold it all within myself.

"What is it, Nora? What has happened?"

"It's useless. Absolutely useless."

The scratching was joined by sobs.

Ranjani grabbed my hands and held them tight.

"But this isn't going to help."

I tried desperately to wrestle my weapons free. I had to do something to lessen the frustration, and causing myself pain was pleasant compared to feeling out of control. Still clutching one of my hands with hers, Ranjani reached for her walkie-talkie.

"Hey, could I get someone to see if Bev is still here, please?"

While we continued our struggle, whoever it was on the other end of the line went searching. A minute later, we had the response."

"Yep, she is here in her office."

"Could you ask her to come to Nora's room please?"

We could hear the conversation in the background and the confirmation that Bev would be there in a second.

And that is all it seemed to be. It was like she must have run or flown. I thought seeing her would bring relief. I don't know why it made me wail. She came and cuddled on the other side of me, clutching one of my hands while Ranjani gripped the other. There I was, wedged between these two wonderful women, imprisoned in their integrity.

"Thanks, Ranjani.", said Bev to the first responder.

"Now, Nora you need to stop. Just stop everything. Stop moving. Stop scratching. Listen to me. Just stop. We've got you, so just stop. Can you do that?"

She cuddled in tighter and pulled my hands away, so I had no choice. But I still wanted to do it for her. So I stopped. I stopped rocking, resisting, wailing and writhing. I just stopped.

"Great job, Nora. Really good. Now we are just going to breathe, OK? Take some really nice big ones with me."

Hers were beautiful and bold; mine jumped around and jerked for a while, but after several, they settled into a stable rhythm.

"You've got this, Nora."

I wasn't sure what this was, but I could feel myself returning to a sense of my weird kind of normal.

As I kept breathing, Bev explained that this appeared to be one of those intense times that usually triggered a dive into dissociation. I had just learned there was another option, and that was to stop and breathe. It was simple but so effective.

As we all kept breathing slowly, silently, the storm subsided into a shower. Then Bev spoke.

"Nora, what happened?"

"I got a message from my boss. It was so scathing. I just feel stuck. I don't know what to do."

"I see. What I want you to do is observe what you are feeling and tell me what emotions are jumping out at you. What are you feeling, Nora?"

"I'm feeling confused, Bev. So confused."

"Anything else?"

"And angry, really angry at myself and for being like this, and him for being such a bastard. I am feeling so guilty for letting him get to me. And I feel like I have no control; powerless and useless. It's all useless. I'm so fucking useless."

"Nora, I know it doesn't feel like it right now, but what you have just done shows you do have the power. You have pulled back from the brink of another breakdown. You have tapped into how you are feeling. And now you have the chance to move forward mindfully."

"But it still feels so messy."

"Yes, it is. But you are forgetting what you were like a few minutes ago. And I have every faith that if you keep breathing and caring for how you are feeling, it will be much less messy again in a few more minutes.

I have an idea. I am desperate for a chai. How about we go down to the café and chat down there?"

A chai sounded like heaven, like warm gloves in the winter wind.

"OK."

"But first we need to get those scratches covered. Ranjani, could I get your help to grab some band aids?"

"Absolutely."

Ranjani left, returning shortly with a medical kit.

"While Ranjani is doing this, I will go and get my bag and meet you back here in a few minutes."

Ranjani was so gentle but could not stop the sting of the antiseptic or the thoughts running through my head that said, "That's what you get, you stupid bitch."

Bandaged up, she helped me off the floor and sat me on the bed.

"You're going to be just fine, beautiful girl."

"Thank you, and I am so sorry for this."

"Nonsense, that is what I am here for."

Bev returned and got Ranjani's order for a beverage for us to bring back for her. Then she bundled me into the elevator, her arm around my shoulders as I slogged forward. We scored the corner couch, which was not only cosy but concealed, and I began to feel very comfortable. Bev was so smart; between the change of scenery and personal accountability in a public place, my perspective was bound to shift. The chai came, and it was all I had hoped for: creamy, spicy, soothing, supportive.

"I think I need to date a guy named Chai."

We both chuckled.

"There's my girl, Nora. There's that sense of humour back. Brilliant. Are you feeling a bit less messy?"

"Yeh, thanks Bev. I am so sorry if I wrecked your afternoon."

"Not at all. I was desperate for a chai." She gave a wink, and I hope my smile showed her how much I also appreciated her sense of humour.

"Nora, no one said using your voice would be easy, and I will not apologise for that. People have gotten used to you pandering to their needs, so they are bound to push back when you start asserting yourself. They don't want to give up the good thing of you being a pushover. You will have to find ways to deal with the backlash. I do promise, though, that it will get easier with practice.

And here is another important thing to remember: You are only responsible for your actions, not anyone else's reaction. If this is right for you and if you have been respectful, then you cannot let their games sway you from it.

Instead of taking their reaction to heart, let's consider it a great source of intelligence. What did their response tell you about them and how they work?"

"They are manipulative; they say all the right things but in a sneaky, sinister way. They really don't care about my health, only their own success. That they want to burden me with blame for things that are way beyond my control. That they are great at being cruel."

"Does this sound like a place you really want to be a part of? Does this sound like a place that is going to be good for you?"

"No."

"I know this might be hard to hear right now, but you are sensitive Nora. And despite what these narcissistic nobs may think, it is a gift. But you need to be in the right place, where people appreciate it, and where you can use it to make a real difference, not be forced to suppress it, deny it or be punished for it."

I understood what she was saying. I was not the first person this corporation had crushed, and mine was not the first suicide attempt by a staff member. The saddest thing was that some had been successful. Were these people sensitive, too? Just then, I noticed how much the scratches hurt.

"Now, if your compassionate friend was here having chai with us, what would she say?"

"This is a great opportunity to find myself, so don't let the assholes spoil it for you."

"Gosh I like your friend, Nora. She is so very wise."

We spent the next little while talking about mum's place. It had been over a decade since I had seen it. I had organised new paint and carpet before it was rented, but by now, it would be looking a little shabby for sure. And I had no idea if the tenants maintained the garden.

"It sounds like a really great project, Nora. It will be really nice for you, and I think more than just what you want, it is what you need.

Speaking of need, I do need to start making a move. Are you going to be OK tonight, Nora?"

"Yes, thanks, Bev."

"But you know to call me, right. Promise you will if you need me?"

"Yes."

"Good, so let's get Ranjani's chai and get going."

Back in my room, I was so sad to see my sky torn up, so I started another one. As the colours crept over the page ideas for my bad qualities popped into my head. Impulsive. Afraid to stand up for myself. Emotionally immature. Runs away from problems. Self-deceiving. Flip-flops between black and white. Does not trust others. Has no friends. The first item opened the floodgates, and soon, the left side of the circle was full of over forty faults. I don't know why I found this funny, maybe because I had been so irritated at the thought of other people finding me faulty. Yet, here I was, quite capable of doing it very well for myself.

I looked in the mirror again.

"You are a stupid bitch, Nora." But this time was said with a smirk. Dinner came at a very convenient time before I had to think about the other side of the ledger. And tonight, there was soup, pumpkin soup, again. I knew the doctor would think it was stupid. Still, I took it as a sign that mum, the universe or whatever power was out there supported my way forward and was suggesting that I did need to push on with my positive qualities. Which I did, but very slowly. The analogy of a camel going through the eye of a needle popped into my head and honestly felt like a more preferable task.

Organised. Intelligent. Smart dresser. Healthy.

I wanted to put down caring, but thought my past relationships would suggest otherwise, so added disrespectful to the negative list instead.

Dependable (when it comes to work), articulate, quick learner, tries to think the best of people.

That was painful. Eight seemed enough. I probably shouldn't have, but I went for sedatives, secretly so happy that

Ranjani was not there. She would know I didn't need them, but with this new nurse, I could slip by unchallenged. I justified my decision with the thought that they would not be providing any when I left. My consciousness crept into bed beside me that night, reminding me that the sedatives were a crutch that I was going to have to let go of. I promptly told her I knew this already, then kicked her out and closed my eyes. I did think I saw her sneak over to my circle and write "comfortable with crutches" in the only tiny space remaining.

Grateful. What was there to be grateful for about today? Chai and chats. Definitely chai and chats.

I was also becoming thankful for the dragon in my dreams. It had shifted from a sinister prison guard to a gentle, albeit clumsy, companion. I was concerned when I saw it had built another cave. The new one though was open, looking out over the cliff to the expanse of the ocean and the sky that surrounded it. It was not there as a stockade but as a shelter. And it made no attempt to shove me in and secure the entrance. I was free to seek shade in there when the sun got too hot and sit outside to watch it fly. The dragon started decorating it with purple flowers, and I joined it, collecting them from across the countryside. It had not made another hell but a home.

Chapter 14

I awoke on the last day with not only my usual dose of heaviness but also, this morning, with a medication haze. At that moment, I hated myself for giving in to the offer of sleep assistance. I took the easy way out and sacrificed clarity for comfort. And I had missed witnessing the last night of the torch light touring routine that showed me someone cared. Right then, I decided I would no longer take medication for things I could figure out myself, and I made a note to discuss this with the doctor. There was one blessing, though, and that was the dream. Decorating the cave with the dragon confirmed my priority; creating a place to find peace. While I drank my tea I watched the world outside. I will be back in it the next day. This thought made my whole body tense until I was distracted by the first purple shoot of the jacaranda, and then the doctor.

"Good morning, Nora. Today is your last full day. How are you feeling?"

I actually felt like providing a sarcastic retort, something like, "No shit, Sherlock", but my respectful self stepped in, and all he got back was, "Fine, thanks."

"So, what happened yesterday?"

Geez, these guys were good. They probably recorded every snore and fart they heard overnight as well.

"My boss was just being a jerk and I let it get to me."

"Please don't dismiss this event so easily, Nora. I have seen people like this cause so many problems for my patients in the past. They like to wield their power like a weapon, and it can, if you let it, undo all of your great work here. I need you to remember this – they are not doctors. They cannot contest what I am recommending. Do not look at them, do not engage with the games they are playing. Take your eyes off them and put them on me, got it?"

"But they might try and push me out. I have seen it happen before."

"Yes, they might. But they can't while you are in this process, being supervised by a medical professional. Let's get this leave locked in and just concentrate on that; then, we will take each step as it comes. If you get an email that worries you, hold it over to discuss it with either me or your DBT counsellor. We are no experts on industrial relations am sure we can help you see through their bullshit.

OK, so, clear? Eyes on me and your DBT counsellor."

"Clear.", I said, feeling grateful for his strength.

"Until you start getting some benefit from the DBT, your work relationships and intimate relationships are going to be a real source of stress for you. These are where you seek validation and place your attachments. However, you are sensitive to other people's opinions, and to the thought of them leaving you. You swing between black and white and have difficulty with distressing emotions. All of this combined, make these relationships potential minefields. That is why I am recommending that for the next year you do not get involved intimately with anyone."

"You mean stay alone."

"Yes. How does that sit with you."

"Honestly, it sounds fine."

"Yes, it may now, but from what I have seen, Nora, it may become more difficult in a few weeks. It is really important that you give yourself the best chance of this treatment working. So please, if you can, make this promise to yourself."

The doctor looked so serious, almost pleading. Although after what he had heard about my love life in the past it was pretty clear that any other option would be ludicrous.

"I understand. And I will."

"Great. We are booked in for next week, and you have DBT, so these will be some good milestones for you. And I am sure you will be kept busy with the move. But do you have any questions?"

"Yes, actually. This insurance form. What is my illness, exactly?"

"It's best to keep it simple. Just put down depression and anxiety. These are the symptoms most relevant to the treatment you are taking time off for."

"And the cause?"

"Put down life stressors. They don't need to know more than that."

This doctor was clever. The contents of this form would now be correct, just not complete; enough, just not exact.

"Thanks. And one more thing. It's about the medication. It makes me feel dull. Even when I don't take the sleeping pills, it just feels like my brain is not working properly. Do I need to keep taking it?"

"Simply, yes. And you need to give it at least four months to really do its thing. You will need to work with your GP to monitor progress with this, but you must not just stop it by yourself, OK? That would be really dangerous."

Why did this second plea from the doctor sound like a promising pathway? What the hell was wrong with me when a descending spiral and self-harm still seemed like it would give some satisfaction. My head followed my heart, and I looked downwards, only to notice the doctor's socks. Black with red smiling sausages.

I pointed at them and then tried to make sense of this psychiatrist.

"Um, why?"

"Why not?" he said, returning my smile.

"OK, we will wrap up any last bits tomorrow. Until then though, have a good day, Nora."

"Thanks, doctor. You too."

I set about using the time before breakfast to finish my second sky. It was shaping up to be much better than the first, so I decided to give it to Bev as a present. She was taking my other ones to display, but his one would be for her. Then I thought about Ranjani and how she was such a steady ship during my storms. I sketched out a bouquet of flowers, which I would colour that evening. That would be Ranjani's present. But what about Mark? I really should make him a thank you card. And Jess? Wow, I really did have a lot of jobs to do today.

Tom was at breakfast but had his head stuck in a book. I knew that trick well. It meant, "I have to be here, but it is under protest. Please leave me alone." I granted his wish and stayed clear. Mark was not there either, and there was still no Jess. So, it was another rapid porridge breakfast, pencilling notes for the letters that I would leave when I departed.

Back in my room, Ranjani came to check on me, which gave me a chance to ask about Mark and Jess. Mark was on leave. When I expressed my hope it was somewhere nice, she informed me that it was actually for chemo. He was battling prostate cancer and was very open about it, offering his experience to help others. Suddenly, I felt so bad. Here I was, taking every bit of kindness he had, not thinking there was so much more he needed.

And when I asked after Jess, Ranjani said she could not breach patient confidentiality. All she could say was that she had been moved to somewhere that would afford her the added attention she needed. My heart sank, repressed with the reminder that this place was no panacea, just part of a process. At that point, I would have given anything for it to be the former, to have my faults forced out and my conditions exorcised. I did not care how excruciating it would be. I wanted to walk out of here well. But the fact that Jess needed more help made me realise that being here may only be the beginning. This broke my heart and began another round of despair.

I brought this hopelessness into the exercise class and left it feeling sad but at least a little comforted. The first class was on crisis management, a recap of what Bev had done with me the day before. It appeared there were so many other ways to help you break a crisis cycle, but the most important part was becoming aware that it was beginning. I added meditation to my list of things I would like to learn. Ben was always banging on about the benefits, but there never seemed to be enough time in the day to sit around and do nothing. Now, there would be, at least for a while, and if it was a way to gain more power, then it was definitely worth a try.

In the next class, we set about planning our first week back in our homes, working through every aspect of our lives and slotting in spaces where they would be addressed. Financial and career came first, and it took a lot of discipline not to take this as a personal reminder of my incapacity to fulfil my professional duties. I would spend the week finalising the insurance paperwork, paying bills, and doing a budget for the move and the next six months. In the mental arena I listed out all the classes I would explore. In the health section, I noted the appointments with the doctor and DBT, my commitment to start the day with exercise and to prepare a healthy menu. If getting well was now my job, then I was going to do it well. The social aspect I left blank. It was best that I absent myself from the mainstream. Family? I had none but was intent on setting up my new home. And in the spiritual arena, putting myself into retreat sure counted as a spiritual process, so the plan was done.

At lunch, Tom was there with a book again, so I spent the time writing my thank-you note to Mark. Back in my room, I finished Ranjani's bouquet and rolled up Bev's sky, tying it with a ribbon I nicked from the art room. It was always wonderful to see Bev, but today, when she walked in, I wanted to cry, and she could tell.

"Hey, Nora. How are you?"

Her soft and gentle tone gave me permission to be upset. So, I sat, cried, and told her about Jess, Mark, and Tom.

"And what about you, Nora. What are you feeling for yourself?"

"I am so sad, Bev. I am sad for myself that I have to now spend years trying to restore some sense of sanity. It seems so daunting, and depressing."

"So, what you are witnessing is where you fit into the picture of what we call common humanity. You care for, and want the best for all those people you just mentioned. You, just like them, are going through the suffering of dealing with health conditions. You are not alone in this, Nora. There is nothing you can do for any of these others right now. But you can turn this wish to ease suffering towards yourself. You are hurting, just like them. So, what is the kindest thing you can do for yourself right now?"

"Give you a hug?"

"You betcha! Bring it in!"

After a wonderful warm hug, Bev pulled back, with a serious look on her face.

"But tell me, Nora. What will you do next week when you feel like this but are aloe in your apartment? Or when you are way out at your mum's next month?"

"I'm not sure."

"I will give you a hint. What would Frida do?"

"Ah, now I understand. I would draw it out, express it."

"Yes, perfect. This may be the way you can prevent your emotions from slipping into crisis mode. Caring for your art can become how you care for your emotions.

The thing is, throughout much of your childhood, with your dad and at school, you were taught that emotions were stupid, so you stunted them and shut them off. Really, though, our emotions hold such wisdom. We will learn so much if we stop and listen to them.

Oh, and that reminds me. Could you write something in your notebook before I forget? Just two words – somatic therapy. Exercise makes us feel so good because it works out the emotions we hold in our bodies. I am not sure whether anyone back at your mum's might offer bodywork, but I think it would be worthwhile for you. So, just something else to explore.

Now. Let's look at your list!"

I produced the circle, weighted heavily towards the wrongs.

"Wow, Nora. You really went to town on yourself! The first thing I need you to know is that this is completely normal. We are all such self-critical creatures, and live in a culture where confidence is seen as conceited. In this context, the imbalance you have here is expected. It does not mean you have more negatives than positives, it's just that this is what you have been told you should see. My question to you then, is this - are there any negatives sinking your boat? There are lots of little niggly bits that are annoying but are there any gaping holes here that are bringing you down?"

I scanned through the list. There were so many damning entries, but which ones were drowning me?

"I am afraid to stand up for myself – to use my voice.

I am emotionally immature.

I run away from problems.

Self-deceit.

I don't trust anyone."

"Yep, they are biggies. But they can all be changed, and the work you will be doing with DBT will help you out with these. I want to challenge one though, and that is running away from problems. There is this view that backing away from a tough situation is a sign of weakness. Sure, not standing up for yourself is not helpful, but there is also no use running into battle when you are facing a massive enemy and you are not armed. In that situation it is absolutely sensible to pull back, regroup, and find a better way to fight the battle. Running away when you have the resources to stand up for yourself is cowardly. But retreating is a very wise military strategy when you need time to get your shit together. I just don't want you to see taking this time off as running away, OK?"

"OK."

"However, there is a catch. You are smart, but you need to dig deep to be honest about whether you are deceiving yourself. Only you will know then whether your retreat is warranted, or whether this is a time when you need to, and can fight."

Bev was so right. I had used the retreat strategy so many times. It was the easy option — so much easier than figuring out what I wanted and using my voice to tell others of my needs.

"Let's look at the other side of the ledger. Which of these are the wind in your sails? What are the big things that are going to propel you forward on this journey?"

"I am organised. I would class myself as intelligent. And I guess I am pretty dedicated to being healthy."

"Perfect. These are fantastic. Can I play devil's advocate for the moment, though. You are intelligent. No doubt, hands down one of the smartest people I have ever met. Just have a look though on what is a hole for you. Emotionally immature. They say that overthinking is under-feeling, and I see this playing out for you. You have supressed a key source of intelligence – your emotions. In their place you have built up huge cognitive abilities. Yes, use your nous, your smarts, and perhaps you can employ these to find ways to balance the thinking-feeling scale."

"Thanks, Bev. That does make sense."

"I see so much emotion in your artwork, Nora. Please never let that go. Now, tonight is your last night, and I am sure you have a lot of things to do before you leave tomorrow. If you would like to though, there is one last assignment. And it is to use every colour we have already worked with; in whatever way you want. This will be something you can take with you and continue next week to provide some continuity between here and your home."

"Awesome, I can do my mandala!"

"What a magnificent idea. I don't know whether this interests you, but here is some background to why I used the colours with you. Have you heard of chakras?"

"Only a little."

Bev passed me a postcard with a person sitting in meditation pose and seven coloured circles embedded vertically within them. Ben had talked about his chakras regularly, and was even getting reiki to balance some of them. He seemed to really buy into it, telling me which ones he believed were blocked in me. Ben used to get really excited talking about it, but honestly, my mind was less on the theory of this ancient awareness and more about how I could use it to get closer to him. Perhaps he could lay his hands on those ones that needed stimulating? No, I couldn't be that forward. Maybe he could take me for a reiki session? He thought that was a wonderful idea. We never made it, though. I messed it up before we could embark on this exploration. I wondered what might have ensued if I had just let things evolve.

"Well, just don't mention them in front of Dr Dempsey. He thinks I am a weird old hippie head, but I know in my heart that every colour has energy and stirs different emotions. It may be something you want to look into further in the future.

"That's great, Bev. Thanks. Yes, I will for sure. I have something for you too."

Passing over the roll, tied with ribbon, made me feel so proud.

"Oh Nora, thank you. This means so much. It is so beautiful. There is something more meaningful for me though, and that is the fact that you redid it."

Another hug, and then we worked through my plan for the next week. When all was confirmed, Bev left me with a congratulations, but also a foreboding of what tomorrow would bring. She had forgotten to ask about my grateful, but I hadn't. I still felt the warmth from the chai and chats.

My messages today were less messy. I scanned and emailed the insurance paperwork and advised HR and my boss that they were coming. I would stick to notifications, nothing more. I confirmed with my real estate agent that I would leave my apartment in three weeks.

Then I saw a message from Calli. She had received the letter, and it had made her cry. She told me to take care of myself and that I could call anytime. I was forgiven — absolutely, and Grace and her would love to see me. I closed the door gently on her offer, advising that I was going away for a while, thanking her for all she had done and wishing her and her daughter well.

I turned away from my phone and looked in the mirror. I did not like what I saw, but at least I did not want to destroy the person standing there.

I was so excited to start my mandala that I jotted down ideas for the layers during dinner and sketched out the symbols I would use. This task would take time, effort, thought, and emotion, so it was purely perfect. And my grateful? I was grateful for colours — all of them.

And colours came into my dream that night, too. The flecks in the dragon's eyes that were once so fierce now flowed between blues, greens and golds. Its scales, which I had seen as a singular, stale grey, now refracted the light, revealing a rainbow sheen that would morph whenever the dragon moved. The chest into which I cuddled was no longer constant but chromatic. There was something else: the sound of the dragon's heart, like both a rousing call and a reassuring rhythm. Then, there was the sensations of its skin. What was once like dry, neglected leather was now like a luxurious blanket. My head lay against it, and I was at peace. I reached out and touched its wings. They were as soft as a butterfly's but as strong as a bat's. My fingers traced the bones that bent around me, and with my palm, I stroked the skin. I felt secure.

And here, surrounded by the shifting solidity of the dragon, I slept.

THE LOVE LIFE OF A CHAMELEON

Chapter 15

Two weeks ago, I walked in here with such resistance; now, I lamented having to leave. I came in under protest but have paved a new path forward. I have a clear job ahead and new role models for productive relationships. I know these people interacted as professionals, and yet they showed the qualities that I needed in my life. For the short term, though, I will stay alone and seek these qualities from myself; that is safer. That is sensible.

The doctor came and went through the final instructions, taking me to the nurse's station, signing out my meds and providing another prescription. He reminded me to stick to my discharge plan and that I would see him next week. Then he reached into his pocket, and handed me a pair of socks.

"Sorry I didn't get to wrap them."

Now, this was a surprise. Had I finally conquered this man, or had I simply made a connection? It felt like the latter and so significant in its simplicity. The socks were bright multi-coloured stripes with teals, pinks, yellows, and greens. On the side, it said, "Ssh… I'm overthinking."

"Oh, these are wonderful. Thank you doctor."

"Well, I noticed yours are getting a bit worn."

He was right about that. I was still wearing the awful orange ones Maria had given me. That was an act of kindness

I would never forget. And so, I would never give up these socks, but yes, they sure needed a wash.

Before more needed to be said, he reminded me about our appointment next week and went on his way. I took Ranjani her picture, which she pinned on her desk and gave me a huge hug.

"You've got this, Nora. Just never be afraid to ask for help, OK?"

"OK."

"Promise?"

"Promise."

"Pinky swear?"

I joined her in this primary school play, thinking how such a juvenile promise still held so much power. Linking little fingers, I replied.

"Pinky swear."

There was another hug, and then I handed over my thank you card to Mark. Ranjani would see that he got it on his return and told me that she was sure it would bring him to tears. She had not known of anyone giving him a thank you card before. I could not believe that. He was such a source of brightness; I found it sad that no one had let him know the positive effect he had on their lives.

Back in my room I stripped my bed, ready for the cleaners to prepare the space for the next poor soul.

I could not sit in the dining room to eat breakfast. Something was telling me that this was not my place anymore, and it had already started to feel foreign again. Without Mark or Jess there, I could make my way in and out without being noticed, grabbing some banana bread and yoghurt and spending the last precious time in the room that had held so much revelation, remorse, rebellion and resolve. I wondered if they did some cleansing ritual between patients, like waving smudge sticks in the corners to expel negative energies. I'm sure Bev would be suggesting it, but I was also sure that the doctors wouldn't have a bar of it.

I asked Bev when she arrived, and she said it had been suggested but quashed due to allergy concerns. Ah yes, that is why you wouldn't find nuts in the porridge bar or emotional support cats roaming the halls. I thought it so interesting that what can help one person can be such a harm to another. We chatted about that for a while and went through the week ahead. Then she, too, passed over a present. It was an art journal, but not just a boring black one like you get at the discount shop. This one had a shiny emerald-green cover embossed with a gold mandala.

"Oh Bev, it's beautiful."

"I thought you might like it. And yes, it is gorgeous, isn't it. But so is what is inside."

I flicked through the pages but could not see anything remarkable.

"It is the white pages, Nora. White holds every colour, and each of these pages is waiting to see which one you will choose. These are your blank pages, and just by themselves, they are beautiful."

"You are so right, Bev. I see what you mean."

And I did. I was the creator of my life. And I could choose my colours.

"Oh, Bev, before I forget, here is your book back."

I handed her the Diary of Frida Kahlo. I already had it on my to-do list to buy when I got out.

"No, you keep it, Nora. We have another one, and I would like to know that you have it for when you need it."

"Bev, I really have got so much out of our session. Do you offer private appointments?"

"No, I don't, Nora. I thought about it but there is only so much time in a day. Believe me, there may be days that you don't feel like it, but you do have all that you need."

There was a long, warm, close, and comfortable hug. Then I picked up my bags, and we walked to the elevator. There were waves from the nurses as I left and then an awkward silence in the lift, like we were at the theatre and a new act was about to begin. Only here, there was no applause only tears as Bev helped me into a waiting taxi, and a wrenching in my stomach as I waved goodbye.

It was a bright and sunny day, and I could not help but notice all the trees along the streets. Had I ever noticed them before? If I did, today they hit differently. Today, these trees were not just side-lines to my journey, but each one a work of art along the way.

I was so nervous arriving at my building, afraid of seeing someone I knew or being asked where I had been. The building manager was brief, welcoming me back and then getting back to his work. Opening the door of my apartment felt like stepping into a lost world. I had almost forgotten what it looked like. It was so clean, so simple, and yet so stylish.

"Wow girl, you have good taste."

It smelt clean too, not harsh bleach clean, but fresh lemon scented. The dead pot plant was replaced by a very good plastic replica. This must have been Calli. It was so kind of her to put in some colour, the lasting kind. There was a note telling me that there were some essentials in the cupboard and fridge. Yes, there was tea, coffee, long-life milk, cereal, tuna, baked beans and crackers. In the freezer there was bread and ice cream. And in the fridge was cheese and chocolate. Calli always believed chocolate was essential, and I remembered her bringing it to bed and enjoying it as we snuggled together. It was a luxury I could never have with Stephen, needing to stay lean to satisfy his tastes.

I was sure my bedroom was a mess when I left; now it was pristine. There was no washing in the basket; when I checked in the wardrobe, it was all done and put away. There was Ben's t-shirt taunting me. I tore it off the hanger and took it straight out to the rubbish chute. Now my room was clean. There was no time for sentimentality here; it was never my strength anyway. I wondered whether my lack of attachment to things was a consequence of my stunted emotions. I know mum's friends were surprised when I sold or gave away all of her things after she died. Didn't I want to keep anything? The simple answer was no. However, there was one exception, mum's rosary beads. These held mum's heartbreak and hopes and have stayed with me ever since.

I decided then that apart from a few other basics, they would be the only thing coming with me back to her home. I opened the windows, revelling in the fresh air, watching the breeze move the sheer curtains and being inspired to take some action myself.

The week's menu was written up, and the online grocery order was completed. It was great to be back in control of what

I ate and to have some time so that cooking would not be a chore. I also ordered some art supplies from Amazon, just enough to last the next few weeks. I would only go to the shops if I really had to. I did not want to risk meeting anyone and having to explain my absence.

Then the stocktake began. All of my possessions were recorded in a spreadsheet with a tick to be placed in one of three columns; take, sell or give away. I took photos of the sale items and ordered some boxes and bags for the things I would take with me, and for those things I would donate to the op shop. I knew I had three weeks to get sorted, but a force was driving me forward. By the time the day ended, I was surrounded by piles of clothes, superfluous kitchen supplies and cosmetics that were unnecessary and so would be trashed. The plastic plant, while so deeply appreciated, also had to go. It would find a new home, one that would not be haunted by the hurt like I was.

I really did not know what to do with the dildos. Would I need them where I was going? Well, I certainly could not hand them over to charity. And besides, I would be alone, and they could deliver some delight on long, lonely nights. Sure, the pleasure was second-rate, but they also simplified life. I had often thought that all a woman needed was a dog and a dildo, and maybe now I might get to find out. I put them in the pile that would be transported to my new home and just hoped it wouldn't feel too awkward having them in mum's house.

Tomorrow, the boxes and bags would arrive. This was the convenience of living in the city. But for now, I was beat.

I ordered takeout from my favourite Indian place and tucked up to catch up on current affairs. It was so strange thinking that there would be no meeting with the doctor that I had to be prepared for tomorrow morning and no work meetings to get to. I would have tomorrow to myself. What did that even mean? I was looking forward to finding out.

There were no dreams of dragons in this place but there were nightmares of Ben; the look of fright in his eyes when I tried to seduce him, the fury when I showed up at his front door. There were many reminders here of the hurt I had caused him and myself. Waking up, I decided that all the furniture would be sold. The day before, I had put the basics like the bed, couch and dining table on the "to take" list, thinking I would get a mover to bring the bigger items. Now, I never wanted to see them again.

Ben and I had chatted on this couch. I could still picture him cuddling his knees to his chest as we contemplated the world and its craziness. This lounge still held his lingering laugh, and this would take more than sage smoke to erase. The fridge is the one he filled with fresh food, encouraging me to eat healthier. The dining table was where we had our last supper and where I had sat upon him and started to kiss him. These memories were too painful to carry with me, so the possessions that held them would be disposed of. I did love my bed, but I had once wished to share it with Ben, so I now considered it sullied. It all went up for sale.

While waiting for the groceries, art supplies and packing materials, I sketched. Not in the book Bev gave me. That was far too good to use yet. I found a good exercise class and did that, too, and found a meditation one to try that afternoon. The groceries came to save some boredom, as did the bags and boxes. I loaded up all the charity stuff and took it to the drop-off point, so pleased that this big job had been done. I was so tempted to look in the shop. Mum loved second-hand shops, believing one man's trash was another man's treasure. It was funny that this was what I had been thinking about yesterday when it came to nuts and cats. But I did not want to be tempted. I was trying to get rid of stuff, not collect more, so I just went home.

It felt so good to get rid of stuff, and seeing the empty space where all those wares had been so satisfying. The rest of the day was spent messaging back and forward to potential buyers and making arrangements for payment and pickup of all my items. This administration was tedious and exhausting but for a good end. The bed would be collected in a few days, so I ordered a blow-up mattress online. This would have to do until I could get settled elsewhere. Given that I would not be seeking any romantic interludes in the interim, it would be a suitable solution.

The next week, I put the final pieces in place to dismantle my life in the city and create another out west. The meeting with the doctor went well, nothing different, but an important chance to reinforce the pathway forward. I needed reminders when I was alone, so I made a list of the key points to put on the wall. These were placed on post-it notes with the words "stop", "self-compassion", "meds", "eyes on the doc" and "what would Frida do?" visible from every key vantage point.

The DBT counsellor was lovely, and I could see how this treatment was so well targeted to the difficulties I was experiencing. The first class, though, was horrific. It was a group session, and we all had to sit in a circle and share. I hated group work, and being able to be seen in this circle was extremely uncomfortable. I was glad that the next one would be online so I could avoid eye contact. I know that the sessions were meant to help us reduce our distress, but they seemed to only add to mine. I heard how others were struggling with their career and relationships, and this only made me despair for mine even more. I know the aim was to make us feel like we were not alone, but I walked away, only feeling more anxious. Although I did get a clearer understanding of the causes of my condition and began feeling less of a freak and more like a fruit that had been planted in faulty soil. It was now up to me to find the right place to grow.

Thanks to my superior organisation skills, I was ready to move a week early. I was living with only the essentials, spending my days doing the DBT homework, online classes and making my mandala. While there were things to do, it felt so weird. Here, again, was the sense that another show was about to begin. It was like the actors were waiting behind the curtain; the audience was seated and silent, too afraid to start a conversation because at any moment the curtains could open.

This sense of suspense and abeyance accompanied me through all of the activities and had me postponing starting anything too serious. I wanted to work on a large-form, painted mandala but found myself "saving" this for mum's place. I wanted to start a language class but thought it best to wait until I was settled. I spent the last few days in this apartment meddling around the middle, making stuff but nothing too meaningful, investing only what was necessary and saving the significant for my new space.

Four hours. Four hours was all it would take to traverse a distance that had not been covered in over a decade. As I headed out of my building for the last time, my car laden with the starting kit for the next six months, I knew that what I was doing was heavy, even if I could not feel it fully.

Soon, soaring skyscrapers were replaced with roadhouses and bustling streets with broad meadows. The up of the mountain to the panoramic views was followed by the descent into the valleys and plains. All along the way, I was making note of the shifting colours, from the cement of the city to the golds of the crops, from the corporate blues to the leafy hues. Ben had often asked me to come to the mountains with him, but I was always too busy. Maybe now was the time I got to play explorer.

Coming into the town, my stomach started cramping, and I hid behind the sun visor, hoping I didn't see anyone I knew. The last thing I wanted was some school reunion ruining my plans. By the time I reached the suburbs, I had second thoughts. Was this really the best idea? Then, driving down mum's street, I knew I was stupid. There was nothing here. This was not romantic it was absurd.

Then, pulling up in front of the house, I felt like I had finally made it home. Seeing this place, all of my doubts disappeared. They were drowned out by the memories of me and mum sitting on the front porch, watching the trains and laughing about her love of romance films.

The white metal archway was still above the front gate, although it was now missing the red flowers that mum had grown through it. The bare bum of the fountain cherub was still there, bold and brave but needing some brightening. The garden was bland and brown, largely dead, I guessed from the years of drought. The house itself looked old and tired and in definite need of a touch-up, just like the real estate agent who walked forward to greet me.

His welcome was polite, but I could tell he was perturbed. I felt sorry for him losing income from this property. Still, he may have it back in six months.

We walked through the house, and he highlighted the repairs that needed to be done. None were urgent, but it would be recommended to address them early. He summarised them on a list he left on the kitchen bench, and then, with a nice farewell, he left me alone.

I went into the backyard, brown and bare except for a clothesline and chicken coop. Mum said she would get some chickens one day but never got around to it. I stood still and breathed in this air. And I listened. It was so quiet. A few cars were cruising in the distance, but otherwise, all I could hear was the spontaneous songs of the birds and the constant buzzing of the cicadas. I could feel my body billowing with my breath and my feet solid on the earth. This is exactly where I needed to be.

But there was so much to be done. I brought in everything from the car, made up my blow-up bed, packed away the kitchen stuff and set up my art supplies. The cupboard was tiny, so I was glad I didn't bring many clothes. The summer ones just fitted in. The winters would need to stay in suitcases for a while, along with the dildos. I would not yet dare to put them in my drawers, feeling that they were slightly disrespectful. The fridge that came with the house was old but clean and ready to be stocked so I took the shopping list and headed out.

My first stop was the furniture shop, where the manager was very complimentary of my choice of couch, bed, and table. He knew exactly what I meant when I said simple yet stylish. The order was completed quickly and would be delivered in a few days. I left with a microwave, though, knowing this might be needed sooner. I popped into the paint shop and collected a whole set of coloured cards, excited to put together ideas for revamping the walls.

The art shop was small, but I was on a mission to see what they had and to check their prices. The lady who greeted me was lovely, and her child, who was drawing in the corner, was so cute. I did not go in there to chat, but I ended up talking about canvases and a tube of coloured paint I had not seen before. She brought out her ordering book, and a new world exploded before me. There were metallics and matts, satins, and sprays.

"I only get a few special ones to keep in the store, but I can get anything you need. Grab a seat and take your time."

While I was looking through the book, the little girl ran up to me. I was not used to children and felt a little uncomfortable.

"Hello. I'm Mandy. What's your name?"

"I'm Nora. Pleased to meet you, Mandy."

"I'm special needs."

Mandy's mum shot me a look that said sorry for the intrusion.

"That's because you are a very special girl."

I was a little shocked when she slammed her body into mine and whacked her arms around my head to hug it tight.

Her mum came to sit on the seat next to me, pulling Mandy away and cuddling the little girl into her side."

"Thankyou. I am sorry, I have not introduced myself. I'm Sam."

"Hi Sam, I'm Nora, but you knew that already!"

We shared a chuckle.

"Sorry about Mandy. I am trying to find her a school that will suit her but there's not many options out here."

"Please don't apologise. She is really cute, and I can see from her drawings, very creative."

"She sure is. Speaking of which, we do have classes here too. I get different local artists from time to time. Here is the schedule for the next few months."

She went and grabbed a brochure off the counter.

"Thanks Sam. I am just getting started though, just setting myself up at the moment."

"Well, the offer is always open! Tell me, do you have something to set your work up on yet?"

"Oh no, I just moved in. Your right, I don't even have a table yet. I guess I will just do it on the floor. Oh, of course, I am going to need some plastic sheeting."

"The reason I ask is that a friend dropped in her own easel last week and asked me to sell it for her. It is an awesome one and would set you back way less than buying something new. Sure, it has some paint on it, but I consider that simply more inspiration."

We went out the back to look at it, and Sam was right. It was sturdy, like a supportive friend, yet just a little bit fancy too, with gold nobs, decorative clips and laced in bright colours.

"You are a wonderful saleswoman, Sam. I'll take it."

Mandy had followed us in, and with those words, she started jumping up and down.

"Yay! Sold! Sold!"

She dived in and gave me another hug.

There we stood, two women and one wonderous girl, all smiling.

The smile remained while I shopped and was still there as I packed all the groceries in the aging cupboards. It had receded only a little by the time I set up the easel.

Then I sat on the floor with a cup of tea and stared at the walls. The smile slipped away, replaced with a sense of weightiness.

What do I do now?

Work, of course. There was so much to do if I was to do this house justice and make it a true testament to mum's memory. I started prioritising the list of repairs, choosing a colour for the wall paint and researching DIY kitchen makeovers. It was well past dinner time when I finished the plan for the garden and the list of soils and supplements I would need to bring it back to life. After a quick baked beans on toast, I lay on my bed of air and wrote down what I was grateful for this first day. There was no struggle with this; there were several things. The space, the work to be done, the art supplies store and my blow-up bed.

Chapter 16

I did not set an alarm for the morning, nor did I need to. Behind the concrete and thick glass of the city buildings I never got to hear the birds. This morning, I was blasted with a cacophony of crows, the piercing call of the currawongs, the melody of the magpies and a symphony of smaller tweets and chirps that I could not identify. There were spontaneous strident screeches of the cockatoos, so confident in their call. Had I heard this chaos all those years ago when I was here mourning my mother? I do not remember, for I was far too deep down in my heartache to hear anything else. What would Bev do right now, I wondered? She would listen, and so listen I did. There was nothing more urgent, so I lay and listened, seeking some understanding of the meaning behind the music and attempting to find patterns to placate my need for order. Of course, there were none, and I admonished myself for my arrogance in thinking I could analyse these creatures.

After a quick breakfast it was straight to the nursery to gather soil, mulch, fertiliser, gloves, shovels and edging for the two spots in the garden I had picked to prepare first. The back was where the vegetables would be; the front would be for flowers. I had to work quickly before it got too hot. It was still only spring, but it felt like it would be a scorcher. Gone were the consistent climates of airconditioned buildings. Here, I would be at the whim of the weather, but it was exactly what I wanted.

By lunchtime there were two neat, tidy and nutrient-rich sections of soil, watered, bordered and ready for stage two. I had also earmarked the place for the compost heap and, while cooling down, researched what I could put in it. Lunch was lots of greens and proteins, adhering to the commitments I had made in my discharge plan, and which I had followed rigorously every day.

The afternoon was earmarked for inside jobs. I organised the roof repairs, found a plumber to fix the leaks and the seals and an electrician who could source and install a new stove. Then, there was the wall paint to decide upon. That came easily; it would be white, knowing that there were all the colours I needed within it and that, like this place, it was a new canvas. The door though, the door needed to be green. Why? This is where the light and the love would come in. This is where I would find my wings.

But what would I do with the floors? The carpet was old and downright depressing. Pulling up a corner I could see the floorboards seemed sound. It would be wonderful to have just polished boards. I knew it was impractical for the cold winters, but that could be overcome with Ugg boots and beautiful rugs, like the warm softness I felt on the dragon's chest. I found a floor man and he would be out the next day to prepare a quote. Easy.

It was only when I stopped for afternoon coffee did I cry. Sitting on the front step, where mum and I would watch the trains, I could not stop sobbing. Tears fell for every triumph and tragedy of the past thirty-seven years, for all that I had achieved, and all those things I had to let go of. They flowed for my fears of being faulty and the uncertainty of my future. And I wept for my mother and the lack of memorial that I had made for her. This would be it. This home would be her honour. But she needed more. I went to the suitcase and dug under the jackets to pull out my photo of mum. I had taken it a few months before she died, sitting where I had just been, watching the afternoon sun, sipping her tea, and sharing a scone. She was already suffering from the cancer and the chemo. Yet, her eyes were still sparkling, and the scarf around her head was a beautiful bright white like a halo. Why had I resisted bringing this out before now? Was it that I was still in denial at her death. Could this still be the case a decade later? Or was I wallowing, comfortable with my crutch of victim – the poor orphan girl who needed a partner to care for her. Mum would never allow this self-pity, so I placed her photo on the mantlepiece. With this I was not only answerable to myself, but to this very special and first compassionate friend.

I had to compose myself for the DBT session, which was helpful. Distressing emotions were the day's topic, and it provided wonderful guidance for what I could do to help me work through the remainder of this crisis and the ones that I knew would come next. I did pride myself on how well I was at distraction. This was definitely my strength. I still needed a lot of practice with the self-compassion part.

Dinner was a simple vegetable stew, but the smell of the spices stirred my spirits, and after eating, I felt exhausted but more at ease. Now, I would plan my art projects. Looking at the coloured chakras Bev had given me; the schedule became clear. I would work with one colour a month, using this to guide my work around the house and the massive mandala I was wanting to do. Each layer of the mandala would have a microcosm painted on its own canvas and then join the rest on one large painting. I would use the smaller ones to perfect the patterns and place them on the larger picture. That was my plan. I knew it sounded stupid, a colour a month. But I needed structure, and this plan was simple enough, yet allowed so much scope.

There were only two days until November, so I would begin then. I listed the red I would bring into my life over the next few weeks. I would plant tomatoes, chillis and capsicum in the back garden and put grevilleas, hibiscus and azaleas in the front. I would include red metallics in the middle of my mandala and make it feel solid, supportive, sturdy and secure. At the end of each month, I would make a plan for the next, and so I had my next six months of creativity mapped out.

Mandy was so excited to see me when I entered the shop again. Her little legs raced toward me, her arms wrapped around my legs and her head buried into my thighs. This one precious child just held so much positive energy. Sam was impressed when I asked about red metallics, wanting to know what I was working on. When I first entered this place, I thought my art would be my personal project and not something I would share. Yet it was so easy to talk to Sam, and she had great advice about techniques to use with the paint to get the effect I was looking for.

"Nora, I can't wait to see how it turns out. Will you take some pictures and show me?"

I would have preferred not to. Honestly, I was petrified of judgement.

"Sure. It might take me a while though."

I thought that this proviso gave me enough time to let her forget the request so I may not have to follow through on my promise.

"You know some of these classes might be really good for you too, if you are interested."

"Thanks, Sam, just not quite yet."

"Well, I hope you don't mind if I just keep asking."

"Of course not, Sam. Thank you for thinking of me."

And ask she did. Every time I went into the store, she mentioned them again. Not in an annoying way, more like she was checking in with whether I was ready to come out of my shell and socialise. When I went in for shades of orange and some more linseed oil, we chatted, and it was clear that she did care for me more than just a potential source of cash. I did not want to get close to anyone, yet Sam and Mandy made my day every time I saw them. I felt special, I felt safe. She asked me what I was planting that month, and we discussed how to care for my carrot, sweet potato and pumpkin plants. I promised that I would bring her soup made from my crop in the winter, unwilling to admit that I may not be here by then. She asked what flowers I had chosen, and we chatted about birds of paradise, ixora and kangaroo paws. The weather had heated up significantly, so I asked her where it was good to swim, and she directed me to the best local pool.

"Much less kiddies piss in this one.", she declared.

"Mummy swore, Mummy swore!" said Mandy, literally making a song and dance about it. She was such a dear girl and gave great hugs.

January came, and I was back to get yellows, golds, and more good brushes.

"Do you have any pictures of your paintings yet?"

Damn, I thought she might have forgotten.

"Not yet. But I will."

"I want to see your pictures, Nora," Mandy said, stamping her foot to show the force of her demand.

"Ok Mandy, I promise."

"Yay, Yay, Yay!" she said, leaping around.

The deal was done, and I would bring some next month. Besides, I was really happy with how the red and orange had turned out. Maybe I would like someone to see them after all.

Then came conversations about the lemonade we would make with my crop once the trees had grown and the bouquets of Portulaca and Rudbeckia I would bring in. I was getting quite proficient with my plant names, and Sam was very impressed. I was also impressed with how fit I was becoming. I was swimming every second day, and my arms and legs looked very athletic. I would show mum's picture my biceps, and I could hear her respond, "Bravo!"

All the repairs were done by February, and I had beautiful new furniture, kitchen cupboards and polished floors. I did not have any guests, but if I did, they would be greeted by a deep green door with a bold black circular knocker. I had not dreamed of my dragon for months. Maybe it was the meds finally kicking in, or perhaps it was that each day, I felt more sure that the dragon was alive and well within me. The roof was renovated, so it no longer leaked when it rained. And it was repainted, as were the walls. I was surrounded by brilliant white, which I will admit was a bit bright when the strong sun hit it, but then, I needed all the brightness I could get. For in February, the hounding had begun.

I was four months into my six-month leave. The green leafy level of the mandala was coming along well, and the green capsicums and Asian leafies were planted. There was so much foliage on the flowers out the front that no extra green was needed. This was also when my boss, via HR, started to send regular messages, wanting to know what my plan was. Would I be coming back, and if so, in what capacity? Or would I be taking more time off? They needed to know for their resourcing schedules and, at first, asked nicely. Then, when I responded that I had not yet decided, they became spiteful. Surely, I knew I was being very inconsiderate? They may need to send me for an independent assessment. They might insist I take more sick leave if required, without pay. They needed an answer by next week, or they would take matters into their own hands. Of course, I would understand that this is reasonable, given their need to manage complex resources.

Take matters into their own hands? I think I knew what that meant – medical redundancy. They were not beyond using this trick to push people out. They did not want weak people who could not be relied upon, so they employed "reasonable management" policies and biased assessors to show they could not fulfil their duties. Then, the person had two choices. Jump or be pushed. A few years ago, one man I knew made the decision to jump, literally, from the top of the office building.

Before this breakdown got too far, I had stuck my head in an ice bucket. It helped. Calling on my compassionate friends also helped. I would distract myself and let the extreme emotions subside. This would be best dealt with when I was calmer. I don't know what made me head straight to the art shop. I could have survived a bit longer without any more green paint, but I knew this was not the point.

"Nora, sorry for saying this, but you look horrible. Are you OK?"

"Oh Sam, not really. I think I have to go back."

"To where?"

Over tea, I told her the backstory. She only interrupted periodically to say, "Those bastards."

Mandy had come over a minute in and sat on my lap, her head cuddled into my chest. With this, suddenly, it all didn't feel so bad. What was it about the touch of another that could settle the greatest storm?

"Do you know what you are going to do yet? I mean, you can't leave, you haven't even showed me your paintings yet."

We both smiled, mine quite a bit smaller than hers.

"I just thought I would have time, but it just doesn't feel enough."

"Could I make a suggestion?"

"Yes please."

"Go and see my GP. She is fantastic and I know she will find a way to help you. I think between her and your psych you can manage these guys. Just don't try and do it alone. I came from the corporate world too, many years ago, and I know that these guys are cruel, and cowards. Don't let them push you around, Nora. I'll get the doctor's number for you."

Mandy and I chatted about her favourite colours while Sam scavenged through her handbag for a business card.

"Here you go. Give her a call OK. Promise?"

"Promise."

"Actually, I have a better idea, let's do it now."

Sam took the card back to the phone and dialled the number. Within a minute, she looked at me and asked if I could do 1 p.m. the next day. I nodded.

"Excellent!" she said as she put down the phone. "I can't wait to hear what you think of her."

"Ask her now, Mummy, ask her!". Mandy's began some very loud begging that was matched with bobbing, causing my whole body to bounce along with her.

"Ask me what?"

"Oh, I'm sorry, Nora. Now is not a good time for you. I don't want to impose."

"Nonsense, I need another distraction to keep me going until tomorrow's appointment. What do you want?"

"I have a wedding in the city in two weeks, and I can't find anyone available to take care of Mandy. Really, I don't expect you to at all, but I was wondering if you might be available to come and stay with her for the weekend?"

A part of me wanted to say no, to show that I was unreliable. But Sam had helped me so much that it was the least I could do. I decided not to express my concerns about my lack of capability with children, especially one with special needs, but surely, I could return the favour and do this for her.

"I would love to."

"Thank you, Nora," Sam said. "How about we swap numbers, and I will send you the details?"

"Yay, Yay, Yay!" said Mandy and bobbed some more. I swore my legs would end up bruised from her bony butt, yet there was no way I wanted to stop her. I thought about all the times my father told me to settle down when I was too happy, too excited, too scared or too sad. I would not impose the same injury on this precious spirit.

I grabbed some beautiful new greens, again rejected her request to join the art classes, and went home to get lost in some leaves. Before bed, I started feeling bad again, so I did one of the loving kindness meditations they had recommended in the hospital. I went to sleep sad but soothed, and for this, I was grateful.

The doctor was all Sam had said and more. I took her my previous paperwork, explained the situation, and she knew exactly what to do. She agreed that there would be a day when I had to make a decision but that, as of yet, I was not in a position to do this well. I was to leave it with her and come back in two days. When I did, she had spoken to Dr Dempsey and completed the paperwork to extend my leave for another three months. I would now have more time to finish the DBT sessions and make sure I was strong enough to deal with the stress that would be awaiting me.

I mentioned the possibility of going off my meds, to which she responded, "Don't be ridiculous", and gave me another prescription. She booked in weekly catchups for the next little while and offered me a jellybean.

"Sorry, I have eaten all the black ones already."

"With all due respect, doctor. You are a weirdo."

"Ha! That's what they all say."

Grabbing a few green ones, I started to head out.

"Oh, I almost forgot. Dr Dempsey says to say hello and that he hopes you are liking the socks! What's that all about?"

"Dr Dempsey seems to have a sock fetish."

"And you think I'm a weirdo? Bye, Nora. See you next week!"

I saw March in by sending a letter back to HR and my boss advising them of the extension and sending that the insurance would be in touch. March was the month of blue. Blue, the colour of the throat chakra and communication. Perhaps I should use my assertive communication skills to make it clear that I did not appreciate their tone or their threats.

What would mum do?

She surely wouldn't waste such energy on those who would use it against me. Instead, the message was kept short, sharp, and simple. Now, I could return to my regular rhythm: swimming, shopping, gardening, painting, reading, DBT sessions, and cooking awesome dinners. It did feel like there was starting to be some space for something different. I just had no idea what yet.

The blue beards, agapanthus and flax lilies were all planted, and I was well on my way with the blue layer of my mandala when it was time to spend the weekend with Mandy. Their house was on the other side of town but looked like mum's. I soon realised that the similarities ended on the outside. Inside was a colourful chaos; a house strewn with art supplies and children's toys but framed with fantastic fabrics. The curtains, the rugs, the wall hangings, the tablecloth, and the sofa throws made me feel like I had arrived in a beautiful bohemian bedroom. They immediately wrapped me in warmth and made me feel like I wanted to explore more. Sam showed me around, with Mandy in tow, adding her important details to the descriptions of her mother. We ran through the menu for the next few days, bedtimes, favourite activities, the things that cause anxiety and what to do if she had a panic attack. I was well out of my comfort zone though, so I was sure not going to take her out of hers.

While we sat and had tea, Sam had something more to ask.

"Nora, you know a lot about business, right?"

"A bit, yes, why?"

"Well, the shop is doing well, and the classes especially. It's just really cramped in there. I'm thinking of getting a loan to move to a bigger space, but the bank needs a business plan to support it. Do you know anything about business plans?"

"Absolutely. There might also be some government grants out there too that might work. That way you don't have to take on the burden of too much debt."

"Oh, Nora, that would be so wonderful. Do you think we could spend some time on this when I get back?"

"For sure. I would be really glad to be able to help. In the meantime, I will do a bit of research and see what I can find."

Sam gave me a hug and then went to give one to Mandy. It was time for her to leave. Mandy held my hand as we waved Sam goodbye, and then we were on our own. We spent the rest of the day walking and gathering supplies for a nature collage; Mandy's idea. We baked brownies, Mandy's idea. Ordered pizza for dinner, Mandy's idea. And then sat and watched some movies; again, Mandy's idea. I didn't have to do anything except facilitate her desired agenda. She was such wonderful company. So curious, so clever, so cuddly. It was over six years since I had watched an animated film, the Lorax, with Calli, and I was enchanted with the ones Mandy chose. We started with Frozen, and I laughed with Mandy as she sang, "Let it go." There was only time for one more before bedtime, and she chose Tangled. Right there in front of me was a cute, confident, caring and cheeky chameleon. I was captivated and spent the show scanning for it, spying on it and assessing its actions.

"I love that lizard.", said Mandy after it gave the intruder a wet willy.

"It's actually called a chameleon, and it has a very special skill of being able to change colour."

"Then I love that chameleon."

"You know, Mandy. I am actually a chameleon."

"Really?"

"Really."

"Then you are special too."

There it was. The one thing I needed to hear. How much I had wanted to be like this gorgeous child, and she had, with those words, invited me into her world.

Mandy wanted to sleep in her mum's bed. She missed her already, so we cuddled together until she fell asleep, and then so did I. I awoke to Mandy tracing lines on my forehead.

"You're getting crinkles, Nora."

There was no way I was going to correct her. Thinking of my face like a potato chip was far too funny. The day was wet, but Mandy did not seem to care. There was still so much to do. We went outside, jumped in puddles, made pancakes for breakfast, painted rainy-day scenes, and then watched movies. We were almost about to have a nap on the lounge when Sam arrived home. She was very weary after a late night and a slow, grey, wet drive home. She plonked on the lounge, cuddled up with Mandy, and started a conversation, which came to an abrupt conclusion when she fell asleep, and then Mandy did too. There was nothing to do except join them, so I parked myself on the recliner and rested my eyelids.

When we all roused, it was dinner time, so Sam and I set about making a simple vegetable pasta. After the clean-up, it was time for me to go, with the promise that I would head to the shop the next day to advance the finance plans.

April saw the planting of passion fruits, society garlic, brachycomes and delospermas. It saw the weekly checkups with the doctor spread out to fortnightly, along with the feeling that I had found my footing. And it saw the first submissions of the small business grant to fund the art shop expansion. We would know within a month if it was successful. But we also had a Plan B, with the business case ready to prove to the bank that her vision was sustainable.

When she mentioned that I was good at this and so many other small businesses needed help, it sparked an idea. There could be another source of income I had not thought of. That night, I went home and set up my own business. I wanted to call it Chameleon Consulting, but that did not seem the right thing to do; a tad too childish, and probably confusing for the clients. Instead, it simply became Nora Jones Consulting. I set up my profile on some outsourcing sites and would start exploring the world of freelancing. This month also saw me spending more time with Sam and Mandy, and I suspected I was getting close to accepting the offer of joining a class. They came around to my place to see the paintings in person, and Sam said she was blown away. She begged me to consider translating this experience into a class I could offer at her store. It sounded like a wonderful idea, and I promised I would think about it.

May was white month, and I only had the edges of my mandala to finish, and the black borders between layers to represent the letting go required to move outward, but also to let love in. Its near completion was timely, given I had picked up a substantial freelancing project, preparing strategic management training materials for a client in Saudi Arabia. There was a whole new world out there that I was unaware of, full of variety, energy and purpose-driven people. It was also full of cheapskates who didn't want to pay for the value they were receiving, but I could weed these out pretty quickly. On the weekends I planted cabbage, cauliflower, pansies and impatiens. Now, the garden was complete. Not all the plants had survived, but a significant amount had. I was becoming more confident in my caring ability; it was time to consider a cat.

First, though, I had to work through the taunting and teasing from my boss that came via HR. There were now less than eight weeks until my return, and they seemed intent on tainting every remaining moment. Before coming back, I would be required to undertake a medical assessment by a specialist to be assigned by them. Only once this had been completed, with a positive result, would I be able to assume my duties.

The next day, a follow-up asked me to confirm receipt and recognition of their previous message.

The day after, another message asked me to advise them of my availability in the second week of June.

The day after that, another message provided the timeline of events between now and mid-July.

To round out the week, I got one more email from my boss telling me that they are incredibly busy and that he looks forward to my return.

Between distracting myself with delivering on freelancing deadlines, the remainder of the month was spent caring for my distressing emotions and continuously consulting with my compassionate friends. By the end of it, I had decided to resign. One part of me didn't want to. I didn't want to let them think they had won. But the doctor was right. My health was more important; if I cared for that, I would be the real winner.

June was the month of brown, an addition to my schedule and not shown on any of the chakra charts, but a colour I thought needed celebrating. Stability, security, and a sense of dependability were exactly what I needed beside me as I sent my resignation letter. When this period of income protection ceased, I would no longer be employed. I provided my bank details for any entitlement payouts and wished them all well.

Then I went and sat in the chilly garden, on the ground and cried. It was over. It was all over. As I felt a bitter breeze on my face, I realised that now I could be here fully. I could commit to this place. I could live here and not feel like I was holding the fort for a future tenant. This was the home I had been looking for. All the work I had done to date was so significant and even spiritual, but now I could settle with certainty and let my soul sink into it. Sure, the freelancing work was not bringing in anywhere near the income I used to make, but here, I only needed a little, and I still had substantial savings. I went inside, made tea and sat beside mum's photo.

"I'm home now mum, I'm really home."

June was also the month that the business grant was approved, and I started helping Mandy move to bigger premises. I also cancelled the DBT classes. I could not continue to afford them without my professional income. This place would be my therapy. I had all the support I needed right here.

Sam had spread the word amongst her business peers about my planning abilities, so I had also scored some work with other owner-operators in the area. My days were full, but with the change of seasons, very dark. It was too cold to swim, and when Sam mentioned a friend had set up a hot yoga class, I had to concede defeat. It actually sounded like heaven. Sunday morning was spent sweating, followed by chai and chats with a bunch of ladies at the café next door. Mandy would wait in the foyer and fall on my lap when we sat down for chai, counselling me about what kind of cat I should get.

We were both surprised one day when the owner came out with a cake lit by sparkly candles. I thought it must have been someone's birthday, but Sam announced it was for me. It was to celebrate my staying, and everyone gave applause. Mandy helped me wipe away the tears and insisted on feeding me some of the cake with a fork.

"For my special friend, Nora."

In July, the colour was to be grey. Sam, Mandy and I went to the shops and got everything I would need for a kitten. Then we went to the breeder and picked up my Russian Blue. She was so gorgeous; grey, but not the dark and brooding shade of the winter sky, but a bright one that hinted at mischief. Her eyes were iridescent green, ringed with gold, making it seem like she had knowledge beyond her few months and tiny frame. She was so helpless, and I was afraid Mandy might crush her. Still, the child was so careful, and the kitten so calm, only mewing intermittently as we drove her home. Mandy wanted me to call her Pascal, after the cartoon chameleon, but it sounded a bit too harsh for something so heavenly. So, Layla it was, LayLay to Mandy.

With my mandalas completed, July was time to start my next project. It was to be my dragon. It took me days to decide how to do such a complex character justice, but with Layla on my lap each evening, it came together. It would take a long time, though, as most of my days were now full of freelance consulting work, with special white space dedicated for visits to Sam's new shop. Mandy was in school so I timed my visits in the afternoon to make sure she was there. I heard how she was enjoying meeting new kids and learning so many fantastic things. She did not like the boys, though; they were bullies, except for one who was nice but was allergic to nuts.

August was pink month. I was not sure why. I just felt like it was such an important colour but was not given the credit it deserved. So pink was woven into the dragon's scales, and places were found in the front garden for daphne's, hellebores and camellias. My days were now dedicated to my consulting work and my nights to painting. Weekends were for gardening, Sam and Mandy, more painting and making meals for the week. This felt meaningful. This felt exactly where I was meant to be.

Then came September and my birthday. I had shown I could care for a garden, an independent consulting career and a cat. Maybe now was the time to consider a child. I really needed to get cracking. I was about to turn thirty-eight, and the clock was ticking. Did I have to have one of my own, though? Maybe I could foster or adopt? I had felt the specialness of being with Mandy, and I just might make a good mother. Sam agreed as she served up the special takeaway dinner she had brought over to my place, and Mandy made me unwrap the ten presents she had made me. Sam encouraged me to drink too much champagne, so by the time they left, I was full of Thai stir fry, Italian chocolate cake and Dutch courage. I figured I deserved some delight, so I pulled out the dildos. It really was the takeaway version of sex; all over in a few minutes and not often completely satisfying. There was some more champagne left, which I consumed while checking out some dating sites. What the hell. It had been almost a year. I had put myself in a really good position, maybe it was time to find a partner and move forward with the plans for children.

There were very slim pickings around this area, but I finally found a guy who was close and quite good-looking. He was a few years older than me, but he was a widower with a child. This could be my Sleepless in Seattle, for real this time — just a rural version.

THE LOVE LIFE OF A CHAMELEON

Chapter 17

Brad was waiting eagerly at the café already when I arrived. After a polite kiss on the cheek and some nervous introductions, we were away, talking about what we were looking for and our success on the site so far. While I had just started, Brad had been on there for a while. He had not found anyone suitable yet, for as he told me, he was a loyal man, and most of the women only wanted a root. I found this admirable, but it also made me anxious. We both agreed it would be wonderful to have someone to cuddle, to know and be supported by. He said excitedly that we were obviously on the same page and looking for the same thing. I thought this was a shallow assumption, but I didn't want to burst his bubble. He seemed very excited, and I would feel so bad bringing him down. I asked about his history, and we walked through his upbringing in a town an hour away, how he had come here for work, lost his wife and was now raising his son alone. He asked how long I had lived here, and I told him I had only been here a few months. He did not ask for any further follow up.

He asked me what I did for a living, and I explained my consultancy. He said, "Cool," but he did not continue to investigate further.

He asked me what I did on the weekends, and I told him I painted. That was great, he said, and stopped with that.

There was no what, no why, no wanting to find out more about me. Maybe he was just nervous.

He, of course, was busy on the weekends with his son and housework, but he was willing to make time for the right woman.

He showed me a picture of his son, a cute four-year-old just a bit younger than Mandy.

"He needs lots of love and attention."

I could not help but think he was talking about himself.

It did not take long for the conversation to turn to sex. There was something Brad had to tell me. He was a Dom and knew that this scared some women. What did I think? I was honest and told him I had previously enjoyed the role of a sub. Would I like to replay, to see if there was a spark? Sure. Saturday night was booked in. His son would be at a sleepover, so I would meet him at his place. There were texts regularly over the next few days, telling me that he couldn't wait to see me, that he thought I was beautiful, and that he couldn't wait to show me his toys. Why was I not finding this thrilling? And why was I planning on going through with it?

Maybe, just maybe, this might be the one. And I would never know if I didn't try. My compassionate friends suggested I steer clear of this guy, but I was willing to give him a chance. It was not as if there was much other choice out here in the country. I left little Layla with her favourite toys and the promise that I would be back soon and set out for what I thought would be a romantic rendezvous.

However, my role as submissive started as soon as I walked in.

His excitement to see me was followed by a hard, hot kiss, and then he asked, "Are you ready, Nora?"

Right then, I realised I should have given Sam this guy's address or at least alerted her to the fact that I was going on a date. We never discussed our romantic life, so it just never came up. But now, I began chastising myself for my stupidity. Still, phone records would be held somewhere, so if it all went to hell, he would be caught.

Brad ordered me to strip.

"Oh, you are beautiful, Nora." I could not deny that these words made me feel warm and wanted.

He fondled my breasts and kissed my lips.

"Kneel."

I knelt.

"Spread your legs."

I opened my legs.

Brad licked his fingers, bent down and ran his fingers gently around, then thrust his fingers inside.

I gasped, both out of shock and pain. That made him smile. Taking his fingers out, he put them in my mouth.

"Do you like the taste of yourself, Nora?"

I nodded. I never did, but it was always what they wanted to hear.

Then he kissed me.

"I like the taste of you, Nora. Now it is time for you to taste me."

He pulled down his shorts and sat in front of me.

"Suck me, Nora."

And I did.

"Oh my god. You are brilliant."

Again, I could not deny that I found this anything but enjoyable. I had come a long way from my first clumsy lessons with dad's friend, and now with my confidence came a sense of control and absolute achievement when I made him cum.

"Clean me up."

I did.

Then he placed a collar around my neck and a blindfold across my eyes. He helped me up and led me to his bedroom."

"Now the real fun begins."

He tied the ropes tight, securing each arm to the shin on the same side. My genitals and my breasts were laid bare. He scratched around my anus, saying:

"We will save this for next time, when I can prepare you properly."

I felt a wave of relief. There would be a next time, which meant I would make it out alive.

"Stick out your tongue."

I did, and he sucked it.

"Keep it out."

I did, and he put a gag over the top, which had a hole for whatever he wanted to shove down my throat. He was right. He did have quite a collection of toys.

"Now Nora, let's go through your safe words. When I ask, you will tell me green, orange or red. Green I will go harder. Orange I will go harder, and don't you dare use red. If you do, I won't stop, I will only back off until the session is complete. Got it."

I got it. I knew how this worked, so I nodded.

I had forgotten how much the whipping hurt. It had been two years since I had felt the sting from Stephen's toys, and this guy was serious. The beating on the breast was bearable, but on the vagina was excruciating. My wail was real, and so was the recoil of my legs and the attempt to cover it from further cruelty. In between strikes, Brad would lick the red-hot skin. I thought he actually cared until I remembered Stephen would use this trick too; it would make the next lash hurt even more.

When the final ten-count came, I knew I could make it through. The rope burns that came with the untying made it clear that he was either unskilled or negligent. Still, he knew how to hold me afterwards and to tell me I was a good girl. Despite the punishment he had doled on me, this made me feel special. It always did when Stephen said it too. I wanted to be Stephen's good girl then, just like I wanted to be Brad's good girl now. When Brad asked me whose slut I was, I told him.

"I am your slut, Sir."

When Brad asked me who owned my body, I answered, "You own me, Sir."

And when he asked me what I wanted to say to him, I said,

"Thank you, Sir."

"Good girl. We will get on very well."

Then he rolled me over on my stomach, told me to get on my knees, and he fucked me hard, squirting his cum all over my back and rubbing it into my butt, and then whipping it as well. Not for long, though; he was spent after his orgasm, and so we cuddled some more.

"You are awesome, Nora. I really enjoyed that."

"Me too.", I said.

Liar. I knew I was lying, but I said it anyway.

It was not long before Brad fell asleep. I quietly got dressed and scribbled a note saying I was sorry I had to go and hoped he had a great sleep.

"See you soon." It said at the bottom with a smiley face.

"You make me sick, Nora. You liar." That's what one side of my head was saying. The other replied:

"But I am just being nice."

It was when I was back home with Layla, cuddling with her in my bed, feeling her soft fur, and hearing her tiny purr, I decided that this was not what I wanted. This was not what I was willing to do to become a mother. Brad was not the environment that would bring out my best colours. I felt glad that I had tried it, but I was satisfied with my resolve.

The next day a text arrived, with Brad asking me when we could catch up again. My first instinct was to block him, run and hide like I had done so many times before. Bev, though, would be furious, in her funny, frowny kind of way. What was all the assertive communication training for if I was not going to use it? Her voice in my head had a point. Besides, retreat was a perfect option when you did not have the resources to fight. Here, I had the yellow - I had the power; I was in control of my destiny and had all the support I needed to stand up for myself. Team this with the blue of communication and I would achieve the green of love, of self-compassion. This is what I attempted with my reply, which was apologetic but assertive.

"I am sorry Brad. This is not what I want, and I am sorry that I have only let you know now and not earlier. I am not ready for a relationship and don't want to waste your time any further. I wish you all the very best and hope you find what you are looking for."

The next few days were a barrage of messages back and forward. Brad begged, believing that we were great for each other. He belittled me, stating that I was obviously only after sex. He would compliment me and tell me how much he cared for me. He also attempted negotiation, suggesting that we could just meet up once a month for some mature adult time. He was so full of contradictions, so desperate, and, as much as I hated to admit it, so much like me.

What should I do? He had left the door open for ongoing dates, and in a way, he was a bit better than a dildo.

I needed to paint this one out. What appeared was my answer. After hours of standing at the easel, I was exhausted, yet what stood before me was enlightening. The picture was dark and brooding. On the floor was a black leather collar, and the hand above was letting go of a blindfold. Only part of a lady's body was shown—a strip of her back buttock, thighs, and arm, all laced with burning red licks.

Sitting down, I stared at this painting and took in what it told me. I blocked Brad and added "begin art class" to my to-do list. I was grateful that I had never given Brad my address.

THE LOVE LIFE OF A CHAMELEON

Chapter 18

December was here again, and between swimming and yoga, I was feeling really fit and well. I had built up a nice client list for my consulting work and was almost finished my dragon. I did love him so.

When Sam came around one weekend, I mentioned to her I had started scratching out some ideas for an art class. She immediately pulled out her schedule.

"What about February? So far, I have a silversmith in January and a portrait artist in March, so you could go between them? Should we call it making mandalas?"

"Oh, Sam, that is crazy good. Are you sure?"

"Absolutely. But first, we need to put on an exhibition. You know, to show everyone what you can do. This will build up the excitement and get people interested. Would you be OK if I put up your work in the show space next month?"

"Oh gosh. I am not sure, Sam. I don't think it is that good. I really only do it for myself."

"Nonsense. I know art, and this is definitely worth a public showing."

"Ok then, but only if you are sure."

Sam shot me a look that told me to shut up, that the deal was done. Now I just had to concentrate on finishing the dragon in time.

She walked over to the canvas where the black one was stashed.

"Oooh, Nora. This one is new, and so dark. Please explain? Actually, no don't worry, I think I get it. It is really different for you, but truly excellent. You don't mind though if I keep this one away from the window when I put your paintings up in the store?"

"No, Sam, that's fine."

There was no use arguing with her that it should probably not be shown at all. I was just glad it would not be in clear view of the children walking home from school. That would make for some very awkward conversations with their carers.

"Sam, did you say silversmithing?"

"Yes, in January. Are you interested? Nora, could this finally be the first class that you do?"

"Honestly, I have always wanted to try it. So sure, sign me up!"

She ran up and gave me a hug.

"About bloody time! It has only been a year. I was almost getting tired of asking."

It was surreal seeing my paintings hanging up in an open space, and even more overwhelming fielding all the questions on opening night. Where did I learn to paint? Well, I learnt the basics in school, but the rest is self-taught. How long have I been painting for? Seriously, only about a year. What was the motivation behind the mandalas? I really just wanted to express the process of personal growth. Who was my artistic inspiration? Frida Kahlo, not so much in style, but in substance. What would my class be covering? The theory and practice of constructing mandalas. Did I have an art degree? At which I felt very out of my depth. No; there was nothing more to be said. Sam saved me from further interrogation by taking me away to introduce me to someone I had to meet. His name was Jase, and he was the silversmithing teacher.

His brown eyes were simply beautiful. But I successfully covered the sparks with small talk.

"Nora, your paintings are fantastic. And Sam tells me you will be joining my class next week."

"Yes, I am really looking forward to it."

"And I am really looking forward to having you in it. You work so much with circles; I can't wait to see how that translates into the metals for you."

"I actually had not thought about that before."

"Seeing how you weave all these wonderful shapes together; I think you would be a natural at jewellery making. I am always on the lookout for new designs, so maybe we could do some work together?"

"Wow, that is really nice of you, Jase. How about I do the class with you first though. You might change your mind when you see how clumsy I actually am."

"That sounds like a deal. But in the meantime, feel free to start jotting down some ideas. We will be making a ring, earrings and a bracelet, so there will be plenty of scope to try some different things."

"Thanks, Jase. I will. I do have to go now, but next week will be great!"

I caught Sam and said I was leaving, waiting until I got to the car before condemning myself.

"No, Nora. No. No. No. No. No. Just don't do it. You stupid girl."

Then I realised Sam was standing at the window. I rolled it down to be met with a look of concern.

"Nora, are you OK? You left kind of quickly."

"Yeh, just getting a headache, that's all."

"And it had nothing to do with Jase?"

"No, not at all."

"Nora! I know when you are lying."

"OK. Maybe just a bit. I just can't start anything, but I did feel sparks."

"So, you had to run away?"

"No, it was more the headache really."

"Nora. I am not going to let this go. Pop by the shop tomorrow and we will work it through."

"But..."

"No buts. See you tomorrow, gorgeous girl."

And with that she gave me a kiss on the forehead.

"Drive safe," she yelled as she walked away.

Gosh it was great to see Mandy when I made it in the next afternoon. I missed her so much. Between my work and her school there was just not enough time together. Sam made tea, put up the closed sign and started the counselling session. I had stopped in at home and got Layla on the way, so that Mandy could play with her while Sam and I talked. To ease my discomfort, I sat beside Mandy, colouring in with her and watching Layla explore everything on the table.

"Well, let me begin by saying that Jase was very impressed by you, Nora. He would not stop talking about you after you left."

"OK."

"And you said there were sparks on your side?"

"Yes."

"So, what's the problem. You are about the same age, he is divorced, you are both creative and live around the area. I think you should ask him out on a date."

Mandy had to chime in then with a rendition of "Nora and Jase sitting in a tree, k-i-s-s-i-n-g."

"I can't Sam. I just can't."

"Why not. Please explain."

"OK. I'll tell you why. Before I came here, I found out I had Borderline Personality Disorder. It really screws around with my thinking and makes relationships really difficult. I did try again a few months ago, but it is just no use. I just don't feel safe."

"Nora, you know I love you dearly, but that is downright the biggest load of bullshit I have ever heard."

"No Sam, it is true. Sometimes I do feel really crazy, and I don't think it is fair to involve anyone else in it. It could take years to get my head on straight."

"But you can take care of Mandy, right?"

"Of course."

"And you can take care of Layla, right?"

"Yes."

And you can take care of your clients?

"Yes."

"And you can take care of yourself, right?"

"Yes."

Now I could see where she was going with this.

"Then why the hell can't you take care of a relationship? If it is with the right person, you will have nothing to worry about."

"It's not that simple."

"I think it is."

"I just don't feel safe."

"What is that supposed to mean?"

I hung my head.

"Honestly, I just don't know."

There was a silence only disturbed by Mandy's humming of the wedding march.

"Look, Sam. Jase does seem awesome. Why don't you ask him out."

"First, stop deflecting attention. Second, surely you know I am a lesbian! What? Are you kidding? You really didn't know?"

She started laughing and Mandy starting chanting, "My Mummy likes girls."

"Oh gee. I was going to go for you too! There were some days I came damn close, but I realised I would much prefer to have you as a friend then to lose you as a lover."

Then we both laughed.

"Look, all I am saying is that I get your need to be alone. I really do. It takes a lot of strength to do what you have done. But there is also nothing wrong with letting someone love you, Nora. Because you really are so easy to love."

"I love you, Nora.," sang Mandy as she threw her arms around my neck almost knocking me off the stool and scaring Layla off the table.

"I would just hate to see this sanctuary you have built become your solitary confinement. Will you just promise me not to shut anything down before it has a chance to bloom?"

"OK."

"If I see you doing it, I am going to be seriously cranky and cut off all your access to art supplies. Got it?"

"Got it."

"Now, tell me how your garden is going."

****

The silversmithing lessons were fantastic. There was something so cathartic about banging out metal, and I found actually making instead of merely painting circles, even more magical. I had to stop myself from looking too often in Jase's eyes so that I could concentrate and curb my desire to get close to him. This happened naturally though, as he came to check on how my work was progressing, suggesting alternate techniques and looking at all of my designs. I had prepared a few pages full, moving to these before starting another mandala.

Closing up after the last lesson, Jase came up and asked me what I thought of silversmithing. I told the truth, that I really enjoyed it and would love to do more. This was not a come-on, but finally some honest communication.

"That is great, because I would really like to talk to you about using some of your designs. Would you be free for a coffee tomorrow to chat about how we could work together?"

I could see Sam glaring at me from the corner, and I could feel my heart pushing me forward.

"Absolutely. Would the afternoon be OK? I just have a few clients to catch up with in the morning."

"That would work great! Perfect!"

Everything was perfect with this man. I wondered if it was actually just the way he spoke, or whether he really did believe it. We exchanged details and I departed, to be met in my car by a "ping" and thumb-up emoji from Sam in my messages. Gosh she made me smile.

Coffee was only the beginning. We agreed a design deal that day and a night to meet for dinner each week where we would plan out our cooperative collections. All of a sudden, I was in a partnership, just not the kind of one I had expected. Jase's ideas inspired me, and so did his eyes.

It took us six months to finish our first collection. We had spent our sparse time together over weekly dinners designing really impressive items, based on the natural world and incorporating mythical symbols. Then for the rest of the week we worked alone, juggling our time between other commitments.

Sometimes, dinners would stretch beyond business. We shared our views on spirituality. Jase subscribed to the Universe model, one which saw a positive energy providing for us. That sounded nice, and I agreed with the positive energy bit, I just was not sure what I would call it. We also talked about children, and how wonderful Mandy was. His wife had lost three children through miscarriage and was too scared to ever try again. The story was so sad. He would love to have a kid, but reckoned he would make a crap father. I told him I agreed, especially if his jokes were anything to go by. Sometimes he would pop in during my afternoon at the art shop. He would hold Layla so close and gently and tell me he always wanted a pet. Maybe now he was not travelling around so much there could be a chance. He would have a dog though, and he was sure it would appreciate his jokes. And we laughed. Jase had a great sense of humour, and his wit was so quick. He would often wave his arms around while telling his jokes and that made them even funnier. He certainly made for great competition when it came to comedic quips.

Was I coming to love this man?

Yes.

There were moments when I felt Jase meant the world to me. That he was everything I wanted and needed; he was my sage and superhero. My head and my heart were wrapped around and within him and I would be on such a high thinking about how we would, one day, come together. I would text him with updates and innocent messages such as "Happy Wednesday" with a smile emoji or "Go team!" with a jumping cheerleader.

A few hours later though, I was loathing this man. He was too busy to give me the love and attention I needed. He obviously didn't like me if he hadn't yet asked me out on a date. And why didn't he call during the week? He did not care, and I did not feel safe. I would not message him again, and I would not return his.

My work during the day would keep me too busy to dabble in this black and white thinking. But during the night, it would violate every waking moment. Right after leaving our dinners, I would snuggle up with Layla and tell her how wonderful Jase was. Two nights later I would be brushing her and explaining to this tender little kitten how one specific word he used was clear evidence that he was actually a manipulative bastard.

And so, this swinging continued, and only ceased when I tried to capture it in some paintings. Black and white collided together, their conflict intent on causing cruelty. Standing back and surveying what I had titled the 'Shunt Series' I felt I had adequately captured the chaos.

Sam would ask me how it was going, eager to know if we had moved beyond business.

"I don't know, Sam. Some days I feel like I am going crazy."

"What do you mean, Nora?"

I explained the demon of dichotomous thinking and how it was doing my head in, and how, in my mind, it was clear evidence that I should not be in a relationship ever again.

"Nonsense! I think it just means you need some help. If you don't deal with this, then it is clear evidence to me that you are just too chicken shit to try. Promise me you will mention it to the GP. I am sure she will have someone you can speak to."

I did. And she did. And I began catching up weekly with a psychologist. It was a man, which I did not want, but he was surprisingly astute, helping me see things from a completely different perspective. He congratulated me for being aware of how my thoughts were driving my behaviour. This awareness was a sure sign that I had made significant progress. And now with this huge leap forward I could build on this and learn how to help myself through. He showed me how to use logic to challenge my catastrophising.

Coming home from one session I pulled out my purple circle. Here was evidence that I was a whole human being, with gifts and faults. Now I must do the same for Jase; he was neither heaven nor hell, merely human. The 'Shunt Series' was expanded and renamed the 'Shade Series' and was added to with canvases where black and white converged into silver-lined greys.

With the revelation that I was actually on the right track, I could let go of the thought that I actually was a lunatic and invest this energy on loving myself more. I looked back through Frida's diary and saw the little girl at the door. I would care for this child, for me, just like I did for Mandy. I would not make her put on a show just to chase a colour that she already had. And I was going to give this connection space to breathe and to become whatever it was meant to be. I did not push forward, and neither did he. We just flowed.

Jase and I were at our regular burger joint for our weekly dinner, and planning the release of the 'Magic Mandalas' collection when it all threatened to fall apart. I placed our marketing plan out on the table and walked Jase through it. He responded by leaning over and kissing my cheek.

"You truly are amazing. I have something for you, Nora."

He pulled out a small blue jewellery box. Oh god, please no. I was just feeling comfortable, I did not need this now. I could feel myself starting to shake.

"What's this?" I asked hoping for some assurance.

"Just a little something I made for you."

And there it was, and there came my outbreath. I hoped he did not notice how heavy it was.

It was a silver pendant in the shape of a leaf, with a green circle gem set within.

"Jase, this is so beautiful, thank you. This means so much."

My words were genuine. He had paid attention to how much leaves meant in my work, and he had listened when I explained why green was one of my favourite colours. And he had combined both into a gift that I could wear as a reminder of what was truly important to me.

"Nora. I really like you. Not just as a business partner, but as a person. Our time together feels so special. I can talk and joke, and create with you in a way I have never been able to do with anyone before. I would love us to be more than just friends, but I don't want to burn any bridges. I just wanted to let you know because it was kind of eating my heart out. Now I have said it I can let it rest. I only hope you don't think I expect anything different than what we have already."

This man was so generous, and so gentle. There was a sensation I had not felt in such a long time. My heart was being squeezed and crevices covered over with thin sheets were now ripped open again.

"Jase, you are truly wonderful. You are, without a doubt, the most incredible man I have met. You inspire me every day, and like you I really treasure what we have. You have no idea how thankful I am for you, and for this, and for you not pushing for something more."

"Would you like something more, Nora. Or not?"

"I would Jase..."

My pause said it all.

"I can feel a but coming on."

"There is. I am dealing with some stuff that I worry would mess things around if we were to move forward. I also have a tendency to be impulsive, and think far too much instead of feel. So, could I ask a favour?"

"Anything at all!"

"Could I have a week to process this? I don't just want to think about what my response will be. I would really love some time to tap into my feelings around this. Does that make sense?"

"Absolutely. And I think that is a superb way forward. I have no expectations, Nora, only the hope that we get to keep creating together for a long time to come."

I got up from my chair and gave him a hug. It felt like this confirmed our commitment to care for each other, no matter what came next. In my mind I heard my mum say "Congratulations, darling," and my other Nora say, "Nice one."

Jase was genuinely upbeat. I could tell that he was not covering over any insult. As I returned to my chair he continued with the business at hand.

"Now, let's get back to the planning a successful showcase. Oh, and designing the next one, which, with your permission I would like to call 'The Love of Leaves.' I am thinking the piece you are wearing would take centre place. Then I am thinking the collection after that could be called 'Into the Dragon's Den,' inspired of course by your incredible painting. And the one after that, well that could be 'Flight of the Fairies,' to incorporate your love of wings. What do you think?"

We both shared large smiles, and I put the necklace on, holding it against my chest. Hand on heart. What is the kindest thing I can do for myself right now? Breathe in, breath out. I believe in you, Nora.

About the Author

Belinda Tobin is a researcher, author, producer, and avid explorer of the human experience, with all its challenges and complexities. Her works span fiction, non-fiction, poetry, TV and film. However, they all share a common purpose, to foster a more conscious, compassionate and connected future.

Find out more about Belinda and her projects at www.belindatobin.com.

For more titles go to:
www. heart-led.pub/bel-house-books

www.ingramcontent.com/pod-product-compliance
Lightning Source LLC
Chambersburg PA
CBHW022142010726
47493CB00002B/303